Nick Bleszynski was born in Scotland and grew up in central and eastern Africa.

After returning to the UK and graduating from Anglia University, he went into television and for the past 25 years has worked as a writer, producer and director for many of the world's biggest broadcasters. This is Nick's third book, following on from the success of *Shoot Straight You Bastards!: The Truth Behind the Killing of Breaker Morant* and *You'll Never Take Me Alive: The Life and Death of Bushranger Ben Hall.* He is married and lives in Sydney, Australia, with his wife, Jill, and son Stefan.

To contact Nick or to find out more about his books log onto www.blackrosemedia.com.au.

BLOODLUST

The Unsavoury Tale of
Alexander Pearce,
THE CONVICT CANNIBAL

NICK BLESZYNSKI

WILLIAM HEINEMANN AUSTRALIA

A William Heinemann book
Published by Random House Australia Pty Ltd
Level 3, 100 Pacific Highway, North Sydney NSW 2060
www.randomhouse.com.au

First published by William Heinemann in 2008

Copyright © Nick Bleszynski, 2008

The moral right of the author has been asserted.

All rights reserved. No part of this book may be reproduced or transmitted by any person or entity, including internet search engines or retailers, in any form or by any means, electronic or mechanical, including photocopying (except under the statutory exceptions provisions of the Australian Copyright Act 1968), recording, scanning or by any information storage and retrieval system without the prior written permission of Random House Australia.

Addresses for companies within the Random House Group can be found at www.randomhouse.com.au/offices.

National Library of Australia
Cataloguing-in-Publication Entry

Bleszynski, Nick.
Bloodlust.

ISBN 978 1 74166 700 4 (pbk.)

Pearce, Alexander, ca.1790-1824.
Convicts–Tasmania–Fiction.
Penal colonies–Tasmania–Fiction.
Cannibalism–Tasmania–Fiction.

A823.4

Text designed and typeset in 11.5/16.5 Sabon by Post Pre-Press Group, Australia
Printed and bound by Griffin Press, South Australia

Random House Australia uses papers that are natural, renewable and recyclable products and made from wood grown in sustainable forests. The logging and manufacturing processes are expected to conform to the environmental regulations of the country of origin.

10 9 8 7 6 5 4 3 2 1

Dedicated to the memory of

Roy 'Rocky' Williamson
(1959–2006)

Andrew Briscoe
(1961–2008)

My liege has been slain in battle, but I see not his wounds nor his bloody countenance, the grim messengers of his untimely death. I see him as he was when first we met, young, lion-hearted and with all the world at his feet. We shall mourn his passing thence make ready our hearts for that glorious day, in the realm beyond, when we will be young again.

I'd yield to the Devil instantly,
Did it not happen that myself am he!

      J.W. Von Goethe, *Faust: A Tragedy*

Author's note

In the special collections section of the State Library of Tasmania in Hobart I came across an extraordinary but little-known collection of documents. According to the Library records, this material was bequeathed to the library in 1909 by John Bisdee of Battery Point, Hobart. It consists of six items.

ITEM 1

One black leather-bound accounting ledger consisting of 300 bound pages. Cover badly worn and scratched, displays signs of weathering and the binding is loose. Ledger originally intended for accounting purposes and the pages are divided into columns and lined accordingly. Paper spotted, mildewed and watermarked. Ink faded, but legible. Author identified as Alexander Pearce, a convict at Macquarie Harbour from 1822–23. The document describes his time at Macquarie Harbour, his escape, and the subsequent events leading up to his death by hanging on 19 July 1824 at Hobart gaol.

ITEM 2

Various newspaper clippings from Hobart and Sydney newspapers circa 1824–32 and a partial transcript from the Select Committee Report on Transportation held in London, 1838 have been glued into the pages following Pearce's account to form an addendum.

ITEM 3
One leather-bound daily journal for the year 1850–51. Owner identified on the inside cover as Mr Daniel Ruth, Druim Moir, Chestnut Hill, Philadelphia, United States of America. Black leather cover is scratched and marked, but binding is in good condition. Paper is heavy bonded manila 8" × 5" but shows signs of water damage. Ink faded but legible.

ITEM 4
A personal letter and envelope dated Macquarie Harbour 19 June 1851 from Mr Daniel Ruth to Miss Caroline Vandenberg. Address on envelope given as Montichello, Devon St, Chestnut Hill, Philadelphia, Pennsylvania, USA. White writing paper 8" × 5" bearing the letterhead of the Customs House Hotel, 1 Murray St, Hobart. Badly weathered and evidence of damp and water damage, Fold marks visible. Ink badly faded, barely legible.

ITEM 5
A letter written by Mr John Bisdee (Jnr) dated 28 October 1909. Address given as 9 Cromwell St, Battery Point, Hobart, Tasmania. The letter is written on two sheets of standard size 8" × 10" manila bond paper in the same neat, copperplate handwriting as items 1 & 5. The first sheet has a formal letterhead with author's address. Fold marks visible. Ink faded, paper slightly discoloured with age.

ITEM 6
A collection of correspondence between Mr John Bisdee (Jnr) and various persons in America and the United Kingdom between 1907–09 attempting to ascertain the

particulars and whereabouts of various persons named in Items above.

I have pieced together the following story using these sources. Make of it what you will.

Nick Bleszynski

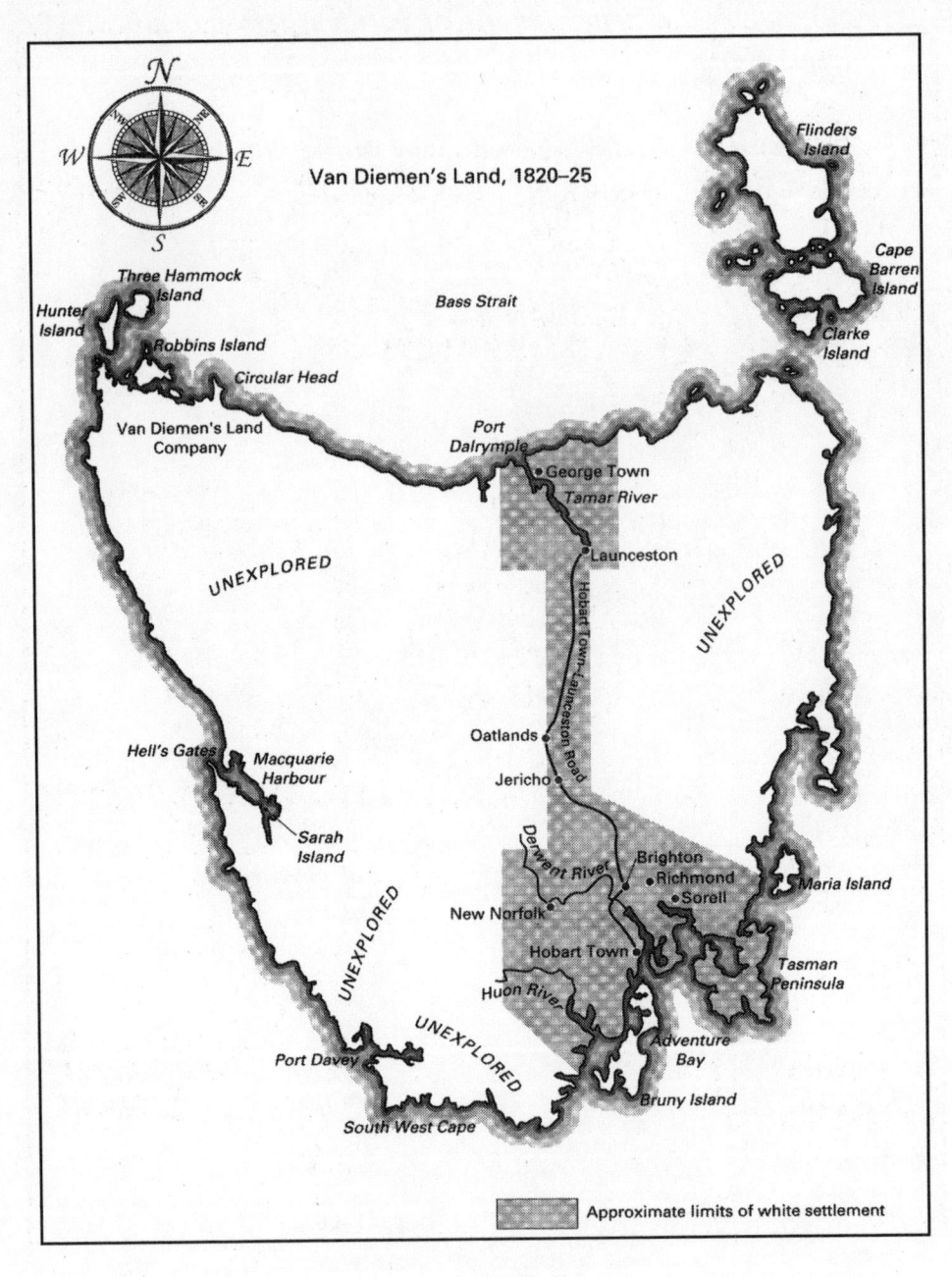

Reproduced from *Hell's Gates: the Escape of Tasmania's Convicted Cannibal* by Paul Collins with permission of Hardie Grant Books

Detail of Macquarie Harbour area

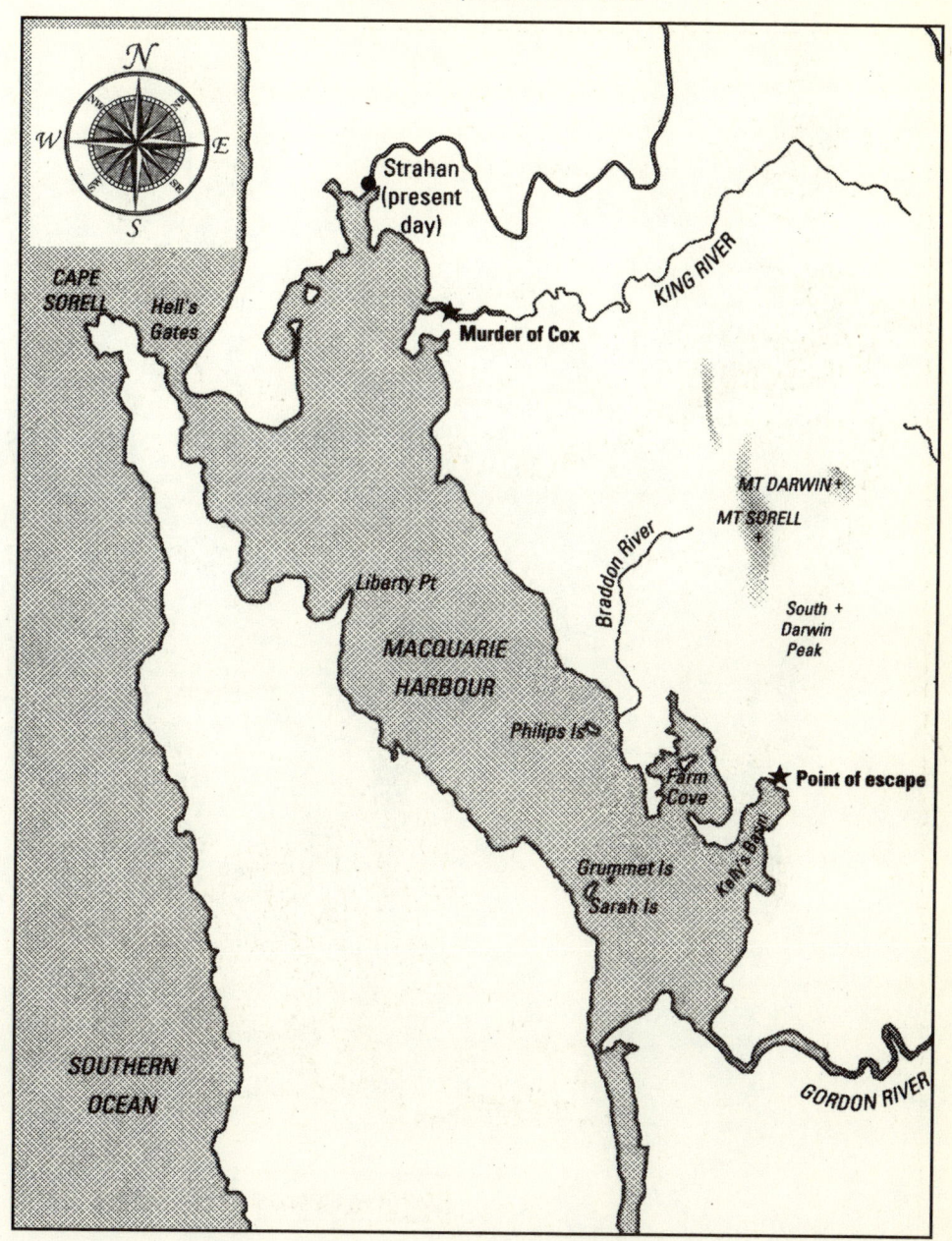

Maquarie Harbour detail reproduced from *Hell's Gates: the Escape of Tasmania's Convicted Cannibal* by Paul Collins with permission of Hardie Grant Books

Pearce's possible escape route

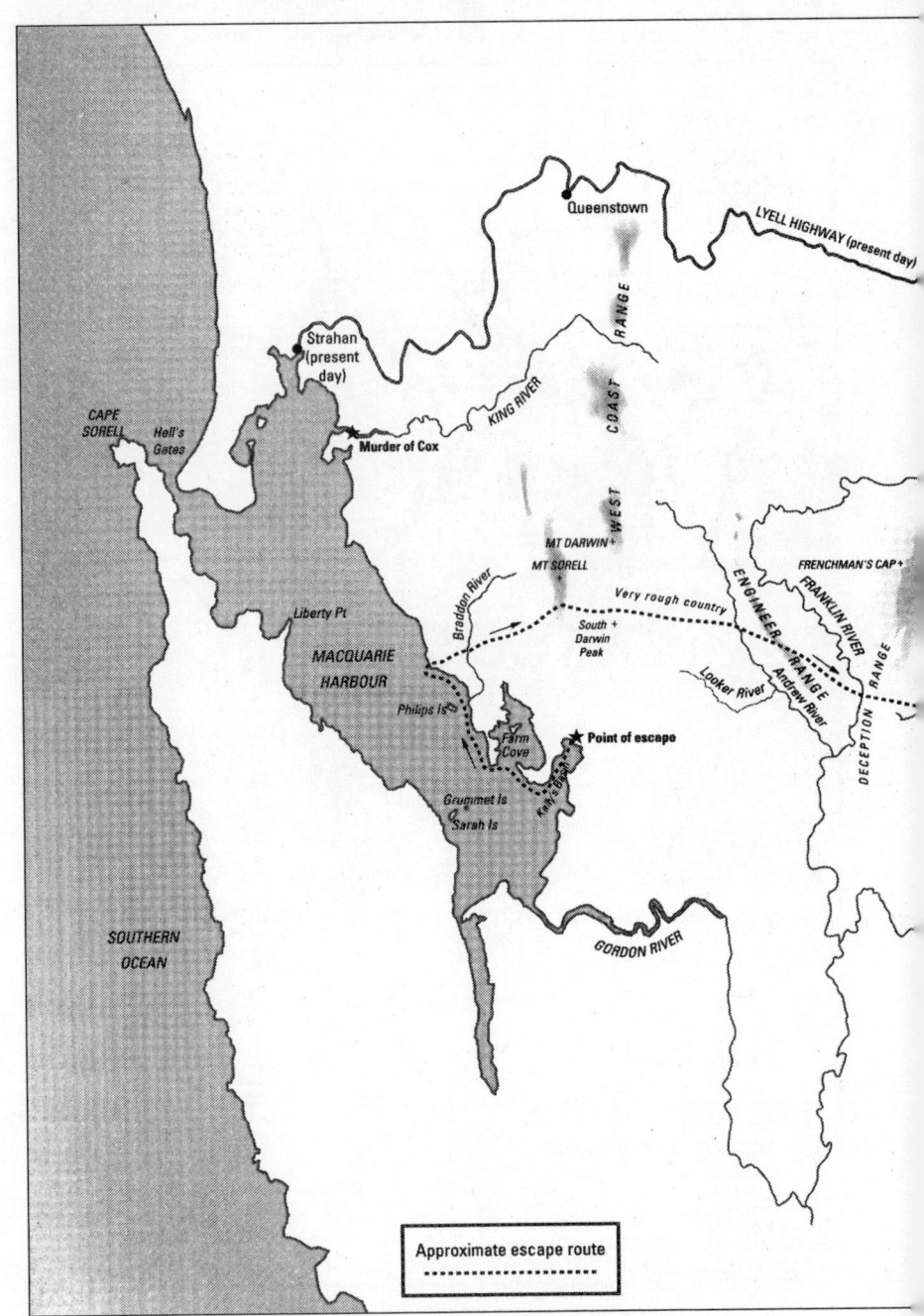

Reproduced from *Hell's Gates: the Escape of Tasmania's Convicted Cannibal* by Paul Collins with permission of Hardie Grant Books

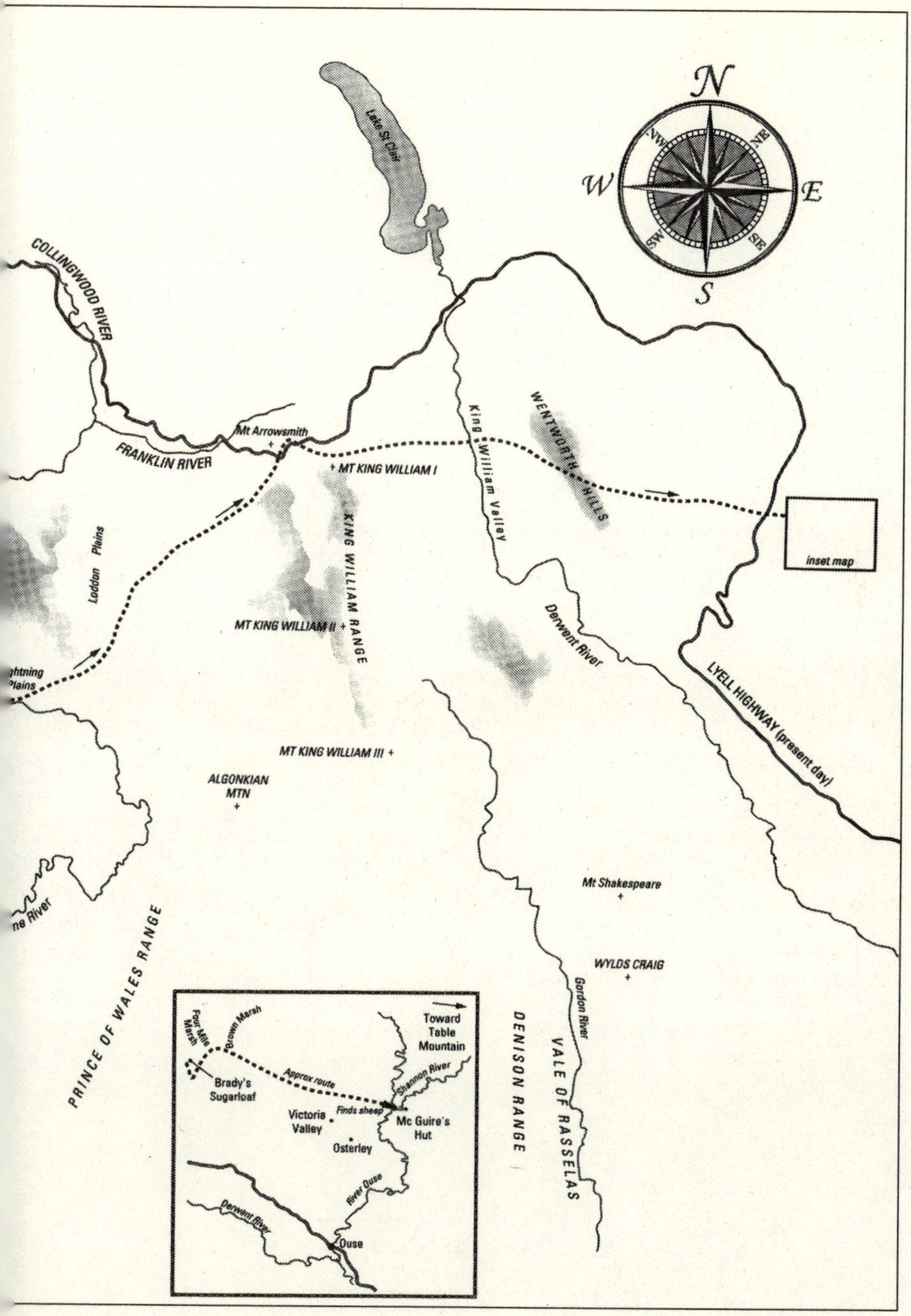

N
E
S
W
NE
SE
SW
NW
Lake St Clair
COLLINGWOOD RIVER
FRANKLIN RIVER
Mt Arrowsmith
MT KING WILLIAM I
KING WILLIAM RANGE
MT KING WILLIAM II
MT KING WILLIAM III
King William Valley
WENTWORTH HILLS
inset map
Loddon Plains
ghtning Plains
Derwent River
LYELL HIGHWAY (present day)
ALGONKIAN MTN
ne River
PRINCE OF WALES RANGE
Mt Shakespeare
WYLDS CRAIG
Gordon River
VALE OF RASSELAS
DENISON RANGE
Four Mile Marsh
Brown Marsh
Brady's Sugarloaf
Approx route
Toward Table Mountain
Shannon River
Finds sheep
Mc Guire's Hut
Victoria Valley
Osterley
River Ouse
Derwent River
Ouse

Chapter 1

The Proposition

Chestnut Hill, Philadelphia, 10 December 1850

DESPITE MISSING ITS BOTTOM jaw, the skull sitting in the palm of Daniel Ruth's elegant hand seemed to grin malevolently up at him. The bone had yellowed slightly, but he knew from his medical studies that discolouration wasn't a reliable indication of age. The incisors and some of the rear molars still remained fixed in the rear of the upper jaw. Why had the doctor called him out on a wintry night and wordlessly put a human skull into his hand, he wondered, as he poked at the points of the small, slightly rounded canines and waited to be enlightened by the older, soft-faced man sitting opposite him.

'I'd be careful, they belong to a cannibal,' said Dr Samuel Morton flatly. His sharp blue eyes watched with keen interest as his young charge sat bolt upright. 'I thought that might get your attention,' intoned Morton, his thin lips stretching into a knowing smile as he slid his gold-rimmed, half-moon glasses up his aquiline nose and admired the way that grace and beauty lay so effortlessly upon his young guest.

A thoughtful frown, just visible beneath his foppish fringe of brown hair, creased Daniel's brow. 'Where did this specimen come from?' he demanded, turning the skull in his hands.

'Australia,' the doctor replied.

Realising he was being tested, Daniel used his fingers to measure the circumference of the skull and then the distance between the mouth and the eye socket, as he'd been shown. His brow furrowed as if somehow his calculations had gone awry. 'Well then, I guess this fellow would be . . . would've been . . . a species of Aborigine,' Daniel said tentatively, his uncertain tone betraying the confusion the doctor's trained eye had already noted in his face.

The young man groaned inwardly as Morton slowly shook his head; he was about to receive one of the doctor's lectures. 'No, he's not an Aborigine, but a Caucasian.'

Daniel's brooding displeasure turned to wide-eyed amazement. Turning the skull in his hands again he said, 'I confess your reference to cannibalism deceived me.'

'You heard the word "cannibal" and naturally assumed that the skull must be Negroid,' Morton admonished him. Daniel didn't argue as craniology and phrenology, new sciences dedicated to proving that a person's racial type, intelligence and moral behaviour could be determined by the size, shape and characteristics of their skulls, were Dr Morton's areas of expertise. During the past decade Morton had amassed a collection of almost a thousand human skulls, which he'd dubbed the 'American Golgotha' and published two well-regarded and much-debated books, *Crania Americana* and *Crania Aegyptica*, which detailed his key scientific findings. He'd filled 637 skulls of different ethnic types with seeds and measured their mean cubic inch capacities, which had the Caucasians at 88, the mulatto at

75 and Negroids at 71. This, Morton claimed, proved that Caucasians had larger brains, were more intelligent and more highly evolved than either mulatto or Negroid peoples.

Daniel lifted the skull. 'Where did you get it?'

'I procured it from some unscrupulous surgeon by the name of Crockett through a Calcutta agent who deals in such . . . curiosities. This surgeon dissected the fellow following his execution some thirty years ago and liberated the skull, thinking it might have some novelty value. He was right about that. It cost me £50 sterling,' revealed the doctor, running a hand through his short silvery hair.

'Did they dissect criminals over there in Australia?' Daniel asked, his flat Philadelphia drawl making the distant land seem more alien and faraway than ever it was.

'Oh, sure. The British colonies never spared the lash or the rope where transported convicts were concerned; still don't. New Holland, as it was known back then, was run by a military administration ten thousand miles from London. Unlike Europe, there was no liberal conscience to disapprove and pass obstructive laws to prevent the procurement of bodies and halt the advancement of science. The judges in Van Diemen's Land simply decreed that the "worst of the worst" be "atomised" after execution and that the parts be given to medical students and researchers. Clearly God's retribution was not sufficient for His Majesty.'

'A-tom-ised, I like that,' Daniel laughed, rolling his tongue round the word as he continued to study the skull in his hand. 'So Doctor, what do you know about this white cannibal?'

'Crockett told the agent that it belonged to an Irishman by the name of Alexander Pearce, the so-called "cannibal convict of Macquarie Harbour", who was executed in Hobart in 1824.

Apparently, he was an escaped convict who lured his victims into the forests where he said others were waiting to escape, but instead killed them and devoured their flesh.'

'Where the hell's Macquarie Harbour and Hobart?'

Dr Morton rose with some effort, crossed the spacious, tastefully furnished room, and stopped at a large globe that sat on a solid side-table. Daniel was behind him, his face flushed with excitement. His boyhood fascination with globes and exotic faraway places with strange-sounding names had never left him. Spinning the orb, Morton allowed it to run eastwards through his fingers from America, across the vast continents of Africa and Asia, before tilting it upwards until the white of the Antarctic was visible. Daniel frowned. Like most educated Americans he knew Australia was somewhere in the southern hemisphere but couldn't rightly say where it was. Dr Morton tapped his bony finger on a small, heart-shaped island just off the south-eastern coast of Australia at the very end of the world.

'Van Diemen's Land is to Australia what Sicily is to Italy.'

'Van Diemen's Land. It has a ring to it. Is that where all the demons live?' Daniel added flippantly.

'It's actually spelt D-I-E-M-E-N,' the doctor corrected him gently.

'I think I prefer it my way.'

Morton smiled. Daniel Ruth had always liked things his way and had gone to enormous lengths to establish his own individual character. He wore the latest foreign fashions, but they were always discarded once others started copying him. Despite being a powerfully built six-footer, he eschewed the usual student sports of football and baseball for tennis, and was a founding member of the Chestnut Hill cricket club. But these were just minor mutinies against the establishment and the Ruth fortune to which he was linked. His mother, Catherine Peirsol, a Philadelphian socialite, had married William Ruth, an English capitalist with extensive shipping interests in America and the British colonies. Such a boy, ready to rebel against his destiny, was perfect for the task Morton had in mind, and an ideal *protégé* to carry on his work once he'd passed away.

'So why are you so interested in this Pearce? Daniel asked, 'Surely the very notion of a white cannibal runs contrary to your theory that Caucasians are the most evolved of all the races?'

Morton nodded. The sharp, fearless question confirmed his instinct that Daniel Ruth was the right man for what he had in mind. Lifting an index finger, as he always did before making an important point, the doctor said, 'A true scientist never rests on his laurels and is always prepared to test his own theories. It's always intrigued me – what turned him into a cannibal? Australia is something of a wild frontier and the convict system extremely harsh. Was it something to do with the penal institution, the harsh environment, or maybe he became deranged . . .'

'Or perhaps he's living proof that Caucasians can also be cannibals,' interjected Daniel.

Morton shrugged and smiled, 'Perhaps.'

'Why not simply request the particulars of his case from London or Australia?'

'I already have, but received no reply. Such reticence usually suggests something unsavoury that no one wants to talk about.'

Daniel nodded. The doctor was no stranger to such matters. Josiah C. Knott and George Gliddon, the two Alabama scientists who funded Morton's research, used his findings to argue that slavery would uplift Negroes and to substantiate the so-called polygenetic theory that they were not human beings. Morton claimed he was just following a line of scientific inquiry and that the British had already compared the skull size of the Irish to primitive man in order to justify their enslavement. But with the issue inflaming social and political tensions between the northern and southern states, many of his peers felt any association with such bigotry was a stain on the doctor's otherwise impeccable reputation.

Despite being a committed Christian, Morton had also contended that the human race didn't spring from two original parents, Adam and Eve, as described in the sacred scriptures, but from five separate sets of racially different parents. This caused much controversy in ecclesiastical circles and saw him accused of heresy.

'The principal task of science,' Morton continued, 'is to peek behind the veil of religion and superstition and inquire into the true nature of this world and its workings. Only ongoing scientific inquiry will ensure mankind's continued evolution.'

'Count me in, Doctor. I don't believe in God or the Devil. That gallery of old curiosities holds no fears for me. I believe in science and the modern world.'

'That's because you're twenty-three, believe yourself immortal and have yet to stare death in the face,' retorted Morton. Suddenly he clutched his chest, his face flushing bright red.

'Doctor, are you alright?' cried Daniel in alarm.

The older man slumped back in his chair, closed his eyes and concentrated on his breathing until he'd got it under control. 'Never got used to breathing with just the one,' he whispered, tapping his chest. His left lung had ceased functioning three years earlier following a bout of pleuro-pneumonia and damn nearly took his life into the bargain.

'Whisky, not water is what you give an ailing man,' Morton said, imitating his late father's thick Irish brogue, his outstretched hand gesturing towards the cocktail cabinet. As he brought over the glass, Daniel noted with relief that his old tutor's breathing was now regular and his skin had returned to its normal pallid hue. The doctor continued as he sipped the strong spirit.

'I've laid the foundations, but future research must focus on individual character traits. Americans are fascinated by the study and classification of human body types, especially theories that connect how people look to their basic character, intelligence, moral sense and capacity for leadership or violence. Just think of the society we could create if we could recognise a genius and nurture him, or reform a criminal before he committed a crime. The story of Alexander Pearce, the white cannibal, will be a sensation and the making of the man who writes it.'

Daniel furrowed his brow. 'You said, "the man who writes it" as though . . .'

'I'm ailing.'

'But you . . .'

'Have never seemed fitter?' said the doctor, finishing his sentence. 'Death is the greatest fillip known to man as it teaches you just how precious time is, but the rigours of a trip to the Antipodes is out of the question. That's why I'd like you to go,' concluded Morton with a flourish as he delivered his punch-line. He smiled as the young man opposite him looked momentarily stunned, his usual nonchalance shaken.

'Me? Why?'

'Oh Daniel, do you really need me to damn you with faint praise?' It was more a statement of fact than a question. He'd recently graduated with first-class honours in medicine and swept the prizes for academic achievement.

Daniel balanced the skull in his hand and sighed, 'I'd go in a minute, but I doubt my parents would approve.'

'Then don't tell them,' came the sharp reply.

'Dr Morton, are you suggesting . . .'

'I realise that your father is one of the university's most important benefactors, but a man's purpose is to meet his destiny, Daniel. He who fails has wasted his life.' Morton knew that grandiose pronouncements demanding Biblical zeal and the valour of a questing knight usually had the desired effect.

Morton was well aware of what he was asking. Daniel was an only child and sole heir to the Ruth fortune. As a result, from a young age his every whim had been indulged and he'd been discouraged from following his friends into military service or entering risky professions such as archaeology, which fascinated him. The smooth, untroubled arc of his life had already been determined before it had been lived. Unless cruel fate intervened, influence and money could almost guarantee that Daniel would get his doctorate, achieve tenure at the university, marry his sweetheart Caroline Vandenberg, and produce heirs to continue the Ruth tradition. At a mature age he'd succeed his father as the head of the Philadelphia Shipping and Trading Company. While most people in the world railed against cold, hunger and poverty, this young man was trapped by wealth and privilege like a proverbial bird in a gilded cage.

As Daniel peered into the log-fire crackling in the hearth, he knew that Dr Morton was right. Under the firm tutelage of his father he'd learned that people of their class didn't take gambles, they took calculated risks. Impetuosity was best left to the poor who more often than not fared badly in life. This journey would be a risk, an uncalculated risk, and he resolved it was going to be his adventure, his triumph, not some foreign sojourn stage-managed by his parents. Lifting his head, Daniel revealed a strong, square, clean-shaven jaw offset by thin lips, a narrow nose and high cheekbones; a curious mix of masculine strength and feminine delicacy. As an anatomist, the human form never ceased to fascinate him.

'Well then Daniel, what say you?' pressed Morton, finally breaking the silence.

The young man stroked his chin and then fixed the doctor with his dark green eyes. 'I'll go. As you say Doctor, it might be the making of me and I'll get to see Van Diemen's Land. Who'd go there for a vacation?'

'I can assure you it won't be a vacation,' warned Morton, his index finger upraised, 'people can be very touchy about the past, particularly concerning matters they'd rather forget. You'll have to tread carefully and use some of that native Ruth cunning.'

Daniel nodded as Morton added, 'I would ask for your discretion in this matter. There are more jealous, small-minded people in the scientific community than in any hick midwestern town. Certain gentlemen will feel their experience and academic standing should warrant them going to Van Diemen's Land in your stead. I look forward to hearing the story of Mr Alexander Pearce before I die.'

'Nonsense Doctor! You've got years left in you.'

'Let's hope so. I'm betting it's one hell of a story,' Morton replied with a tight smile. He noted Daniel biting his lip and fielded the awkward request before it was voiced. 'I'll smooth things over with the university. This sabbatical is related to the completion of your doctoral thesis and might result in a discovery that will make them the talk of the scientific world.' After four years as the professor of anatomy at Pennsylvania University and the serving President of the Academy of Life Sciences, Dr Morton was not without influence.

Now that Daniel had made the decision to go, Morton noted

he'd become restless. 'I won't detain you any longer, you have arrangements to make,' he said, getting up and seeing his student to the door. After donning a knee-length black frock-coat and placing a brown felt hat on his head at a rakish angle to crown the fashionably long hair, which he wore to the shoulders in the style of the London dandies, Daniel turned to leave.

'I've always maintained that clothes are one of the crude measures we humans use to identify social classes and announce our station in life,' said Morton with a little laugh, 'but maybe if they flattered me as they do you, I might be differently inclined.'

As he pulled open the front door an icy blast of winter air chased them back into the warmth. The villages of Chestnut Hill, Germantown and Mount Airey, home to Philadelphia's most wealthy and influential residents, were perched up in the hills above the city. Although much cooler during the hot summers, they were also colder and more snowbound in winter.

'In the Antipodes the seasons are about-face and it will still be warm when you land there,' Morton said, handing Daniel an envelope containing five hundred dollars. The young man immediately handed it back, his face flushed, but his expression sombre.

'Sir, I couldn't.'

'A noble gesture Daniel, but take it anyway. Through you I will be able to make the journey I always dreamed of and it only seems right that I should share the expenses.'

Daniel knew that to protest was polite, but to refuse would offend so he bowed his head in supplication. 'Thank you, I'll spend it wisely.'

'I'm sure you will,' the doctor said charitably, despite knowing that Daniel was a dissolute dandy and cocksman of some repute.

'Look after yourself!' Morton called out as Daniel stepped over the threshold and disappeared as though he'd stepped behind a black curtain.

'No need Doctor,' came the cocksure reply from the darkness, 'as you yourself said, I'm twenty-three, believe myself to be immortal and have yet to stare death in the face.' Standing in front of Dr Morton's two-storey Italianate-style house as warm, yellow light slanted through its curtained bay windows, it was easy for Daniel to believe that the world was his for the taking.

During the half-mile walk past his beloved cricket club back to the west side of the suburb where his parents' estate commanded stunning views of the Wissahickon Valley, Daniel didn't regret his decision to send his father's Hansom cab home. He didn't feel the crunch of snow beneath his feet or winter's icy fingers clutching at his face. His spirit was soaring and his mind racing with the thrill of adventure at the far side of the world and the endless possibilities that awaited him there. At a single stroke he could save years of tedious waiting for old men to die and jump the long, shuffling queue of mediocre academics waiting patiently for their dues. This story could catapult him to fame and fortune, a professorship, tenure at the university, if he would only go through the door of opportunity that now stood ajar before him.

At the end of Willow Grove Avenue were the wrought-iron gates leading to Druim Moir, the grey stone and granite Gothic mansion his father had built complete with tower and battlements. Peering through the railings past the skeletal outlines of chestnut, beech and oak that lined the long avenue, he noted that the lights were still on and pictured his mother in the sitting-room, pretending to read as she awaited his safe return.

As Yuletide approached Daniel continued to play the dutiful son and devoted suitor. He accompanied his mother to the five-storeyed Lits Brothers department store in the city with its distinctive white iron-clad façade and took Caroline skating on the frozen millpond at Wissahickon Park followed by a hot chocolate in the quaint, old Valley Green Hotel. He also carefully and quietly laid his departure plans.

On discovering that one English pound was worth eleven American dollars, Daniel went to the bank and liquidated all of the $10,000 in bonds and shares he owned, but didn't touch any of the money in his trust fund as he knew that Mr Shaeffer, the officious Swiss-German manager who handled his father's business accounts, would alert him at once. With a wink he told Miss Lambert, the kindly teller he'd known since boyhood, that he needed the money to make a down-payment on a house. Daniel knew from her flushed, dimpled cheeks that Miss Lambert assumed he was going to propose to Caroline, but as discretion was 'always assured' at the Philadelphia National Bank, she'd keep her little secret until the formal announcement appeared in the *Pennsylvanian* or the *Gazette*.

Daniel also booked his return passage from New York to Sydney via London where he'd organise his onward trip to Van Diemen's Land. He didn't want his destination revealed by a simple check of the passenger lists, so when the booking clerk asked for his name, he cheekily replied, 'Pearce . . . Mr Alexander Pearce.'

His last night in Philadephia was New Year's Eve. On the

stroke of midnight at an uptown ball Daniel drew Caroline close and kissed her with uncommon passion in full view of all the other guests. The local gossips were certain that a proposal of marriage would soon follow, but little did they know that Daniel had carefully and quietly laid his departure plans. After taking Caroline home and making hard, fast passionate love to her one last time, Daniel posted short notes to his parents and Caroline, explaining that he'd gone on a short trip to pursue the opportunity of a lifetime and would return within the year, but giving them no details. He knew he should have told them the truth, but reasoned that his father would've forbidden him to go and Caroline and his mother would've drowned him in their tears.

On New Year's Day 1851, just three weeks after Dr Morton had made his proposition, Daniel Ruth was pushing his way along Manhattan's South Street where most of the shipping activity in New York was centred. Amid the clamour of clattering hooves, rumbling barrels and gangs of men straining to hoist heavy loads into the yawning holds of waiting ships, Daniel had to constantly sway, side-step and change course. In the close press of warm humanity his senses were assailed by dirty river water, horse shit, tobacco, unwashed bodies, rum and cheap perfume. Towering over the throng were forests of masts festooned with tangled webs of rigging and tightly rolled white sails which would gracefully unfurl like a bird taking to flight once they caught the first stiff breeze.

Daniel followed the East River down to Castle Clinton which was built to guard Manhattan's southern tip during the War of Independence. There he boarded the White Diamond Line's

Toronto along with vacationers, immigrants, business people and fellow adventurers.

Daniel staggered sideways when the ship suddenly lurched away from the dock, frightening the seabirds whose garrulous protests rose as passengers and well-wishers released their paper streamers. Watching the brightly coloured bunting drift over the rows of flat-topped warehouses and the tight ranks of Manhattan red brick and brownstone, he felt strangely euphoric, and impulsively joined his voice to the joyous hymn issuing from the throats of a thousand passengers.

As a strong, following breeze filled the billowing folds of white canvas above their heads, he watched the distinctive curved promontory of Sandy Hook quickly pass them on the starboard side as they left New York and soon became a mere speck in the greyish blue expanse known as the Atlantic Ocean.

He was on his way and no one and nothing could stop him now.

Chapter 2

Under the Rose

Hobart, Van Diemen's Land, 9 March 1851

AFTER A GRUELLING THIRTEEN-WEEK journey from one side of the world to the other, Daniel Ruth finally stood in Macquarie Street in the centre of Hobart, under the glowering, craggy gaze of Mount Wellington. Hobart was the capital city of Van Diemen's Land – if it could be called a city. By American standards, with a population of only 23,000, it was more of a small, provincial town. He noted that Hobart's wide dirt streets, neat parks, fine sandstone buildings and partisan street names had been made in the image of Mother England, as were its citizens with their profusion of Victorian bustles and gowns for the ladies and stiff, horizontal bowties, white shirts, dark jackets and deep-cut waistcoats for the men.

Daniel stopped at the corner of Argyll Street as he heard the dull rattle of chains. *Too slow to be a horse and cart* he thought as the sound grew steadily louder. On the next street along a group of ten yellow clad prisoners in iron leg fetters shuffled along under the watchful eye of two armed redcoats. *The British still transport convicts to Van Diemen's Land* Daniel reminded himself. This stark historical image belied Hobart's polite, genteel veneer, but provided a tangible link to the man he'd come to find. Bobbing about in the ocean on the far side of the world, this island described by a local historian as '. . . sacred to the genius of torture where prisoners lost the aspect and the heart of man' seemed fantastical, some wild figment of Dr Morton's imagination. Now, for the first time, it felt real.

Before he could start his work he needed rest and recuperation. He found a clean, comfortable billet in the middle of town at the Custom House Hotel on busy Murray Street, which ran down a steep hill to the harbour. He crawled gratefully into bed and slept for a day and a night. It had been a long, exhausting journey.

After boarding the *Eden* in London, Daniel had quickly tired of the endless tea parties, games of bridge and piano recitals which the British passengers took to with gusto. Noting trysts forming amongst the ship's captive population, Daniel observed that the rising levels of boredom corresponded with an increase in sexual activity.

Whilst lounging on a deckchair reading Thomas Lemprière's *The Penal Settlements of Van Diemen's Land* and writing in his day journal, Daniel spied two sisters who'd been observing him from afar. There had been no chance to meet them because their every move was shadowed by a tiresome, overweight female chaperone of advancing years.

He bribed the head steward to ensure that he was seated close to them at dinner, and during the course of polite conversation was able to discover that the sisters' names were Alice and

Elizabeth Bond and that they hailed from a wealthy, landowning family in Leicestershire, a rural area of middle England. They were on their way to visit relatives in New South Wales where they'd doubtless be shown off like breeding stock to potential suitors.

They'd rejected the stiff, formal advances of the young Englishmen aboard, so Daniel laid on his easier colonial charm. Finally, one balmy afternoon, just east of Madras, he coaxed them into an energetic *ménage á trois* in a surprisingly roomy lifeboat while their overweight, perspiring chaperone rushed hither and tither shrieking their names in her high-pitched, theatrical voice.

By the time the long low coast of Java and the monstrous bulge of Krakatoa, the famous volcano, were sighted off the port side, he'd moved onto the wife of a Swiss industrialist who preferred to spend his days and nights drinking and gambling in the gentlemen's lounge. Daniel even had the impudence to take £10 off the man at blackjack a mere ten minutes after leaving his wife on all fours begging him for more cock. The *double entrée*, so to speak, appealed to his rather sardonic sense of humour.

By the time the *Eden* had passed through Sydney heads, Daniel had chalked up an impressive tally. He'd also run through a governess to a wealthy Sydney family, the wife of a British army officer, and caused a young Franciscan nun of exquisite beauty to question her calling.

After a couple of days' rest, Daniel began his quest in earnest. The best place to get information on Pearce was the local newspaper, the *Hobart Town Gazette*, though he knew he'd be appearing on their front page if they ever discovered he'd been sent from

America by the controversial phrenologist, Dr Samuel Morton, to discover what turned Alexander Pearce into a cannibal. Scandal and controversy were a journalist's stock-in-trade the world over.

Aware that Philadelphia had long been at the forefront of penal reform in America, the *Gazette*'s genial editor, Henry Thomas, accepted Daniel's explanation that he was an American journalist from the *Philadelphia Gazette* researching an historical piece on convict transportation and the opening of the so-called New Model Prison at Port Arthur, the penitentiary built to replace Macquarie Harbour. Thomas found him a desk, granted him access to the paper's archives, and introduced him to the journalists who were a ready source of local information. Before he did anything else, he looked at a map to acquaint himself with the locations and distances between his various points of interest.

Daniel learned that Van Diemen's Land was about the same size as the state of Pennsylvania. Hobart lay in the south-east on the Derwent River with several small towns dotted around the eastern hinterland. After some minutes searching, he finally found Macquarie Harbour on the remote west coast. There were no settlements within a hundred miles of it, it was surrounded on all sides by forests and mountains, and was inaccessible over land. This was all implicit in the notation 'unknown' that stretched along the whole length of the west coast.

He started his archival research in 1824, the year of Pearce's execution. On his third day he found an article dated 25 June that gave an account of Pearce's trial in Hobart's Supreme Court.

It's true, Pearce was a cannibal, thought Daniel triumphantly as he lifted his head from the newspaper. He was barely able to contain his excitement as he read it again. The following day he came across an account of Pearce's execution. From those articles he assembled a list of characters with connections to Pearce.

One of the *Gazette* journalists, John Vickers, a single man of a similar age, was happy to visit old pubs like the Whalers' Return and the Hope & Anchor and let Daniel 'stand' him beers while he talked about Hobart's murky convict past. Peering through the fug at the roughly hewn characters who frequented these places, all speaking in richly flavoured English accents and supping strong-smelling ale, Daniel could easily imagine Pearce slipping in for a pint or a nobbler of rum.

When Vickers had drunk his fill, Daniel would walk back to his hotel through the narrow, darkened streets around the harbour area, which were frequently cloaked in thick fog. He drank in the fresh, briny smell of the sea, the sound of creaking timbers, horses and carts clattering past on the unmade roads, and the bleary voices of sailors swearing and singing somewhere out in the darkness.

One night he said casually, 'John, I came across an interesting story about a character called Alexander Pearce.'

Vickers nodded, 'Oh aye, the cannibal convict,' he snorted, 'bit before my time though. I wasn't even born when they hanged him.'

'There must still be people who remember it. I mean, it's only been twenty-five years.'

Vickers thought a moment and then said, 'Well, Reverend Knopwood who took his confession has passed on, Chief Justice Pedder who sent him to the gallows and the prosecutor, Attorney-General Tice Gellibrand, both returned to England, but I'm sure John Bisdee is still alive and in living in Hobart.'

'Bisdee?' Daniel couldn't recall the name on his list.

'He was the gaoler at Hobart gaol when Pearce was hanged. Lives up on Battery Point, I believe.'

Daniel nodded politely, but was careful not to betray his interest.

Unlike the vast city of Philadelphia, it was easy to find someone in Hobart. In less than twenty minutes he'd walked down Murray Street from his hotel, along Salamanca Place past the rows of new red-brick warehouses that lined the harbour front and up Kelly's steps to the little plateau widely regarded as the most salubrious area of Hobart. He stopped to admire the splendid views across the city, harbour and sea before wandering through the narrow streets past the mansions of the rich and wealthy and the modest cottages festooned with sweet-smelling roses of every colour and shade.

He paused at a cramped corner shop and found that a Mr John Bisdee, formerly the Hobart gaoler, lived just around the next corner at number 9 Cromwell Street. It turned out to be a neat, sandstone cottage with a grey slate roof, small windows and a lush front garden. Knocking on the front door, he hoped that Bisdee would give him a first-hand impression of Pearce and maybe have a diary or access to written records.

To his disappointment, there were no footsteps on the other side of the door, no signs of life. Daniel pushed his *carte de visite* through the heavy brass letterbox and re-traced his footsteps to his hotel.

The young American waited impatiently for two days and returned twice more with the same result.

Unaccustomed to being ignored, Daniel decided to wait the old man out. He was up early the next morning, before the mist had lifted off the harbour, and took up a position opposite Bisdee's house. Two hours later the front door finally opened and a tall, thin, white-haired man emerged. Daniel waited until he reached the wooden gate before he came forward. 'Mr Bisdee?'

The old man nodded. 'That's me.'

Daniel extended his hand and introduced himself. 'Pleased to meet you, sir.'

Bisdee ignored his hand and peered into his face. Daniel could see his own reflection in the man's rheumy blue eyes, which sat beneath a pair of wispy white brows that curved upwards like gull's wings. His manner could best be described as brusque.

'You're the American who's been putting the cards through my door, aren't you?' he demanded sternly.

'Yes.'

'Well, now you've bailed me up, what do you want?'

'To talk to you about Alexander Pearce.'

Daniel noted Bisdee's eyes suddenly widen, startled. 'I haven't heard that name spoken round here in a long time. What's your interest in him? Are you some sort of damn newspaper man writing an article about freaks? Isn't that what you call such people over there . . . freaks?'

Daniel, sensing the old man's growing hostility and any prospect of help fading fast, decided to come clean. Taking a deep breath and making placatory gestures, he nodded, 'We do and it's a very unkind practice. Sir, believe me, I don't approve of such exploitation. I'm not a journalist, I'm a scientist from the University of Pennsylvania. My tutor, Dr Samuel Morton, came into possession of Pearce's skull some years ago . . .'

'So that's where it went. Sold like a novelty item, I suppose.'

'Dr Morton is an eminent physician and scientist of international renown with a special interest in phrenology . . .'

Lining him up in his sights like a marksman, Bisdee delivered a clear warning in a sharp tone, 'Take my advice Mr Ruth. Don't go looking for Alexander Pearce and leave that place well alone, if you know what's good for you.'

'What do you mean?' cried Daniel, hearing both fear and excitement in his own voice. The stern-faced ex-gaoler slammed the heavy gate on him and retreated down the neat path flanked on either side by heavy-headed roses, cursing as he fumbled with his keys.

Daniel spent the next few hours walking the streets, his head full of riddles. *What did he mean by 'leave that place well alone?' What's he afraid of?*

Though unaccustomed to being snubbed, his agitation abated and Daniel started thinking logically about who might hold Pearce's records. Bisdee mightn't be willing to help him, but Hobart gaol might.

Filled with new purpose, he marched along Macquarie Street, turned left onto Campbell Street, started up the hill and followed the high, spike-topped sandstone walls of the gaol that ran for almost two city blocks. It was bordered at its southern end by St Matthew's Church and at its top end by the old Trinity Church or Penitentiary Chapel, a beautiful Georgian-style building, complete with clock tower.

Returning to his guise of an American journalist, Daniel interviewed Governor Brein, a cheery, avuncular man who'd succeeded Bisdee on his retirement. Escorting Daniel across the cobbled prison yard past groups of yellow-jacketed, sullen-looking convicts, he showed him the damp, dark cell where Pearce had spent many months and then the gallows in the large open courtyard where he was hanged. Brein even allowed Daniel to stand on the trapdoor and gaze up at the red-brick and sandstone prison buildings. Pointing to a set of double doors at the far side of the prison yard beneath a large carved stone cross, the governor proudly explained that a convict could pay for his crimes in prison and atone for his sins in the adjoining Penitentiary Chapel.

Finally, almost bursting out of his skin with impatience, Daniel was taken to a small airless room where the prison records were neatly filed in rows of shelves that lined the walls together with weighty tomes detailing prison regulations and matters of law. Judging by the hot, stifling atmosphere, the smell of leather and the dead flies collecting on the sill beneath the sun-bleached blind, the fate of previous convicts was something few people concerned themselves with. In the middle of the room was a wooden table piled with folios.

'I had Mr Lowndes take out everything we have on Pearce to save you some time. He knows our records front to back.'

Daniel inclined his head towards the elderly officer. 'Thank you, Mr Lowndes.'

Sensing he was finally getting close to his quarry, Daniel started going through the files. But pretty quickly he realised that he wasn't going to find anything of great interest. There was the order of execution, a copy of the trial transcript, a letter from Lieutenant-Governor Sorell confirming the sentence, and a note stating that the sentence had been carried out. The only items of real interest were the various charge sheets detailing Pearce's trail of petty crimes in Hobart from the time he arrived in 1820 until 1822 when he was sent to Macquarie Harbour. They included: absconding, disobedience, drunkenness, theft, and forging his name on a money order. But there was no hint of the murder, violence and cannibalism that followed his transfer to Macquarie Harbour.

It was dark by the time a dispirited Daniel took refuge in the Whalers' Return and sought solace amongst the familiar babble of voices, the smell of pipe tobacco and a pint of dark, flowery ale he'd developed a taste for. He'd barely taken a sip and settled in to record the day's events in his journal when a tall, familiar-looking man of around twenty-five years came through the door. *Where have I seen that face before?* Daniel wondered.

He didn't have to ponder long because the man came right over to his table and solved the puzzle for him. 'John Bisdee,' he introduced himself.

His son? 'What a coincidence!' Daniel exclaimed. 'This morning I was . . .'

'No coincidence. I knew you'd be here. You've upset my father with your talk of Pearce.'

'I'm sorry . . .' started Daniel, but Bisdee was in no mood for apologies.

'I know your sort, you'll be back. You won't leave him be until you've got what you want so I'm going to tell you everything now and have done with,' he said, with what Daniel was coming to recognise as characteristic local bluntness.

Daniel nodded, his spirits soaring again. 'Okay, can I get you a beer?'

Bisdee shook his head and remained standing, hat in hand, as if to remind Daniel that this wasn't a friendly visit.

'My father was Pearce's gaoler.'

'I heard that.'

'Took him to the gallows; Pearce even confessed to him I think.'

Daniel sat bolt upright as he considered this new piece of information. 'Did he ever talk about it?'

'No.'

'Never?'

'Whenever some bad news leaked out of Macquarie Harbour, the newspapers would recount its dark history and rake up the Pearce story again. My father would get angry and say they'd no idea what they were on about, but never explained what he meant by it.'

'Do you know if he still has any papers or letters from that time?'

John Bisdee, who Daniel imagined was the image of his father in his younger days, looked thoughtful for a moment then shook his head. Daniel felt his heart sink to the pit of his stomach.

'No, nothing. He took it all back to Macquarie Harbour.'

Daniel jolted upright again, earning himself a dark look from a nearby sailor whose beer nearly ended up in his lap.

'When?'

'Oh, years ago. Macquarie Harbour was finally closed in 1833, once they'd opened the new prison at Port Arthur. I was about twelve years old when my father was ordered down there to help close the place up and transfer all the prisoners. He didn't want to go and tried everything to get out of it but Lieutenant-Governor Arthur was adamant. My father had seen some rum things in his time and had dragged men screaming to the gallows, but I'd never seen him afraid before.'

'What was he afraid of?' Daniel noted Bisdee avert his eyes for a moment before replying. Either he was lying or didn't want to say.

'I couldn't rightly say, but I heard him tell my mother that he was taking it all back to where it belonged and that he wanted nothing more to do with the damned place. He resigned from the prison service shortly after he returned. That's all I know.'

'Thank you,' said Daniel as sincerely as he could, but Bisdee's face remained closed.

'Thank me by never calling at our door again.' With that, he nodded curtly and left as quietly as he had arrived, hat still in hand.

After a few celebratory nobblers, Daniel took a walk around the battery on his way back to the hotel, heady from the strong liquor and the endless possibilities. Something had frightened Bisdee and if he'd returned items to Macquarie Harbour, Daniel was going there to look for them.

He allowed his mind to drift beyond his doctoral thesis. Outside of academia there was an America hungry for fresh sensation. His published tale of the white cannibal supported by a public exhibition of convict relics and photographs could make his name and help him launch a career as an adventurer and public speaker outside the narrow confines of university life. Dr Morton would be disappointed, naturally, but he'd find a way to smooth things over. He smiled to himself. His father would be proud that he was thinking big. William Ruth always considered that Daniel would be wasting his intellect as a poorly paid academic and wanted his only son to follow him into the shipping business. He was sure he would be able to convince his father to use his contacts to get the artefacts sent back to America, if he could only get them to Hobart.

Holding this thought Daniel turned around and went back to the Whalers' Return to ask the barman, with whom he now had a nodding acquaintance, if he knew of any boats for 'private charter'.

'That depends guv'nor.'

'On what?'

'Whether your business is above board or not. If it is, see Captain Osborne,' he said with a nod towards a man sitting on his right, wreathed in tobacco smoke.

'But if you're wanting no questions asked then Captain Byrne is your man,' he added, gesturing towards a large buccaneering type skulking in one of the snugs with two of his crew at a table crowded with empty jugs and swimming with beer slops.

Daniel opened his mouth to assure him that everything was above board, but the barman held up his hands. 'Truth be told guv'nor, I ain't interested, but if it's of any use to you Byrne's ship is the *Isabella*.'

Early the following morning Daniel went down to the harbour and easily located the three-masted brig *Isabella* lurking behind a tangle of masts, almost as though she didn't wish to be found. She was the only one with a black hull, which enabled her to lie up, undetected, at night.

He waited until ten o'clock, commonly regarded as a respectable time to call, but obviously not for sailors of dubious repute. After standing on the wharf calling 'Ahoy there!' for five minutes, Daniel went aboard and called again, but still to no avail. The *Isabella*'s holds were barred and her shutters closed up tight against prying eyes.

He was about to give up and go home when a needle-sharp steel point was pressed into the back of his neck. The reek of sour breath and strong drink announced Captain James Byrne before he even spoke. The hoarse, rustic-sounding English, which he later discovered was Cornish, carried an unmistakeable hint of menace.

'Who you be boy?'

'Daniel Ruth,' he replied.

'What business have you here, Mr Ruth?'

'I have a proposition for Captain Byrne.'

'And what would that be?'

'I want to charter his boat.'

The point was removed from his neck. 'Turn round slow like and keep your hands where I can see 'em.'

Daniel turned around and saw the large bearded figure he'd glimpsed in the Whalers' Return the previous evening now standing before him. At over six feet tall, Captain James Byrne was an imposing figure. His coarse black hair was pulled back from his face and twisted into a rat's tail that stretched halfway down his back. His dark eyes, still bloodshot after his night of revelry, took Daniel's full measure.

After what seemed like an eternity he asked, 'Where you bound for?'

'Sarah Island in Macquarie Harbour.'

A frown crossed Byrne's face as the destination registered in his still-befuddled brain. 'What in Christ's name would a gentleman such as yourself be wanting in such a godforsaken place?'

'None of your business, Captain,' Daniel replied curtly, anxious to get on even terms with him.

Byrne nodded stiffly. 'That's your sovereign right and rest assured that whatever passes between us is "under the rose",' he said, motioning with his blade at the rose motif carved into the beams above their heads.

The American blinked uncomprehendingly. 'Under the rose?'

'Whatever business we transact here will remain secret. It will never be told to another living soul.'

Daniel nodded, a prickle of excitement raising every hair as he felt Byrne drawing him into a shadowy world of secret codes and silence.

'The outward journey will take four to six weeks depending on the weather, the return as little as four days with a following wind,' Byrne continued, 'What's our cargo?'

'That's none of your concern,' said Daniel, feeling bolder knowing he was now 'under the rose', but it'll be a quick turn-around, no more than a day.'

Byrne showed him a row of discoloured teeth, 'Very well, but silence has its price, Mr Ruth.'

'How much?'

At the mention of money, Byrne suddenly had the look of the fox about him. His eyes narrowed as he looked him over, trying to discern Daniel's desperation and how much he might be prepared to part with.

Daniel had done a rough calculation of wages and supplies for eight men and a fair premium for their silence, then settled on a figure. He recalled his father's mantra: *Never pay more than the figure you have in mind. If you're holding the money, you're holding all the cards.*

'It'll cost you £150,' Byrne said. Knowing that was half a year's wages for a professional man, Daniel shook his head.

'Captain, I wish to charter your vessel not purchase her. £100.'

'You're surely not a seafaring man, Mr Pearce. £125.'

'That matters little, Captain Byrne. £120 and not a penny more.'

'Done.'

Byrne spat on his hand and offered it to Daniel. It was less than he'd expected, but enough to make it worth Byrne's while. 'I'll have some expenses, food, supplies and suchlike,' Byrne continued. Reaching into his pocket, Daniel palmed him a thick roll of paper notes. 'Half now, half on our safe return.'

'Fair play,' said the seafarer.

'When do we sail?'

The captain thought for a moment. 'We'll set sail in a couple of weeks, but you won't be aboard.'

Daniel's mouth twitched, but Byrne intercepted his question. 'Too many pairs of eyes on us. If we leave together the British redcoats will be down here for a looksee the moment we put back in.' With a tilt of his head he added, 'There's a boat called the *Southern Star* berthed on the other side of the harbour. I heard it's taking some piners down to Macquarie Harbour in a day or two. Tell Captain Wilkes I sent you, give him ten quid and he'll take you to Sarah Island with no questions asked. That should give you a few weeks to attend to your business.'

'That should be enough. Piners? What are piners?'

'Men who cut down Huon pines, Mr Pearce. The finest wood for shipbuilding in the known world,' he declared rapping his knuckles on the *Isabella*'s wooden rail. 'This handsome vessel was built at Macquarie Harbour twenty-five years ago with that very same wood.' The knocking brought six other men up on deck, swarthy, unwashed and as hard as tack.

'Lads, this is Mr Ruth. We be going on a little trip with him.' They stared back at him impassively. Pleasantries were not required in their line of work.

As he leapt back onto the quay Daniel had a sudden thought and turned around. 'How do I know you'll come and not just leave me stranded there?'

Byrne looked at him sombrely, his coal-black eyes unblinking.

'Because we shook hands on it and a gentleman is only as good as his word.'

Daniel must have blanched a little because Byrne allowed a smile to split the lower half of his bearded face before yelling across the divide, 'But most importantly, you've got the other half of our money and Captain James Byrne always collects his dues!'

Howls of laughter blew him back towards the town.

Having secured his passage on the *Southern Star*, Daniel purchased food supplies and items such as a canvas cover, blankets, an axe, a crowbar and a tinder; everything he would need to survive for a few weeks in the open as well as a good stock of paper, ink and pens. He also understood the novelty and power of the new art of photography, which Dr Morton had used to illustrate his own books. Daniel dug deep into his cash reserves to purchase a new daguerreotype camera of English manufacture, fifty half-glass plates and the chemicals needed to coat them so that they could capture the images. He could see how photography might help validate his scientific findings more reliably than drawings and sketches.

The *Southern Star* sailed at sunrise on the twenty-second day of April with Daniel and a dozen burly piners on board charged with the task of felling five hundred of the tallest, straightest Huon pines they could find. He'd read in the paper that the Van Diemen's Land shipyards were working to full capacity and were now building more ships than all the others in the colony put together.

Daniel stood on deck where he would eat and sleep for the next month or more and admired Hobart's pleasant aspect. Its orderly cluster of mostly single-storey buildings and tall church spires were squeezed onto the green wedge between Mount Wellington and the River Derwent. He felt satisfied with his quick progress and knew that Dr Morton would approve.

There was precious little activity at that early hour, which drew his attention to the lone figure standing at the furthest point of the harbour out by the beacon. As the boat drew level, Daniel caught only a glimpse of his face in the grey half-light, but realised with a start that the dour countenance belonged to John Bisdee Junior who he caught in the act of crossing himself. *What the hell is he doing here at this hour? Why did he make the sign of the cross?* Before Daniel could turn around, seized by a momentary tremor of foreboding, the figure had given him his back.

Five weeks later the *Southern Star* came in close to a hostile, iron-bound coastline made of rust-streaked rock. He recalled reading descriptions of its bleak character and how it was frowned over by huge mountain masses of such a desolate aspect that the British navigator Matthew Flinders had looked upon them 'with astonishment and horror'.

There was a swell and some motion around the narrow gap through which Captain Wilkes was trying to pilot the ship. A few men crossed themselves when it was remarked that they were about to pass through Hell's Gates, the name the convicts gave to the entrance of Macquarie Harbour. Daniel recalled a passage from his reading, 'It was their proverb that all who entered there gave up forever the hope of Heaven.' Captain Wilkes plunged the ship into the foam, and riding in on the frothy swell, the *Southern Star* fairly 'creamed in' to the wide expanse of still water in the harbour beyond.

A half-day later the small, squat shape of Sarah Island appeared on the horizon. It was vastly different to the exquisite pictures he'd seen in the Hobart library by William Buelow Gould and other convict artists. They'd depicted a well-ordered settlement, designed and planned with typical military efficiency to make full use of every spare inch. Modern boatyards and workshops lined the shores, well-tended agricultural areas were interspersed with impressive stone buildings, there were proper roads, and large sections of the island were encircled by high wooden fences to mitigate the freezing winds and divide the island into smaller, more secure sections.

The order and symmetry he'd admired in the pictures had all been lost. It no longer appeared like the walled castle or fort, as some had described it, though the turreted stone structure of the penitentiary was still clearly visible. Man's fortress in this harbour had quickly crumbled and been softened by a green fringe of trees that defiantly sprung back up out of the ground as though nature was reclaiming what was rightfully hers. The ground was littered with the rotting, rusting relics of Sarah Island's convict past while young saplings poked out of the cracks in the stonework and the roads had been overtaken by grass and weeds. The wooden sheds and workshops had been invaded by the weather and now collapsed in on themselves. Only sections of the high wooden fence remained.

However, the jetty on the southern end of the island showed no signs of wear and tear and was obviously made from the prized wood that the piners had been sent to harvest. Wilkes' crew unloaded Daniel's supplies and cast off again with uncharacteristic haste. As they pulled away there were no farewells or shouts of 'good luck', just a sullen silence.

Even though Daniel was generally regarded as a genial sort,

the piners had viewed him with suspicion from the start. They went silent whenever he approached and then rapidly dispersed. He put it down to the clannishness often found in these tight-knit little fraternities and thereafter kept his own company. Only at the very last did one address Daniel directly. A young deckhand, not yet out of his teens called out, 'Mr Ruth . . .'

'Let it be, Jack,' warned Captain Wilkes sharply, 'it's not our place to be interfering in this gentleman's business.'

'What is it?' Daniel asked, 'do you have something to tell me?' But Jack looked down at his feet and shook his head. *What in the universe was going on?*

'I'll be headed back to Hobart in a day or so. Signal me if you want to leave,' the captain shouted down from the wheel. Puzzled as to why Wilkes thought he'd want to return so soon, Daniel nevertheless waved in acknowledgment. But as he'd noted when they'd passed through the heads, mariners were terribly superstitious and probably thought it bad luck to land on an island where men had been imprisoned and killed.

Alone, and with four or five hours of daylight left, Daniel started looking around the now-abandoned island. He poked about in the bakehouse and tannery, which had been built with pink, under-fired bricks made along the banks of the Gordon River wherever the convicts had found clay of the right consistency. Despite signs of weathering, both still looked quite sound, as did the prison block whose rusting metal doors now stood open. Daniel wandered through the empty offices and cells and peered into the rancid darkness. If any place should have ghosts, this was it.

It reminded him of the Wayside Inn in the picturesque village of Merioneth, just outside Philadelphia. It had been a prison and a military outpost during the War of Independence and was reputedly haunted by a headless, moustachioed Hessian soldier, a young British officer and an American general. Edgar Allan Poe used it as a retreat to drink, smoke opium and pen his dark, Gothic tales. Daniel and his friends had enjoyed a drunken weekend searching the haunted basement and jumping out of shadows at each other but without seeing or feeling any other-worldly presence.

'Where are you, ghosts of Sarah Island?' Daniel called out boldly. The only sounds were his footsteps on the flagstones and the echo of his own voice reverberating back at him off the walls, so he laughed and answered his own question, 'You all died long ago!'

He lay down in one of the tiny solitary confinement cells into which they'd once crammed three men and tried to imagine the suffocation and panic they must have endured. He read the names of the poor souls who'd whiled away the hours carving messages in the wall to sweethearts and families they'd likely never see again.

As Daniel wandered across the island he was assailed by the aroma of wild mint. Looking about him he noted that sage, thyme and sweet briar had also broken out of the once bounteous, well-tended gardens and run wild with the native vegetation. Stands of tall, straggly apple trees still produced fruit, though the apples were now tasteless and gnarled like some Garden of Eden gone to seed.

Down by the shoreline the slip docks had been removed, and rotting pillars and broken wooden fencing was all that remained of the mighty shipyards where eighty-three barques, brigs and cutters, jollyboats and schooners had been built during the turbulent decade of their existence. Chalked on the posts of the sections still standing were the names of those ships: *Tamar*, *Cyprus* and *Frederick* which, he recalled, had been pirated by the convicts and sailed to China and South America in desperate bids for freedom. Byrne's ship, the *Isabella*, which he was now depending on to help him complete his mission, was also named there.

The light had started to fade and Daniel looked up at the two-storey penitentiary that had been built with local stone on the western edge of Sarah Island four years after Pearce was executed. It was also the administrative centre where any records would have been kept and Daniel felt sure his prize lay within.

He found the solid front door barred against him. He'd bought a crowbar in Hobart for just such an eventuality, but no amount of prising or poking would shift it. Built on the edge of a cliff there was no back door and the windows had bars on them, except for those on the second storey. Daniel estimated that it was twenty feet up the sheer wall to the lowest window and searched around for something to help him climb up, but most of the loose wood had been rotted by the persistent damp.

Finally, he stumbled upon some sail-maker's fids, long wooden spikes used to make holes in the thick flax sails so they could be sewn together. Using the blunt heel of his axe, Daniel drove them into the mortar between the sandstone blocks and using them as footholds started upwards.

He was ten feet up when the one below his left foot gave way. The world spun around him as he crashed back to earth. Somehow he managed to land on his feet, but yelled out in pain as he turned his ankle and red lights flared behind his eyelids. Gingerly he tested it and found, to his huge relief, that the joint took his full weight.

Seized with sudden anger and frustration, Daniel picked up the crowbar and started smashing the hooked end against the door. After a dozen blows he was breathing hard and the muscles in his arms burned. Staggering backwards with fatigue, he suddenly heard a jangle and whipped round, ready to confront whatever made the noise.

There was nothing there, only the wind in the trees and the distant sound of waves breaking on the shore. *What did I think it was, a convict ghost jangling its chains?* he smirked, embarrassed at his own fright and how the atmosphere and history of the place were affecting him.

Moving back a step, he looked down and saw a small bunch of keys on the doorstep. Then, peering up, he noticed the stone lintel above the front door that stuck out a few inches making a small ledge wide enough for a set of keys; his hammering must have dislodged them. His father, who'd been brought up in very modest circumstances in the mill city of Halifax, had recalled such quaint British customs from his childhood, but he hardly imagined it would apply to Her Majesty's harshest prison and laughed out loud at the absurdity of it.

At the second attempt, he found the right key and to his relief the lock turned as smoothly as if it had been oiled the day before. He pushed the door open with a creak, releasing the smell of dead air and gathering dust. Fetching up his oil lamp he noted his hand shaking nervously as he clicked the tinder and lit the wick. A warm yellow light flared in the glass and illuminated a stone staircase just in front of him.

He climbed it slowly, axe at the ready, every one of his senses fully deployed. At the top he found what had been offices and cells all open, but there was no sign of the records Bisdee had mentioned.

There was one final door. He tried the handle.

Locked.

His mouth went dry as he told himself, *This is it. Records or bust.*

He found another key that slotted into the lock and turned it clockwise. There was a click and a creak as the door swung open. As he lifted his lamp he felt the breath leave his body. Piled high in that final room was the story of Macquarie Harbour. Trembling with relief and excitement, he entered the room.

The yellowing, mildewed records detailed every aspect of its decade-long existence, of what some historical accounts described as, 'The most brutal penal colony in the history of the British Empire.' Opening a folio at random, he came upon a convict's confession to a murder he had committed, which gave a chilling insight into life at this hateful location.

I am very uneasy in my mind; the Devil terrifies me both day and night, so I never have a moment's rest. I have committed murder! As I and Saul were wandering by the water side, he caught a snake, which he cooked, and of which he only gave me a very little piece. I asked him for some more, and on refusing it, I struck him with the knife above his eyebrows and then in the cheek. The blood then ran down his clothes and he cried out, 'Oh Allen, do not murder me! You may take all my clothes, but don't kill me.' I then stuck my knife into his heart, and ripped his bowels open.

Daniel started moving the wooden crates and sorting through the boxes, opening every folio and checking its contents. Slow and methodical, that was the scientific approach.

By the time the first light split the dawn sky he'd sorted

through hundreds of requisition forms, convict complaints, budgets and official decrees from all three governors and lieutenant-governors Sorell and Arthur, but though desperately tired Daniel wouldn't rest until he'd found what he was looking for. As the pile of unsorted records receded, he began to fear that they weren't there. There were still a dozen identical wooden boxes with the British Royal crest and the notation 'HR' on their sides, but one had no markings.

His breath came in short gasps as he pushed the other boxes aside. *Surely this time.*

He felt his heartbeat speed up as he opened the top folio and found a copy of the official execution notice for *Alexander Pearce, 19 July 1824*. Digging further down he found a folio with four neatly written and bound statements. On closer examination he saw that they were confessions made by Pearce to various people: Commandant Cuthbertson, who Daniel recalled from his reading, was the first governor of Macquarie Harbour; Reverend Knopwood, the magistrate who investigated Pearce's case; and Father Conolly who'd ministered to his spiritual needs once the execution order had been signed. Under these lay other papers related to Pearce's conduct and trial and one last folio at the bottom of the box.

It was the moment of truth and Daniel knew it.

The last item was a leather-bound ledger which was heavy to lift. To his disappointment, he saw it had something to do with accounts, but when he opened it he realised it had been used for a different purpose. As he read the first page a cold shock passed through him and the words swam before his eyes; he'd found more, much more than he'd ever dare dream. *This was Pearce's story written in his own hand.* The thick paper smelt slightly damp and musty, the pages were dog-eared and black where they had been thumbed many times. Daniel ran his hand over the ledger, savouring the thrill of discovery. The past had unexpectedly come to life between his fingers. This was why he'd come.

He closed the heavy, musty smelling book, put it carefully back in the box, and left the room. Walking out into the cold, grey dawn he helped himself to a lungful of salty sea air, which left him as heady as a glass of good wine. Down by the shore he washed his face with handfuls of cold water until his head stopped thumping and the pall of tiredness had lifted from behind his eyes. His blood humming through his body, he looked around the deserted island and recalled the stories of astonishing brutality and despair he'd read in Hobart. *I know something of the world Pearce inhabited, and by God, I'll know a whole lot more by the time I finish his story.*

He walked back up the penitentiary steps and sat at the table. Having travelled from the far side of the world for this moment, Daniel Ruth took a deep ceremonial breath, opened the personal account of Alexander Pearce, the convict cannibal of Macquarie Harbour, and began to read.

Chapter 3

Ghosts of the Dead

Hobart gaol, 18 July 1824

The cadaver lies at full stretch on the table before me. His face is covered with a white napkin. Judging by the bluish tinge blossoming on his snow-white skin, death came some hours ago.

I am something of an expert on the nature of death.

Although I can't see the face, I know it is a man because he is naked. His arms are folded across his chest in the Christian tradition. He is laid out on a long, formal dining table made of dark, polished wood. Mahogany, I think. The faint smell of beeswax mingles with melting candle-wax from the silver candelabra that sits in the middle of the table.

The table is situated in a grand dining room, the like of which I have never eaten in. It's set for dinner. The cadaver rests on a starched white tablecloth with knives, forks, spoons, platters, bowls of fruit and vases of long-stemmed white lilies arranged around him. Black-suited servants lurk in the alcoves and window nooks, ready to be of service. Their faces are obscured by shadow.

One steps forward and pulls out a chair for me. As I sit down I ask him, 'Where are the others?'

'You'll be dining alone tonight, sir,' is his crisp riposte. No one has ever called me 'sir' before.

'But there are twelve places set,' I protest.

Brandishing a large carving knife, he ignores my concerns and asks, 'Would sir prefer leg, breast or offal?'

I look at him aghast.

Opening the cadaver's folded arms, he inserts the point of the knife into his forearm and draws the sharp blade across his flesh. The wound gapes open but to my great surprise there is no rush of blood. As he carves a portion of pinkish flesh onto a white china plate and sets it before me he remarks, 'If I may be so bold, sir, the choicest cut on the human body is the soft meat on the inside of the forearm.'

'What ghoulish monstrosity is this?' I shout, my outrage building as I try to overcome the shock.

The servant looks puzzled. 'Are you not Alexander Pearce of Macquarie Harbour recently convicted of murder and cannibalism? Didn't you tell the Reverend Knopwood that you preferred human flesh to chicken or pork?'

To remind me of my disreputable past, the white-gloved servant carefully removes the napkin from the face of the dead man. I recognise his face and the gaping wound on the side of his head instantly.

The corpse opens its eyes and turns to look at me. A broad smile splits his lips. 'Remember me Alec? Alex Dalton. You killed and ate me not a year since. The twenty-seventh day of September it was. I believe you had a portion of my liver, some thigh, breast and one of my cheeks.'

'No ... no,' I stammer, my heart racing and breath

coming in short, sharp bursts.

Dalton smiles at me with no hint of malice or rancour, just sadness tinged with regret. He reaches out and grasps my wrist. His touch is as cold as marble. 'You only did what you had to. It was the others who hatched the plot and made you turn against me.'

I sit there and shake like the last leaf of autumn.

'Ah well, you can eat your fill tonight,' he muses and turns his head away again. The servant replaces the napkin.

'Bon appetite,' calls Dalton in that sing-song accent God had gifted the people of Cork, muffled slightly by the cloth covering his face.

'Alec, Alec . . .' I hear a faraway voice calling my name. I tear my attention from the ghoulish repast that has been laid before me and struggle towards the sound like a drowning man to the light.

As I break the surface of my delirium, I greedily gulp down great lungfuls of dank, musty air. Despite the damp and chill that seems to emanate from the stone walls that surround me, I am drenched in sweat and my whole being shakes as though I were in the grip of some virulent fever.

The horrible sight of Dalton presented to me like a turkey dinner re-awakens the terrors of my conscience, which refuse to be stilled. I've had the same dream every night of late as the ghosts of the dead continue to visit me. *Are bad dreams a sign of madness?*

While I ponder this question I slowly unclench my fists and let out an anguished wail as I see I've driven my fingernails deep into my palms, drawing blood.

'Bad dream was it, Alec?' says a deep baritone with a flat lilt that hails, like mine, from the northern counties of Ireland.

As I drift on the uncertain tide between wake and sleep, my eyes adjust to the gloom and I see the fleshy, disembodied face of Father Philip Conolly peering at me from the darkness. I blink and wonder if he is real or part of the same terrible apparition. Still lost halfway between this world and the other, I hold up my bloodied palms and cry, 'I'll die for your sins?'

Exhibiting the patience of Job, the priest sighs at my blasphemy and addresses me in an urgent voice very much from the world of the living. 'Alec, this is no time to mock God. I urge you to confess your sins and repent. He is merciful to those who repent, even with their dying breath.'

The sombre reminder of my impending fate lands in the pit of my stomach as I wake from one nightmare to find another awaiting me.

I am going to die, but for my own sins and no one else's.

In the wide, cobbled yard above my prison cell, bounded on all sides by tall, sandstone walls, I can hear the hangman making ready for my dispatch.

The English, being the great nation they are, have a procedure for everything, the gruesome business of execution included. By decree, the noose must be tied around two sandbags, each weighing approximately half my body weight, and dropped through the heavy wooden trapdoor twelve times to test its readiness. The trapdoor snaps open on well-oiled hinges with the monotonous regularity of the prison clock, whose merry chimes at each quarter hour recall a life beyond this hell made in sandstone and lime plaster. Each discordant crash reminds me that my time is on the ebb.

Tomorrow I die.

*

My executioner comes to see me in the forenoon to obtain the necessary measurements to prepare my dispatch. Solomon Blay, an ex-prisoner from Oxfordshire, is the Hobart hangman. He is one of the great characters of the colony, known and feared by all. Whenever he gets word that there are men to hang, 'Old Solomon', as he is known, takes to the road dressed in a long black coat and hat, carrying a small leather bag. It looks similar to a doctor's except that his dispenses death. He is a common sight on the roads between Oatlands, where he lives, and the prisons at Richmond, Hobart and Launceston where he plies his grim trade. He walks because superstitious coach drivers refuse to pick up a 'merchant of death' and his wages are so low that he can't afford a horse.

Bringing with him the smell of fresh rain and open fields, Solomon Blay enters my cell. A tall, wispy fellow with wild white hair, wrinkled, pock-marked skin and a pure white beard that tapered to a point some way below his bow-tie, he is a far cry from the rough, cold-eyed brute of popular imagination.

Showing no fear of my reputation, he draws near and pushes his face close to mine to examine my neck. Working with death has ploughed deep furrows into his face. Fixing me with dark eyes that are almost hidden beneath his tangled eyebrows, he withdraws a neatly coiled tape-measure from his little bag.

As my hangman fits me for my hempen cravat he discusses my execution as other men would the weather, interspersing anecdotes with my measurements, which he mutters out loud. Death is a craft like any other.

'Neck, ten inches . . . We use the so-called "English drop", he explains as he slashes the tape through the air like a rapier, then winds it round my neck. 'It relies on a fall through the trapdoor to break the neck, rather than the old method of removing the chair from beneath the victim's feet and letting them expire by way of slow strangulation, which is still favoured on the European continent, I'm told.'

I nod as he places the cold metal tip of the tape against the underside of my chin and lets the roll flutter to the floor.

'Four foot eight inches ... We only use the best here,' he assures me. 'The rope is three-quarter-inch manila hemp boiled, dried and cured with melted paraffin. It must be short enough to prevent your feet from touching the ground at the bottom of the fall.' Motioning me to stand on the scales they use to weigh out wheat and corn, he carefully places and replaces round lead weights until he is satisfied a perfect balance has been achieved.

'Nine stones and two pounds ... The noose must be heavy enough to bring you to an abrupt halt in mid-air, but not so heavy as to tear your head from your shoulders.'

I stop listening to his patter as, truth be told, it matters little. Chief Justice Pedder has also decreed that I be 'atomised' after death, an ignominious fate reserved only for the 'worst of the worst'.

Once my neck has been broken and Colonial Surgeon Scott is satisfied that life is no longer extant, the prison surgeons will cut me down, joint me like a chicken and send the portions to the eager quacks in their subterranean morgues where the stench of chemicals and decaying flesh nip the nose. In the tradition of the wizards and witches who came before them, they will attempt to discern what made me a monster from my lumps, bumps and the shape of my limbs. This voodoo is grandly called science which, apparently, is excuse enough for any act of barbarism.

Solomon Blay leaves me with an assurance that he has attended to at least a hundred successful executions. I shake his hand and thank him for his consideration, even though I know that my suffering is of little consequence. Prison scuttlebutt has it that the newly installed lieutenant-governor of Van Diemen's Land, Colonel George Arthur, will attend my farewell party. Such a distinguished gentleman will not wish to be embarrassed by a slipped knot or a sudden decapitation, especially in front of the scribes. They will be present to describe, in florid detail, the last moments of the 'cannibal convict' who, as they've so colourfully put it, 'is laden with the weight of human blood' and has 'banqueted on human flesh' for the titillation of readers at the four corners of the British Empire.

No, your eyes do not deceive you. I am a man-eater, a cannibal. At first, I did it out of necessity but, as with all habits, it took a hold of me and I started to crave human flesh.

For the last time, through the bars of my cell I watch the red and gold rays of a winter sunset disappear behind the wide, slated roof of St Matthews as darkness spreads out over Hobart Town. I still have one sunrise left.

Conolly sighs, as though divining my melancholy thoughts. Though it is customary when sentencing a man to death, in my case Chief Justice Pedder did not ask God to have mercy on my soul. This duty was handed to the lugubrious Conolly on Friday last after the lieutenant-governor announced I would be hanged on Monday morning.

The condemned are allocated a priest to help them come to terms with their crimes and to accept the justice of the courts. On the gallows the British want shows of repentance not defiance, as has been the fashion with bushrangers. At least Conolly is a Holy Roman and an Irishman to boot. During the first years of the colony, the English refused to allow priests to minister to the needs of Catholic prisoners. Those requiring ecumenical guidance had to make do with a Presbyter unable to take a confession, offer absolution, or give Holy Communion. Given their history, the English, of all people, should know the difference between the two.

This afternoon, after we'd done much praying, Conolly read me the 'condemned sermon' and exhorted me to 'throw myself on the mercy of God'. 'Confession,' he assured me, 'would be followed by absolution and Holy Communion.'

I demurred, but still he persisted. 'Alec, as long as there's life, there's hope of God's mercy.'

Last-minute conversions are not unusual as the notion of good and evil finally becomes clear to those about to enter the hereafter. The magical ritual of confession and Divine forgiveness is apparently proof of God's intervention in human affairs. Why he doesn't intervene sooner is simply covered by the catch-all, 'God moves in mysterious ways.'

I managed to hold out on Conolly for nearly three days. The need to retain my dignity, a small measure of control over the last thing on this earth I can call mine, was my main reason. They've locked me up, judged me by their rules, condemned me to death, lampooned me in the press and now are preparing to hang me. Everything is on their say-so, according to their rules, but my soul is still mine and they can't make me give up its secrets. But for all my failings I've never been a difficult or quarrelsome man and I realised that Conolly was genuinely concerned about my fate. I relented.

'Father, I'm ready to confess,' I said with a sigh, though, in truth, I have no desire to make peace with a god who has shown me precious little mercy in this life. I suspect Father Conolly knows my true feelings, but he takes his vocation seriously and believing he'd saved my soul from purgatory would be more of a comfort to him than it would to me.

I confessed to all my mortal crimes, but did so in Irish so no one could hear me; I also insisted he write it down in Irish so no one but he could read it. I think my discretion and the shocking nature of my sins convinced him I was truly baring my soul to him.

Finally, another long day in the service of the Good Lord over, Conolly stands with difficulty. His short, stout legs and creaking knees are barely able to raise his portly form from the rough wooden bench he's been warming since the departure of my executioner.

Now that the hour of his liberty has struck and he's saved my mortal soul from the Devil, Hellfire and suchlike, the good Reverend has better places to be. A warm at the hearth followed by a hearty repast and fine wines at the Reverend Knopwood's table, finished off by the port and cigars I can smell on his breath in the mornings. I don't begrudge him these temporal pleasures; 'Life is for the living,' as we Irish are fond of saying.

From his standing position Conolly looks down and again exhorts me in his rich baritone, 'Spend this last night in prayer, Alec. I implore you.'

I nod as he turns to go. 'Good night, Father.'

'Bless you my son,' he replies and makes the sign of the cross just as Governor John Bisdee, my gaoler and true confessor, arrives to take over the death watch. The priest, if he but knew it, had obtained from me a second-hand confession, not nearly as detailed as the one I'd already given Bisdee.

*

Not yet thirty years old, John Bisdee is a man full of enterprise and purpose. He arrived here from Somerset as a free settler only four years ago. In that short time he has been appointed governor of Hobart gaol, has received a generous land grant out at Jericho where I was taken by the redcoats, has bought up other leases and established a market garden. The contrast between the enterprising, God-fearing gaoler and the condemned cannibal couldn't have been greater, yet we've struck up a friendship of sorts.

Bisdee feels sorry for me because the whole world is my enemy; no one has a good word for me, not even the convicts. I am facing certain death, but have expressed some measure of repentance; he also knows I didn't commit those terrible crimes of my own volition.

Most condemned men feel the need to make their peace, despite having lost whatever faith they once had. Consequently, gaolers hear more confessions and confidences than any priest. With an extra lump of meat, a blanket and the odd nobbler of rum, they do what little they can to ease the difficult final passage.

Seven months ago, following my capture and hasty dispatch to Hobart, I told him things I never told Conolly or any of the others I had confessed to. As I spoke he clasped his hands tightly together and whispered prayers under his breath.

He came back to me some hours later in his nightshirt. Worry was etched into his young face and fear sunk deep around his tired eyes. 'Make a clean breast of it to the lieutenant-governor,' he implored me.

'Why would he grant an audience to a mere convict?'

'I am not without influence as regards his Excellency and if he understands the delicate nature of your request, I'm sure he'll agree.'

'But they'll hang me,' I protested.

Almost demented with dread, he clutched my hand with a fierce strength, fixed me with his pale blue eyes, and petitioned me again with all the Christian conviction he could muster. 'It's deep within you, Alec,' he breathed with a tremor in his voice. 'That terrible hunger will return again, but stronger than before. As it says in the Book of Joshua, "Choose this day who ye shall serve". Rest in peace or live in torment, it's up to you.'

Having done all that he reasonably could for me, Bisdee returned to his sleepless bed and left me to scribble down my story as I would want it told in the old accounting ledger I purchased for a gold sovereign from a well-known scallywag a few days after my arrival here. I'm certain that my tale will be written many times by unknowing strangers in whatever manner best suits their ends, but 'tis better you hear it straight from the horse's mouth.

The following morning, 13 December 1823, I took the half-mile walk from Campbell Street, in the company of two redcoats, to have an audience with the previous lieutenant-governor, Colonel William Sorell, who, amid some controversy, had been recalled to London, despite vigorous local protests and a petition.

His palatial residence was set in spacious grounds at the eastern edge of 'Hobarton' – as the locals call it. As we crunched over white marble chips up the long driveway, I couldn't help but admire the sandstone building with its red-tiled roof set in a perfect emerald-green oval of grass and garlanded by a wild profusion of English vegetation: oaks, beeches, willows and roses. It looked to me more like a perfect vision of heaven than a mere governor's residence. If I thought heaven looked anything like it I'd petition the Good Lord for forgiveness on my bended knees.

We were met at the front door by a black-liveried servant and ushered through an impressive reception area across a vast expanse of chequerboard-tiled floor. I had never seen such opulence in all my life, and like a curious child took it all in. The walls were lined in rich oak panelling and decorated by large canvases of English landscapes, great moments in British military history, and portraits of Sorell. A horseshoe-shaped staircase swept elegantly upwards to where someone played a sad, reflective minuet.

Our guide stopped at a solid pair of double doors and rapped a military tattoo on the polished oak. A strong, refined voice called 'enter' and we walked through the doors into what I took to be the lieutenant-governor's study. Bookcases lined every wall and at the rear of the room sat Colonel Sorell smartly attired in a navy-blue frock-coat, white shirt and breeches, as befitted a man of his station. Piles of fine, leather-bound books were stacked on almost every surface in the room. He'd already begun the painful process of packing his belongings for the long voyage back to England.

The redcoats delivered me to his desk, saluted, then retreated to the doors where they stood with their muskets raised over their chests. He stood and waved them away, knowing that I might be less inclined to speak in their presence.

As we came face to face I saw him take my full measure, perhaps wondering how such a small, ordinary-looking man could possibly be capable of such barbarity. Although he was some six inches taller than me, he was not what you'd call a big man. Slight, almost slender in build, I put him at somewhere over forty, his soft, refined features the product of centuries of good breeding. Peeking out from beneath his carefully coiffed and teased white hair was a pair of startling clear blue eyes the colour of cobalt.

As this was hardly a convivial business meeting and I was a convict not a gentleman he did not offer me his hand, but nodded politely. 'Please sit down,' he said, motioning to a generously stuffed armchair that almost swallowed me up as I sank into its soft upholstery. I noted that it had been covered over to protect its lustrous fabric from the dirt, nits and fleas that might be found on a convict.

Sorell perched opposite me on a small couch. 'So Pearce,' he began, 'Mr Bisdee petitioned me, with some passion I might add, early this morning to see you about some confession you wish to make. What's this all about then?'

I confessed to twice killing and devouring my fellow convicts and told him that I feared I might do it again.

Once I'd related my terrible tale Sorell nodded, his face noticeably paler than when I'd first entered his study. He staggered a little as he crossed the room to an ornate, highly varnished cabinet of English design, but without losing the poise or natural grace that had characterised his popular but colourful tenure. I expected him to dismiss me immediately but he was in need of fortification. He poured two large brandies, excessive for the early hour, but justified given the extraordinary nature of the confession I'd just made. Forgetting I was a convict, he handed me one glass and drained the other as if it were water. The strong spirit seemed to return the colour to his cheeks and some equilibrium to his legs and he spoke at last.

'I admire your candour Pearce, and understand your need to unburden your soul of such terrible deeds, but you realise that a confession of this nature will consign you to Hell?'

I looked him straight in the eye and nodded. 'Hell's Gates hold no fear for me. I have passed through their grim portals before.'

Chapter 4

Hell's Gates

Off the west coast of Tasmania, May 1822

A VIOLENT SHUDDER SEIZED the timber hull of the *Duke of York* as two weathered, barnacled fangs of rock suddenly came into view. Through the mist and spume that kicked up off a black sea, the narrow gullet we were headed for resembled the maw of some slavering beast. These sentinels of stone, known as Hell's Gates, guarded the narrow, eighty-yard entrance to Macquarie Harbour, the most remote and southerly point of human habitation in the entire Empire. We truly were at the bottom of the world. The only thing beneath us was the frozen extremity of the earth.

The *Duke of York*, a square-rigged barque of no more than three-hundred tons, had fifty-nine convicts aboard, all 'men of bad character and incorrigible conduct', a badge we wore with defiant pride. We had all been transported from some part of the British Isles for greater or lesser acts of criminal behaviour, which we continued on arrival in Van Diemen's Land. After a few trips to the 'bloody triangle' had failed to convince us to mend our ways, we were consigned to Sarah Island, 'a place of secondary punishment' for the remainder of our sentences, so that we might be reformed by more 'traditional' methods.

We had embarked at Hobart almost six weeks before, journeyed down around the South Cape and come halfway up the west coast right into the teeth of the 'roaring forties', the ferocious gales that constantly buffet the western seaboard of Van Diemen's Land. Its terrible power had forced us to ride at anchor south-west of the heads in a sheltered spot between Olsen's Reef and Trumpeter Rock for the past two days where ships have been known to wait more than two weeks for a more favourable northerly before daring to tackle the straits. It was a necessary precaution as the hidden reefs and sandbars that guard this narrow approach are reputed to be amongst the most treacherous on the high seas; its secret depths are littered with the wrecks and bones of the unwary and the unlucky.

A ferocious wind tore at our sea-drenched clothes, its icy fingers numbing our faces and ripping at anything not firmly battened down. The ship's crew and redcoats, soaked through with cold sea water, scurried here and there securing the canvas covers that protected the precious supplies from the ruinous sea water. Everything had to be supplied from Hobart. If even one shipment was lost people in the settlement would starve as the colony hadn't yet been long enough in existence to harvest a single crop.

It was unusual for convicts to be transported on deck but the *Duke of York* was a cargo ship and had no accommodation below – if one could describe the regulation five feet six inches per man on the outward passage from Ireland as such. In a true measure of our lowly station, we were forced to make our beds down in the hold on top of the stone ballast or in the so-called 'star hotel' on the open deck amongst the flour sacks, barrels, boxes and livestock also bound for Macquarie Harbour. The unholy terror of being trapped in a pitch black hell, if she went down, convinced most of us that the deck was the safest billet. As the planks pitched and rolled beneath us, we swayed about like Saturday-night drunks. All of us to a man – convicts, soldiers and sailors – would have bargained away his soul for a warming tot of rum. The sour stench of animal shit and vomit violently assailed my nostrils as it ran down the deck and swirled round my boots before the next wave thudded into our bows, came in over and sluiced it over the side.

There was an ominous creaking as the keel suddenly listed dangerously to port extorting fearful brays, honks, oinks, shouts and squeals from every man and beast on board. Feeling my feet lose their purchase on the sea-soaked timbers, I grasped the taff rail and felt a heavy presence arrive at my side, not purely of its own volition. I turned to view a tall, strapping figure in a heavy army greatcoat clutching at the rail next to me. Even doubled over, he had the bearing of a military man. I'd a feeling I'd seen him before, but couldn't recall where.

'Hell's Gates,' he said dryly, his strong Irish brogue to the fore.

'Aye, and well-named by all accounts,' I replied with a grimace. Though he'd only spoken two words I knew his lilt was from southern Ireland, Cork or Kerry perhaps. I wasn't surprised to hear my own tongue spoken so far from home. It was said that one out of every five men transported to Van Diemen's Land was Irish. Now that both it and New South Wales had been settled, the new colony badly needed labour and Ireland had plenty big, strapping lads and a poor system of justice eager to exile them.

He untangled his long limbs and drew himself up to his full

height, a good foot taller than me, making him a few inches over six feet. He had broad shoulders and a solid build, normally an advantage in the hurly-burly of convict life, but hard to maintain on the meagre convict rations we would doubtless receive at Macquarie Harbour.

Like most convicts he wore his thick mane of black hair below the collar and his beard full, which gave him the wild look of a pirate. But beneath his unruly growth he had a handsome, what my mother called a 'well-ordered', face. That is to say, his nose, eyes and ears were small and in proportion to one another, something that couldn't be said of we Pearces of Monaghan. His prominent cheekbones and solid, square jaw gave him a look of determination and strength. In my experience, a man's countenance generally gives some indication of his soul and Dalton proved to be a case in point.

The big man bowed his head and fixed me with his deep blue eyes, which I imagined once danced with mischief and life. Now all there was was a weary glimmer of resignation common to most so-called 'government men'. He extended a hand, the size of a shovel, which covered mine as he took it in a tight grip. I felt hard callused skin on his palm, a man used to hard work. There was none on mine. A thief doesn't get calluses on his hands, only on his soul.

'Alex Dalton, Cork,' he yelled so I could hear him over the gale, the crashing waves and the seabirds that wheeled and shrieked across the rain-leaden skies.

'Alec Pearce, Monaghan,' I called back. 'We were sentenced at the same hearing in Hobart, so we were,' I added, suddenly recalling where I'd seen him before. 'The same hearing, the same boat and the same first name, to be sure. Maybe our destinies are linked.'

Dalton's mouth twisted into a sad little smile. 'Two Alexanders. Our fathers surely had great hopes for the pair of us.'

'Never knew mine,' I demurred.

'Never?'

'Well, I was only six years when he left. One Saturday he got his coat and went out the door. I can see him yet, a wee man, thin and pale, an older version of me. Through the rain-streaked window I watched him lift his collar and put his shoulder to the cold wind that always gusted down our narrow close. It was then I saw the small suitcase in his hand and thought it odd. I looked over at my ma who was, as always, in the kitchen stirring a pot of broth. "Where's da going?" I asked. "America," said my ma matter-of-factly as though he was just away to get a paper from the shop. We didn't sugar-coat things in our house. As you know yourself, we Irish are a straightforward, fatalistic people and life is just as it appears, hard and unforgiving, a struggle to be endured.'

'Aye, right enough,' concurred Dalton with a grimace.

'I went towards the door, tears in my eyes, but my ma stopped me. "No son, let him go," she said sharply, making no allowance for my tender years. So, I watched from the window until he disappeared from sight. He never said goodbye, never looked back. "Surely he must be away to make his fortune, our fortune, and then he'll be back," I offered. "Aye, that'll be it," said my ma.

'I lived on that hope for years, but he never came back. Years after, I heard my da had worked the wharves in New York, never made a penny, and died of some disease. Though I hadn't thought of him in years, he was still my da whatever else he wasn't.'

'That's a sad tale, Alec, so it is,' said Dalton, but he wasn't in the mood for reflection and after a decent pause allowed a mischievous grin to split his lips. 'Monaghan is the holiest county in all of Ireland, is it not? Did Saint Patrick himself not build a church there?'

'That was Armagh,' I replied, instinctively jabbing my finger northwards as though I were standing back in Market Street blathering to some stranger.

Undeterred, Dalton ploughed on. 'Aye well, I never went as often as I should on a Sunday, but I've heard it said that Monaghan has the prettiest girls in all of Ireland.'

'Ah well, you're right there now,' I conceded, 'but there's plenty of ugly sisters left for the rest of us.'

Dalton threw back his great, bearded head and laughed. That's one of the joys of being Irish. A fellow countryman will always find something nice to say about your county, whether it's true or not.

'Took the King's shilling,' I said nodding at his campaign greatcoat, which had seen better days.

Dalton's mood suddenly darkened. My question had obviously stirred up bad memories. He shrugged. 'Wanted to see what the world beyond Cork looked like, so I did.'

'See any action?'

'Nah, but I was stationed in Iberia and then Gibraltar.'

I nodded though I'd never heard of those places. Like most Irish men of my generation who weren't convicts or immigrants, I'd never travelled more than five miles from the place I was born.

'How did you land here then?'

'I stole some money, absconded, got drunk and then punched an officer,' volunteered Dalton, seeing little need for discretion given the striated circumstances of our meeting. 'Got fourteen years,' he added. A dull light had now replaced the sparkle that had briefly lit up his eyes when we first met. He waited for my story. I took a deep breath.

'I liked shoes.'

'Shoes?'

A violent gust of wind snatched the words from my lips as it tried to tear the sails from the masthead above our heads. Incredibly, some of the jack tars scampered up the rigging and started taking in all the canvas, bar the foresail, in preparation for one of the captain's famous manoeuvres. The boom of the waves as they broke against the great pillars of rock was deafening, but Captain James Kelly had been the first to navigate a ship through these straits into Macquarie Harbour some ten years before and knew all of its wiles. Having slowed her progress as much as possible, he brought her round hard to starboard to get the wind behind us, drenching all on deck in cold brine as she fairly skated towards the narrow gap between the heads.

'Maybe we're to blame!' shouted Dalton over the cacophony as we clung to the rail of the pitching brig as rogue currents tore across our bows.

'How so?' I yelled back.

'Back in the days of King James the First, a man was executed for causing a storm at sea with the intention of drowning a member of the royal family. At the time it was believed that storms were caused by the Devil, the prince of the power of the air, and by those who assisted him.'

Having no earthly idea of the trials that lay ahead of us, I held all such notions to be superstitious nonsense and laughed out loud. 'Well, that would explain why every convict ship bound for Macquarie Harbour gets tossed by a storm.'

'You know, of course, that on its outward journey a sailor aboard the *Prince Leopold,* one of the ships that established the settlement for which we are bound, fell from a mast to his death. A bad omen some would say.'

'For those who believe in omens and suchlike nonsense.'

'You don't then?' challenged Dalton.

'I believe only what I see with my own eyes.'

'Don't mock what you don't understand. As the bard himself said, "There are more things in heaven and earth, Horatio, than are dreamt of in your philosophy."'

'A man of education, a man of war, and a deserter from His Majesty's army; you're a rum mix Mr Dalton and no mistake!'

My newfound mate didn't share my humour, his face set in a brooding expression that indicated a character with many hidden depths. Judging by his speech, deportment and education, he was a cut above the common foot soldier. Perhaps he was a disaffected son of the gentry or a black sheep? The colonies were full of such exotic, tragic types who threw over wealth and privilege for a buccaneering life of adventure. I expected I'd hear the full story by and by.

The fury of the tempest intensified as we prepared to navigate the narrow channel through Hell's Gates, bringing matters of heaven and earth to the forefront of our minds. The foresail cracked louder than a ringmaster's whip and the ship's timbers groaned in protest as the gale again tried to tear her apart. It was as though nature herself was trying to discourage us from entering, but man being the creature he is listens to no reason but his own.

Just when it seemed that we must be dashed to pieces against the unflinching, stony face that now filled our vista, Kelly showed his guile by suddenly tacking hard to port and piloting the flimsy timber hull clean through those treacherous straits. A loud hollow grating echoed up from below as the hull scraped across the top of a ruinous reef that lay just beneath the surface. It had been a close-run thing, even for a ship with a shallow draught.

'Like threading the eye of a needle,' muttered Dalton gripping the taff rail hard enough to make his knuckles whiten. *A soldier who'd lost his nerve,* I observed.

Thankfully, Captain Kelly held his. I looked up to the wheel and saw him brush his fingertips across the brim of his naval cap in a mock salute to the forces of destruction that he'd just cheated once again. Judging by his jaunty step as he descended to the deck to take stock of the damage, he was a man who enjoyed his sport.

Our dramatic entrance was but a purview of the trials that lay ahead of us. If I could have foreseen the events that were to follow, I would've lifted my hands from the rail and let myself slip quietly beneath the white foaming waves. Drowning would have been a more merciful fate.

Chapter 5

A Purview of Hell

As soon as we'd squeezed through the bottleneck, the noise and the storm suddenly abated and we found ourselves bobbing on a wide placid lake. After a spell, a light wind finally rippled the surface and filled the sails while Dalton and I hung onto the rail and silently surveyed the surrounding landscape.

From its narrow portal at the top, Macquarie Harbour opens out to form a wide body of water a mile or two across, which I'd heard many mariners insist was one of the best natural harbours yet discovered. Illuminated by a weak sun that struggled through the brooding clouds above, its mirrored surface stretched away as far as the eye could see to a towering mountain whose bald, rounded peak was swathed in grey mist.

Still wary of rocks and shallow waters, Kelly hugged the right-hand bluff taking us past the pilot's home, a small, shuttered, red-roofed cottage of English character that sat atop the heads. It and a jumble of smaller huts, housing his boat crew and the redcoat guards, nestled next to a solitary pine whose ancient, gnarled limbs had been bent over by the wind and whose wild foliage stuck out at all angles like an unruly haircut. The pilot, Captain James Lucas, had watched our progress from up on the headland and lifted his hand in salute, a gesture that Kelly returned. Lucas had four redcoats next to him, their muskets unslung, in case any of us were game enough to go overboard. Their distinctive tunics were a welcome if ominous splash of colour on a dreary canvas of brownish buttongrass, the only other living thing hardy enough to withstand the terrifying gales that blasted the heads throughout the year.

A mile or two into the harbour the shoreline receded rapidly on either side of us and the thick carpet of buttongrass gave way to miles of tightly packed green forest bounded on all sides by distant, imposing pinnacles of rock that stood testimony to its violent creation in the dark and distant past. I shivered slightly as I was suddenly filled with a terrible foreboding. The silent landscape had an eerie feel, as though we'd entered a lost kingdom that had somehow been suspended in time. Little did I know that this would be the theatre for the most extraordinary of tales.

I pushed such foolish notions from my mind and breathed in deeply. The sight of land, the gentle breeze and the rolling deck were a tonic after being scoured by the elements for the past two weeks.

'It smells as fresh and green as Ireland in the spring,' I waxed, but Dalton grunted.

'They try to soften its harshness with names like the Shannon and the Ouze, but this godforsaken place will only ever be home to tyrants,' growled Dalton, his beard bristling with a deeply held passion. 'Van Diemen's Land is barely twenty years settled and already its ground is soaked with convict blood and a vault for convict bones.' *With a temper like his, it's little wonder he was discharged from the army*, I mused.

I refused to dwell on such melancholy thoughts and instead studied the shoals of fish ghosting through the water below that was stained the colour of tea. They looked the same size as the trout we used to tickle out of the pure waters of the Blackwater River. Oh, what wouldn't we give to have those heady days of summer and youth over once more.

Lost in our pasts, which now seemed more golden than ever they were, we continued in silence for almost the whole length of the harbour, which I estimated to be some thirty miles long and about two wide.

Finally, our destination, Sarah Island, hove into view on the port side. Though it was just six-hundred yards long and one-hundred-and-fifty wide, it was the only island of any size within the perimeter of the harbour. Much heavy clearing and building work had already been progressed and a jumble of low wooden huts was now visible beneath a pall of wood smoke.

'Port over and starboard home,' piped up Dalton, suddenly jocular again, but my mood had soured as we drew near to our destination.

'I doubt there's anything posh, or even remotely comfortable, in this blind hole of a place.'

I was proved right in very short order. In what now, in the re-telling, seems like a terrible portent, we watched fat storm clouds, as black as a witch's hat and laden with rain, come tumbling in over the barrier of mountains that towered heavenwards to the north-east.

'Looks ominous,' remarked Dalton.

Though we had yet to set foot in the place, its short history was already well known to every convict. Following the discovery of the harbour and many years of petitioning the Secretary of State for War and Colonies in London on the need to build a 'place of secondary punishment' in Van Diemen's Land, Lieutenant John Cuthbertson finally arrived at the island last December with one-hundred-and-ten convicts; seventeen NCOs, soldiers and their families; and eleven trusty convicts of 'good avocation': carpenters, ship-builders and sawyers. We were about to witness the fruits of their labours.

The boat came alongside a makeshift wooden jetty whose flimsy construction creaked ominously as the swell lapped against it. We were greeted by an armed detachment of redcoats, the 48th Northamptonshire Regiment of Foot, the so-called 'heroes of Talavera' who introduced themselves from the other end of their bayonets, which they had fixed for the occasion of our arrival.

Their most notable victory since their posting to Van Diemen's Land was the slaying of Michael Howe, the bushranger and self-styled 'lieutenant-governor of the Woods'. A wild, bearded figure who lived out in the forests, dressed in animal skins and wrote his manifesto in his own blood, Howe and his merry men had terrorised the island for six years between 1812–18. When a bounty was put on his head, Howe had the audacity to put a reward on the lieutenant-governor's, though Sorell had the last word. He promised the man who bagged him free passage to England and a big reward. In the end it wasn't a convict but William Pugh, a private in the 48th, who ended Howe's bloody reign by shooting and then beheading the bushranger after a terrific fight.

With redcoats at our front and back, we were herded like stock animals along the wet wooden jetty and onto *terra firma* for the first time in almost six weeks. Buffeted by wind and rain and still suffering from the 'sailor's roll', we staggered up the slippery track, flanked by crude wooden huts and cottages leading to the heart of the settlement.

In one of the adjoining gardens was a welcome sight, a comely young wench bending over as she tended the young plants that had poked their green shoots through the recently tilled soil. We had not so much as seen a woman in many months and the sight of a pair of full, rounded buttocks straining against the seams of a loose-fitting calico skirt was a proper tonic. A low whistle brought her sharply to attention and she turned and eyed her audience with undisguised contempt. With her tall, stately carriage, long dark curls, bewitching black eyes and soft olive skin, there was something exotic about her, a touch of the tarbrush perhaps.

'I'd plough her furrow any day of the week,' muttered someone behind me.

'Only in yer dreams lads,' rumbled the avuncular, barrel-chested Welsh sergeant who commanded the redcoats. 'That there is Sarah Simmons, Commandant Cuthbertson's squeeze.'

The laughter faded as we came up over the rise. The sight that greeted us was not as easy on the eye as Sarah Simmons.

'Holy Mother of Christ,' breathed Dalton as we gazed upon what was surely a purview of Hell. Every tree had been cut, every stump uprooted and the vegetation stripped back to the bare earth, which had been pitted and torn. These craters had filled with water, which had fallen ceaselessly from the leaden skies ever since our landing, to form large, mustard-coloured lakes. The overspill and the constant tread of boots had churned the ground like a ploughed field. Huge roaring pyres, offering a little relief from the biting chill, drifted a thick pall of wood smoke across the devastation, further adding to the primitive, unearthly feel of the place. It was as though every vestige of the old world had been erased and civilisation re-born here.

I quickly observed that there was not a draught animal in sight: men were expected to do their brute work. As if to illustrate the point, the dull rattle of chains gave us our first sight of the convicts who inhabited Hell's Gates. Six men harnessed to a wooden cart piled high with sacks of flour from the ship appeared over the rise, their muddy boots slipping and sliding as they struggled to keep their footing. We recoiled in shock at the sight of the scrawny, toothless men dressed in filthy, sodden rags looking as starved and wasted as desert castaways. Exhaustion was clearly visible in their pinched faces as they shuffled past us dragging fifty-pound balls with their right legs or weighed down with heavy iron collars around their necks. A blue-jacketed overseer urged them on, making free use of every profanity in the convict vocabulary. Others carried full wicker baskets on bended backs like slaves, their yellow uniforms, known as 'canaries', streaked white with lime. Hard punishing labour was obviously viewed as the antidote to villainy.

In the absence of trees, which usually form a natural wind break, fifteen foot-high wooden fences had been erected along sections of the shoreline to moderate the biting gale which whipped across the harbour. Out in the bay, beyond those wooden ramparts, a large, sixteen-oared whaleboat crested white-topped waves as it towed rafts of logs towards shore, the shouting curses of overseers carrying across the water to us. Once they got close in, a gang of fully clothed men waded into the freezing waters up to their waists, manhandled the huge logs ashore, and with block and tackle dragged them across the freshly churned earth to the saw pits.

Down in the pits, rows of ragged figures were crammed together, shoulder to shoulder, stripped down to the waist. Faces shrouded by pointed, calico hoods with eyeholes cut in them, they looked like some secret religious order. They drew long, double-handed saws through huge logs, the heat from their sweating bodies rising in a steamy fog. The logs were sliced into thick boards which others planed smooth, the smell of the fresh white pine shavings, scented with cloves, perfuming the air.

All this effort was being expended on Cuthbertson's pride and joy, the first schooner to be built on Sarah Island. Its keel had already been laid down on the slip, the wooden ribbing of its hull sticking upwards like the bones of a huge whale carcass. Urged on by their overseers, men swung hoists bearing the heavy planks into position so other tiny figures could start hammering, sawing and drilling them into place.

All around us, other yellow-clad convicts fetched and carried, cooked, and tended fledgling vegetable gardens where the first green shoots of potatoes and wheat poked through the black soil. I closed my eyes and listened to the rhythm of their labours clashing together in a discordant symphony, but always in the background, keeping time, was the jangle of irons and chains.

Though they never said a word to us, the old hands eyed us newcomers with an undisguised pity that raised all the hairs on my neck and arms.

More huge logs were tossed on the bonfires which caught alight with a roar, sending Biblical pillars of flame shooting heavenwards.

'Is this our Golgotha?' wondered Dalton aloud.

The redcoats poked and prodded us through the slosh and wet to the parade ground where Lieutenant John Cuthbertson awaited us beneath a Union Jack that fluttered in the stiff breeze. According to the murmurs on the *Duke of York*, he preferred the grander-sounding Commandant to his military rank.

Cuthbertson had earned his commission in Spain during the Peninsular War at the Battle of Talavera. Under the supreme command of Lieutenant-General Sir Arthur Wellesley, better known as the Duke of Wellington, the British were attempting to expel Napoleon's forces from the strategically important Iberian Peninsula. A French counter-attack at Talavera pushed the British back until the 48th Regiment rallied and carried the day. Cuthbertson, also survived the slaughter at Albuera was also later wounded during the epic storming of the fortress at Badajoz and again at Pyrenees.

As we neared, I noted that he stood on a small mound of earth lest his polished boots, Wellingtons not Napoleons, got dirty. Resplendent in full military dress – white breeches, red tunic dripping with gold braid, medals and epaulettes, topped off by a black shalako hat with white pom-poms – Cuthbertson cut a faintly ridiculous figure as supreme ruler of a ragged tribe living in a primitive kingdom of wooden huts and mud. There is nothing worse than a man who has had his ration of glory and cannot admit that those halcyon days will never return. Cuthbertson was clearly such a man.

'The English have a fine sense of pageantry, if nothing else,' muttered Dalton, echoing my own thoughts. Aye, we'd seen plenty of his sort since Cromwell's armies landed in Ireland. As soldiers, magistrates, governors, landowners and factory owners, they'd blighted our country and they'd blight this one too.

'I feel sorry for the blacks; they don't know what's comin' to them,' I replied.

'Don't worry about them, worry about us,' grunted Dalton as we drew within earshot.

Captain Kelly himself brought the dockets detailing our

names and crimes to the commandant who enquired about our conduct during the voyage. Pursing his thin lips and nodding, he seemed more than a little put out when the captain gave us a good reference. The deep lines etched around Cuthbertson's tight mouth suggested it was regularly pinched in annoyance and he had to content himself with a cruel jibe.

'Ah well Captain, the sluicing they got on deck will have freshened them up a bit and rid them of any lice,' he mocked, loud enough for us all to hear. To his credit, Captain Kelly didn't take him on. He simply saluted and left.

'In my experience they either believe in God or the lash and Cuthbertson is of the latter persuasion,' I whispered to Dalton. 'His military record has him down as, "a sadistic bully with unnatural tastes", that's why, at thirty-nine, he has not been promoted for fifteen years and was chosen to pioneer a penal colony at the arse-end of the Empire. You only get posted to places like Macquarie Harbour when there's nowhere to go but down.'

Dalton risked a glance at me. 'You seem to know a lot about him.'

'Aye, I know him well enough.'

We stood in silence as he inspected our ragged ranks. In his immaculate white-gloved hands he held a thick, leather-bound ledger, the infamous 'Black Book', where all transgressions and punishments were recorded. I'd heard it said that he had no qualms about entering the maximum one hundred lashes and then ordering the scourger to hand out a dozen or two more on top. He muttered each name and studied each face for the distinguishing characteristics described in the dockets, as if committing them all to memory.

By the time he arrived in front of Dalton, who stood next to me, our commandant looked as though he had just sucked on a lemon. His hard, grey eyes were the colour of granite, which appropriately announced the unflinching character that lived within. His face was lean and ruggedly handsome, though the ravages of middle age had begun to take their toll. A distinguished grey had started to fleck his mutton chops, but looking beneath his tall shalako hat I noted he combed his hair forwards over his brow in the style of the Roman emperors. This, I fancied, had more to do with vanity than the dictates of fashion. Time had caught up with him as it does all men. A long, white scar traced the curve of his jaw, which must have been sustained in the Spanish wars or in some duel of honour.

When Cuthbertson spoke, a hard-edged Tyrone brogue underscored the carefully cultivated English accent, which he'd hoped would enhance his prospects with the English officer class who were famously disdainful of provincial accents and those who spoke with them.

'Alexander Dalton is it?' sneered Cuthbertson.

'Yes sir.'

Without taking his eyes from him, the commandant proceeded to recite his life story. 'Private, 64th Regiment of Foot. Court-martialled in Gibraltar 1822 for the theft of money, desertion, striking an officer and transported for fourteen years,' he trumpeted, announcing Dalton's private disgrace to all present. He knew full-well that a man who'd taken the 'King's shilling' would always be treated with suspicion by other convicts.

'Did you ever hear the roar of the cannon, Mr Dalton?'

'No sir, I signed on after the Spanish campaign.'

'No sir. See this?' trilled Cuthbertson, stabbing with his index finger at an ornate silver badge pinned to the breast of his red tunic. Under a crown and a scroll inscribed with the word 'Peninsula' was the number 48, which sat atop two oak-leaf clusters and a second scroll bearing the word 'Talavera'. 'That's where these boys gave up their lives to carry the day for King and country. You're a blackguard and a disgrace to the army and His Majesty.' A speck of white spittle escaped from the side of his mouth as he leaned close to Dalton and growled, 'Watch how you go, Mr Dalton. One slip and I'll have the skin off your back.' He glared at Dalton for fully half a minute before lowering his gaze a good foot to run his searching gaze over me.

I imagined my record would have simply said, 'Convict 102. Born Carrickcross, county Monaghan, 1790, convicted of petty theft at Armagh Assizes, 1819. Five feet and three inches, brown receding hair, grey eyes. Pock-marked skin and mutton chop sideboards. Unmarried. No distinguishing marks' – the sum total of my existence so far. However, there was one more item of interest and Commandant Cuthbertson showed he was blessed with excellent recall.

'Mr Pearce, I believe we met last year. After trying your hand at banditry, you and a number of other Vandemonians took advantage of the lieutenant-governor's amnesty and surrendered yourself to me at the Coal River.' He fixed me with those flinty grey eyes and stood his ground until I acknowledged he was correct.

'That's right, sir,' I conceded. *No mention though of how you blew poor Atkinson's hand off when he didn't raise it quickly enough for your liking.*

'Don't entertain any such foolish notions here. I don't give amnesties. Ever,' he growled. There was a dangerous edge to his voice that suggested this was no empty threat. It was our first and by no means our last sighting of Cuthbertson's true nature. He may have been Irish, but it was clear his fellow countrymen would get no favours.

Having inspected his new subjects, our Commandant returned to his mound and from his tunic produced a scroll. He very carefully undid a scarlet ribbon and unfurled an official-looking document, holding it up for all to see. It was written in a neat hand and sported an impressive red wax seal and ribbon at the bottom. Clearing his throat, Cuthbertson spoke in a firm voice with as much gravitas as he could muster.

'I wish to read to you from a letter sent to me by Lieutenant-Governor Sorell, who charged me with the task of founding and administering this new penal colony.' He paused a moment as he found the pertinent passage: '"Nothing I can imagine is more likely to lead to the moral improvement of the most abandoned characters in this colony than a rigid course of discipline, strictly and systematically enforced at the penal colony of Macquarie Harbour. You will consider that the constant active unremitting employment of every individual convict in very hard labour is the grand and main design of your settlement. Banishment to Macquarie Harbour must not only be felt but considered by a whole class of convicts a place of such strict discipline that they may absolutely dread the very idea of being sent there. Never lose sight of the continued, rigid unrelaxing discipline and you must find work and labour, if it only means opening up cavities and filling them up again. Unceasing labour, total deprivation of spirits, tobacco and comforts of every kind, the sameness of occupation, the dreariness of occupation, must, if anything, reform the vicious characters who are sent to you."'

Just as carefully, as if afraid his edict might crumble to dust and divest him of the powers it contained, Cuthbertson rolled up the scroll and secured it with the red ribbon. Then, holding it aloft, he curled his top lip in a cruel sneer and said, 'This is my mandate and my Holy Book. As Commandant, Magistrate and Chief Justice, my power is absolute. I am the law in this settlement and I intend to use it to its fullest extent to bring you to heel. You're far from Hobart and even further from Sydney where that bloody Scotchman, Macquarie, would have you believe a convict is as good as a free man.'

Publicly cursing the Governor of New Holland would ordinarily earn you a striped back and spell in gaol, but out here he was beyond all reproach and Cuthbertson wanted to apprise us of that fact. It seemed to me more than mere irony that they'd named this place of punishment after the most liberal-minded governor the colony has ever had. Far from a compliment, it was a well-aimed dart. He raised his right hand aloft and performed a little pirouette on his mound.

'What you see all around you is a "fortress of nature". This is a prison without walls or bars but the sea, rivers, mountains and impenetrable forests form a natural barrier that cannot be breached. Two months ago eight of your fellow convicts took off into the bush with two of my regiment, two kangaroo dogs and three convict workers in pursuit. None returned, not even the dogs which, I'm told, the natives regard as something of a delicacy. Their fate I shall leave to your own fertile imaginations.' Cuthbertson paused for effect and then ended his welcome speech with a piece of advice: 'Work hard, obey orders and you will have nothing to fear, but transgress and I warn you right now my scourger's lusty right arm will have the skin off your back by the fourth stroke.'

This was his cue for a struggling convict to be pulled out of a nearby wooden hut and dragged down to the place of punishment. Three wooden triangles stood on a flat piece of ground to the side of the jetty, their posts driven into the shingle just above the high-water mark. We were poked and prodded across the rocks to witness the spectacle. By the time we arrived the man's arms had been raised up and lashed to the pole above his head, his ankles to each pole and the shirt ripped from his back.

The burly scourger, his head shaven like some medieval torturer, had a cat draped over each shoulder. 'That cat looks to be double the weight of the one they use in the army,' observed Dalton, 'they mean to cause him as much pain and damage as possible.'

Dalton was right. Having been tied to the halberds a few times myself, I noted these cats each had nine tails. Each one was about four feet long and made of three strands of leather woven together using nine overhand knots. One was tipped with wax, the other with bits of metal for extra bite. It was known as the 'thief's cat' and altogether worse than anything the redcoats or jack tars would ever have to suffer.

Next to me Dalton started snorting and hacking softly then, without warning, pursed his lips and sprayed the scourger's broad back with a stream of greenish spit. Dalton gave a little self-satisfied smirk. A justified but reckless gesture of defiance. He didn't react or try to wipe off the spittle, but turned to face us in his own time. An ugly specimen of humanity, there was not a trace of pity or human compassion in his lined face, which had been deeply scored by time and hardship. 'All the worse for him,' he said with malice, tilting his head towards the unfortunate lashed to the triangle. He turned his back on us and flexed his great shoulders. The message was clear. We might be able to defy them here or there but they would have the last word, always.

Like some dandy in a music hall caper, Cuthbertson strolled on stage holding the infamous Black Book open. Moving a white-gloved finger down the list of the vanquished, his brow creased and in his carefully refined English accent said to the flogger,

'This man has been punished before, but doesn't seem to have learned that sleeping during the hours of work is not acceptable conduct.' Pointing to the worst of the two cats he said, 'The wire-tipped one today, I think Mr Flynn. Teach this wretch a lesson he'll never forget.'

'Aye, sir,' grunted the flogger, brushing his brow with his fingertips in a mark of deference. It obviously paid to stay on the right side of Cuthbertson.

A scourger was a good position for a certain type of man. They performed no hard labour, were allowed comforts the rest of the convicts were denied, and got better rations of food. Mind you, if we ever rose against our gaolers, he'd be the first one to go down.

This little bit of theatre also gave us our first sighting of Dr Spence, a thinning, flame-haired Scotchman, a Highlander I would have said from his accent. Though slight in stature, he was not short. He only appeared so next to the large, brawny soldiers and convicts to whom he now ministered. Spence was still the right side of thirty but despite his relatively young age, the crimson blush of the hard drinker had already bloomed on his face. It had blurred his once-fine features and given him a permanently dazed air. Like many of the soldiers and convicts we'd seen on the island, he had a worn, hollowed-out look about him, as though he'd seen too much of life already. In a place like this, grog and laudanum was the only refuge for a man of conscience powerless to stop the brutality he had to bear witness to then fix up each day.

The victim had been hung so as Cuthbertson and Spence could see his face and back alternately, as they promenaded up and down the jetty, each stroke being delivered as they turned, This gave the flagellator ample time to 'season' the cat by dragging it through the sand so he could inflict even greater damage with the next stroke. As Assistant Colonial Surgeon, Spence could call a halt to the punishment, but he daren't cut across Cuthbertson and hated himself for it. Consequently, any man who got a 'canary', the maximum one hundred strokes, would be at the triangle for over an hour and have to endure double the time and double the pain.

Flynn took a perverse pleasure in his work, delivering the first stroke with a great, round-shouldered swing. The slap of leather on skin resounded so loudly that men tending the gardens some distance off stopped their labours and looked up.

'One,' shouted Cuthbertson briskly, up on his toes. Clearly, he relished the crack of the cat.

There are two types of convicts, the game ones and the screamers. The poor unfortunate lashed to the triangle belonged to the latter fraternity and his piteous cries began when the first stroke landed, sending squalling seabirds skywards. As we watched the convict get a 'red shirt', Dalton muttered out of the side of his mouth, 'Had much air and exercise, then?' as we convicts called a flogging.

'A bit.'

'What's the worst flogging you've had?'

'Two bobs in five days,' I whispered back a little boastfully, not wanting him to think that because I was small I couldn't hack it.

He gave a low whistle. 'A hundred strokes in less than a week,' exclaimed Dalton, a new respect in his voice. 'What was that for?'

'The first time I was drunk and disorderly and the second time I got drunk and disorderly and stole a wheelbarrow with two turkeys and three ducks in it.'

There was a low rumble in Dalton's throat, 'You're naught but a common thief.'

'That I am.'

Flynn had a strong arm but was no master of his craft. As he landed each stroke the steely tips of his tails curled around his victim's front leaving angry red weals around the ribs, neck and stomach. It only takes five or six strokes to break the skin and that is punishment enough for most men. However, this flogging was not punishment but instructive like the display of bayonets, to educate us recent arrivals in the ways of Sarah Island. The transgressor was due to receive a 'Botany Bay dozen', prison cant for twenty-five strokes, but by the time the cat had been laid across his back fifteen times, it was as raw as a bullock's liver. Blood covered his back and stained his breeches but mercifully, he'd lost consciousness – not that it spared him further punishment. Our commandant's only action was to shout, 'Come on Mr Flynn, take another half pound off the bugger's ribs,' and meticulously enter the tally in the Black Book once the final stroke had been delivered.

We'd all been lashed and seen plenty men experience the same but what happened next staggered even the older hands. Instead of allowing the medic to wash his injuries, slather some hogs' lard on a bit of tow and cover his ruined back, Cuthbertson flicked his fingers signalling an overseer to dump a bucket of briny water over the bloodied and crumpled figure, making him cry out again. This was known as 'getting salty back'. Then, with his lip bitten back in a cruel curl, the commandant yelled at the redcoats, 'Get him back to work. If he complains or refuses, bring him back and give him another dose of the same.' Cuthbertson glanced over in our direction to ensure his point was made then turned on his heel. In Hobart gaol this settlement was often referred to as 'the Devil's Island' and now that I'd met the Devil, I knew why.

We were prodded back towards the huts where we would be billeted, slipping and sliding on the slick of mud that seemed to cover the whole island. A constant drizzle drifted down from the low, scudding clouds.

The settlement, such as it was, was a dreary clutch of buildings. Care and better materials had been lavished on the soldiers and officers while we convicts were housed in wretched huts made from green shingles and badly fitting boards; in truth they offered as much shelter from the elements as a picket fence.

Our possessions were searched and any food items, tobacco, grog or anything that could be deemed a human comfort were confiscated. They would doubtless be sold back to the hapless owner at a handsome profit once the deprivation became too much to bear. Just because convicts were forbidden from having rum, tobacco and food it didn't mean they couldn't have them. All this and more was freely available from the freebooters, petty thieves and frauds who'd put their old skills to good use making life here a bit easier. During the voyage we heard they brought in their booty under the hulls of the supply ships with a whipping line attached so they could pull it ashore under the noses of the redcoats who knew all about it and were all in it. The odd shipment was seized to fool the commandant into thinking that his men were vigilant.

I had nothing of interest or value bar the few gold sovereigns I kept in the false toe of my left boot – a little cushion should I ever find myself in a tight spot or, God willing, ever make it back to civilisation.

Our convict numbers were called in ascending order and

one by one we entered the quartermaster's hut, were ordered to strip and put on our 'canaries', also known as 'slops', while they burned our own clothes. The winter issue was a yellow wool shirt and jacket and canvas trousers with broad arrows painted on them. Like the bayonets and the flogging this little ritual also had its meaning - we were no longer men, we were government men.

The light dimmed quickly as the sun dipped behind the distant hills and the air took on a chill as men began to return from their work gangs. The roaring fires were stoked up so they could take some heat and dry out before dinner and curfew. The old lags entrusted with this task showed us how to treat our clothes so that they afforded us some protection from the rain. They told us to stuff our jackets and trousers up the bakery chimney until they were properly 'smoked' then cover them in animal fat, which would dry and harden to form a shield against the water which, they assured us, fell from the leaden skies for more than three hundred days of the year.

We were but babes in the wood.

Before the sun had set on our first day I learned that punishment on the island was as natural as living and breathing. While smoking my canaries I made the acquaintance of Mordecai Cohen, a short, soft-spoken Jew with mournful eyes and a rapidly receding hairline who looked more suited to a bank or a courtroom than a gaol. Though his education and bookish knowledge had not spared him the same fate as the illiterates, Mordecai had the courage of a lion. He told me how, following the first escape, Cuthbertson had exercised his magisterial powers.

'That damned despot convened a court on the jetty and

quizzed the men as they came ashore, one by one. But to his chagrin, each one repeated the same carefully prepared statement.'

'Carefully prepared by you?' I asked.

He smiled enigmatically as he recited it back to me. '"Each of us has a right to escape this tyranny. Nor can we be compelled to pursue those who choose to invoke that right to escape." I was the only one who could be goaded into saying anything more. I knew he suspected I was behind this little show of defiance. After all, who knows persecution better than a Jew?

'"Is that all you have to say for yourself?" Cuthbertson berated me. "Yes," I replied.

'"And you an educated man of faith. If you have no more to say then you must accept without reservation that the punishment you will receive is fair and justified." I stood there silently. Cuthbertson flicked a dismissive hand at me.

'"You had your chance. Take him away." As two burly overseers converged on me, I found my voice. "Sir, your laws have neither justice nor humanity to recommend them," I cried out in bitter rebellion. Holding up a hand to prevent me being seized by the collar, Cuthbertson leaned back in his chair, a sarcastic grin spread wide across his face.

'"Needs must, Mr Cohen," he said. I continued, "We are punished for being hungry, we are punished for being persecuted and we are punished for being banished to this miserable place without hope or comfort. We are prisoners of a Civil War we do not understand, a war we cannot hope to fight or win. We will not pursue those who choose to do so." My point made, I said no more. The commandant brought his two hands together four times in a slow hand clap and in that *faux* English accent he insists on using said piously, "Very well spoken man, but as it says in the Book of Psalms, *I will visit their inequities with the rod and their transgressions with stripes.*"

'He lined up some thirty convicts, including myself, and ordered the scourger to give us twenty-five strokes each for failing to prevent our fellow convicts absconding from their work details.'

Cohen also told me about the libertarian ideals of Mr Jeremy Bentham of London, who openly questioned the effectiveness of excessive punishment. His ideas were gaining in popularity, but I'd wager all the gold in my boot that it will be another hundred years before they reach this bleak anchorage. Cohen's courage under fire gave me hope, which I sensed was a very precious commodity on Sarah Island.

Chapter 6

The isle of Misery

BEFORE FIRST LIGHT THE next morning I started the dreary routine that the authorities intended would occupy the life of convict 102 every day for the next five years – if I survived that long. We were roused by the bell still in the black hours before the winter dawn and made to stumble our way to the parade ground for the muster. Fog had settled like a thick blanket on top of the pitted, ripped earth as scores of ghostly figures slipped and slid through the mud, freezing rain slanting into our faces. All convicts were mustered, military fashion, before dawn every morning, seven days a week, before leaving with their work details. The Sabbath, held sacred even by God, was a working day to Cuthbertson who believed that if man could work on Sunday, he could also be flogged. Our only days of rest would be Christmas Day and the King's birthday.

The first order of the day was gunfire. The soldiers were under strict orders to have their guns loaded at all times, but the damp played havoc with the gunpowder and paper cartridges they rammed down their barrels, so they had to discharge and re-load their muskets each morning. It also served as a reminder to we convicts that they were always in good working order.

The roll was then taken under Cuthbertson's watchful eye. Any man who failed to respond when his name was called, was late or disturbed the count could bet on getting twenty-five strokes. Dr Spence, clearly a slave of his own desires, would sometimes be called to the muster to examine a sick man before he had sufficient time to repair the abuses of the previous night. The man would nearly always be declared fit.

The dull clank of heavy chains and the shuffle of feet heralded the arrival of the unfortunates we'd first seen upon our arrival – the 'out and outers' from Grummet Island who were brought under heavy guard to Sarah Island every morning to work. They were so-called because they would use any means to escape this place, even a hangman's noose.

The diet of fear kept most convicts cowed, but there were those who would never yield, never learn, even in a place like this. For this class of offender, the so-called 'hard men', a separate, more severe place of punishment had been established on Grummet Island, a small dome-like rock that lay to the north-east of Sarah Island. It too had been shorn of every tree, leaving all who resided there exposed to the cruel vagaries of the weather.

At the end of each day they rowed in their whaleboats back to the small island whereupon they jumped overboard into chest-high water, waded ashore and spent the freezing winter nights in wet clothes crouched like hermits in cells that had been gouged by hand into the seaward cliffs.

By the time we'd had breakfast, which consisted of a thin porridge made of flour, water and salt known as 'skilly', and sat in our whaleboat until the sun came up, we were already frozen to the marrow by the driving rain and the cold, howling wind. A number of lucky convicts had 'billets', light duties such as gardening, cooking, acting as overseers and tradesmen. They stayed in huts with only two to eight men, copped better rations and were allowed comforts like rum and tobacco that were denied the rest of us.

We could be assigned to any number of hard, unpleasant tasks such as timber-felling, coal-labouring or burning charcoal for the blacksmith's forge. Coal was mined at the aptly named Coal Head on the north shore of the harbour. At first they thought it would at least keep the colony supplied with winter fuel, and although it turned out to be low grade and smoky, it was free and required heavy labour so they kept mining it.

On the banks of the Gordon River convicts also made bricks from river clay and burned limestone to make mortar which would be used to construct the more substantial stone structures that Cuthbertson had planned for Sarah Island.

I was glad to find that Dalton and I had been assigned to the same logging detail even if the others weren't. They'd been told two were to be added to their number and were mighty glad to see big Dalton who could pull his own weight, but their faces fell when they saw me, five foot three, balding, with a pigeon chest.

'Looks like we've come up a bit short,' snorted Robert Greenhill, a swarthy sort. His lined, weather-beaten face looked markedly older than his thirty-two years, and told of a man who'd seen all the glories, hardships and tragedies of life. His thinning brown hair, shot though with a hint of Hibernian red, was scraped back from his forehead and worn in a ponytail in the style of a pirate. I knew that the first time I let them down he would be right at me.

I'd heard Greenhill had been a mariner and he made enough fuss about re-arranging the boat to make allowance for me. Unless there was a proper balance of strong and weak rowers, the boat would go skewing from side to side. He sat me in the middle of the boat opposite the oldest-looking cove in the party. I gritted my teeth and thought to myself, *I'll show the bastards.* As a small man you always have to prove yourself. That's your lot in life.

While our overseer got his orders a couple of the more amenable lads introduced themselves. William 'Little' Brown hailed from the apple and cider county of Somerset. The thinning crop of light brown hair on his pate and the silver that had woven itself into his wispy beard announced the arrival of his middle years. He was taller and broader than Dalton but something of a gentle giant.

Greenhill's restlessness was contrasted by Welshman, William Kennelly, who was a cooper by trade. With his fine features and brown doe-eyes he would have made a handsome man, but the ravages of time and convict life hadn't been kind to him. He was now bald except for a thick fringe at the back of his head like a friar's. Though he was a big, broad-shouldered man, he was the oldest and slowest in the party. Like Brown he was an old lag who'd spent many years in English prisons before being transported.

Little did I know it then, but these were some of the men who would accompany me to the very precincts of Hell.

As we rowed away from Sarah Island, the hook of the ironically named Liberty Point visible in the distance, the sun rose over the ridge of mountains on our port side, casting a soft golden light across the harbour. We surprised a mob of native black swans, which had been dipping their daggered beaks into the water in search of breakfast. On seeing us approach they opened those vivid red beaks and honked out a warning. We stopped rowing and watched as they spread their magnificent red-tipped wings and did what every one of us wished we could do: lifted themselves up off the water and away. It was a rare moment of grace and beauty in a harsh place.

Constable Malcolm Logan was our brutish overseer. A short, squat Lancastrian, he was a good head and a half shorter than Dalton. Beneath his barrel chest a fat paunch squeezed over his thick leather belt, testimony to the superior rations he received for his treachery. Though little of his ginger hair was left, a secret he kept hidden under his blue peaked cap, Logan sported a thick pair of mutton chops that had been razored at an angle halfway down his face so they met his luxuriant greying moustache, which sprouted from his top lip. Sunken deep in his fleshy face, creased by age, worry and the hardships of life, was a pair of small blue eyes, which were either darting around or narrowing in suspicion. He knew what the convict class thought of men like him and worried we were plotting against him. While the commissioned men had no choice but to follow orders, Logan was a convict who'd volunteered for this duty, which made him the object of much derision.

'Never mind watching the fucking birds, pick up the stroke!' he boomed.

'Fuck off you fat bastard,' the lean, rangy Bob Greenhill drawled, leaning on his oar and fixing the overseer with a defiant stare. Though he revelled in his little bit of power, Logan was still a convict and not trusted with a firearm.

'Start rowing, or I'll have you on report,' barked the overseer, following this up with an evil little sneer that said, *You'll do as your told or else* . . . Logan's power lay not in armaments but in his ability to report us to Cuthbertson, which would result in a flogging or a spell in irons on Grummet Island, or maybe both. That was his hold over us – the fear of merciless punishment and the terrible pain that would follow.

Not wanting to be the one to get us all the lash, Greenhill lifted his oar and threw Logan one last icy stare that left no doubt as to what he'd do to him given half a chance. The rest of us followed in short order.

'That's better, now . . . stroke,' called Logan, turning to gesture south-east with an outstretched arm, as if we were embarking on some great odyssey.

As we got into a rhythm, the men picked up the rate and I stroked strongly to prove that I was as capable as the rest of them. I matched them stroke for stroke until Kennelly, his face red from exertion, finally gave way and shouted out in his sing-song voice, 'Slow down boys afore me bloody heart gives out!' There were a few grudging nods and a sly wink from Dalton. I'd passed their first test.

After rowing for an hour or so we reached the far end of Macquarie Harbour, which narrowed to half a mile as it merged with the wide meandering Gordon River. We'd been cast asunder in such a miserable and inhospitable place and travelled such distances daily because the highly prized and very rare Huon pine grew along the banks of the Gordon River which spilled its clear mountain waters into the harbour.

This tree grew only in a few parts of the known world. Yet out in this ancient wilderness, untouched by man 'til now, great stands of them rose some seventy feet into the air, each one reputedly taking two to three thousand years to grow. The wood's lightness and durability was prized by shipbuilders. They claimed Huon pine did not absorb water, or rot, and even after fifty years in the brine it could be re-planed and come up as new. Cuthbertson wanted three thousand trees taken out each year as he believed this precious wood was the currency with which Macquarie Harbour would more than pay for itself.

As we neared our destination the river narrowed further until we were flanked on both sides by silent stands of trees that stood over us like sentries barring our escape. We were dwarfed by nature and in awe of it. It already seemed to me that this was a strange, sinister land that had been colonised by the British but would never be governed by their rules.

Logging was one of the least-favoured jobs and I soon discovered why. We spent the early part of the day cutting notches into the great trunks of the chosen trees, which measured up to fifteen feet wide, and inserting lengths of wood into them, which were used as steps to climb ten to twenty feet above the ground. Then, three at a time, we wielded long-handled axes and felled trees, some of which were five feet in diameter.

Though we took it in turns, John Mather, a dark-haired blue-eyed Scotchman who'd only recently come into manhood, was our best axeman. He exhibited what I'd call an 'agricultural build': solid jaw, thick neck, broad shoulders and powerful arms. He'd been a bread-baker in the town of Dumfries until he was convicted of forging a £15 money order.

We also trimmed branches, stripped the bark off the trunks or cut a swathe through the forest, which was lined with small logs. Known as the 'slipway' or 'pine-road', we used our handspikes and cant hooks to roll the logs over the top of them down to the water. Then we had to wade into the freezing water up to our chests and tie the logs together into rafts of ten. Our arduous labours were punctuated by two short breaks for a mug of tea. All food was kept on the island to deny escapees any form of sustenance.

It was hard, dangerous work. None of us had any experience in felling trees and many men had been caught by falling trunks, trailing branches or rolling logs, each one weighing twelve tons and therefore impossible to stop. A couple of weeks before I started I'd heard that a rolling log had slipped out of the block and tackle and crushed a young lad, leaving him crippled. By all accounts he was lucky to be alive and though he was shipped back to Hobart because of his injuries, there wasn't a man jack that would've changed places with him.

We worked until the light started to fade at about four o'clock then rowed the six miles to Sarah Island. At the end of a long day, our muscles aching, we arrived back long after dark. We could hardly stand, far less plot or carry out any mischief. Cuthbertson had promised us 'unceasing labour, total deprivation of spirits, tobacco and comforts of every kind, the sameness of occupation, the dreariness of occupation,' and was true to his word.

Whenever we caught a following breeze and arrived back before dark, we were forced to witness the flogging of some poor unfortunate, usually for the most trivial of offences or as a result of severe provocation. The thrice-daily floggings served to sate Cuthbertson's 'unnatural tastes' and to remind us to stay in line. John Douglas, the Commandant's clerk, let it slip that 9100 lashes had been dished out during this first year of the colony, which amounted to forty apiece for every one of the 230 men in the place on account of there being a tariff for every indiscretion.

Neglecting your work or insolence to overseers earned you a 'Botany Bay dozen'. Cuthbertson would ask the overseer if the convict had not been insolent as well as neglectful of their work. It is easy to imagine the reply, which generally saw the punishment doubled. Losing any part of your 'slops' was also worth a dozen, unless the thief was identified.

The next tariff was generally double the previous one, making the next a 'bob', or fifty strokes, which was meted out for breaking any tool, no matter what circumstances you might plead. Cuthbertson, of course, didn't acknowledge accidents, only carelessness.

The same punishment held for those caught in suspicious places or in a compromising position with a woman or another man plus three months in irons.

The maximum punishment any magistrate in the colony could hand out was a 'canary' and six months in irons. It was sixty-one strokes more than the Biblical thirty-nine, the maximum that black slaves in the Americas could receive, which was a true indication of our station.

The 'canary' was generally reserved for more serious crimes such as robbing a hut, the King's stores, taking to the bush or striking an overseer, but would also be arbitrarily dished out to coves committing more than one indiscretion, such as a neglect of work, insolence and theft.

Once the show was over, we had our one proper meal of the day. A slab of slimy, heavily salted pork or beef was our reward for a hard day's graft. Much of what arrived from Hobart was so soft and rotten that you could stick your finger through it, but no one complained. There was nothing to be done and you'd get 'a dozen' for your trouble. Only officers enjoyed fresh meat: roast swan, baked wombat and stuffed echidna graced their menu.

Dalton wolfed down his meagre rations like a dog, confirming my earlier impression that he would find it hard to sustain his large frame on this starvation diet for long.

'We're were supposed to get ten pounds of bread, seven of beef or pork, four ounces of oatmeal, salt and vegetables each week,' he complained. 'Little' Brown, a solidly built citizen like Dalton, allowed his big face to wrinkle as he chuckled in a rich, melodic Somerset accent, 'Save your breath soldier. We ain't never gonna get anything like it because the supplies from Hobart are always short.'

'No wonder we've all got malnutrition, scurvy and bad guts,' I piped up.

'Aye, but the punishment, the hard labour and the starvation is the way Cuthbertson keeps order in this colony,' offered Kennelly.

'He started here with seventeen redcoats and eleven trusted convicts, but lost two soldiers and three convicts going after the first bolters,' added Thomas Bodenham, a slightly built, glum-looking Yorkshireman with a long thin face and short fair hair who looked much older than his twenty-two years. 'Four of the remaining fifteen redcoats guard the pilot's station at Hell's Gates. The *Duke of York* brought another fifty-nine men, which means there are now only eleven soldiers guarding one-hundred-and-seventy convicts, including about twenty women. Twenty to one is dangerous odds in any game.'

I had been surprised to discover that Bodenham was a farm labourer turned highway man, though you'd scarcely credit him with it; he didn't look fit to say boo to a goose far less brandish a pair of irons and call on some cove to 'stand and deliver'.

I went to put a piece of bread in my pocket for later but the sharp-eyed Greenhill, who missed nothing, hissed at me, 'Eat it up now, boy.' When my brow creased in puzzlement he explained, 'They put ergot[1] in it to make it go off quicker. In this damp it'll be a lump o' mould by daybreak.'

'It's a blight that grows on the stalks of the rye,' added Matthew Travers, the last one in our party to cut the King's English with me. Only a little taller than I was and slightly built, Travers was a farm labourer and butcher from London, and a long-time mate of Greenhill's. He'd been transported for life for the persistent theft of livestock. With his wispy fair hair and pug-face, he reminded me of a little dog as he shadowed Greenhill's every move. 'They put it in to stop us hoarding it for an escape,' he added with a nod.

I spat into the dirt and said unguardedly, 'Bastards! I reckon those boys who bolted two months ago were just the first of many.'

Greenhill fixed me with his piercing green eyes as if deciding whether to say something, but after a long moment opted to keep his own counsel and turned away.

No matter what straits men find themselves in, they will establish a natural order so that like the beasts in the field everyone knows their place in relation to the others. Prestige in this blind hole of a place was proximity to the fire. After being soaking wet and out in the cold all day, a warming at the fire before it was extinguished at 8 pm was one of the very few comforts we had. The biggest, the strongest and the most brutal took their place at

---

1 Unbeknown to the authorities and convicts at the time, ergot also has hallucinogenic properties. It contains ergotamine, which Swiss scientist, Dr Albert Hofmann, used to make lysergic acid diethylamide, better known as LSD, in 1938.

the hearth while the rest sat in behind them and absorbed whatever heat they could get.

While many of the men sent here were just common but persistent thieves, laggards and confidence tricksters, there was also another class of prisoner: hardened criminals who spoke little but said plenty with their tough-eyed stares. Back in England, some of the older ones had been 'glimmed' or branded with a hot iron on the flesh part of the hand or the cheek before the practice was outlawed at the end of the eighteenth century along with pillory, jibbeting and other suchlike medieval practices. Murderers copped an 'M' and brawlers an 'F' and had their ears cut off. You didn't cross them if they took your rations, blanket or used you for their pleasuring.

Nothing moves a man as powerfully as his sexual impulses. There is no other urge to which he will devote as much time and energy. There were only about twenty women in the settlement. Ten of those were the wives of the soldiers and government officials who administered the settlement and of the other ten, half worked in the hospital on nearby Grummet Island and the rest as servants for the soldiers and officials without wives. They were far more interested in hooking someone who could give them a better life than a worthless convict. In the absence of women, men buggered each other and in the absence of men, lonely shepherds buggered the beasts in their charge.

Never was sodomy so condemned by the British government yet so well facilitated by the living arrangements on Sarah Island. We had to sleep on our sides because there was no room to sleep on our backs and this convenient crush made the 'Mollies', young, slim, pretty boys who could be taken for a woman, easy meat for the depraved. The rapist merely lay down next to the Molly of his choice and to avoid being kicked by flailing feet or fists, the nearest man would reach out and grasp onto a limb until the ordeal was over. Once the beast had been sated, the men around him could enjoy a peaceful night's sleep without further fear of molestation.

Though well past my prime and never pretty enough to be a Molly, during my first week I was accosted by one of these buggers, a roughneck ex-soldier by the name of James Dalway.

These queers all had men to run their errands, give them extra rations from their plates, fetch and carry messages and contraband, and to satisfy their depraved whims. They used rape as a way of putting the fear into them. Dalway had pegged me as a new boy with no allies and made it clear he wanted me to serve him.

At over six feet tall and mean with it, Dalway was not a man you said no to. His shaven head was criss-crossed by white ribbons of scar, his ears were torn, his nose flattened, and the few teeth left in his head only added menace to his slow, twisted smile that slid like a serpent across his battle-scarred face. His boxer's arms and chest were decorated with blue India ink. The murmurs were that before being transported for fourteen years, he'd spent some considerable time at His Majesty's pleasure for theft and violence.

With a fierce grip on my shoulder, he dragged me to the far side of the barracks one night after lights out. 'Lie down and do as you're bid,' he growled, grabbing my throat with one hand and pulling down hard on my shoulder with the other. 'Don't make a fuss neither, or I'll cut ya.'

My heart was in my mouth as Dalway flattened me on the bare boards where I could feel a cold draught blowing up between them. *What should I do? If I cried out would anyone help me?* The other men knew what was happening but stayed clear. Dalway mocked me in his musical Welsh burr, 'I know you Irish lads ain't fond of the cock but maybe some o' this will change yer mind.' There was a rustling as he pulled down his breeches and he began to pant. In a voice that had dropped to a throaty rasp he whispered urgently, 'Come on, get 'em down.' My hand trembled as it went to the drawstring holding up my breeches and then I felt the sharp point of his jib at my gut. 'Do it now boy.'

Oh Christ, oh Christ.

I did as I was told and felt his calloused hand start to caress my arse and his finger roughly probing inside me. Then I was face down on the hard floor, arm up my back with his heavy weight bearing down on me. I braced myself for the worst indignity a man can suffer.

I felt a rush of air, sensed a blur of movement in the pitch black around me then heard an agonised cry. Suddenly, the weight was gone, my arm was free and I rolled away. Bodies rumbled around me as protesting voices shouted and swore and then there was silence. A familiar voice called out, 'Alec!'

Dalton! Thank bloody Christ! 'Aye, here.'

I felt a strong hand pull me to my feet and lead me away. 'Are ye alright, Alec?'

'Aye,' I said trying to get some feeling back in my twisted arm, 'and not a moment too bloody soon.'

As I lay back down in a safer spot, still shaking, I thought it strange how history sometimes comes round full circle. Dalton wasn't the first big lad to save my bacon.

I remembered the squat, grey-stoned school in Carrickcross with its low sloping slate roof and rain-slicked, cobbled yard; it was as much a living hell for big Tam Peden, son of a local Scotch merchant, as it was for me. 'I'll fight ye then,' were words that struck fear into my early years. The Irish are quick to anger, but slow to forget and like primitives we settle our arguments with fists and weapons, not words, as our brutal history will surely attest. I was often scolded for coming home with bloody noses, cuts and bruises as if I, the smallest boy in the town, with no Da to fight his battles for him, would go looking for trouble.

Tam took after his ma, a hefty, rosy-cheeked woman with soft white arms as thick as a man's leg, but never said much and got called names like 'dummy' and 'eejit'. Tam was dropped on his head as a bairn, which is what they say about anyone a bit slow or simple. He also had the misfortune to have a wandering eye, which made it hard to know when he was looking away or right at you.

At playtime he stood alone, back to the wall, his hand dipping in and out of his pocket, or *pooch* as Tam called it in his slow, hard-edged Scotch accent. He always carried a bag of boiled sweets, something none of the rest of us had.

Red-headed Michael Corrigan, one of my principal tormentors, caught a whiff of peppermint and went right up to him. 'Here dummy, gie's a sweetie.'

Tam didn't take him on. He just stood there unconcerned like a cow chewing the cud.

A fiery character and quick to anger, Michael punched Tam hard on the shoulder. Quick as a flash, every child in the school was in the loud, raucous circle of frenzied faces that surrounded them chanting, 'Fight, fight, fight . . .' Michael enjoyed his moment in the sun, dancing about with his dukes up like Tom Cribb, the champion boxer of the day.

Tam measured him up with his good eye, and with a speed you wouldn't credit him with, caught Michael with a vicious left hook that landed with a slap like the ones we received from the headmaster's cane. It was a knockout punch.

A river of red rushed from Michael's nose and mouth as he wobbled about like a newborn lamb and sank to the ground. By the time the teachers arrived only Michael, Tam and I were left.

Mr McCreadie, who taught the fourth class, pointed at me accusingly and demanded, 'You boy, what happened?'

I put on my best face and replied briskly, 'He fell over, so he did.'

'You sure?'

'Aye, I mean, yes sir,' I said giving him a little salute.

McCreadie looked up at Big Tam, opened his mouth then thought better of it. From the scowl on his face I could tell he didn't believe me, but his expression softened as he considered that Corrigan was a born troublemaker and probably got his due.

I was about to follow Michael and McCreadie when I heard a rustling; I looked over to see Tam holding out his bag of sweets, his squint eye fixed on me. I took a big black and white peppermint humbug, stuck it in my cheek and put my back to the wall next to him.

During the next few years those humbugs rotted almost every tooth in my head, but at least it was the dentist and not the bullies that knocked them out.

I knew that a beating was nothing to Dalway. He'd been getting them and dishing them out all his life. He was a prisoner of his terrible urges and would persist until he nailed me. I couldn't always rely on Dalton to be there so I decided to fix him up. It had to be something big, something he'd never come back from.

One night a few weeks later there was a scuffle in our barracks, two men fighting over whose turn it was to sit near the fire. It started out with fists and feet, the usual roughhouse stuff, but then one jibbed the other in the guts. The redcoats were soon in amongst us, but no one saw anything. However, I saw the bloody jib, which was no more than a piece of metal sharpened at one end, being dropped through a crack in the floor.

The next evening I crawled underneath the hut and got the knife. Dalway had a lovely kangaroo coat sewed for him by one of his Mollies. I slipped the jib into his pocket as we queued for supper and gave the word to O'Donnell. They did a search of everyone present. Dalway just sat there thinking he had nothing to fear until O'Donnell stuck his hand into his pocket and pulled out the bloody blade.

'What's this then?'

Dalway's face flushed an angry red and he started raging, 'It's not mine. Some pimping bastard's put it there!'

'Tell that to the commandant,' said Waddy, unslinging his musket. Dalway bunched his fists, but when he heard flintlocks cocked all around him he dropped his hands and went meekly. Having been a foot soldier in Spain, one of Wellington's so-called 'scum of the earth', he knew what a Brown Bess could do to a man at close quarters.

Dalway had a long history of violent conduct and Cuthbertson removed him to Grummet Island where he'd spend a year butting heads with other like-minded men.

A little later, when everyone was outside having a sly smoke before curfew, Dalton sidled up to me. 'That was lucky for you.'

'Aye, right enough.'

Lowering his voice, he leaned in close and said, 'That was down to you, wasn't it?'

I nodded. 'Being a wee fella I learned early on that guile is the best way to settle scores. In late summer when the bully boys were up in the orchard at Rossmore Park, I'd tip the wink to McTavish the gamekeeper and watch as my tormentors learned the first rule of war – there's always someone bigger than you. Listening to their cries for mercy was almost as good as landing one on them yourself. In Hobart, I'd been running with a gang of petty thieves who thought it was a smart idea to cut the wee man out of the takings. "What you gonna do about it?" they sneered. The next thing they knew they were in the dock listening to me turning King's evidence and testifying their many misdeeds.'

Dalton clapped me on the shoulder with a big hand and joked, 'I'd best not get on the wrong side of you then, Alec.'

Little did he know, little did we all know, what lay ahead of us.

The Sabbath provided the only break in our dreary routine of work and sleep. On Sundays we worked a half day and were compelled to attend a religious service of sorts in the afternoon.

I noted at our first assembly that there was no man of God on Sarah Island, the British authorities wisely reasoning that the Almighty could not be party to such brutality. The lesson, invariably on the theme of redemption, was read by Dr Spence who held the leather-bound Bible in his small shaky hands, his eyes watery and his voice tremulous. His words had passion, but made little impression on anyone except the small knot of recent converts who prayed loudly and sung the hymns with gusto. There was a rumour that Lieutenant-Governor Sorell saw religious conversion as an act of penance, which they hoped might lead to shorter sentences. On Sarah Island the only Holy Trinity we knew was cold, exhaustion and hunger. As Bodenham, the former farmer boy, put it, preaching forgiveness and tolerance on Sarah Island was 'like ploughing in the rocks'.

Though Cuthbertson appeared to have no Christian spirit, he sat in the front row every week. Mind you, back in Ireland, most of the tyrants were God-fearing men of one persuasion or the other. Attending church and declaring themselves to be men of God made their spite seem just and noble, part of some higher, yet-to-be-revealed purpose. God, in name at least, was in harness here too.

We continued with our labours through the cold, dark winter months, praying for the warmer weather to come. During that time we saw every aspect of this island's grim character. As Mordecai Cohen had famously remarked, most of our commandant's laws had 'neither justice nor humanity to recommend them' and Hell's Gates soon justified its terrible celebrity.

The daily floggings continued apace, 1700 being delivered in one black week alone. It was well beyond the limits of human tolerance. An old cove by the name of William Halliday was sent to hospital in a weak, sickly state one morning, but that afternoon appeared before Cuthbertson charged with trying to impose on Dr Spence. It was hardly an incident of note, but there were spies who prospered by telling tales to the commandant. Sergeant Waddy was summoned to Cuthbertson's quarters where he was pacing the floor in a terrible rage. Halliday was found guilty and sentenced to fifty lashes. Even Waddy, a deeply religious Welsh Methodist who believed that convicts got what they deserved and that every man chooses his own destiny, pleaded very hard for him to be forgiven on account of his illness.

'He's very sick and quite old,' protested the soldier, but Cuthbertson was the sort who never forgives a lash.

'Needs must sergeant. I've given you an order. Old or sick, that sort of behaviour is bad for discipline and encourages skiving. I won't tolerate it. Summon Mr Flynn.'

Waddy knew from the dangerous edge in Cuthertson's voice that he wouldn't be dissuaded. He saluted, turned and marched from the room. Best he could do was to ask the scourger to lay the cat easy on him. But that plan was thwarted by Cuthbertson who did not take his usual stroll during the flogging, but stood over Flynn, measuring every stroke.

'Come on man, hit him harder! I mean to see a red shirt, hit him harder . . . harder!' And when he thought the scourger was going easy on him, he warned him, 'If you hold back on one more stroke Mr Flynn, I'll finish the job myself and then give you double the dose.'

The flagellator responded to the threat of punishment with a volley of full-blooded blows that had Halliday arching his torn back in agony. Each blow was now met with a raw, open-throated scream.

Finally, five strokes short of the total, his back red ribbons of raw flesh and the dust beneath him stained with blood, Halliday fell silent and slumped against his bonds. Flynn looked at Cuthbertson for guidance yet the commandant impatiently gestured for him to continue. 'Get on with it man. The punishment must be paid in full.'

Dr Spence went to him straight after the last stroke had landed and ordered him cut down. He turned Halliday over, placed his forefingers on his wrist and neck and finally put a mirror close to his mouth. After a minute he saw no misting on the glass, looked up at the commandant, shook his head and said, 'He's dead, sir.'

'Then get a burial detail and plant him in the ground,' said Cuthbertson sharply, not even sparing the recently departed man a decent pause. Sniffing the air like a cautious fox, our commandant sensed rebellion and retribution were abroad and ordered his soldiers to 'present arms'.

As he filed past us I noted that the expressionless mask he habitually wore hadn't altered one jot. In fact, glancing round our gallery of shocked faces, he actually seemed quite pleased with the impression he'd created. 'As you gentleman are so fond of saying, it's the fortune of war,' he remarked. Even during wartime, seldom can there have been such a display of callousness.

William Halliday was the first convict to die on Sarah Island. Given Cuthbertson's plan to turn the island into a boatyard, there was no room for a cemetery so he ordered the burial detail to wrap him in tarpaulin and row him out to a small rock that lay half a mile due south-east of Sarah Island. As we watched the oars of the burial party dip rhythmically in and out of the water, I recalled Dalton's comment about Van Diemen's Land being "a vault for convict bones". It was true now of Sarah Island too and I thought it a fair wager that Halliday would not be alone for very long.

They landed on what became known as Dead Man's beach and covered him over with rocks, but laid no marker and said no grace. Not a very Christian send-off, but at least he left his name for posterity. Although it doesn't appear on the maps as such, the rock was from then on known as Halliday's Island.

The murmurs amongst the men were that the late convict copped the last five lashes after he was dead and Cuthbertson ordered an early curfew.

As we lay in the pitch black of our hut listening to the harsh words said against Cuthbertson and the redcoats, a terrible gale blew up in the harbour that rattled all the buildings and threw great waves thundering onto the beach. I'm not a religious or superstitious man by nature, but it was hard not to imagine this storm as God's vengeance.

As if eavesdropping on my thoughts, Dalton's voice came sailing through the dark, 'His wrath is in the thunder and the lightning, the roaring of the seas and great winds. He sees all, hears all. Nay, nothing can escape Him, not even the unspoken secrets of the heart.'

Aye, a rum mix right enough, I thought to myself.

As we stood in the cold, wet gloom the next morning, the mood was still sullen and resentful. Cuthbertson consulted his fob watch. It was after five o'clock and there was still no sign of the prisoners from Grummet Island. *Was something amiss?*

We got our answer in very short order.

The dull clang of the warning bell sounded from the summit and all eyes went immediately to the small island that glowed red as if ablaze. A column of smoke rose up from the small island into the drab grey early morning sky. The sounds of shouting and singing carried over to us.

'Christ,' breathed Dalton as loud murmuring broke out in the convict ranks.

'Guard present arms!' shouted Cuthbertson in an attempt to restore some semblance of order. The nine redcoats that flanked our commandant brought up their muskets in a warning not to entertain any notion of riot or chaos. Barely able to control his rage, the commandant frothed at Sergeant Waddy, 'Take three men, get over there and note the names of those responsible. Rioting will not be tolerated in this colony!'

'Aye, aye sir. Ferris, Marshall and Taylor with me!'

Our attention returned to Grummet Island as they traversed the narrow channel, the volume of noise increasing as the boat neared but didn't land. It seemed to be stuck about ten to twenty yards offshore.

'What's happening?' gasped Mather, a tremor of excitement in his voice.

Only Cuthbertson knew as he had his spyglass stuck to his eye, but the curl of his lip indicated that the landing wasn't going to plan. He pulled down the instrument, snapped it shut, then impatiently summoned a redcoat and roared, 'They're throwing rocks to prevent them landing. Private Cahill, have the signalman send Sergeant Waddy a heliotrope as follows: Re-take island at all costs. Treat prisoners as hostile. Fix bayonets and fire at will.'

A deathly hush fell over the convict throng. Our own commandant had just declared war on us.

The private, too young to have been seasoned in the Peninsular War, boggled at the enormity of what he'd just been ordered to do. But saluting crisply and bringing his heels together with a snap as he'd been trained to do, he called back, 'Aye sir!' Yet the pitch of his voice betrayed more than a hint of trepidation.

As Cuthbertson went towards the signalling device he was stopped in his tracks by another voice.

'It's not a riot, sir.'

'Who said that?' demanded Cuthbertson.

'I did,' said a young private by the name of O'Donnell, a farmer's boy from Armagh, the next county up from Monaghan. He was a decent sort, as redcoats go, and we'd nod and exchange the odd word.

'Then, Private, would you kindly tell me what it is?' seethed Cuthbertson.

'A wake sir. I've seen something like it back home. There'll be a few sore heads at the end of it, but nothing more.'

Cuthbertson squinted hard at the soldier as he mulled over the information. Being an Irishman, he should've recognised this himself, but the trooper's plea allowed him to rein back his order without appearing weak. Redcoats shooting convicts was a drastic measure and would not be well received in Hobart, Port Jackson or in London for that matter. There would be an official inquiry.

After a long moment the commandant nodded. 'Very well. Recall Sergeant Waddy. We'll give them some rope, but if order is not restored by tomorrow you'll lead a marine party ashore and re-take the island.'

But O'Donnell was right and the following day the prisoners' sore heads were swiftly complemented by sore backs. With the constables, hutkeeper and cooks all guarding the hospital, the women and the stores, and no one willing to name the ringleaders, Cuthbertson lined them all up, chose twelve at random and gave them seventy-five lashes apiece for riotous behaviour. With Cuthbertson urging them on, two flagellators worked the 'heavy cat', turn about, from noon 'til dusk. The screams jangled the nerves of even the hard men. According to the prisoners detailed to carry those who'd passed out to Dr Spence, bodies were strewn around the triangle and the rock pools overflowed with blood.

Rumour had it that Cuthbertson's mercurial temper was a consequence of the syphilis he'd caught dallying with convict girls like Sarah Simmons.

Known to be free with her favours, she was sent here from

Hobart where she was notorious for escaping the gaol at will to enjoy nights on the town, and climbing out of her cell window and shinnying up the drainpipe and onto the roof. There she entertained her friends on the surrounding hillsides with song and dance and ordered in food and alcohol items which somehow always found their way to her. Here, Sarah was a freebooter, known to be heavily involved in the supply of smuggled items. One night she even climbed up on the roof of the store hut and in plain view of all proceeded to barter with the soldiers. Dr Spence had gazetted her for dispatch to the Female Factory in Parramatta where she had also distinguished herself, but Sarah didn't want to go. Variously described as a 'forthright' woman or a 'succubus who fed on the desires of weak men', she set about changing her destiny. Many men, good and bad, had come to grief on the dangerous curves that hugged her rounded hips and ample bosom.

Sarah had been assigned to cook and clean for Cuthbertson and Dr Spence who were forced to share a cottage due to the lack of accommodation. The scuttlebutt was that she wore no undergarments and used flirtatious displays of her quim to lure the commandant. He resisted for almost a week but one morning he finally showed himself to be as mortal as Adam by affecting a so-called 'maritime entry' while she bent over the tub washing his shirts.

It was a short hop across the lane from her cramped little hut to the commandant's cottage. Once installed in his bed there was no more scrubbing and cleaning for Sarah who remained on the island as Cuthbertson's plaything. The good doctor didn't care. He kept his own secrets at the bottom of a whisky bottle, which doubtless also helped him sleep through Cuthbertson's carnal cavorting. We convicts joked that the commandant was so bewitched that he named the island after her though, in truth, it was named after the wife of the ship-owner whose vessel first discovered Macquarie Harbour.

Sarah, what a sweet-sounding name for Hell.

Had any of us dallied with a convict woman, the tariff was fifty strokes of the cat. Though they were not asked to endure the lash, women were punished nonetheless. On New Year's Day 1822, the first ever spent on the island, the Superintendent of Convicts reported that some soldiers had been seen loitering near the living quarters of the five women convicts who worked at the hospital on Grummet Island. Without further inquiry, Cuthbertson summoned the coxswain and ordered him to load a whaleboat with a week's supplies and to row the women to the Long Beach, which was situated along the main coastline ten miles outside Hell's Gates. When they arrived the shocked misses were informed they were being banished there for consorting with soldiers. They protested their innocence and charged that privates Cahill, Leech and Walsh had arrived in a stolen boat vowing to 'ramp the whores' and had made drunken and unwelcome advances towards them. He waved their pleas aside and said that a large fifteen-ton launch would come for them in a week, but if they didn't fill its hold with oyster shells, which would be crushed down for lime, they would be left there another week.

When they said they were afraid the natives might attack them, the coxswain relented a little and gave them one musket and twenty rounds of ball cartridge with the recommendation that if attacked they save the last five balls for themselves. With that sage advice, he rowed away leaving the weeping damsels abandoned on the lonely shore.

Mercifully, when the launch arrived the following week, the

women filled the hold to overflowing with shellfish and, contrary to everyone's expectations, returned alive.

As always, there is one rule for kings and another for commoners.

A week after Halliday was planted, Greenhill addressed our logging crew after first looking round casually to make sure that Logan wasn't within earshot. It was clear from the intensity of his voice that this subject had been agitating him for some time.

'Do you all want to die here?' His charge was met with silence, which Greenhill took as a sign to continue. 'Then let's get out o' this accursed place,' he hissed urgently under his breath.

I met his gaze. 'I'll go.'

He nodded, turned away from me and said no more.

'Better dead than in fetters,' murmured Dalton who had been listening in and decided to throw his hat in the ring. We all revealed the same tattoo inscribed on our forearms, chests or shoulders with gunpowder and a pin – the letters 'D' and 'L' enclosed in a circle signifying 'Death or Liberty'. The phrase had become the convict catchcry following the Vinegar Hill rebellion of 1804, the one true revolt mounted against British misrule. Philip Cunningham, a stone mason from County Kerry, had led the mostly Irish convict force of two-hundred-and-sixty men who'd broken out of a government farm at Castle Hill, near Port Jackson, with the intention of seizing Parramatta – the colony's second settlement. But faced by a better-armed British force, the convicts had lost their nerve, broke ranks and fled.

Cunningham was taken some time later at Green Hills. When asked by the redcoat commander what he wanted, Cunningham replied, 'Death or liberty!' They granted him his first request and hanged him summarily on the stairs of the nearest public store. But it was more than just a rebel cry; it became the first commandment in the convict Bible.

Dalton had his tattoo on his chest next to a 'D' which had been branded on his skin close to his armpit. He saw our eyes go to it.

'The D is for deserter,' he explained and shrugged his shoulders. 'I deserted from Ireland, from the British army, and now I intend to desert from Macquarie Harbour too.'

My eyes went to Greenhill who nodded, but said nothing more.

Something was brewing and he'd tell us in his own good time.

Like Cunningham, we knew that death might find us, but we were all prepared to risk it for liberty.

Dalton showed that we were prepared to do more than jaw about it. One night a few weeks after that exchange, Dalton spotted an unoccupied jollyboat next to us when landing our whaleboat on Sarah Island. It was known to be an old boat in poor repair used by soldiers to row back and forth to Grummet Island. It was good enough for the harbour but would flounder in heavy seas. This didn't deter Dalton who took his time securing our boat. While Logan was distracted, counting all the tools to make sure none of the axes had been stolen, he pushed the jollyboat into the water.

'Are you mad? You'll never reach safety in that old tub on your own,' I hissed at him.

'Jump in and help me then.'

'No. I'll bide my time and go when . . .'

'See you in Ireland then,' he laughed as he took up the oars.

I looked over my shoulder to see Logan turn, and realising Dalton would never have enough time to get clear, cupped my two hands and called out loudly, 'Throw me the rope, I've got it!' Dalton saw Logan come tearing down the hill, his face like thunder, and was quick-witted enough to do what I asked. I caught it and pulled the boat back to shore.

'What's all this?' demanded Logan, his face flushed with anger, 'you were attempting to steal this vessel weren't you?'

'No, the boat started to drift and Dalton jumped aboard and threw me the mooring rope.'

'A likely story. That's piracy, that is.'

'Then we're the first pirates in history to bring a boat back. If we were going to make a break d'ya think we'd take a jollyboat? We wouldn't get past the heads in that.'

Logan pondered this for a long moment then grunted. The commandant might take a dim view of a vexatious escape report in which prisoners returned a boat. He looked at us, suspicion still clouding his heavy features, then waved us away. 'Go on then, get out of it,' he growled.

As we hurried up the hill to join the others Dalton said, 'Thanks, I don't know what I was thinking, but lucky for me you got one over on Logan.'

'God didn't make me big, but he made me quick,' I replied.

Chapter 7

Death and Liberty

I awoke one night and found myself choking. Something was being forced down my throat. Pushing myself upright, to the vocal displeasure of those around me, I tried to cough it up. Finally, just as I thought my lungs would burst for the want of air, the offending object came up into my mouth accompanied by the coppery taste of blood. A tooth, a gnarled, rotted stump, had uprooted itself from my soft gums and lodged in my throat. The salt diet and lack of proper nourishment meant the loss of teeth was a common condition and a strange blessing: one less to torment me when it rotted through and one less for Dr Spence to pull.

During August, my fourth month on Sarah Island, a terrible pall of despair descended on this outpost of lost souls, threatening to engulf us all. It caused the anger, misery and sullen hatred that burned within us to erupt forth in a spectacular show of violence that left no man untouched.

News of a death usually comes as a shock, even if you're not acquainted with the victim, but not on Sarah Island. Our labours were interrupted one grey afternoon late in August by a spiral of black smoke that appeared like a dirty smudge on the clear horizon. Because it rose in the west, we knew someone had lit the warning fire on Sarah Island: the signal for all boats to return. We looked at each other, questions writ large on our faces. Had there been a prisoner revolt or another escape? Had a work party been attacked by blacks?

Logan also looked apprehensive. If there was an uprising he'd be the first lynched. He ordered us into the whaleboat and we set course for home. Our tired muscles found new vigour and we stroked the six miles in double-quick time.

We were met by anxious redcoats who I now knew to be sharp shooters normally stationed at the heads.

'Something is badly amiss here,' murmured Dalton.

We were herded to the parade ground where all the other prisoners had mustered, guarded with fixed bayonets by the redcoats. Cuthbertson was atop his ceremonial mound barking orders at the overseers, Sergeant Waddy and the superintendent of convicts, as the whispers flew thick and fast between the prisoners. Murder was the word on everyone's lips.

Mordecai Cohen told me that the ancient Greeks believed that the day you became a slave you lost half your soul. But for some like Thomas Hudson, who had lately been employed at the coal diggings, the daily grind of cold, hunger, hard work and punishment had claimed the other half too. That fateful morning, without provocation, Hudson had hit his overseer, Constable Thomas Hisp, over the head with a shovel. Such was the force of the blow that the man died instantly. Hudson did not resist arrest.

Some days before the murder, a deep melancholy known as the 'black dog' had settled on him, a condition that afflicted every man on Sarah Island, convict and gaoler alike, at one time or another. During the interview that followed, it was reported that Cuthbertson had asked him, 'Why did you do it, man?' Hudson shrugged, apparently unconcerned at the magnitude of his crime or the serious predicament he was now in. 'Was there any bad blood between you?' the commandant pressed.

'No, I've nothing against the man. He just happened to be standing there.'

'Then why did you hit him?'

'I can't rightly say.'

'What sort of answer is that, man?' bellowed Cuthbertson. 'What did you hope to gain by it?'

'I'm tired of this world and I want to be released from it,' he conceded.

Hearing that one of his men had lost his life for no apparent reason, Cuthbertson reportedly seized the edges of the table and gripped them until his knuckles turned white. 'I'll make bloody sure your wish is granted,' he snapped back.

'Better the gallows than living like this,' was Hudson's retort.

Another muster, another early curfew with the commandant declaring that anyone seen out after dark would be shot without warning. As we were marched back to our quarters the atmosphere of fear and uncertainty was thick in the air. *Why had Hudson tired of life and become an 'out and outer'?* We sat there with that unanswered question hanging over us, but no one was game to give it form lest it somehow infected us too.

But that wasn't the end of the disruption. In the confusion that followed two pairs of convicts, William Allen and William

Saul, followed by Francis Oates and James Williamson, escaped from their work gangs and headed in opposite directions.

The island was in uproar once again when a thin, ragged Allen returned of his own volition two weeks after his escape much the worse for his ordeal. He was reportedly wearing Saul's clothes, which looked as though they had been pierced by spears. Under close examination from Cuthbertson, Allen confirmed that natives had attacked them and killed Saul. Suffering from lameness and starvation after days of walking, he was sent to the hospital on the small island. While there he asked another prisoner to cut his hair and as he did so confessed to murdering Saul. He reportedly said, 'I'm uneasy in my mind. The Devil terrifies me day and night and won't let me rest.'

'Why did you murder him?' pressed his convict barber.

'We'd gone days without food then William found a dead snake. He cooked it on a fire but instead of sharing it, gave me a very small piece. When I asked for a bit more he said no and a terrible dark rage came over me, the like of which I have never encountered in my life. I took my knife and stabbed him about the face and neck, then, after he had begged me not to kill him, I stuck the knife in his heart, ripped open his bowels and then cut his balls off for good measure. I was quite frenzied. Then, as quickly as it had seized me, the frenzy released me and I was confronted by my terrible deed.'

When the man cutting his hair tried to elucidate on what had seized him, Allen shook his head and came over all melancholy, 'I can't rightly say.' Then, as if he felt relieved of a great burden, the miserable convict lowered his chin onto his chest and started to cry openly. 'God forgive me, I'd rather die than live.'

After persuading Allen to reveal where the terrible deed took place, a search party was dispatched to Birch's Bay at the north-western end of the harbour towards Hell's Gates. No sooner had they returned with a grim cargo – which, by all accounts, confirmed Allen's story – than an escapee from the other party, Francis Oates, also returned alone in a dilapidated state, bearing a similar tale of madness and murder. He claimed he and Williamson had fought over a dead fish, which his partner had eaten while he searched the shore for more. Enraged by his mate's greed and his own desperate hunger, he smashed Williamson's skull in with a heavy stick.

Deprivation and hunger, it seemed, could drive men to terrible extremes.

In a tumultuous aftermath, the three murderers were shipped off to Hobart for trial. Given the parlous state of affairs and the number of redcoats to prisoners, Cuthbertson stopped all work and put us under close guard until passions cooled.

We whiled away the dead hours whispering and talking wildly about the uncanny atmosphere that hung about this place and how it had infected us all with some strange madness. It was now being spoken of as a 'bad place' where evil gathers like mist in a hollow. Little Brown's great shoulders shook as a shudder passed through his huge frame.

'All this loose talk of devils, madness and murder gives me the shivers,' he confided in his booming baritone.

'Me and all,' added Bodenham, making the sign of the cross on the front of his calico shirt for good measure.

'I tell you true, I've travelled the wide world and whenever there's a forest there's legends,' mused Dalton raising his eyebrows mischievously.

'And what legends would they be?' I challenged him.

Seeing he had an alert audience he threw open his hands,

looked round at the circle of faces and chided me, 'Alec, didn't those wandering folk-tellers we call *seanachies* in Ireland ever come in for a warming at your fire and tell you stories about the *conriocht* and the *faoladh*, the *werewulf* creatures that live out in the woods and prey on lost and unwary children? Did your ma tell you never to go into the forest on your own?'

'Sure she did, but that was just a ruse to scare the bairns.'

Dalton cut me off with an upraised finger. 'It's said, is it not, that the *seanachies* learn their storytelling from the *bean si,* the banshee messengers from the dark side sent to warn people of death and disaster? Your ma did well to pay them heed.'

I laughed, 'You're a case Alexander Dalton and no mistake. I have often wondered how superstition gained such mastery over such a practical and hard-headed race as we Irish, but it is a land of great imaginations. There's scarce a town, village or hamlet that doesn't have a legend of a beast on the bogs or a *faoladh* in the forest, which the locals will swear is true on the graves of safely dead ancestors.'

'Load o' bulldust more like,' grunted Greenhill, clearly unamused by our banter.

'What's that Bob? Don't you believe in otherwordly things?' riled Dalton. 'Surely the sea has its legends and you'd have a tale or two?' Greenhill shot him a slit-eyed glare and growled to signal his disgust, 'Bedtime stories for children.'

But arguing against superstition is like arguing against religion. You can't see God but you sense His presence, and if God is there so must the Devil. Once men have made up their minds that some place or thing has a curse upon it, no amount of logic can ever persuade them to the contrary.

Mather steered the talk back to more earthly matters. 'What'll happen now?' he wondered aloud.

'It's Cuthbertson's play,' said Greenhill steadily, his angry stare still glued to Dalton. There was some chaff between those two.

If we convicts had been afflicted by some mysterious malady then our commandant had a ready remedy – kill or cure. A couple of weeks after we resumed work, the sensational news reached us that Allen, Hudson and Oates had been found guilty of murder in Hobart and were on their way back to Sarah Island to be executed.

'Why here? Why not string 'em up in Hobart?' pondered Kennelly, concern creasing his large brow.

Dalton, as ever, had his own theory as to why justice had taken such a circuitous route. 'This will be the first ever execution on Sarah Island and Cuthbertson means to use it to restore order and put the fear of God into us.'

'I've heard it said that Sorell has given Cuthbertson leave to build a gallows out by Badger Rock,' added Travers.

The rumour was confirmed by a gang of sawyers and carpenters from the shipyard who spent a week erecting a scaffold large enough to take three men at once.

The day after they finished, the *Duke of York* arrived under the cover of darkness with the three condemned men and the sheriff of Hobart on board. According to the *Hobart Daily Gazette*, which Cohen got for a kangaroo skin, Allen, Hudson and Oates all cited their harsh treatment at Macquarie Harbour in mitigation, to no avail. Their plea was denied by Chief Justice John Lewes Pedder, a stentorian-voiced judge who many of us had appeared before at one time or another.

*

All work was suspended at noon on execution day so we could attend the hanging. One-hundred-and-seventy convicts stretched themselves out on the side of a hillock overlooking the gallows and dozed in the sunshine, making the best of the rare break from our heavy work schedule.

But far from being a sombre theatre of retribution, as Cuthbertson had intended, the hanging had the air of a country fair about it. The fat black clouds that had been dumping cold buckets of rain on us for weeks had parted early in the morning and the sun, now at its zenith, shone down on us from a peerless blue sky. Without so much as a whisper of wind, the surface of the harbour was stilled and shimmering.

Someone passed round a bladder filled with rum, stolen from the supplies the *Duke of York* had just delivered. It wouldn't be missed as a certain amount was always allowed for vaporization, which also known as "the angels share".

Before long the mood was festive, almost merry.

Cuthbertson tried to add some theatre to the occasion, waiting until the sun started to turn golden before the bugler appeared on the wooden platform and began to play a lament as the men were brought up the steps to face the gallows. Though the moment of reckoning was at hand for these three men, solemnity had long since departed the scene and he was drowned out by raucous cheers and shouts of 'Good on yer boys!' and 'See you in Hell!'

Hudson, shaky and weeping, looked in dire need of a priest, but Allen and Oates' remorse was evidently short-lived because they almost danced up onto the platform, waving to their cheering mates and shouting 'Cheerio!'

'It's more like a parting of friends going on a distant land journey than men about to be separated forever,' remarked Dalton.

To shouts of encouragement they took off their boots and

tossed them into the tight knot of humanity that had now gathered at the front of the gallows. The items that were caught were held aloft like trophies. Spying Cuthbertson, surrounded by redcoats, Allen and Oats winked at him and called out, 'Goodbye Jack' – Jack being flash cant for the Devil. The row reached a crescendo when they took the chance to vent their feelings. Francis Oates, by far the best orator of the three, stepped forwards and delivered a rousing requiem.

'All of our lives in this place are but days in Hell. Far better this, to die by axe or rope, than to wake each day in fear and tremble and wish you had not waked.'

Sergeant Waddy tried to introduce some solemnity to the proceedings by singing the hymn, *Nearer Thy God to Thee* in his deep, rumbling baritone, but was shouted down.

Cuthbertson took to the stage and stood defiantly in the face of the noise, his white-gloved hands behind his back, raising himself up and down on his toes, seemingly unperturbed, almost basking in their hostility. He knew he'd have the last word.

He gave a curt nod and three redcoats stepped forwards, directed the prisoners to stand on the trapdoors, bound their hands, placed white hoods over their heads and stepped back. Cuthbertson nodded again.

Sergeant Waddy's big hand slammed down on the lever which released the bolts. The trapdoors opened one . . . two . . . three and they disappeared from sight. The swinging trapdoors slammed against the gibbet in quick succession, sounding like a volley of gunfire.

But the drop didn't break their necks cleanly.

Waddy's men had not tied the nooses properly and there was a violent drumming of feet on the wooden planking as they danced on air beneath the gallows. The loud tattoo lasted fully half a minute before it slowed and finally stopped as each was strangulated.

There was a long silence, as the enormity of death registered in grog-addled minds and whispered prayers were sent heavenwards to accompany their departed souls. Then Cuthbertson, who'd remained standing in plain view throughout, nodded at the tight press of convicts as if to say, *That's my answer*, called out 'needs must, gentlemen, needs must,' and turned on his heel. A loud hissing and spitting followed him all the way up the muddy track to his cottage.

Dalton muttered, 'The score of the lash is enough to keep order for now, but those damned redcoats might yet need every one of the ten cartridges they keep ready in their kangaroo pouches.'

The arduous daily routine of chopping, stripping, rolling and floating logs took our minds away from the hangings; the work was an almost welcome diversion from the poisonous atmosphere that now infected the island. The redcoats were jumpy and Cuthbertson punished every indiscretion ruthlessly, however small, in a bid to reinstate his iron rule. Whatever plot Greenhill was hatching still remained a secret, but we waited patiently, having no other flotsam to cling to in this sea of despair.

A new worker was added to our logging party, a tall, earnest young man of no more than nineteen. He went by the name of Peter Ellis and hailed from the Broads of Norfolk where he had been in service at a grand house belonging to a rich landowner.

'What brought you here?' I quizzed him at tea on his first day.

He looked at me dubiously.

'We've all landed up on the wrong side of the law. I was sent here for stealing shoes,' I said, trying to make light of it.

He kept his head down, so I shrugged and watched Logan filling his tin mug with four heaped spoons of sugar, as he did each morning. *Gluttonous, fat bastard.*

'I was in love with her,' Ellis said suddenly, pulling my attention back to his troubled young face.

'What's that?'

'Susan, my intended, worked in the same house as me. Young master Horsley had his eye on her, but she wouldn't have anything to do with him.'

I nodded sadly. I had heard such stories before.

'One day he sent me into Norwich on an errand to collect a suit he'd had made by a tailor there. I thought it odd because I was sure I'd seen it hanging up in his wardrobe, but it was not my place to question so I went.' Peter bit his lip and hesitated.

'Did something happen when you were gone?'

He nodded his bowed head and when he finally looked at me I saw the tears shining in his eyes. With a loud sigh he said, 'I got back after dark without the suit, which had been collected the week before, to find Susan had locked herself in her room and was saying she couldn't see me no more. I kept on knocking and eventually, afraid that I'd wake the whole house, she opened the door. Before she even opened her mouth I knew what all the commotion was about. The sparkle had gone from her eye.'

'That bastard,' I spat.

'He'd cornered her in the laundry and said he intended to have her. He was too strong and she couldn't fight him off. I ran all over the place, swearing all sorts of vengeance against master Horsley, but Susan sat me down and very calmly explained, "Peter, there's nothing you can do. The older maids told me not to fuss and that I'd have to get used to it. The gentlemen upstairs would have their sport with the young servant girls downstairs. It was almost customary out in the country."

'But I told her, "I don't give a bugger! We're not their chattels. I'll take up the matter with Lord Thomas Horsley himself." Though she begged me not to interfere my blood was up and nothing would dissuade me.'

I pictured Peter running up flights of darkened marble stairs, ready to defend his maid's honour.

'But his Lordship flatly refused to censure his son, roundly berated me for having the effrontery to accuse the young master of such a vile deed, and dismissed me from his service forthwith.'

He again fell silent and again I prompted him. 'Did you go after him?'

Peter took a deep breath, his pulse throbbing in his temple as he recalled the scene. 'When he returned from his hunting the next morning, I warned the heir to the manor to keep away from Susan, but he just laughed in my face. "I'll have her whenever I want," he sneered in that hoity-toity voice. I challenged the young master to a fight, which his vanity wouldn't allow him to refuse, and gave him a sound thrashing in a leafy forest clearing.'

I sighed. 'But that wasn't the end of it?'

He shook his head. 'I was arrested. The local magistrate, an acquaintance of Lord Horsley, found me guilty of attempted murder even though both fighters had been attended by seconds and I had withdrawn when requested. I was transported for seven years and on my arrival in Van Diemen's Land discovered a letter had been sent ahead to Lieutenant-Governor Sorell warning him of my "disturbed and violent nature" and recommending that I serve my sentence in the harshest facility on the island.'

His misery at his own misfortune was compounded by the fate of his beloved. 'There's no one to protect Susan now,' he lamented, 'the young master will continue to press his affections on her until she is with child and she will be sent from the house in disgrace with a bastard in her belly.'

I'm afraid Peter's luck improved little on Sarah Island. In Norfolk he'd been a kitchen servant and was unaccustomed to hard manual labour, so it wasn't long before his soft hands blistered and split. Working outside in all weathers at this southerly latitude he soon caught the chills and started shivering. Logan denied his request to see Dr Spence, his mean little eyes narrowing in suspicion. 'There's nowt wrong with you lad, least nothing that a day's hard work won't put right,' he grunted.

'But . . .'

'Draw yourself in, or you'll get a raw back to show the doctor,' warned Logan.

Wisely, Peter said no more about it and clambered into the boat. Logan smirked. We all thought plenty, but kept our own counsel through gritted teeth.

We started felling trees on a steep slope that ran down into the Gordon River, which made it easier to get the logs into the water. By noon the poor lad was pale and staggering. The sweat poured off him and his brow was as hot as a branding iron. We had rotated the axe work carefully without Logan noticing, so we could keep him on light duties, such as stripping bark and chopping branches.

'Peter's getting worse,' said Mather, his brogue strained with genuine concern.

'We're doing our best to cover him,' muttered Greenhill. 'He'll just have to grit his teeth 'til the shivers pass.'

Up on the platform above our heads we watched 'Little'

Brown give a massive Huon trunk three broad-shouldered blows, spraying wood chips to the wind. Sensing that the tree was about to topple, he paused, sweat streaming off his balding head, and called out, 'Here she comes!' This simple rule allowed the rest of us get clear and avoid any mishaps.

Working out in the forests these past couple of months, we'd developed a keen ear for the death-knell of a tree. Just before it comes down, it gives a mournful groan, as though announcing its doom to the rest of the forest. Then there is a short silence followed by an almighty crack as it snaps, and a roar as it suddenly descends. Some go over slowly and others tumble straight down. We were attuned to these sounds and the likely result, but Peter wasn't and his illness had made him sluggish on his feet.

The still forest air was rent by sharp cracks that echoed like gunfire. I was momentarily dazzled by a ray of bright winter sunlight that slanted through the thick green canopy as the huge trunk leant forwards. Then this force of nature plummeted to earth with a mighty roar and nothing in this known world could have stopped it.

As this tree grew on the side of a hill it simply toppled over, its roots unable to anchor its hefty beam in the soft peaty soil. With a terrible ripping sound the earth started opening up around us as tangled coils of ancient roots, thicker than a man's leg, tore through the ground, showering us with black soil. Men started shouting and charging around as they scrambled to get out of the way. My foot caught on one of those uprooted strands that sent me sprawling. I scrambled to my knees, looked up, and knew I couldn't get clear in time. So wide was the girth of the rapidly approaching trunk that it cast a shadow over me. I closed my eyes. *So this is how it ends.*

Just before the huge trunk pounded me into paste, a heavy

body hit me hard around the middle and propelled me backwards. As we tumbled in a heap there was an almighty crash and the ground shook as if struck by the very hammer of the gods. Then there was silence, bar the distant squalling of frightened birds and a soft rustling as thousands upon thousands of green leaves spiralled gently down to earth like green confetti. We looked round dazedly, thankful we'd managed to get clear.

'Where's Peter?' said Bodenham, an edge of panic in his voice.

Then we heard sobbing from behind the huge girth.

Oh God.

We ran to him but his legs, from the knees down, were pinned beneath the huge tree. It didn't take much imagination to know that they would be crushed to pulp.

Greenhill was the first to snap out of the shock. 'Right, let's see if we can shift him.'

'Leave him, he's a gonner,' growled the fat-bellied Logan who, to our disappointment, had also come through unscathed.

His face flushed with anger, Greenhill rounded on him. 'If, by the good grace of God it was you under there, we'd fucken leave you, but he's one of us!' Greenhill's rasping Cockney accent grated harshly on the ears as he spat the words into Logan's startled face. The Lancashireman was well aware he was a scab and a traitor, but due to Cuthbertson's tight rein he didn't get told too often.

'You can't talk to me like that,' he protested, 'I'll report you.' But for once his threat rang hollow and having stopped Logan in his tracks Greenhill now turned to us and with great emotion added, 'He ain't dead 'til he stops breathing!' It was the first time I'd seen the aloof and sarcastic Greenhill show concern for anyone, except his constant companion, Travers, who he'd known back in England. He took the sobbing Peter under the arms and tried to drag him clear, but he was too tightly pinned and the pain set him screaming. Greenhill knelt and covered his face with his hand, thought a moment and then, as if he and not Logan were in charge, barked out instructions to the rest of us who stood by, uncertain what to do.

'Get over here and start digging.'

We all did as we were bid and burrowed into the heavily bloodstained soil around Peter's legs using the axes we got from the boat and our bare hands. Logan stomped about in the background, grumping about it being 'a fool's earn'. When at last we were able to free him, there was nothing but two soil-blackened stumps below his knees. He'd lost a lot of blood and was beginning to fade. Seeing us transfixed by the awful injuries, Greenhill stripped off his canary jacket and wrapped it around Peter's stumps. None of us had any experience in dealing with such injuries and the best we could do was to get him back to Dr Spence as soon as possible.

Urged on by Greenhill, we pulled savagely on the oars until our muscles burned. Fortunately, this journey home was assisted by a stiff northerly, which rippled the harbour. Yet even with the elements in our favour it took us over an hour to get back and raise the alarm. We stood up and waved our arms so that the spotters up on the summit would see something was wrong through the spyglass.

When we landed, Cuthbertson, a retinue of redcoats and Dr Spence were all in attendance. After a night of turbulent pleasures the medic still appeared a little misty and confused and his hand shook as he examined Peter's shattered legs. I noted he wore the same grim countenance as the day he examined William

Halliday after his flogging. Spence felt for a pulse and even when he found one he gave us no cause for celebration.

'He's alive, just. Bring him,' he ordered with a slight quaver in his voice.

In keeping with the primitive nature of Sarah Island, the doctor's surgery was no more than a small bare room with a wooden table. We laid Peter on it without being asked.

'I've no chloroform or laudanum to dose him up with, mind. They're bobbing about off the head on that supply boat that has been waiting four days for a fair wind. You'll just have to hold him,' Spence warned as he donned what looked like a white butcher's apron and slipped a wooden bit into Peter's mouth. It wasn't going to be pretty and just about as methodical.

Spence then opened a small leather bag and produced a small sharp saw. 'Stand ready boys,' he said grimly and without ceremony began to saw briskly through flesh and bone. Peter tensed as he felt the steel teeth bite and started thrashed and moaning feebly as the pain intensified. Greenhill clasped onto his hand and spoke to him throughout the procedure. Fearing the spread of gangrene, even if he survived this butchery, Spence took both Peter's legs above the knees and sealed the arteries with a smoking branding iron brought inside by a soldier. His screams could be heard right around the island.

Gagging from the bloody butchery of the operation and the smell of burning flesh, we tumbled out the door, many, myself included, spewing on the ground. Only Greenhill seemed above it all. I supposed that riding the perilous oceans hundreds of miles from the nearest shore and medical care, such basic surgical procedures were commonplace.

No sooner had we regained our balance than Dr Spence appeared in his bloodied apron, wiping his stained hands with a damp rag. 'He's gone,' he said with no surprise or hint of regret, 'nature could do no more.'

No further explanation was needed nor given. We were aware that Peter's terrible injuries would most likely cost him his life. Maybe Logan had been right, but we'd done the best we could by him.

In the race to get Peter back to the settlement I hadn't time to consider how close I'd come to joining him. I grabbed Dalton, who happened to be standing next to me, and offered him my hand. 'You saved my skin again, Alex,' I said solemnly, 'and I'm forever in your debt.'

He accepted my hand and nodded his great bearded head. 'You'd have done the same for me.'

'One day I'll repay the favour,' I croaked, Peter's sad passing getting the better of me.

'Your hand and your thanks is reward enough,' he said modestly.

They dispensed with Peter's body quickly. As we watched the burial detail once again plough a lonely furrow out to Halliday's Island to lay Peter the broken-hearted to rest next to Halliday, Allen, Hudson and Oates, tears stung my eyes for the first time in many a year. But for Dalton I would have been making the short trip with him. I wondered whether I should give over a gold sovereign to get a letter written to Susan, his girl in England. I decided against it. There's enough misery in this world as it is.

The sight of them rowing Peter away into the glory of a red sunset was the mainspring for Greenhill to finally tell us what had been occupying his thoughts for the past couple of months. Perhaps recent events had impressed on him how cheap a commodity life was here, and that none of us could be sure how much time we had left.

I'd discovered that Greenhill and three others had already tried to stow away and then steal a schooner. Maybe he was anxious to get back to England to settle with his wife who'd caused him to be transported by reporting to police that he'd stolen her coat. Evidently, Mr and Mrs Greenhill had both been cut from the same rough cloth. He was not short of a plan, just the men to make it work, and now he was about to start recruiting.

'Was there ever a better invitation to leave this place?' he challenged, nodding at the distant silhouette of the boat.

'What have you in mind?' I asked.

'Seize a whaleboat and make for the open sea.'

'Where would we go?'

'Timor, Java or Batavia even.'

'Has anyone else tried it?'

'A few years ago four government men took a schooner from Hobart and made it to Java, sunk it and disappeared. Probably livin' the high life while we rot here. If a bloody woman can do it, then so can we. What say you?' growled Greenhill.

The 'bloody woman' was none other than Mary Bryant, a Yorkshire lass who made the first and most legendary break for freedom back in 1791, barely three years after the First Fleet had landed. She, her husband and son stole Governor Phillip's cutter at Port Jackson and reached Timor after drifting in an open boat for sixty-nine days. Despite losing her husband and son on the journey, she made it back to England on a series of cargo ships only to be arrested at Portsmouth and committed to Newgate prison on a charge of piracy. The reformer and author James Boswell took up her cause and she was spared the death sentence and later received a full pardon. Stories like Bryant's and Cunningham's gave us hope and inspiration, which burst forth now.

'I'm in.'

'I'll go.'

'Nothing to lose.'

'Me too.'

'Aye.'

'Aye.'

With himself and Travers he now had eight. Greenhill had found himself a crew.

'When?' demanded Dalton.

Greenhill turned his searching gaze on us one by one, trying to detect any hint of treachery before he parted with his secret.

'The fourth day of October.'

'That's twenty-one days from today,' confirmed Travers, his tongue flicking in and out of his mouth like a reptile in pursuit of a fly.

'Why the fourth?' cut in Kennelly.

Greenhill hesitated a moment as he stole a look at Travers, who nodded and grunted before he continued in a low voice, 'That's when the next supply ship is due. There'll be plenty provisions for the taking and everyone will be occupied with the unloading and the newly arrived convicts.' The shipping schedule was a closely guarded secret, precisely to prevent the formation of plots such as ours.

We nodded.

It was settled.

Chapter 8

Escape from Hell

Macquarie Harbour, 20 September 1822

On cold, clear days the frost was cruel first thing in the morning. It held everything in its iron grip, including our bare hands, which stuck fast to the oars as soon as we lifted them. Usually, the only way to get any feeling in them was to row like the Devil, but that day our blood was running so high that we didn't even feel the cold.

The hour of our liberation was at hand.

We'd been forced to bring our escape date forwards two weeks when the *Waterloo* put in to Macquarie Harbour early due to a very favourable confluence of elements. Just our luck. Due to prevailing winds and weather conditions, outward voyages normally lasted four or more weeks, whereas the return could take as little as four days.

As we prepared to crest some brackish waves on our daily run to Kelly's Basin, I stole a sly glance at Logan. As usual, he sat up at the bow like some hideous figurehead sucking on the clay pipe he kept clenched between his teeth, whistling tunelessly between puffs. *He'll not have much to whistle about shortly*, I mused with no small satisfaction.

No sooner had the thought left my head than the stench of rotting flesh suddenly overwhelmed us and we stopped rowing as hands were quickly clamped over mouths and noses.

'What in the bloody hell's that?' moaned Mather.

I spied the bloated white belly of an upturned fish bobbing on the surface, decay already well-advanced. It was followed in short order by many others and soon we were surrounded by hundreds of stinking corpses – eyes straining out of their sockets, mouths wide open, their last gasping breaths fixed by the rictus of death.

'Christ almighty,' cursed Bodenham, crossing himself. It would not have seemed so eerie or portentous had we not planned to flee that day.

After pulling his thumb and forefinger from his red, bulbous nose and depositing a generous mouthful of phlegm over the side, Logan explained the Biblical plague that surrounded us. 'After heavy rains tons o' rotting herbage gets washed down from the mountains into the harbour and poisons the water.' Returning to his usual harsh, hectoring tone he growled, 'Now, put yer backs to them oars ye buggers and we'll soon pull clear o' them.' For once we snapped to it and soon left the malodorous fish in our wake.

I chanced a glance at the others. It was nothing more than dead fish and as Logan said, it was a common enough occurrence, but when you are carrying a guilty secret everything appears fateful.

We go today.

An additional complication was that Cuthbertson, sensing unrest brewing amongst Peter Ellis's workmates, posted Greenhill to coal duties. He was a man of war and knew that the feud between Greenhill and Logan would fester. It was a blow to our plans, but we were determined it wouldn't stop us.

I stole another glance at Logan's bulky outline and allowed myself a grin. *We're fixed on today and we'll stick to it come what may.*

We ensured the day started just as normal and did nothing to arouse Logan's suspicion. We worked for the usual hour-and-a-half before we stopped for tea. While we supped strong unsweetened black tea, Logan made a great virtue of piling up a pyramid of sugar on his spoon before carefully tipping it into his tea and stirring it noisily, repeating the process four times. The sweet smell drove us to distraction.

Corporal Logan was so absorbed in his petty show of privilege that he didn't see the bunched fist that rammed hard into his mouth, depositing him on his arse in the still-wet grass. It was served up as afters by 'Little' Brown. Dalton, the military man, took up a stout pine pole, which he'd cut and stripped for just such a contingency, spun it expertly in his hands and had the thin end to Logan's throat in a flash. With one short, sharp poke he could've crushed his throat.

Momentarily stunned, a look of fear crossed Logan's face, but wiping his bloodied mouth with the back of his hand he tried to recover using a threat. 'Get that away from me now,' he snarled, trying to brush away the pole, but Dalton held firm. Logan then tried to gain his feet, but Bodenham swept his legs from under him. He sprawled on his arse and again attempted to restore order. 'Let me up and I'll say no more about it,' he pleaded.

'You're a lyin' bastard Logan! You'd shop the lot of us as quick as look and we'd end up with more stripes on our backs than a maypole,' spat Travers, getting in on the act.

A terrible rage seized us at the very thought of Logan's

treachery and we crowded around to give him our answer with boots and fists. Small stones scrunched beneath our feet and our breathing grew heavy as we laid into him with our boots. At first he gamely resisted, grabbing at our legs and lashing out with his feet, but Dalton swung a well-aimed kick into his mid-region and there was a sharp crack as one of his ribs broke. He stopped struggling, his face contorted with pain, but we kept on booting him until we drew blood.

As we stood around him catching our breath, Travers stooped, rummaged in his pocket and relieved him of his tinder stick, which would be useful on our journey. 'You won't have much use for this now,' he smirked.

We further soiled his smart dark-blue jacket by rolling him in the dirt like a pig and binding his arms behind him with some rope from the boat.

'You'll hang, the lot of yers!' Logan roared, and got a straight fist in the face from Brown which burst open his bottom lip.

'Oh, we're not stayin' about for that,' jeered Bodenham as we dragged Logan to his feet and lashed him to one of his precious pines. Sill Logan struggled, his great barrel chest heaving and straining against his bonds. 'You'll never get past the marksmen at Hell's Gates. They'll put more holes in you than a rusty bucket.'

The standard British army issue was the Brown Bess musket, which fired four shots a minute. Little wonder the British army killed 10,000 Frenchmen at the Battle of Talavera. As we waded into waters that had suddenly lost their chill, I calculated that we would have to dodge sixteen bullets every minute and that it would take us an hour or so to steer a small boat through the narrow channels and monstrous swell that always lapped at Hell's Gates. The odds were against us.

'I'd sooner take my chances with the sharp-shooters than spend another day as a government man,' shouted Dalton, assuaging my fears and raising a small cheer from the others. Turning to face Logan he jeered, 'Whatever happens to us, it's nothing compared to what Cuthbertson will do to you. You'll be lucky if you don't end up in irons.'

A pained look crossed our overseer's – our former overseer's – face as he watched us jump into the whaleboat and start pulling on the oars. His lonely figure receded into the distance and was then lost beneath the waterline as we moved away from the shore.

We rowed the six miles to Coal Head where we could see Greenhill anxiously awaiting us. He'd overpowered the one constable overseeing his detail and tied him to a heavy log.

'What fucken kept you?' he yelled as we beached the rowboat.

'We was just saying our goodbyes to Corporal Logan like,' joked Kennelly, but Greenhill was in no mood for levity.

'We're not home free yet,' he cautioned as he led us to the bolted door of the pilot's hut. A few hefty shoulder barges from Dalton and Brown and an assortment of boots from the rest of us buckled the door at its hinges. Pulling it clean off we darted inside. There was just ten pounds of flour, six pounds of salted beef and an axe, which Greenhill immediately slipped into his belt. 'It's a start,' he said, 'we'll grab this and head for Lucas's hut where there'll be plenty more. Those bastards don't starve themselves.'

As we lugged the supplies outside, the other convicts in Greenhill's party began to drift towards us, a Scotchman called Chas McCurdy to the fore. He had a reputation as a hard nut with a brawler's face to prove it. A once-thin pointed nose had been flattened and pushed to one side by the force of fists. Set deep into his warrior's countenance was a set of intense blue eyes that flashed with violent intent. Though now approaching his middle years, he was as lean and muscled as a robber's dog.

'Can we get some of yer grub boys?' drawled McCurdy. Though worded as a request, his aggressive Scotch tenor made it sound like a demand.

'Sorry shipmate, we're bound for freedom and we'll need every scrap we can carry,' said Greenhill shaking his head.

'That disnae seem right to me.'

'Aye,' piped up another. 'We've been on short rations for the past six months.'

The coal party, which consisted of nine other men, formed into a phalanx between us and the whaleboat. There was a stand-off. We were well-matched but did not want to waste precious time fighting our own race. We might yet have to take on the redcoats.

'Gie us half that beef,' demanded McCurdy with a sneer.

Greenhill responded by pulling the axe from his belt. 'Then you'll have to come and get it.'

They didn't advance in the face of a weapon, but held their ground.

'Come on boys,' said Greenhill and we edged forwards.

There was a dangerous moment as Greenhill and McCurdy came face to face. Our man raised the axe and said, 'Are you going to step aside, or am I gonna cleave your skull with this?'

They held each other's stare for a long moment, neither yielding. Whatever McCurdy saw in Greenhill's stare was enough to convince him that he would use the axe. Having defied the greater odds long enough to retain his hard-won reputation, the Scotchman nodded, took a reluctant step back and said in his strongly accented brogue, 'Let them pass boys.'

'Douse the warning pyres,' ordered Greenhill sharply as we pushed through their sullen ranks. The former master mariner had rapidly assumed command of our party. He was cocksure, but had been in a few tight spots and once we were out on the open seas we'd be relying solely on his navigational and survival skills.

After we'd poured sea water on all the timber, we got into the boat and started pulling towards Hell's Gates, a mindful eye on Sarah Island which lay just two miles to the south of us. So far so good.

As we inched towards Hell's Gates we ticked off each landmark as we passed it. We'd gone past Kelly's Basin, Farm Cove, and could see the familiar shape of Liberty Point on the port side. But that's when things began to go wrong.

To our horror smoke started billowing up behind us from the shore we'd just left. Our fellow convicts had managed to light a signal fire to warn the redcoats that something was amiss. The tariff for failing to prevent other convicts escaping was a 'Botany Bay dozen' and they weren't going to cop the lash on our account, especially as we hadn't shared our food.

There was meant to be a code of loyalty between convicts, but it was often sacrificed to self-interest. Places like this bring out the best and the worst in men, usually the worst.

'There'll be extra rations on their plates and a tot o' rum in those bastards' mugs tonight,' spat Greenhill. Our worst fears were confirmed when we saw the sun hit the mirrors of the heliotrope as a message was dispatched to the sharp-shooters at the heads. There'd be no extra supplies there for us now and the redcoats would have plenty time to prepare us a hot reception.

'If we're taken, I'll kill every man jack o' 'em, that bastard McCurdy first,' vowed Dalton, breaking the silence.

'Will they come after us?' asked Mather fearfully.

'Cuthbertson will be launching the whaleboats right now, as sure as eggs is eggs,' confirmed Greenhill grimly.

We looked towards Sarah Island and imagined boats, crewed by redcoats and the stoutest convicts, cresting the waves towards us. Cuthbertson would be standing on the bow of the leading boat exhorting them to catch us before we reached Hell's Gates.

'Head for the shore,' commanded Greenhill decisively, pointing to a small beach area on our starboard side near the mouth of one of the many mysterious, unnamed rivers that snaked down the surrounding mountains.

Glad of a firm hand, we turned hard right and began pulling in a well-ordered rhythm, which we'd built up over the past months of rowing out to work. By the time the bow thumped hard into soft white sand there was still no sign of the pursuing whaleboats.

'What about the boat?' fussed Bodenham, the anxiousness we all felt surfacing in his voice.

If Greenhill felt the same, it wasn't evident from his. 'Cut her up and hide the sail in the trees.'

'Let's just leave it,' beseeched Mather looking longingly at the thick green screen of trees which we could quickly melt into.

'No, leave no trail. We'll need all the start we can get. They'll be out with the dogs. Better they don't know where we started from.'

'Just do it,' said Travers backing up Greenhill. 'Bob's had experience in these matters.' *He'd also been re-captured twice*, I thought to myself, but kept my own counsel.

Little Brown grabbed up the axe in his great, gnarly hands and started hacking at the boat's ribbing. Taking it in turns with the axe, we soon reduced the boat to matchwood.

'There's no going back now,' piped Mather as he watched the debris being tossed into the undergrowth.

'What about our footprints?' asked Bodenham.

'The tide will take care of those,' Greenhill replied as the first small wave of brownish water lapped up past the tide mark and wet our boots. Cocking his head to one side, our commander watched the retreating water wipe the sand clean of footprints. 'No one will ever know we were here,' he added. The same terrible foreboding I felt on entering Macquarie Harbour came over me at that thought, though none of the others seemed concerned by the prospect. Once again, I pushed it aside.

'Which way?' asked Kennelly. We all looked round for guidance and Greenhill waited until he was sure all eyes were on him.

Standing directly beneath the sun which was quickly rising towards its brief midday zenith through the ever-present clouds, Greenhill turned hard left on his heel, military style, raised his extended hand over his head and sliced through the air. *He was cocksure, no doubt about it. He's just made himself our leader without so much as a word being spoken.*

'Due east gentlemen, that's where our salvation lies,' he announced confidently. 'Now, you know no white man has ever crossed this country on foot and the few maps there are describe the west coast of Van Diemen's Land as "unknown"?'

There were nods and 'ayes'.

'I won't lie, it'll be tough going. Are ye all up for this? If not, speak up. I hear there's plenty room on Sarah Island.' His little quip drew a few nervous laughs. He looked round us all, his gaze falling on Brown and Kennelly, the oldest, and me the smallest. He gave me a little smile as if to say *you sure?* Scurvy had shrunken and blackened his gums, making his rotting teeth even more prominent each time he grinned, giving him a hungry, wolfish look. He reminded me of the wild dogs I'd encountered in the bush when I worked as a shepherd around Hobart. I stared right back at him. *I'll show you, mate.*

'Good,' he said, the condescending little smirk still on his face.

It was a solemn moment. We were at the start of a great adventure. We all shook hands. *Eight of us are starting, but how many will be there at the finish?* I wondered.

One by one the others pushed through the solid screen of springy green thicket that separated the known world from whatever lay beyond. I took a deep breath, parted the herbage and plunged in after them. Just before I disappeared from view I glanced backwards. The waves had erased our footprints behind us, leaving the beach pristine, as though no human had ever set foot on it. Again I was filled with a strange sense of disquiet that I couldn't attribute to anything other than gut instinct.

'Come away, Alec,' called Dalton.

As I moved forwards again, the dense green screen sprang back, obscuring my view of the harbour and closing off the portal through which no man had ever returned.

Daniel Ruth was forced to tear his eyes from Pearce's journal by a loud bang on the window in front of him, the glass rattling hard in its frame as if someone had cast a stone against it. Leaping to his feet, heart in mouth, he peered through the grimy glass, suddenly fearful of what he might see on the other side of it.

There was no one there. The outlook was the same as always:

the swaying treetops just below the window; the harbour in the middle distance, a dark shade of grey or blue depending on the sky above it; and the immovable mountains cloaked in cloud and green moss. He caught a movement out of the corner of his eye and let out a sigh of relief as a stunned brown bird fluttered up from the sill.

'It was a bird, a bird flew into the window,' he said aloud, reassured by the sound of his own voice. Two days before he'd seen Captain Wilkes sail close to the island on his way home and made a point of going to the front door to wave, just to prove he was still alive and that whatever had made them fearful was all just childish superstition.

The young American sucked in a deep breath and rubbed his tired eyes, which felt as though they had grit in them. What he had just read deeply shocked him. Though it was only thirty years ago, the world Pearce described was a savage and primal place where things were done out of necessity rather than reason and with very little regard for their fellow man.

Crime and punishment was a topic of much debate in his native Philadelphia, which was founded by Quakers who didn't hold with violent punishment. In a break with British colonial tradition, they ceased public floggings in 1786 and from 1794 capital punishment was reserved for the crime of murder. The liberal, progressive city fathers believed the deprivation of liberty and life's pleasures was a far greater punishment and that solitary confinement would force a prisoner to think about his crimes and increase the probability of reform. The term 'penitentiary' was derived from the reform institution established at Walnut Street prison, Philadelphia. As Pearce had noted, no such liberal notions had ever been entertained on Sarah Island.

As darkness fell he sat down next to the fire and started mixing up the sharp-smelling chemicals and coating half-a-dozen photographic plates. Later, Daniel lay on his back in his makeshift camp and stared up at the strange sky and the unfamiliar constellations that blazed down on him. He reflected that the sky here seemed to be bigger, with more stars. *Maybe it's because we're so close to the bottom of the world*, Daniel thought idly as a warm feeling of contentment drifted over him. He'd made it to Van Diemen's Land under his own steam, used his guile to find the whereabouts of Pearce's journal, and here he was living the greatest adventure of his short life. As he prepared to crawl into his shelter for the night, Daniel looked around with some satisfaction at the makeshift camp he'd built with his own two hands.

As he lingered somewhere between this world and the next, his thoughts drifted towards home. He felt a pang of regret for Caroline and his parents who he knew would be praying for his safe return. *When I come back with the Pearce story, they'll understand, they'll be proud of me*, was his last waking thought.

As he slept, Daniel dreamt he was back at the University of Pennsylvania during the first year of his medical degree. Professor Mendelsson, who taught a new science called psychology, produced a large drawing consisting of a series of black and white dots and asked the class, 'Relax your mind, look beyond the dots and try to pick out the pattern, as you would if you were doing a puzzle or an anagram. Without conferring, write down what you see.' They all stared at it blankly for ten minutes before the professor gave them a series of clues. 'It's a picture of a famous person.' There was still no response so the professor added, 'He's known to everyone in the civilised world.' When there was still no answer, Mendelsson threw his arms wide and exclaimed, 'His is the most famous face in the history of mankind.'

A hand shot up and a voice called out, 'Our Lord Jesus Christ.'

To Daniel's astonishment, the mass of dots almost magically joined up before his eyes. Mendelsson smiled and concluded, 'As scientists you must approach research with an open mind. Your job is to join the dots, to find the picture in a world of infinite possibilities. It's a matter of asking the right questions until the picture becomes clear.'

Daniel woke before first light with those wise words still rolling around in his head like loose marbles. For breakfast he had a strong brew of coffee and a hunk of damper bread with salted meat whose rough texture and taste Daniel's discerning palate had almost grown accustomed to. He then walked purposely into the stiff breeze and felt the cold, sharp needles of rain sting his cheeks and earlobes as he made his way to Badger Rock, lugging the heavy camera, wooden tripod and plates.

Photography had become part of his daily routine. After using three or four hours of daylight he'd return to the penitentiary to read some of Pearce's memoir and then wade through the mountain of records verifying facts and researching events or people mentioned in Pearce's writings with what Dr Morton would have called 'scientific rigour'. It was arduous work, but Daniel calculated the *Isabella* could arrive any day in the next few weeks. The weather had held, so he imagined it would be sooner rather than later.

As he ducked under the black camera hood, the significance of the wooden 'A' that stood before him was suddenly clear. Against the first flicker of light in the blue black sky it looked for all the world like some pagan totem, but he now knew that it was the so-called 'bloody triangle' where the men he'd been reading about had been flogged mercilessly. He also found a flattish patch of ground where only a few saplings and low bushes had taken root. Thinking this must have been the parade ground where the convicts were assembled each morning, he searched around and found the flagpole from which the Union Jack had once fluttered. Traces of whitewash were still visible on it. The Union Jack was supposedly a symbol of civilisation but it might as well have been the skull and crossbones. As Daniel peered through the lens up into the weeping grey sky it struck him how careful Cuthbertson had been in preserving his dignity even in this little backwater of the British Empire.

Heading back to his garret he no longer felt the childish urge to taunt the ghosts of Macquarie Harbour, or to listen to his own mocking echo bouncing off the walls of the stone chambers. Daniel was aware of a subtle change within himself. At first, he'd felt superior, a man of science laying to rest the dark superstitions of Macquarie Harbour, rather like a missionary stepping onto a native shore, but through Pearce's story he'd begun to see his own life in a different light. While he'd grown up free and easy back in Philadelphia, men here toiled in terrible conditions, treated little better than animals. Punishment at Macquarie Harbour was meant to stop one step short of the gallows, but some preferred to take that final step, rather than live in the purgatory Cuthbertson had created. Choosing death over life was a state of mind he couldn't even begin to comprehend. What made it worse was that many of them were minor offenders, gradually dehumanised by a system of justice devised by the nation that claimed to be the leading light of the civilised world. It had been quite a history lesson and Daniel clattered up the last few stairs, eager to begin the next chapter of Pearce's enthralling tale.

Chapter 9

Tyranny of Nature

AFTER THE EUPHORIA OF our escape, we quickly discovered that there were many miles ahead of us before we reached freedom. We trudged through some thinly populated coastal rainforest, which afforded us some cover from the spotters on Sarah Island only five miles away. Unless they'd discovered the boat, Cuthbertson would still be expecting us to attempt to get out through the straits rather than go overland, but he'd try to cover every eventuality.

To keep up our spirits we sang songs, a mix of old favourites and newly minted tales of convict misery, of which there had been plenty. *The London Prentice Boy* was one we all knew well and we belted it out with gusto, the usually quiet Kennelly's baritone to the fore.

> *Come all you young chaps who live both far and near,*
> *Pray listen with attention to these few lines you'll hear,*
> *I once in ease did ramble, but sin did me destroy,*

So now upon Van Diemen's Land, is the London prentice boy.

Our proximity to Sarah Island and the Gordon River, which they could sail a schooner up, meant we had to head inland and keep up a quick pace the whole day. We followed the course of a rapidly flowing creek and by mid-afternoon we'd arrived at the foot of Mount Sorell, a vast cathedral of stone named after our esteemed lieutenant-governor who would soon be demanding a report from Cuthbertson as to why there'd been two escapes in less than a year from a place held to be 'inescapable'. The time we spent on Sarah Island meant that we started this journey lean and fit, but this was a difficult climb, especially without ropes. Rising up to some 4000 feet, its rocky dome was almost as devoid of vegetation as its venerated namesake was of hair; therefore the higher we climbed, the more exposed our position became. The frowning walls of stone glared back at us but as we were hemmed in by steep, stony ridges, all angled upwards, there was only one way forwards.

Mount Sorell looked solid enough, but its surface of soft, crumbly scree refused us a firm foothold and quickly scoured all the skin from our hands, knees and elbows. Grabbing hold of the few clumps of wiry, scrubby vegetation that doggedly clung to the face of the mountain, we reached a ridge a couple of hundred feet beneath the summit by nightfall, though my legs would've sworn we'd climbed it twice.

With no moon to betray us, we were keen to put more distance between ourselves and Sarah Island, but the path was treacherous and the jagged rocks below unforgiving, so we spent the night in the rocky embrace of Mount Sorell.

Greenhill had decreed we would eat only one meal a day.

Brown looked down at his meagre ration, which sat easily in the palm of his great hand, and mumbled, 'Not much to sustain a man after a hard day's trekking.' Six ounces of bread and meat per man was all the rations we could afford.

Though exhausted, we nevertheless posted pickets, still fearful that the 'heroes of Talavera' might try to add our scalps to their belts. We daren't light a fire in such an exposed position so those with kangaroo coats bundled themselves up and we all huddled close together to ward off the biting wind commonly found at such altitudes.

As day broke, we witnessed the glory of a red dawn. The early-morning mist made the trees look grey as it hung heavy in the glades. As it cleared, we were granted a breathtaking if depressing vista. If Monaghan took its name from the Irish word *Muineachán*, meaning 'the land of little hills', then this was a land of big mountains. Their dark outlines, whose peaks were lost in the fast-rising vapours, stood sentinel on the horizon with a low-ridged barrier of rock running beneath them. At all points of the compass we were surrounded by a tight green crush of trees that offered no hope of a quick escape.

We turned round and risked a glance back towards the harbour. In the near distance, clearly visible, was Sarah Island and we could easily pick out the familiar landmarks in the harbour we had all come to know and hate. By now the logging gangs would be up to their waists in the icy waters wrestling with huge logs.

'I'll stake my davy that the bugger's got his spyglass on us at this very moment and is roundly cursing our mothers,' rumbled Dalton, his mouth twisted into a snarl.

'He can curse mine all he likes,' jibed Travers, but no one took him on. Even on top of a mountain we didn't feel safe. We hadn't seen or heard anything of a hunting party so far but we knew we must keep moving.

We spent the best part of morning trekking down the other side of Mount Sorrell, which was far more dangerous and more wearing than going up it, but it earned us no respite. As we left the coast behind us, the character of the forest suddenly changed. Gone were the thin saplings and wiry brush that could easily be pushed aside; instead, densely packed, rough-edged vegetation thickened and closed in around us. As we parted the foliage to make way, it snapped closed behind us as if to bar the way to our return.

We did see signs of other human life that day, but not redcoats. Mather, the youngest and fittest amongst us, was in the lead when he let out a raw-throated yell. Fearing we were about to be attacked, we took to the bush and grabbed up stones and cudgels. Crouching in the cool shade, the lazy buzzing of insects was the only sound, other than the blood pounding in our ears.

Then came Bob Greenhill's strong voice, 'Out you come, the coast's clear.' Mather had taken fright at a fur kaross left hanging off a tree-branch, still dripping blood. It was proof the blacks had been there that very day. Was it a warning to us or had it just been left out to dry? We cast anxious looks into the shadows beyond the green-fringed path where thin rays of light contorted innocent shapes into the beasts that lived in our imaginations. We all began to wonder what one of those long spears in the guts would be like – the sharp tearing pain and the long, agonising wait for death. It was commonly believed that native Toogee tribesmen had finished off the last party that escaped from Sarah Island and I tried to push from my mind the scurrilous scuttlebutt that they'd been roasted on a spit.

The local blacks were fighting back against their invaders. While their spears were no match for British muskets, the terrain favoured their stealthy war. Renegade blacks led by the likes of Black Jack, Musquito and Wayler were learning to wait until settlers had discharged their muskets then attacking them as they re-loaded. In the British press, Wallola, the warrior queen of the Aborigines, had already been compared to Boudicca, the queen of the Britons, who drove back the Roman invaders. In the end, both lost, but pride demands that you defend your land, your race and your kin, something we Irish had been doing for centuries. Finally, the Aborigines will be defeated and delivered into the hands of God and the government, who will do for them as well as any army.

The unforgiving terrain forced us to plunge downwards into the belly of a deep gorge choked with undergrowth. At the foot of the gorge we entered what I would call very rough country and had our first encounter with the giant local vegetation. The riot of foliage before us was like nothing we'd ever seen before. One thing we'd learned about at Macquarie Harbour was trees, and we knew every one of them. Myrtle, eucalypts, leatherwood and beech seemed to be the most common along with the various members of the pine family: celery top, Huon, King Billy and pencil. The smallest would have been twenty feet tall and the tallest well over a hundred. In addition, there were giant Sassafras: umbrella ferns with huge, feather-shaped leaves of a size I'd never seen before, and another unknown plant of a huge circumference brandishing broad, sword-shaped leaves that tapered down to a sharp point.

The light dimmed as the sky above was replaced by a wild tangle of canopy. The forest took on a fairytale quality as we arrived in a glade where filtered light slanted through the trees onto an ancient, gnarled trunk some ten feet in width, surrounded by fallen trees covered by a colourful array of toadstools, green spongy sedges and mosses. Its giant roots had pushed up through the ground and spread around it like the tentacles of some great serpent. Untrammelled by man and nurtured by the wettest climate on the Australian continent, this forest looked the same as it did on the day God created the earth. When we'd come through Hell's Gates, I'd had the unsettling feeling that nature was warning us not to enter; as I looked around me now, that same sensation visited me again.

As there was no way around the forest we plunged into its midst, but if we expected nature to allow us easy passage we were sorely mistaken: we could barely move in any direction as the springy fronds of the Sassafras fern barred our way. They were the girth of a man's leg and gave no quarter, even when hit with an axe or slashed at with a knife. With Brown and Dalton in the lead, we pushed them back and held on until we'd all squeezed through, only to be confronted by the next and the next. It was like an army of hands snatching at you, shoving you sideways, while their rough hairy skin rasped our arms, faces and hands. The going was made even slower by so-called 'horizontals', thin, willowy trees that preferred to grow sideways rather than upwards. They slammed into our chests and knees while a close-knit assortment of bushes, small trees and vines tied up our feet.

There was a fateful rumbling in the heavens, I felt the cold touch of rain on the back of my neck, and then heard a noise like a drum-roll as heavy drops cascaded down onto the topmost leaves. It quickly turned the ground, which was littered with slippery moss-covered logs, into a treacherous mire that sucked in our boots up to the ankle and further drained our will and strength with every step.

We discovered by painful degrees that the best method of getting through was to crawl on our bellies, the strong smell of damp and rotting vegetation adding to our general discomfort. We also kept an eye out for spiders and snakes, many of which were venomous in these parts.

Just before nightfall we were precious glad to burst out into open country. It was the longest few miles any of us had ever travelled. We spent our second night in the open near a marshy creek, feeling confident enough by this stage to light a fire. The warmth raised our spirits sufficiently for Mather, the first one to speak in many hours, to give voice to our general feelings.

'Surely no redcoat would brave all that just to bring back a convict party? They'll surely expect us to perish in these woods.'

It was meant to be reassuring, but as I watched our rations almost halved in just two days, an uncomfortable feeling came over me. We might have outrun the redcoats but we were pushing further into the unknown each day, testing the limits of this country and ourselves. I couldn't help but worry about what lay ahead of us.

Our limits were further tested on our third day by a great, as yet unnamed spur of rock with a jagged, broken spine that ran across the entire span of our horizon. Behind it lay the imposing snow-capped peak of Frenchman's Cap, which Greenhill was using as a navigational point. Without a compass there was no way around it. We would have to go as the crow flies and that would be no easy assignment.

'Right, we'll spend the night atop that ridge,' stated Greenhill boldly, but my fears of the night before proved well-founded.

Nightfall found us stranded halfway up that precipice, having badly overestimated how much ground we could cover in our severely weakened state.

We'd spent most of the day on our hands and knees attempting a dizzying upwards climb on a knife-edged ridge of hard, crumbly shale. Gripping on with hands and feet numbed by cold, we inched our way upwards towards the blustery clouds that had blown in off the mountains, trying to ignore the slanting rain that drove into our faces and the sudden gusts of wind that contrived to send us over the dangerous precipices. One slip and we were gone.

Mercifully, we scrambled onto a narrow ridge before darkness and collapsed onto an uncomfortable bed of wiry scrub. This high up there was no firewood and the scrub was too green to catch alight, so we were again forced to huddle together for warmth.

The hardships quickly dulled our bright spirits and chaffed our strong characters. Brown and Kennelly, the oldest men in the group by some measure, found the going particularly hard and started muttering that our break for freedom was an act of folly and they wished themselves back at Macquarie Harbour. Greenhill and Travers gave them black looks that left us wondering whether there'd be a challenge to their authority and if some would return to Sarah Island.

By and by I'd become aware of the true nature of the friendship between Greenhill and Travers. On Sarah Island they were always in each other's company, but knowing that they'd run sheep together in England and been transported together I just thought Travers was a lickspittle. However, out here it quickly became apparent that there was more to it than this. At first, I noted intimate looks and discreet touching and later on I spied them slipping off into the bush together just before dark while the rest of us were fetching wood, lighting the fire, cooking and drawing water. It was a strange twist for a cove like Greenhill who prided himself on his manliness, but Van Diemen's Land was a place of strange twists and nothing would surprise me, or so I thought.

The novelty of liberty had worn off pretty quickly. Our escape from oppression by our fellow man had only delivered us into the hands of nature, which quickly proved the equal of any tyrant. Each day, it introduced us to some new and painful feature of its landscape. While descending into a gorge where a great river snaked its way through the green wilderness, we pushed through clumps of tall yellowish grass shaped like swords with edges as keen as shaving razors. This 'cutting grass', as we dubbed it, took every opportunity to inflict small, stinging cuts on every piece of exposed flesh and further reduced our clothing to rags. As edging slowly through them only increased the pain, we covered our faces with our shirts and charged headlong through the gauntlet of leaves as though we were the cavalry and they the cavaliers.

Weariness and exhaustion broke our tight ranks and soon we were strung out across a half-mile. Greenhill, Mather and Travers took the lead and I, determined not to lag behind, tailed them closely. Thomas Bodenham was behind me and further back were the big men: Brown, Dalton and Kennelly. Looking around and seeing immense swathes of green pushing in on top of us from every direction, our big men dwarfed by nature's huge creations, I became acutely aware of our insignificance. Man has always been the master of his domain, but not out here.

Brown and Kennelly began to lag behind and we were forced

to wait for them several times. Greenhill tried to gee them up, but finally ran out of patience and gave voice to his true feelings.

'That's the last time we'll wait on you. From now on if you can't keep up we'll leave you behind.'

'Have a heart Bob,' bleated Brown, drawing his sleeve across his forehead. His chest was heaving and he looked plain worn out. 'We've just done a long stretch and we ain't up to this.'

Greenhill snarled back, 'We haven't come this far to get bagged on your account.'

Dalton, who was leaning against a tree, muttered through clenched teeth, 'Jack Brag's at it again,' and checked him, 'You've a pretty conceit of yourself Bob, but the sun don't rise or set by you, just remember that. You're the only cove here who can navigate, but that doesn't make you the leader. We're all in this together and you might need us before all's said and done.'

It was a dangerous moment. Greenhill clenched his jaw and fixed Dalton with an evil stare. His hands bunched into fists but he didn't raise them. That would have been an act of war that the ex-soldier was far better equipped to win. Dalton drew himself up to his full height and stood his ground, the first familiar stirrings of dark, Irish anger in his tight expression. They eyed each other off for a long moment before Greenhill finally broke the stare and tried to make light of it by gesturing at their small bags which carried their coats and spare clothing.

'Then you carry their luggage, but we ain't holding up for you no more.' Dalton hoisted their two bags up onto his broad shoulders and nodded at him. 'Lead the way then.'

'Watch that cove Greenhill, he's as dangerous as a snake,' Dalton warned me that night.

Our stomachs, shrunken to the size of walnuts by months of mean rations, grumbled continually. We'd had the last morsels of the salted beef two nights before, which was already on the turn. We still had some flour, which smelt strongly of the ergot they used to hasten its moulding, but we kept mixing it with water, which fell aplenty from the heavens, and put the mix on glowing embers to make bread as there was nothing else to sustain us. The taste of mould was strong on my tongue, but I forced my jaws to chew and swallowed anyway. It took two cups of wild green peppermint tea to wash away the aftertaste but I carried a sour churning in my guts for a day after.

The constant daily chaff of cold, hunger, rugged terrain and physical effort began to take its toll on our minds and bodies. Exhaustion worked on you like powerful drink. The only way to deal with it was to go into a trance-like state until a sharp rock came through the sole of your boot, you stumbled into a pot-hole, or a rogue branch or some other hostile extrusion rudely brought you back to your senses. Adding to our misery was the rain, which fell without remission. It was a cold, dense lashing rain known only in Ireland, Van Diemen's Land and a few other bleak places on this earth.

The intense hunger also began to play tricks on my mind. During the past couple of days I had experienced sharp gut pains followed by a feeling of light-headedness, which seemed to magnify everything around me momentarily as though I were looking at the world through a spyglass. Sounds and colours were also received more intensely. In one of his rambling discourses, Mordecai Cohen had told me that many of the religious and mystic visions mentioned in the Bible came to the prophets after long periods of starvation in the wilderness.

I'd also seen Greenhill in a peculiar light the other evening in that small window of blue twilight just before the black curtain of night suddenly falls. He was crouched over the fire baking the loaf from the last of our mouldy flour that would be our only meal of the day, his face illuminated by the light of the flames. With his teeth bared, eyes glittering and grotesquely twisted features I could swear that his face had contorted into that of a beast. I blinked and looked again but the illusion, if that's what it was, was gone and he appeared again as a normal man. I shook my head and stared open-mouthed. *Was it real or just a trick of the light?*

By the evening of the fifth day we were spent. The rough country and lack of food had murdered our spirits. Even Greenhill and Mather, the fittest amongst us, were feeling the pinch. Knowing that no general worth his salt marches his troops until they drop, Greenhill, still mindful of Dalton's scolding, called out, 'We're all done in, lads. Maybe we should rest a day. What say you?' A chorus of 'ayes' settled it.

We were starving, yet surrounded by food and spent our rest day turning over every rock in a vain search for the reptiles we'd glimpsed. We had a dash at a few small marsupials we saw peering at us from the bush, but they were much too fleet of foot, as was the small furry creature that fled into its burrow when we went after it. We tried to smoke it out, but it preferred to die in its lair rather than give us a bite to eat. The native orange-bellied parrots were just a blur of yellow, blue and green as they fluttered past us, dodging our desperate broadside of rock with ease. Opossums squalled and crashed about in the treetops at night, but there was little prospect of us catching any of them either. The Aborigines might be able to find a meal in the array of brightly coloured berries and small nuts we saw along the way but we had no idea which of them were edible and were afraid of poisoning ourselves.

We spent the whole day hunting, but by sunset hadn't a morsel to show for it. It was a very quiet night around the fire as we reflected that we truly were strangers in a strange land.

In the absence of fresh meat, we roasted the kangaroo coats that belonged to Bodenham, Greenhill, Kennelly and Travers. Travers carved them up and served them to us as though it was the choicest Sunday roast. As we looked down at our lumps of tasteless skin and lamented our luck Greenhill said, 'Don't be ashamed. I've seen an admiral eat his own boots and would've come back for seconds had his not been the last pair on the ship.'

I sensed we were rapidly approaching unknown territory in more than one respect.

That evening as we sat around the campfire I experienced the first of many wild sensations. I gaped and looked about me as a murmur welled up out of the tangled green depths of the undergrowth. The vegetation teemed with life after the long winter hibernation. Red in tooth and claw, struggles for survival were being played out on every twig, leaf and blade of grass. Ants, as quick and brutal as native warriors, swarmed their prey, pulled them to the ground and injected them with their poison. Beetles, in their armoured shells of dull bronze, rumbled about like leviathans, battling each other with a fearsome array of fangs, horns and pincers. Even the furry green caterpillars, the most innocuous of creatures, were locked in mortal combat, using every one of their hundred feet as they strained to gain some advantage. *Maybe this is how God views us from the heavens?* I thought as my ears rang with the screaming, high-pitched chaos of war and death.

Their violent bloodlust seemed brutal and senseless at first, but as I watched I saw that there was some method to their apparent madness. It was chaotic and at the same time orderly, calculated even. The warriors singled out the young, who might compete with them for scarce food, the old who were no longer productive, and the weak who consumed food but didn't hunt or contribute.

It was then I first heard the voice, the one that would haunt and torment me almost to the end. The words were indistinct at first, more like the wind soughing through the leaves than a human voice. *It's the way of nature.*

Who said that? I murmured as I whipped around, the hairs standing up on the back of my neck. But there was nothing there, just a gentle breeze bending back the tall green grass that surrounded us. A plaintive groan of branches, then it came again: *It's the way of nature.* I noted that none of the others had reacted. The voice had seemed oddly near, as though it was inside my head.

Then, just as quickly, the sights and sounds of battle receded. I put my head between my legs and wondered, *Am I being deceived by some imagination of the brain, or am I suffering from some terrible fever or madness?*

My glimpse into the secret world around us had shocked my senses. More often, it was man who oppressed nature; having it push back against us was troubling. We'd sensed but dismissed it at Macquarie Harbour, but no one here would deny that this forest had a primitive presence and a power that was starting to affect our characters. *Was it the spirit of the forest that spoke to me?* I wondered as I shook my head in an effort to escape my dreamlike state and empty it of outlandish notions. Greenhill had said something about scurvy causing men to lose their senses and I'd lived on salt meat and little else since I got here. I'd never even seen a potato. Perhaps that was it? I raised my head and found the world as it was, for a moment or two anyway.

I couldn't say whether the others had seen nature in the same close detail but Bodenham made an unguarded comment that, with hindsight, heralded our descent into barbarism.

'God, I could eat a piece of a man,' he sighed, and in doing so unwittingly opened the door that Greenhill had evidently been waiting behind.

'It's not such a wild idea,' he remarked, looking round at Mather, Travers and me to gauge our reactions.

Mather drew in a sharp breath. 'It would be murder to do it.'

'I was placed by fortune in a similar situation when I was a mariner,' Greenhill explained, 'it's known as the "custom of the sea". Such things were only done in dire situations, but sea-faring folk adhere to this code because they know it is better that one man be sacrificed so that the rest might live. What good would it do if all hands starved to death and the very next day a rescue ship arrived? As I'm sure Mr Dalton will testify, in times of war, 'tis commonplace for a soldier to lay down his life so that his comrades-in-arms might carry the day.'

'Have you tasted human flesh?' asked Mather.

'Aye, I have. It tastes very much like pork,' he replied steadily and without hesitation. 'I'll warrant if we do it I'll eat the first part myself, but the rest of you must all lend a hand so that the guilt of the crime is equally shared.'

Greenhill stared at our faces intently, as if searching for a sign that we were with him, but no one spoke up in support of such a barbaric proposition. Nonetheless, the unspeakable had been uttered and taken some form in our minds. I shuddered inwardly at the thought of having to decide who, when and where. It had been three days since we'd finished the meagre rations we'd carried away with us. We couldn't continue such a journey without sustenance, but we were all happy to forgo such a dinner and leave that terrible decision for another day.

Little did we know just how quickly that day would arrive.

Chapter 10

Field of Blood

The wilderness, Van Diemen's Land, 27 September 1822

The following day, our seventh out of Macquarie Harbour, we finally cleared the huge range that had occupied our efforts for almost three days and were trudging through thick forest where we encountered another great unnamed river. As usual, the five younger men, Bodenham, Greenhill, Travers, Mather and I, were out in front, while Brown, Dalton and Kennelly brought up the rear.

Glancing back to make sure they were still out of earshot, Greenhill gathered us in and said, 'This is the fourth day since we last ate decent food. Another day or two and we won't have the strength to fight our way through this sort of country.' We knew what he was getting at, but no one took him on.

With a nervous flick of his tongue Travers continued, 'Come on lads, surely you know we all can't make it through.'

'What are ye saying?' said Mather in alarm, his Scotch brogue sharpened by fear.

'I'm saying we've no choice. It's time we applied the custom of the sea.'

'What? Kill and eat one of the boys?' quavered Bodenham.

Greenhill nodded and looked hard into our faces, his eyes darting from one to the other.

'Naw, I couldn't do that,' said Mather shaking his head.

'Me neither,' piped up Bodenham.

'No,' I chorused my insides shuddering at the thought of it.

'Maybe we're almost there . . .' insisted Mather, wringing his hands hopefully.

Travers, tired of Mather's childish whine, grabbed him roughly by the shoulders and spun him about in a tight circle. 'Look round you man! There's nothing out there but bastard trees as far as the eye can see. We'll all be dead long before we see Hobart!'

Silence descended on us as the terrible reality slowly seeped into our minds. Drawing in a breath Greenhill continued, 'Of course, if we just leave it there's no saying what a starving man might do . . . I mean look at what happened to Allen and Oates.'

Bodenham's eyes widened, 'What do you mean?'

'One of us might be driven to a desperate act. He could strike any time,' Greenhill said, swinging the axe at Bodenham, forcing him to step backwards. 'But if we decide who we'll take, then we've no need to fear each other.'

Oh, Bob Greenhill, you're a cunning fox and no mistake, I mused. *You've cleverly planted the seed of doubt, fear and uncertainty in all our minds.* Up 'til then I'd been happy listening and watching his plan unfold. This had not escaped Greenhill's notice, who now buttonholed me. 'What say you, Pearce?'

I asked the question that was on all our lips. 'Who d'ya have in mind?'

Greenhill smiled slowly. He'd profited from many years at sea and the hard lessons life had taught him; all that worldly experience was at his tongue's end ready to be put into words. He knew it was time to lay his cards on the table.

'Dalton,' he said without hesitation, searching my face for a reaction. My years of thievery had taught me how to make it poker-like though my heart was racing faster than a galloping horse. Behind my calm expression the questions flew around in my head. *Why Dalton? Was it because he fronted up Greenhill? Surely the older, slower Brown or Kennelly would be the best pick, if we have to make a choice.* The next few seconds were an agony as I balanced my terrors. I owed Dalton my life, but if I protested would I be sacrificed in his stead? I opened my mouth, but before I could speak I got some urgent advice from an unexpected quarter. I detected the strong smell of peaty moss, then a voice breathed close to my ear, *Say nothing, Alec. If you do then Greenhill's axe might find you at the end of its terrible arc.*

This time there was no mistake about it. The words were clear. More than that, I recognised the voice. I felt my throat go dry. *Who are you?*

That's right, Alec. You know who I am. A low chuckle followed.

Da?

A heavy silence. Around me were only the serried ranks of the forest giants, looming and still, their gnarled fingers pointing to the sky. Caught wondering whether this had something to do with those wild sensations that had been assailing my mind lately, I found I had neither voice nor words at my command, so I closed my mouth again.

Taking my silence as acquiescence and aware that Dalton and

I had become friends on Sarah Island, Greenhill explained why he'd been chosen for the chop.

'He's the best pick because he volunteered to be a scourger.' This revelation sent a ripple of anger and surprise through everyone, including me.

'Where d'ya hear that one?' I challenged sharply.

'I heard it said by a very reliable source,' countered Greenhill, tapping his nose. 'They prefer the ex-military men. Know how to take orders and more hardened to the sight of blood.'

My mind was reeling. *Was it true, or was Greenhill playing us? It didn't square with what I knew of Dalton, but did I really know him at all? It was true he'd been struggling on convict rations and floggers got lighter duties and better food. He'd deserted from the British army and maybe was happy to desert us.*

'God in heaven, who'd have thought it,' muttered Bodenham, sneaking a backwards look at Brown, Dalton and Kennelly who were still some thirty yards back.

'The pull of the chain and the cut of the lash make men do strange things,' lamented Travers.

Bodenham and Mather nodded and stopped talking. They'd both taken Greenhill's bait to spare themselves the agony of not knowing who would strike when, where and at whom.

Mather gave way first. Unable to look anyone in the face, he poked at the sodden, leafy ground with the toe of his boot and said in what he hoped was a firm tone, 'Right, Dalton it is.'

'When?' said Bodenham jumpily.

There were now four for a feast.

Knowing he had the majority, Greenhill turned his searching gaze onto me. 'What say you, Pearce?' Again, there was that little smirk which asked, *Have you the stomach for it?* It wasn't enough that I'd survived Sarah Island and got this far.

Each day that has passed since, I have agonised over that moment. If I'd been braver and spoken against it maybe the others would have joined with me and we could have overthrown Greenhill at the start. But my stupid pride and my own survival had occupied my whole mind.

Everyone was staring at me, waiting for my answer. There was the patter of raindrops on the wide-leaved canopy above and the same voice I'd heard before advised, *If you want to live Alec, best you say 'aye'.* Then, as if I were standing outside my own self, I heard a faraway voice agree to this terrible proposition, 'Aye.'

Just as the others finally caught up to us, Greenhill paused for dramatic effect and sealed Dalton's fate with a harsh whisper, 'We'll do it this evening, after we make camp. If anyone lets on to him they'll take his place.' I looked back as the other three joined us, knowing full well that Greenhill was staring very hard at me. My mind screamed, *We've just agreed to kill my best friend for food* and I shuddered inwardly as the questions crowded my mind. *How would we kill him? Who would strike the fatal blow?*

A horrible blackness and a deep sense of treachery filled my unhappy soul and I turned away from Dalton before he could catch the sorrowful look in my eye. It was the moment, God forgive me, that I abandoned him to his fate.

'What are you lot plotting?' said Dalton cheerfully.

'We were just arguing about the shortest road out of here,' shrugged Greenhill calmly. With the same authority he'd shown after we'd beached the whaleboat, he sliced through the air with the edge of his hand. 'Due east, that's the only way, and if a mountain comes before us we'll climb it and if a river comes before us we'll ford it.' His speech over, he took the lead and like sheep we followed.

That day was the longest one of my life. The weight of the terrible dread I carried inside almost drove me to my knees on several occasions. I couldn't bear to look at Dalton. I kept telling myself that I would find a way to warn him, to help him escape, but I found my conscience vying with the sinister new voice telling me to do whatever it took to survive.

My agony increased as the hard white disc of light slowly softened and slipped down the sky, dragging my spirits with it. I was lost to God long ago, but in this, my darkest hour, I sent silent prayers heavenwards.

But as we made camp and dusk stole over us it seemed to me that only the Devil answered. In a daze I fetched firewood and carried water, my mind numbed by dread. I thought of running away, but where would I go? I'd die in this dark, unforgiving place, which was as Dalton had said: a vault for convict bones.

Once we were settled around the fire Greenhill nodded at me to create a distraction. My throat went dry and I couldn't think what to say. Dalton sat there gazing into the flames, innocent of the diabolical plot unfolding around him. Then, though he little knew it, he provided the perfect diversion for his own death.

Turning to me with a smile, he asked, 'Alec, when we were coming in through Hell's Gates you started to tell me why you were transported, something about shoes.'

Out of the corner of my eye I saw Greenhill give a little nod and very slowly and casually began to move round behind Dalton. *This is it! Should I call out to him?*

I caught a whiff of pungent leaf mould and the familiar voice murmured, *It's too late to do anything now. Tell your story and live to see another day, Alec.*

I closed my eyes in sudden anguish and silently pleaded, *Who in God's name are you?*

The grass rustled about my ankles. *You know who I am* came the sly, insistent reply.

Returning to the terrible present, I took a deep breath, forced a smile onto my face, stared deep into the fire and cast my mind back four years to Monaghan. I was sure my voice sounded a little tremulous, but I pressed on.

'All my life I'd been given old shoes, small shoes and big shoes, but never good shoes, never shoes that belonged on my feet and not someone else's. Money was tight and to be sure with three brothers older than myself, they'd already seen their best and their worst days by the time they found their way onto my feet. Even our local priest used to declare that the Pope himself must have worn them because they were surely the holiest shoes in all of Ireland.'

My quip drew a smattering of nervous laughter from those round the fire, but I didn't look up, didn't want to see what Greenhill was doing. Part of me wanted to shout out, 'Run Alex, run! They're gonna kill ya!' But I couldn't. The truth was that I was afraid, afraid that if he got away they'd kill me instead. I didn't want to die here like an animal and be eaten, so I took another breath, choked back the dread, and continued with my story, trying to think of happier days.

'Although I'd never owned good shoes in me whole life, I always thought a decent pair of shoes spoke volumes for a man's character. It seemed to me that a man was judged as much by his shoes as what came out of his mouth, as if they were a window to his very soul.' There were murmurs of agreement from around the fire.

'On market days in Monaghan colourful canvas awnings stretched across the Diamond, Market Square and Old Cross Square, which all but made up the town and surrounded the statue of St Patrick, which stands in the middle of almost every town of any consequence in Ireland.'

A quick glance showed Dalton hanging on my every word, no sign of Greenhill. I ploughed on desperately.

'I watched feet all day from my position at the corner of Dublin and Glaslough streets, which runs off the Diamond and is in the very shadow of the gaol itself. Working boots, Wellingtons and Napoleons, brogues and brown and black shoes with buckles, straps, laces and even bells for the dandies all passed by me as their owners went about their business. Whenever I saw a pair I fancied, I followed them home. To avoid trailing muck into the house and attracting the wrath of their good lady wives, most Irish men have been taught to leave their shoes at the door. I'd wait 'til they were safely inside, open the door and pluck them right from under their noses.'

A slight scuffling noise somewhere out beyond Dalton forced my heartbeat to race, so I had to stop and take breath to try and stop its hammering in my head.

'How were you caught, Alec?' asked Dalton. I glanced up and saw everyone listening intently to the tale, tense but glad of the distraction. Greenhill had melted away into the shadows, doubtless awaiting his moment.

'Ah well, one day I stole a pair of lovely patent leather shoes from the local doctor. Bespoke they were. If I was ever seen they'd only come after me for ten or fifteen yards until the cold and rough cobbles persuaded them it was a fool's earn. But this day it was my great misfortune to have stolen the shoes of a man who played on the wing for County Monaghan Irish football team. A grand runner he was and a grand footballer too as he showed when he took me to the ground with a flying tackle just as I rounded Flynn's corner.'

Dalton's big face split with mirth and he slapped his knees with the palms of his hands like a schoolboy. 'And he turned ye in?' he pressed.

'He said he was awful sorry, but he was a Justice of the Peace and it was his civic duty. In the court, when the beak heard the charge against me read out he puckered his lips tighter than a chicken's arsehole and peered at me over his pince-nez glasses. Speaking in a very lah-di-dah Scotch voice that proclaimed his education and good breeding, he said (and here I mimicked the Judge's high-pitched falsetto): "Six pairs of shoes, Mr Pearce? Isn't that rather excessive?"

'"Well, I wanted a pair for each day of the week, your honour," I explained.

'"One for each day of the week?" exclaimed the judge, apparently offended by my display of avarice, "surely you know there are seven days in a week?" he chided me.

'"I know that you honour," said I, "but I never rise on a Sabbath. I prefer to spend it in bed with my doxy and have no need of shoes on that day." There was an explosion of laughter in the public gallery. It's commonly thought that Scotch Presbyters have no sense of humour but this one proved to be the exception to the rule. With a mischievous twinkle in his eye, he waited until the mirth died down, leaned forwards and retorted in his thin, reedy voice, "There may only be six days in your week Mr Pearce, but there will be seven years in the sentence you will serve in Van Diemen's Land. Your doxy will have to find other ways to occupy her Sabbaths, until your return."'

As Dalton threw back his head and laughed long and hard at my woeful tale of misfortune, Greenhill loomed out of the shadows and hit him on the back of the head with the blunt end of the axe. It landed with a hollow thud, its suddenness and ferocity stunning us all. Despite knocking the big man right off his perch, the force of the blow didn't kill Dalton outright as was intended. Lying on the ground, he put his hand to his head and seeing blood he looked up in appeal, a mix of shock and amazement on his face.

'What in the universe was that for?'

Then the penny dropped. 'For God's sake!' he screamed, a terrible dread already in his voice, but the hour for mercy and compassion had long since departed.

He lurched to his feet and tried to run, but Greenhill expertly sliced his hamstrings as if he were a farmyard swine, bringing him down in a screaming heap. 'Get him!' he barked.

Greenhill's brusque tone stirred us to action. All the hatred, anger and frustration that had been forced down by the iron discipline of Macquarie Harbour exploded from our throats in a great frenzied roar. Shouting like savages we swarmed him, our combined weight forcing him to the ground. All about me blurry faces, glittering eyes and gaping mouths rose and fell as we struggled to pin his thrashing limbs.

Dalton fought gamely for his life. He delivered great round-shouldered blows to the heads of his assassins, who seemed to care little.

'Alec, help me,' he pleaded, his voice hoarse with fear and pain.

My name was the last word he ever spoke. His cry for help echoed through my mind for a long time afterwards.

I buried my face in the earth, sick with shame at my own cowardice. I felt a terrible conflict – between doing something you have to do when you know you shouldn't and a strong primitive instinct telling me I must stay alive.

Greenhill, the grim reaper, armed with an axe instead of a

scythe, stood patiently above the sticky, bloody tangle of limbs until Dalton's head popped out of the ruck. He stepped forwards, swung the axe and delivered a swift, sure *coup de grace*. Dalton gave a single, hoarse cry of fear and pain as Greenhill's axe found its mark with an almighty thump. Turning it expertly in his grip, he pulled Dalton's head back and drew the razor-sharp edge across his exposed throat. The clumsy instrument punctured the two arteries on either side of the neck and there was a terrible wet, sucking sound as the blood drained out of him in a red torrent.

'Catch it!' screamed Greenhill, and to my horror Travers leapt forwards and held out the cooking pot. Splattered in blood and fortified by hunger, desperation and fear, we stared and listened to him gurgling like a drain as he drowned in his own blood. Gradually his thrashing slowed and finally he went loose as the life passed out of him with a great shudder. The scene was over like a dream, but as the miasma slowly cleared from our heads we found Dalton in its terrible wake.

The shock of seeing his dead body was cruel. His once powerful arms now dangled uselessly by his sides and his head was twisted round at an impossible angle, the great gaping wound at his throat already black with flies. He wore a shocked, pained expression, his lips parted in a final question that would never be answered. His sightless eyes were wide open and staring heavenwards.

I looked upwards and imagined Dalton's departing soul peering down on us. How ugly our betrayal must look.

Finally, Greenhill broke the silence. Getting to his feet, his face, hands and shirt dripping with Dalton's blood, he grinned at me in a most evil way, 'You spin a grand yarn Pearce. Made it easy on the rest of us.'

If that was meant to be of some comfort, it wasn't.

For almost five minutes there was nothing but the sound of the wind in the trees and the metallic tinkle as Travers expertly bled every last drop out of Dalton into the gourd, which was now full to the brim.

We trooped down to the river in numbed silence, leaving Greenhill and Travers behind to work on the body. On the way I discovered that I'd pissed myself in fear, though no one else seemed to notice. The others all wore dazed expressions, their eyes still wide open and goggling with the shock of the sudden and bloody violence against one of our own.

When we reached the water, Mather and Kennelly fell to their knees and dry heaved onto the bank. As for myself, I cried, great racking sobs of grief and terror that threatened to force my guts up onto the sand at my feet, not just for what I'd been a willing party to, but for something else altogether, something that almost forced me to the limits of my sanity.

During the fray, it had seemed to me that the voice I was hearing was that of my father. But he was dead, and had been for years, his mortal remains rotting in a grave in America. I'd waited until I was a man for him to come back, to hear his voice again, and now here he was in my hour of need trying to help me through. *How was this now possible?* In my abysmal state of mind, I didn't know. And what was more, I didn't care. Perhaps there were no bounds to the spirit world. In any case, from the day we came through Hell's Gates this strange location seemed to me to be very close to the underworld, the world of the dead and damned; 'Pluto's land' as some called it.

Da? I said to myself, searching for him to see if it was true. The trickle of the water in the stream suddenly increased to a rush and the voice spoke again, only this time it was not that of a stranger. It was tinged with distant memories of home and happier times.

See, you do know who I am.

You're dead.

But still looking out for ye. Always did Alec, me boy. You were the runt of the litter, always gettin' bashed up by the tinkers and the farmer boys.

But how?

Just know it's me and that I'll help you through this as I should've done when you were a boy.

Why did you never come back? I asked, but there was nothing except the gurgle of water as it slowed back to a trickle. I knew the answer anyway. My ma let him go to America because she couldn't get rid of him any other way. It was seen as a disgrace to leave your man and the Catholic Church wouldn't allow a divorce. Emigration, the quest for a better life, was the only respectable way to end an unhappy marriage.

I brought my mind back to the present, and in stony silence we washed in the freezing, snow-fed waters of the river. But even its cold shock couldn't wake me from the nightmare. Though Dalton's blood rinsed off easily enough, the same couldn't be said for the fear and loathing we felt for ourselves and each other. None of us could bear to speak or look the other in the eye. There were no words to justify what we'd just done. We'd broken the First Commandment and committed the worst of all God's sins. We were about to commit another, so bad it wasn't even one of the Ten.

It was dark by the time we returned to the camp. Greenhill and Travers had already started working on the carcass by the light of the fire. They hadn't wanted to look into the face of a dead man while they worked, so they'd taken Dalton's head off and sat it up on the trunk of a fallen tree like a trophy on a mantelpiece. They'd stripped his trunk naked, removed his hands, feet, cock and balls so that he no longer resembled a human being, and hung him by the legs from a nearby tree. Travers had been a butcher back in London and had lost none of his deftness with the blade. We watched in mute horror as he skilfully carved up Dalton's cadaver while soberly informing us that, 'Like a fowl the human body has both light and dark meat, each with a different texture and taste. The most succulent parts are the inside of the forearms, the backs of the calves and the cheeks of the face.' Then, thrusting the knife in just below the breastbone, he ripped downwards, opening Dalton's belly with one clean motion, allowing the offal to tumble out in a bloody rush. As he carefully pulled out his intestines, paunch and liver, trimmed the fat of the kidneys and cut through the skirt and lungs, Travers kept narrating, 'Parts of the offal are also amongst the prized cuts.'

In mind of this, Greenhill got down on all fours like a dog, rolled up his sleeves and expertly reached inside Dalton's body, almost up to the elbow. I had the terrible feeling he'd done this before. He grasped onto something, twisted and wrenched hard, then slid his arm back out of Dalton's belly with a wet, sucking sound. In his bloodied hand he held his prize, Dalton's still-warm heart, which had only recently ceased beating.

Without ceremony, Greenhill threw it on the hot coals at the edge of the fire. It immediately swelled in the heat and turned pink while the fire started hissing and spitting as its juices began to run. Within a minute or two the aroma of cooking meat, the smell we'd all dreamt of for the past week, drifted up to our famished nostrils; but it did not inspire any appetite in the rest of us. Brown, Kennelly and Mather all looked very green round the gills.

As he watched Dalton's heart broiling on the fire, I'd swear Travers licked his lips. 'That looks grand,' he whispered.

'Then best you help yourself,' said Greenhill tartly, pointing at the carcass, 'there's plenty choice cuts left.'

'You'd keep the whole heart for yourself?'

'That I would,' said Greenhill, folding his arms in a gesture of finality. But though Travers was slighter in build and shorter than his lover, he wasn't cowed.

'I did my bit and deserve a share of the spoils.'

With that, Travers snatched up the uncooked heart from the embers. Greenhill intercepted him and they wrestled over it like wild animals, the flickering firelight casting their grimacing features in a very sinister light. They tumbled to the ground before Greenhill forced Travers to release his grip by head-butting him in the mouth. His top lip split like a ripe fruit and as his hand went up to his face Greenhill got both hands on the heart. Though it was still half raw, he bit into it like an apple. I felt my empty stomach heave up into my dry mouth and suddenly my head felt light. I put out my hand against a thick trunk to stiffen my legs. I'd seen blood, I'd seen men die, but never such an exhibition of savagery. Greenhill sensed our acute discomfort, grinned at us and flicked out his tongue to catch the juices that ran freely down his grizzled chin. 'Come on lads, tuck in,' he mocked.

No one came forward. One by one we just sat down quietly by the fire, our heads still reeling. I glanced out beyond the circle of flickering firelight where the trees stood still and dark. Greenhill and Travers paid us no heed and set about building a rack out of green twigs onto which they placed morsels of Dalton's flesh. The only sound was the hiss of cooking meat and the angry crackling of the fire. A light rain kept falling on our heads and forks of lightning flickered silently across the night sky as the gods signalled their displeasure.

While they waited for their meat to cook, Greenhill took up the cooking pot, which was full to the brim with blood, and offered it round like a pagan chalice. Holding it out to Bodenham, who sat close by, he coaxed, 'Here, drink some.' The diminutive Yorkshireman's normally pale features turned waxy as he peered into its murky crimson depths. 'His blood?' he breathed, shocked by the very notion, 'I . . . I don't think I could.'

Greenhill shrugged and pulled it back. Travers, crouched by the fire, added, 'Not a hundred years ago in merry old England blood was held to be a tonic able to restore the strength of the sick.'

Greenhill nodded and said, 'After a hanging, the victim was drained of blood, which was given to ailing onlookers who held out cups to receive their share.'

But images of cannibals, vampires and witches loomed too large in our troubled minds and none of us would partake. Greenhill grinned and shook his head, 'Suit yourselves, all the more for us.'

With that, he drank three long draughts of blood then handed the pot to Travers who drained it. They wiped their bloody chops with their sleeves and started on the slivers of meat, which they shared between themselves. Finally, their hunger sated, they reclined with an ease surely known only to pagans and primitives and bared their teeth in a wide grin which, to my horror, were stained red.

I staggered into the dark for a piss and only as I returned did the full horror hit me. Here we were, white Christian men crowded round a fire deep in the forest at the dead of night, partaking of human flesh and drinking blood with the skeleton of our host in attendance. At first sight it reminded me of the hideous tableau of Hades that a priest in my youth would hand round to show what would become of us if we strayed from God's path. The scene before me was surely proof of this. Our degraded souls had surely descended to the lowest circle of damnation.

We were roused from our shallow, fitful dozing before first light by the clamorous drone of flies that had already uncovered our foul deed. Various kinds of maggots, worms and beetles had begun the grisly task that nature allotted them.

Most of Dalton's flesh had been expertly cleaved from his body and what remained was a mere relic of humanity, a headless blood-streaked skeleton minus a few limbs that Greenhill and Travers had decided to save for breakfast.

'We've done all the dirty work, now you can all bury him before he stinks the place out,' ordered Greenhill with a nonchalant wave. In the wake of Dalton's killing I'd noted that the ex-mariner had become increasingly domineering and no one seemed game to argue the point with him. He had the axe, could navigate by the sun and stars, and had shown us that he'd the iron will to get his bidding done.

We buried our former mate without ceremony by scratching a shallow ditch in the soft, peaty earth and covering his headless corpse with dirt. We couldn't even look down at the pathetic grave, far less find the words to utter a requiem. A steady drizzle fell like tears from the leaden skies and I doubt any of us had ever attended a more melancholy occasion in our lives. It was no way for a decent man, any man, to die and we all knew it. In this savage land, where nature is truly in the raw and it was eat or be eaten, the voracious devils that inhabited these woods would soon have Dalton stripped down to his bare bones.

By the time we returned from the burial Greenhill and Travers had parcelled up Dalton's meat in the large green leaves that grew in great profusion around us.

'It won't last more than a couple of days,' advised Greenhill, clutching Dalton's fire-blackened thigh-bone, gore running freely down his chin. I took a deep breath and averted my eyes but I couldn't put the grotesque image of Greenhill out of my mind and spewed. My stomach heaved repeatedly, but there was nothing to dredge up from my guts except some greenish bile, the residue of the tea we'd drunk that morning. Greenhill just chuckled and shook his head.

'Everyone must partake of Dalton. Then, no one can go telling tales if we're caught. Travers and I did the most of it, but we ain't dancing at the governor's ball for you lot.'

With that, Travers picked up a fatty piece of flesh and popped it into his mouth, continuing, 'After the first mouthful it's just meat. Tastes just like chicken or pork. You'll come round to it, if you want to make it out of here.'

A few cold drops of rain wet the back of my neck. *He's spoken the simple truth, Alec. There's no turning back now. There's only one way out and that's forwards. Eat a piece, show him you're strong*, advised my da.

I hesitated, but again he urged me on, *Do it Alec, be the first not the last.*

Still I hesitated. This was human flesh, the body of my friend.

Trust your old da Alec, it'll stand you in good stead for what lies ahead.

What do you mean? I thought, suddenly alarmed, but he was gone.

I chose a smallish piece of flesh that had been thoroughly blackened and charred by the fire and moved it from hand to hand while it cooled. Then I took a deep breath, tried to dismiss any memory of the big, amiable lummock I'd met on deck on the way to Sarah Island and put the morsel in my mouth. As I chewed I remembered the grand Christmas feasts we used to have when I was a boy: duck, goose or some wild fowl, courtesy of his Lordship of course.

Not wishing to dwell on the taste I swallowed it barely half chewed and felt it bump down uneasily into my gullet. I caught a bilious vomit in my throat and forced it back down.

'Good man,' said Greenhill nodding approvingly. 'Come on, let's be having the rest of you.'

No one moved. To a man they looked on wide-eyed, fearful of committing the most barbaric act known to man and violating every Christian principle.

Bodenham crossed himself in an act of contrition, which enraged Greenhill. His face turned puce and contorted into a mask of pure evil. Seizing the hapless Yorkshireman by the collar, he shoved his face close to Bodenham's, grinding his teeth like some sort of wild beast. 'There's no room for your meddling God, boy! Out here, the only law is survival and I don't think He would approve of this,' he snapped, jabbing his index finger heavenwards for emphasis. Rounding on the others, the axe clutched in his right hand, he handed each one a piece of Dalton's flesh and issued his orders.

'Right, every man jack of you is going to eat a morsel right now, or we'll have to consider them a blackguard.'

It was a bad situation. Not to partake might promote another rash act, or indicate weakness that might be used against you at a later date.

One by one, Bodenham, Brown, Kennelly and Mather all took a piece of Dalton and ate it. Like a stern parent, Greenhill stood over each one until they had chewed and swallowed their portion before he moved to the next. Satisfied that we were all now bound by the same guilty secret, Greenhill sat back down. It was quiet bar the crackle of the fire and the rasp of tooth on bone as one by one Travers picked Dalton's ribs clean.

Though my stomach was no longer in revolt, I didn't feel hungry enough to try another morsel.

We left in the sickly first light of dawn when the trees were still an eerie luminous green and the vapours rose up off the grass like steam from a kettle. Shrouded in fog our legion of damned souls trudged silently in and out of the trees, appearing and disappearing like pale, silent ghosts. It seemed a fitting image as we were lesser men than we were yesterday.

Like salmon we ran upstream against the flow towards the source of the great river whose serpentine course we had followed these past few days. Flush with spring water it flowed strongly and I suspected that like the great fish, only the strongest of us would survive. I found my mind drifting back to the arse-numbing Sunday sermons my ma made me sit through, until I got too big to bribe, cajole, or threaten.

'You'll go straight to Hell,' she'd warn me as she went out the door in her best frock, coat and hat.

She was right about that. I noted the white fog billow up before me, then my da spoke.

Ye're ma was right about most things, he lamented.

The early Christians were a bloodthirsty lot and occasionally the priest told a story that stuck in the mind. One such tale concerned Judas Iscariot, the disciple who betrayed Jesus to the Romans for thirty pieces of silver which, thereafter, was known as 'the traitor's pay'. Following the crucifixion of Jesus, Judas, racked with guilt, hanged himself. His thirty pieces of silver hadn't been spent nor claimed by any of his kin and because it was deemed 'blood money' the law said it could not be paid back into the Jerusalem treasury. Town officials gave the thirty pieces of silver to a priest who bought a plot of land to be used as a place of burial for the strangers and travellers who died abroad and had no one to bury them. It was known as the 'Field of Blood'.

I had a terrible feeling this forest would be our field of blood. How many Judases were amongst us and how many of us would find their last resting place here before we reached safety, if we ever reached safety?

Around noon we stopped in a clearing for a feed. Silently, we opened our packages of meat crudely wrapped in the green leaves. Mather started threading pieces of flesh onto a twig.

'What are you doing?' asked Bodenham. They were the first words anyone had spoken all day.

'My grandmother was Russian. She always cured and skewered the meat before cooking it.'

'There'll be nothing to cook it on unless someone gets firewood,' grumbled Greenhill. Secure in his tenure as leader, he made no move to volunteer, but Brown uncoiled his large frame as he stood up.

'I'll go, anyone else game?'

The rest of us were sick of trudging through the forest and had no wish to spend our precious rest pushing our way through any more of it.

'Alright then,' said Kennelly and followed Brown through the trees.

An hour later they still hadn't returned and Greenhill sensed something was amiss.

'Maybe they got lost,' volunteered Mather, 'them bloody trees all look alike.'

Bodenham offered a gloomier prognosis, 'Maybe the blacks got them. They'll surely know we're here by now.'

Greenhill remained calm in the face of the rising panic. Gesturing with the handle of the axe at Mather and me he said evenly, 'Come on, let's go and look for them.'

We wandered around calling their names for a while before Greenhill picked up their trail. Brown's big tramping feet and large frame made a distinctive spoor as he pushed through the tightly packed vegetation.

Judging by the amount of snapped twigs and trampled-down cutting grass, it was obvious they were headed in the opposite direction at speed. We started to follow, half expecting to find them sitting down in a clearing, but after half a mile or so it was clear that they were neither lost nor speared. They had disappeared back into the forest maze that had taxed all our energies for the past week.

Greenhill roared in anger like a beast denied its meat, then spat on the ground, 'Good riddance, they were slowing us down.'

We returned to camp with the shocking news, which was met with alarm.

'We're done for,' wailed Bodenham. He grabbed up a handful of dead leaves and rubbed them furiously between his two palms as if trying to scrub any trace of Dalton's damning blood from his fingers.

'Once they get back to Macquarie Harbour and tell them

what we've done they'll send out a shooting party,' Mather concurred.

'Bulldust,' snapped Greenhill, angrily seizing him by the front of his jacket. 'They'll never make it back alive through that wilderness alone with no food. Furthermore, they ate Dalton's flesh as well as we did and everyone present was witness to it. Cuthbertson could never find us here and might just hang Brown and Kennelly in our stead.'

'Aye, they can't hang us without hanging themselves,' confirmed Travers.

Their logic seemed well-founded and quelled the panic that had infected our ranks. Privately, I wondered if they'd fled not just because we killed Dalton, but being the oldest and the slowest they feared they might be next. At that precise moment, I felt a cold, uncomfortable certainty start to take shape in my mind: Dalton was not the last, just the first. This fear remained unspoken but looking round the tight faces, trying hard to mask their true feelings, I sensed that all bar Greenhill and Travers wished we'd taken our chances on a return journey. Macquarie Harbour wasn't much, but after the events of the past two days, a 'canary' and a month or two on Grummet Island suddenly seemed a small price to pay for your life.

To ensure there were no more defections, Greenhill collected the firewood himself and we returned to our cooking.

Once any hair and skin had been burnt off, Dalton's flesh smelt like that of any other animal, but sheer dread and the renunciation of all that is holy stopped us savouring its smell. My mouth was dry and my stomach tight and constricted, but I looked down at the lumps of meat and told myself that Dalton was dead, and that I could go on living if I ate him. It was that and the terrible gnawing pains in my stomach that finally enabled me to conquer the feelings of nausea and repugnance that had followed my first morsel.

After the first proper feed I'd had in a week my stomach stopped rumbling.

Chapter 11

The Precincts of Hell

The Wilderness, 2 October 1822

IT WAS NOW TWELVE days since our escape. We had eaten the last of Dalton almost two days ago and our stomach cramps had returned. The trouble with human flesh, according to Travers, is that it doesn't have as much fat in it as an animal's.

Macquarie Harbour had hardened us and inured us to the many trials and discomforts, but the constant rigour of travelling through rough country had begun to take its toll on our bodies. We slipped and fell constantly as we crawled, climbed, slid and trudged over some of the toughest and most remote country in Van Diemen's Land. Our clothes had been ripped by the hostile, tightly packed vegetation that barred our way at every turn, leaving the exposed skin on our arms, legs and faces a mass of open, festering sores. Our ill-fitting boots and the hard, unrelenting country we were travelling in left our feet broken and raw.

So far, we'd managed to skirt around any rivers we'd come to, but a branch of what we believed was the Gordon River, which we'd been following for some days, had to be crossed.

The fleeting but welcome appearance of sunshine and blue sky had turned the water from grey to blue and cast a strong, yellow light across the stern, grey rock-faces, turning them from black to a sandy brown. A waterfall tumbled out of the dense green fringe and spilled down into clear, sparkling river. But all nature's beauty and wonders had been lost to us. It was now the enemy.

Fed by melting snows and the continuous rain, the river was full and flowed fast. Over many centuries its currents had gouged a torturous route down through the mountains, making the sides very steep. As neither Mather nor Travers could swim, we spent the best part of the day searching for a way down to the water and then for a spot where protruding rocks and boulders might help us affect a crossing. We made a bridge by cutting down some small, straight trunks and jamming them between the rocks, but the torrent of clear, icy water swept them away and smashed them to matchwood on the unforgiving rapids further downstream.

'Bugger it,' huffed Greenhill, hating to see precious time and energy wasted.

'Let's cut some long, thin poles they can hold onto when they're in the water,' I suggested.

This tactic was more successful. Bodenham, Greenhill and I swam from rock to rock and dragged the frightened looking Mather and Travers across behind us. We reached the far bank just before dark as heavy rain clouds rolled in overhead. We were frozen and exhausted, the exertion of the crossing and the cold water having depleted our reserves of strength.

Greenhill was becoming increasingly driven by tempestuous fits of anger that seemed to erupt from him with little warning. This was well illustrated as we made camp against the side of a cliff that offered some shelter from the incessant rain.

'Gather firewood and fetch water before the sun sets on us,' he commanded, rubbing his hands together, his teeth chattering with cold. Bodenham and I duly obliged but when Mather, guardian of the precious tinder, came to light it he became frantic and started thrusting his hands in every pocket.

'What's the matter with you? Give it over before we all die of pneumonia,' scolded Greenhill. When he saw the stricken expression on Mather's pale face he got to his feet, stuck out his hand and growled, 'Come on, fork it over.'

Mather stood stock still. 'I haven't got it,' he said in a small voice.

Greenhill caught alight at his timid answer. 'You fucking *what?*'

'I had it an hour ago, but both my pockets have holes in them,' he wailed, pulling them inside out to show us.

'If you don't find it now I'll swear I'll do for ya,' raged Greenhill, his face contorting into an ugly mask of hate. I noticed he'd tightened his grip on the wooden handle of the axe he carried in his belt.

A terrified Mather got down on his hands and knees and started scrabbling around in the grass, keeping a fearful eye on our vengeful leader. Thankfully, he found it quickly and handed it over like a child eager to please a stern parent.

Greenhill snatched it from his trembling hand and boomed, 'You stupid bastard!' Such was the frenzy of his rage that I was sure he was about to strike him, but he tossed the tinder to Travers and stalked off into the forest, remaining there until his dark hour had passed. A shudder I couldn't attribute only to the cold passed through me and again I experienced the same uneasy feeling that we were captives of this strange, primal land which kept pushing us to even greater extremes.

Round the fire Mather shuffled over to me, his features clouded with concern. He clearly had something on his mind.

'What do you think will happen now?'

'I don't know,' I shrugged. Though not lying, I nevertheless had grave fears that what had happened to Dalton was going to happen again, and soon.

Although it remained unspoken, Mather was seeking protection in numbers. Greenhill and Travers were inseparable and Mather and I had begun to stick together leaving Bodenham, who was moving beyond the grasp of common reason, exposed.

Robert Bodenham's nerves had clearly been shaken by our ordeal. His bloodshot eyes and haggard face spoke of sleepless nights and a troubled conscience. As often happens in dire situations, Bodenham turned to God and took to petitioning Him loudly as we trudged through this terrible landscape, mumbled fragments of hymns and verses spilling randomly from his lips and unnerving the rest of us. In our situation it didn't do to dwell too long on death or the hereafter.

The following day was spent scaling and descending the vertical rock-faces of yet another precipitous mountain. Mather and I were resting when Greenhill approached us. Not one for small talk, he came right to the point.

'It's three days since we last ate and we're taking a beating on these mountains.'

'Maybe we're closer than we think,' pleaded Mather, but the mariner shook his head. Like a mystic he checked the position of the sun, raised his hand and pointed north-east. 'Table Mountain is still a good distance away and we won't make it unless we take some nourishment soon.'

We knew what he was driving at. Mather and I looked at each other apprehensively. He'd been the first one to give way when Greenhill wanted to take Dalton and now clearly regretted it.

Unable to prise anything from us, he said it outright. 'Look, killing another may not be agreeable to you and I doubt any of you would volunteer to do the deed, but I'd do it again before I'd starve.'

Mather and I glanced at each other again, our faces full of dread. This time Mather spoke up. 'I don't know, it's only been less than a week since . . . we took Dalton,' he blurted, unable to even say the words 'murder' or 'sacrifice'.

Sensing resistance, Greenhill seized Mather by the jacket and pushed his face close in, 'Let's hear your plan,' he snapped, 'come on, what say you?'

Mather lowered his eyes and said nothing, but I spoke up in his stead. 'We're thieves not murderers, Bob.'

Greenhill swivelled his head and flashed me a mocking, rotten-toothed grin. 'Did you really think you could open this Pandora's Box and then just close it again? What a boy you are! Don't you know yet what this life is? There are lions and lambs and whatever the Good Book says they will never lie down together. Best you decide which you are because your fate may yet depend on it!' The wild light in Greenhill's eyes chilled me to the marrow as my worst fears were confirmed: Dalton was not the exception, but the rule.

Then, just as quickly, his rage spent, the strangeness left his eyes and he was Greenhill again. He loosened his grip on Mather and glanced around, perhaps afraid he'd revealed too much of himself. As he got to his feet and prepared to take his leave of us, he seemed to regain his old self and added in a calm voice, 'Needs must, Mr Mather, needs must.'

We sat in awkward silence. It hadn't escaped my notice that

Greenhill had adopted Cuthbertson's old maxim. We'd just exchanged one cruel tyrant for another, but a tyrant on whom our daily survival depended.

'Thanks mate,' said Mather, a slight tremor in his now-familiar lilt.

'What for?' I replied grimly, 'it's not over yet, not by some stretch.'

The following day we edged our way down a series of steep gorges choked with thick cutting grass and razor-edged shrubs, which continued to tear at our skin and clothing. Suddenly, we burst out onto a big wide plain of buttongrass and for the first time in almost two weeks we didn't have to barge our way through hostile country. Our spirits immediately lifted. The country around us began to look more like the settled districts we knew.

Bodenham immediately fell to his knees to give thanks to the Lord for guiding us through the wilderness and fingered the small cross that he kept on a chain around his neck. Greenhill eyed it angrily, his lip curled into a sneer. God and Greenhill had evidently forsaken each other some considerable time before.

'Up off your knees man, we're not there yet,' said Greenhill gruffly, but he couldn't interrupt Bodenham's intimate conversation with his Lord and we had to stand by while he implored Him to deliver us safely to the door of some good Christian soul.

'They'd be few and far between hereabouts,' muttered Travers.

We started off across the plain leaving Bodenham, his knees still muddy and wet from his praying, to catch up to us.

'We're out of the mountains, we'll be alright now, won't we?' he called to us breathlessly.

Greenhill didn't reply and kept on walking.

For once I agreed with Greenhill. Cuthbertson had told us that this forest was our prison and we weren't out of it yet. Far from it.

As if to confirm this fact a black cloud rolled over the top of us and it started to rain. Again.

The open plains didn't deliver the salvation Bodenham had prayed for. There was no sign of the native game we'd hoped for, except for a few fleet-footed marsupials who too easily evaded our lumbering approaches. The seemingly benign vegetation held its own hidden terrors, which further slowed our progress and sapped our fading strength. The entire surface of the plain was sodden with water, the clay soil holding moisture like a sponge. The water poured through our leaky boots, compelling us to use the clumps of grass as stepping stones. To put a foot wrong meant sinking up to your knee in wet, sucking mud, forcing the others to stop and pull you free. We had to spend the night in the open with no shelter from the driving rain or the cruel wind. We also discovered two new tribulations: leeches and foot rot.

It was almost dark before we gained dry ground and slumped over the fire at the end of another long trudge of pushing weary legs uphill, too exhausted to even speak. I'd eaten nothing in three days and hadn't done a shit for two days. There was nothing left in me. Like the beasts of the fields, green juice stained our mouths as we munched grass and nibbled the tender tops of bushes, anything to fill the aching voids that were our stomachs. It was Travers who broke another long silence. 'If I had a nobbler o' rum I'd raise it to us. It's two weeks to the day since we set out from Macquarie Harbour.' Travers paused as he bowed his head and ran his hand through his long mane of greasy brown hair. He was right. This was the original date we'd intended to flee. Had I known what we would become, I would have stayed put and found another way to escape.

Greenhill gave a long sigh. 'I'm sorry boys, I've failed you. I said I'd get you through, but I don't believe I'll get to any port with my life,' he said tremulously. It was a rare display of doubt. No one spoke, but Travers nodded in agreement, flicking his tongue in and out as if in search of a fly, 'Aye, we're almost at the end of our rope.' His voice trailed off and without further preamble Greenhill came to the sharp point.

'Though it pains me to say it, one more of us must die so the rest can go on,' he said, gesturing at the cruel wilderness that surrounded us on all sides to indicate that his hand had been forced. Then he casually pulled out his clay pipe and left us to stew over his words. Mather and I had stiffened visibly while the others looked strangely relaxed in the face of death. My heart pumping, I began to ponder. *Had Greenhill spoken with Bodenham and Mather? Had one of us been set up to die? Who was on the inner and who on the outer?* The Scotchman was also looking very concerned. He'd twice felt the full force of Greenhill's wrath. The ex-mariner had a wry smile on his face as he carefully tapped his pipe on a rock and stuffed the bowl with some baccy. *Maybe he knew what was running about in our heads. Was this how he'd arranged it?*

Finally, Bodenham broke the silence that had settled uneasily around us and asked the question that was on all our minds. 'When was the first time you tasted human flesh?'

Despite myself, I felt the chill of foreboding slowly warm into a glow of curiosity.

Greenhill took his time lighting his pipe and puffed on it until the tip glowed as he cagily tried to discern whether it was a square question or a sly attempt to gain some sort of confession.

Finally, his face wreathed in smoke, he said, 'I went to sea at nine years of age. Boys grow up fast on deck and they're men long before they've any fluff on their balls. Life isn't fair, but whoever said it was?

'About three years after I signed up we were shipwrecked on a small palm island somewhere to the north of Java with naught on it but some white sand, green canopy and a spire of rock rising out of the middle of it. You could walk around it in a few hours.

'We foraged in the forest on the island for whatever we could get: birds, fish, lizards and monkeys. As they got scarcer they also grew warier and we slowly starved. Four or five days after our last mouthful the captain, well seasoned by the briny, sat us all down and said that it was time to enact the "custom of the sea". I was sent away to the other side of the island to build a warning pyre in case a ship was sighted.'

Pausing to spit a long stream of baccy juice into the fire and look around to ensure we were all listening closely he continued, 'I returned some hours later to find them feasting on roasted meat. I was told the mate had bagged some native beast and they gave me my share of the spoils, which I scoffed down. As we lay round the fire, bellies fit to burst, I asked, "Where's Charlie?" Charlie was another young jack tar, a few years older than me. He'd run away from a bad home for a life of adventure. "He's a bit poorly and retired early," I was told. I'd seen him drink sea water, despite being warned against it. They were my shipmates; I had no reason to doubt their word and thought no more of it.

'The next day there was still no sign of him. Given the alignment of stars, moon and tides that governs the seas, the captain reckoned it was the time of the month for cargo ships to pass by. He told me he'd sent Charlie up to the lookout with the spyglass at first light. "Can I go too?" I pleaded. "Nay lad," the captain answered me, "we need all hands here to cut shingles and leaves for a proper shelter."

'"What's the point if we're to be rescued any day?" I protested.

'"That's an order laddie," he snapped and I did as I was bid without further question.

'Secrets have a way of escaping and when Charlie never returned I was finally told that the sea water had sent him mad, so they'd cut his throat and served him to us. When enacting "the custom of the sea" there is an established order. The sick and dying are taken first followed by any savages or slaves, women, the least popular, and then by degrees the weakest. I vomited on the sand until my stomach was empty. Though naval rank is maintained in such striated situations, I berated the captain loudly for ordering such an atrocity. He could've court-martialled me on the spot and had me flogged within an inch of my life, but these were trying times and I was very young, so he sat me down and explained the facts of life.

'"Now lad what good would it do if all hands perished and a rescue ship arrived the next day?" he argued. "You're very young and I sent you away to spare you the pain of saying good-bye. Charlie gave his life to save yours, which makes him the best friend you'll ever have." And with that he dismissed me.

'A week later, a day we would never have seen but for the nourishment we took from Charlie, a Dutch trading frigate appeared on the horizon and were saved.'

Greenhill fell silent and gazed into the fire whose crackling filled the silence that followed. Even more than twenty years later it seemed the memory could still move him.

'Taking a life is against God's will,' groused Bodenham.

'I'll grant you that it's against the law and Christian morality,' countered Greenhill, 'but faced with such a dire situation those soft-faced London do-gooders would act no differently, whatever they may say. The "custom of the sea" has existed since the first men crossed the oceans under wind and sail, but no one has ever been prosecuted for it. We're not adrift in a jollyboat, gentleman, but our predicament is the very same.'

It was very persuasive and after a pause Greenhill trumped it by saying, 'What's more, God forgave us.'

Bodenham's eyes widened at the mere mention of His name. 'He did?'

'On reaching Java we went to see a priest so that we might confess and make restitution to God. He was naturally shocked, but after some thought he said he didn't think God would condemn us because like His own son, one had given his life so that others might be saved.

'We brought the remains of Charlie's body with us so it could be laid to rest in a proper Christian grave and marked by a headstone paid for by the church and his crew. On that pillar of stone was carved the words from the Book of Acts, chapter 7, verse 60: *Lord lay not this sin on their charge.*'

'How would we decide?' asked Mather, still able to muster some defiance without seeming to dismiss the idea.

'In time-honoured tradition we should let God decide who lives and who dies.' He paused again for effect and Bodenham again took the bait.

'How would God decide?'

'We draw lots, the shortest one loses,' continued Greenhill, jabbing his finger heavenwards. 'It will be His will.'

Bodenham mouthed the words 'His will' like some religious incantation. Maybe it was a trick of the light, but I could have sworn Greenhill winked at me. Bodenham then unwittingly sealed his own fate by nodding solemnly and saying, 'It's a harsh outcome for one of us, but it must be faced. God forgive me, but I can't go another day without food.'

'It's the fairest way, but we all have to solemnly swear to abide by the will of Almighty God,' insisted Greenhill, looking round for dissenters. 'If anyone objects or refuses to share the burden of responsibility after the lots have been drawn they will take the place of the one with the shortest lot.'

No one spoke.

Greenhill nodded very soberly and said, 'Then, before we do it I think we should humbly ask for the Lord's understanding and guidance through this difficult time.'

Obediently, we all bowed our heads as Greenhill said loudly, 'Oh Lord God look down upon us in your infinite wisdom. The journey through this vale of tears is a long and difficult one . . .'

I raised my head and met Greenhill's piercing stare. Despite conducting the ceremony, he'd never been much for preaching and praying. He winked at me and this time I was sure it was no trick of the light. Bodenham was next and this clever charade had been constructed to trap him and us. He saw that I understood his clever artifice, gave me a crooked little smile, lowered his head and continued reciting the prayer, which I realised with another jolt he was reciting from memory. My stomach started churning with anxiety. *How many unfortunate souls had heard this prayer?*

His Judas words continued to wash over us, the voice calm, respectful and sympathetic: 'We humbly ask for your guidance during this painful decision and pray you'll deliver us safely back to civilisation where we might make amends for our past transgressions.'

'Amen,' chorused five voices.

We opened our eyes to face the horror that was about to unfold before us. My da announced himself with a faint whiff of rotting herbage before he spoke. *Be strong now, there's nothing you can do. He's weak in the mind and won't stick this much longer anyway. He wanted to turn back first because he hasn't the heart for it.*

No one had spoken since the prayer. There was nothing more to be said.

Greenhill carefully cut five straws of the yellowish buttongrass, which had brought us such misery these past two days, took half an inch off one strand and added it to the other four. He looked away and shuffled them back and forth, spread them out like a fan and held them out towards us. 'Gentlemen, take one each.'

I'll freely confess it was one of the most terrifying moments of my life and my vision blurred as I looked at the straws which would decide my fate. Bodenham had no such reservations. Eyes closed, lips twitching as he recited a silent prayer, he picked out a slender strand and clutched it to his chest in a closed fist. Greenhill, the hint of a cruel grin playing across his lips, picked the next followed quickly by Travers.

Just two left.

I stared hard at them, my mind racing, trying to decide which one held the key to my survival. In that moment of dread I knew I'd do anything to survive and would sacrifice any of the others just to live. *What if I draw the short one by mistake? Should I fight or meekly accept my fate?*

Almost imperceptibly, Greenhill rolled the right strand to one side. *Was it a sign? Should I take it or leave it?* A terrible thought crossed my mind: *What if the winking was a ruse and Greenhill is leading me by the nose to the slaughter?*

'Come on boys,' cried Greenhill, setting my nerves on edge even more.

Go on boy, before he offers the choice of the two to the Scotchman, scolded my da.

Without thinking, I snatched the one on the right and brought it up to my fluttering chest with a thump. Mather, eyes cast downwards, took the last straw.

Looking up, we searched each other's faces, wondering which unlucky soul had drawn the short straw. Feeling that the moment had been delayed long enough, Greenhill drew in a long breath and said, 'Right, on the count of three hold up your straws. One . . .'

I felt patches of sweat break out all over my body as my mind filled with doubts. *This is worse than Dalton,* I thought. *At least we knew he was getting it, but it could be any of us.*

'Two . . .'

'Three . . .' Our hands opened and we held up our straws, our eyes darting from hand to hand to see who had the shortest. I saw instantly that mine was the same size as Mather's and felt a shudder of relief pass through my body, then realised that my good fortune was someone else's bad luck.

Greenhill and Travers also held long straws leaving Bodenham, whose face turned a deathly white when he realised he was the unlucky one. He continued to hold his straw out as if he hoped it would miraculously sprout in his fingers.

No one spoke.

I couldn't look him in the face and studied my feet instead.

A moment later there was a loud snuffle and Bodenham started sobbing. It was a wretched sound that made me sick to my stomach, but I did nothing to save him. If I wanted to see the green of Ireland again I had to eat his flesh and I knew it.

There was a scuffle of feet and I saw Greenhill rise, the axe dangling from his hand. 'Thomas, it's God's will. Everything is, you said so yourself. You have to accept it.'

'Yeah, He's asking you to lay down your life so your mates might have a chance to live,' added Travers.

'Like Charlie?'

'Aye, like Charlie,' said Greenhill rolling his eyes, tiring of the delay.

'But why me?'

'Only God knows the answer to that, but He wants you with him,' soothed Travers.

'I envy you,' cut in Greenhill.

'Why?' exclaimed Bodenham, lifting his reddened eyes.

Greenhill made a little circle with the edge of the axe. 'Soon, all the pain and struggle of this world will be over and you can enjoy all the glories of heaven that you have longed for since you were a child.'

Bodenham gasped, as if Greenhill had seen into his very soul, his eyes shining as fresh tears filled his eyes. He clasped his hands together, looked up and pleaded with his executioner. 'Grant me ten minutes to say my prayers and prepare myself.'

Greenhill nodded, 'Ten minutes.'

Bodenham squeezed his eyes shut, causing another overflow of hot tears. He bowed his head and began to pray, 'Our Father who art in heaven . . .'

He got no further. Without warning, Greenhill brought the sharp edge of the axe down on the top of Bodenham's head. It cut through the air with a murderous swish, the full weight of his body behind it. It made a hollow thump like a drum and sent clumps of hair and scalp flying. The speed and violence of the blow caught everyone unawares, knocking Bodenham to his knees and sending Mather and I backwards off our log onto our arses.

We missed the second blow, which was of equal force, but we heard the dull thud.

Through the angry red flames of the fire we saw Bodenham pitched forwards onto his face and Greenhill standing over him, red, syrupy blood dripping down his bare arm. *He's done him right in the middle of the Lord's Prayer*, I thought with a start.

Bodenham didn't move and Greenhill casually drew the blade across his soft throat, which made a rasp as it slit the skin. Travers was on hand with the pot when the rush of blood came and as he watched it fill he delivered a short requiem, 'Bodenham's better off in heaven. He wasn't for this world.'

Mather cowered at the sight of the copious blood, regretting now that he'd spoken out of turn. Greenhill fixed him with those hard green eyes that had seen many things and in a gentle, almost mocking voice brought our earlier conversation full circle, 'Needs must, Mr Mather, needs must.'

As he and Travers prepared to butcher Bodenham, Greenhill looked up. 'You two get the wood while we attend to him,' he ordered, nodding at the cadaver which was already attracting the attention of busy bush flies.

Him. He called Bodenham 'him'. I noted that since the butchery had begun we'd stopped using each other's names. Perhaps it was easier to eat meat that didn't have a Christian name.

Mather and I walked a hundred yards or so into the forest before our legs buckled beneath us and we tumbled to the ground. 'Oh God, oh God,' sobbed Mather, out of his mind with fear and finally giving vent to his despair at what we'd just witnessed. Greenhill had played a clever hand. Until the end we'd no idea who was for or against us. We sat silently in that clearing, alone in our thoughts, until night drew a discreet veil over our misdeeds.

Later, the four of us sat round the fire and partook of our terrible rations. This time Mather and I did so without hesitation, but without the obvious relish shown by Greenhill and Travers. When I looked upon the steaming portion of meat awaiting me, served up neatly on a green leaf, a wave of horror passed through me, but hard on its heels came hunger.

Don't let sentiment stand in the way of a good feed, boy. He's dead and there's not a thing to be done about it, rumbled my da, his voice strong and insistent.

I picked up a sliver of juicy pink meat and put it in my mouth. Endless days of trekking had worn down any feelings of resistance or repugnance I'd once felt. This was the only food we were going to see and the choice was stark: eat it and get strong or starve and stay weak. Out here the weakest would die first. The civilised behaviour that separates men from the beasts had been stripped away and we had become re-acquainted with our primitive selves, which demanded survival at any cost.

I quizzed Greenhill while we gorged ourselves on Bodenham's offal. 'Was that story about Charlie true?'

He continued working his jaws on the rubbery meat for a moment, then parted his lips and gave me an evil red smile that chilled me to the marrow. 'What does that matter now?'

I realised with a start that there was no Charlie. He'd planned and executed the whole thing with a cold cunning that was quite unnerving.

That's it boy, eat up, stay strong for the fight ahead, advised my da. There was that strong smell of vegetation again and I knew he'd gone. I had now become attuned to his comings and goings.

This time I didn't have to ask what he meant. I knew.

*

The next day we again rested and fed on whatever parts of Bodenham we couldn't carry. Full to bursting, Mather took a purgative that Dr Spence had given him to quell his troubled guts.

'Might help to balance his humours,' Greenhill noted gruffly as Mather scampered off into the bush to squat.

'What?' I said shaking my head.

Greenhill, who loved both the sound of his own voice and presenting himself of a man of the world, proceeded to lecture me on the subject of medicine. 'It is held that the human body is filled with four humours: bile, blood, black bile and phlegm, all four being in balance when a man is in good health. Like the tides they wax and wane according to the time of year, how long you work and what you consume. When they get out of kilter you get sick and your character alters. Too much blood makes a man sanguine, too much phlegm makes him rowdy, too much black bile makes him melancholic like Bodenham, whereas that Scotchman definitely has a touch of the choleric about him, wouldn't you say?'

I shrugged.

'You don't say much, do you?' said Greenhill accusingly. 'Well, whatever he's busy purging is better out than in.'

But his medicine didn't take effect and onwards we struggled, four tiny figures dwarfed by nature's great creations.

Mather had taken my speaking up against killing Bodenham as a sign that I might be a worthy ally. He approached me that night as we sat round the fire and whispered to me in his strong brogue, 'That cove Greenhill would kill his da before he'd fast a day. You and me should watch out for each other.'

'Makes sense.'

'Let's get clear of those two and strike out on our own,' he proposed with the sort of dangerous innocence that can get your throat cut or a spear through the guts. I peered out nervously beyond the shallow arc of firelight where the dense black night was full of secretive sounds: clicks, rustling, scuffles and muffled growls. *What would our chances be if I took to the woods?* Truth be told, I was afraid of the dark, or what waited in it. Maybe the voice wanted me to run. Once I was on my own I would be easy prey.

'It's crossed my mind many times during the past few days to follow Brown and Kennelly's lead, but we don't know the way back and we've no food. We'd be dead in a few days. We've no choice but to push on together and face whatever comes. I know that Greenhill is unscrupulous to the last degree, but hopefully he'll bring us to the settled districts before we need to kill again.'

'We'll take 'em, if it comes to it,' said Mather, displaying the choleric Greenhill had commented on.

'Aye, alright, let's watch each other's backs.'

Perhaps because I come from a country where superstition regularly overwhelms common reason, I've never paid much heed to omens, portents, signs and suchlike, though I knew now that I should.

Two days after we killed and ate Bodenham, we spent the night in a stony cradle between two imposing monoliths whose blank, stony countenance exuded a strange but powerful presence. With their edges all rounded and smoothed they looked more like primitive symbols carved by a human hand than accidents of nature. Their cold, black granite sides were made of huge, tombstone-shaped slabs of rock burnished by the abundant rain water. Round, pock-marked boulders spewed up from the fiery pit of the earth's belly during its violent creation were carelessly strewn around its base like children's marbles.

As we gathered wood and dredged water from the rocky pools, the sound of our feet clattering on the thousands of flat stones that littered the valley floor echoed off the walls of our stone chamber. Darkness began to seep out of every crack, cave and fissure turning blue twilight into black night.

Sometime in the small hours a sharp intake of breath nearby dragged me from my shallow sleep. My eyes snapped open immediately as my frayed nerves had conditioned me to do. Mather was upright next to me as stiff as a guard dog.

Though the fire had burned down to embers, everything was coloured by a strange reddish light. Our eyes were drawn up to the black vault above us where slow-moving clouds had parted like a ragged stage curtain to reveal a huge red moon hanging low in the night sky. We rose and gaped at this portentous apparition and wondered what it meant. I looked around at the others and our hands and faces seemed to be bathed in blood. Broken, drifting clouds cast shadows across our faces as they passed across the face of the moon, changing their shape and form. I reflected that all men are just shades of light and dark when all is said and done.

'I've heard the moon affects the wax and wane of the tides, the turn of the seasons and even the moods of men and beasts, but what strange omen is this?' muttered Mather, shooting me a worried glance.

I had no answer for him. But Greenhill, who always seemed to stand at the centre of his own universe called out irritably, 'Go back to sleep ye heathens, 'tis just the moon moving into the shadow of the world, a rare occurrence, but nothing Biblical or suchlike. When you wake in the morning the world will be just as it was.'

More's the pity, I thought. With nothing more to speculate on we shuffled back to our places round the fire. As I started to doze uneasily again I glanced over at Greenhill who, for all his bluff talk, was still standing there looking upwards, almost basking in the eerie light.

And so it went. By day we trudged through hostile country, ever hopeful of reaching civilisation, and by night we stayed awake, its chafe slowly wearing us down. With each day that passed the rumbling of our stomachs grew louder and the prospect of another killing grew ever nearer.

Despite the biting cold we no longer huddled together for warmth at night. Instead, we sat up round the fire so we could all see each other. We snatched what sleep we could, jerking awake suddenly if anyone so much as turned over, ready to grab up a cudgel to defend our lives.

Greenhill was forever sharpening the axe on a lump of hard spotted stone he found in a riverbed to ensure its edge was always keen. Like some savage tribal god, he wielded it unmercifully. Amongst our little clan it was the symbol of all power, the sole arbiter of life and death. It had the effect of keeping us all on edge, wondering at whom and when he might strike; needless to say, he took some perverse pleasure in this. A brightly coloured parrot landed on a bough nearby and my da warned, *Be careful Alec, his belly's grumbling and he's getting ready to strike.*

There was a flutter of feathered wings and the bird and the voice were gone.

Finally, four days after Bodenham, Greenhill tried to nail Mather.

*

One morning before we set off, Greenhill announced that he was going to gather firewood. A short time later Mather, who'd suffered with stomach pains in the night, took a purgative and went off into the bush. Shortly after we heard the sound of vomiting and then Mather shouting, 'What's this? Would you murder a sick man? Come on then, fight a man who's looking at you.' A moment later Greenhill and Mather came tumbling out of the brush locked together.

Greenhill was an experienced fighter who'd been in a few tight clinches, but the Scotchman showed that he knew how to handle himself. He blocked Greenhill's swing of the axe with his forearm, grasped his right wrist, and with a powerful wrench twisted it back against the joint, causing him to cry out in pain. The axe fell from his grasp and made a hollow rattle as it hit the stony ground.

In desperation, Greenhill swung a wild roundhouse punch, which Mather deftly sidestepped, and slammed his fist into the mariner's face with the force of a prize-fighter. As Greenhill staggered backwards and titled on his heels to regain his balance, Mather pushed him backwards and with a deft sweep of his right foot put Greenhill on his arse. The Scotchman picked up the axe. He looked at its keen blade and then at Greenhill, who wore a primal-looking sneer that peeled his lips back over his rotting teeth. 'Come on then, finish the job. See how far you get.'

Go on, kill him, I willed him, but having claimed the weapon Mather seemed unsure what to do with it. He looked at it, decided he didn't want any part of it and to my complete astonishment handed the weapon to me.

As I fumbled with it he nodded toward Greenhill and said in a very level tone, 'Keep it away from him.'

All eyes went to me. I now held the power. Here was my

chance to avenge Dalton, if I wanted it; but as we say in Ireland, if you go out looking for vengeance, dig two graves. There was a rustling in the thicket and my da counselled, *Don't Alec. Your best chance is to let Greenhill think you're on his side. It's you or Mather next, surely you know that?*

I felt my breath shorten. If I went for Greenhill, Mather would surely back me up and we'd be rid of that tyrant forever.

But would he? teased my da. *What if he's setting you up to die? He took that axe off him awful easy. Are you ready for war?*

As I dithered, Travers threw Greenhill his butchery knife and cocksure once more he gained his feet and advanced on me, shifting the blade from hand to hand. 'Come on then,' he taunted.

My da's voice was calm, but urgent, *Give Bob the axe. He'll think you're frightened of him. If you hold onto it any longer, he'll kill you.*

I'd never fought a duel in my life; in this world wee men survive by avoiding fights. So, rather than attack Greenhill and die, I handed him the axe. He took it, gave me a wink and rounded on Mather, waving it about it about above his head. 'Should've used it when you had the chance, boy.'

He and Travers turned on their heels and walked off, leaving Mather and I alone. I heard my da chuckle as though he was enjoying the sport. *Clever, very clever Alec. You've shown Greenhill you're loyal and put the Scotchman between Greenhill and yourself. That Mather cove is next for the chop and no mistake.*

No . . .

You mark my words, boy. The brush rustled again as he left.

Mather knew it too. He looked at me, his face a mixture of hurt and anger, the bitter taste of betrayal strong in his voice. 'I thought we were going to look out for each other?' he wailed.

'Then you should have killed him and had done with. When you handed me that axe, you forced me to choose. He would have killed me in a minute and you'd be feasting on my flesh now.'

Although unspoken, the trust between Mather and I had been broken and the question crossed my mind: *Had he intended that Greenhill would kill me, so he could save himself?* He seemed honest enough, but this transit had shown me that all men, including myself, have treacherous hearts and will do what they must to survive.

Whatever the truth of it, without so much as a word between us, Mather had been marked as the next to die. He seemed to sense he was now on the outer and from that moment on Greenhill, Travers and I travelled together, leaving him to follow some distance behind. At nights he sat alone at a separate fire, never daring to close his eyes. He kept glancing at the forest as if he was thinking about taking his chances out there, but must have felt the odds of survival were too great because he never took it on. One of us was awake at all times to get up for a stretch or to take a piss, forcing him to take his guard throughout the night.

The hunt was on.

By accident or design we came to a great river the next day. Mather couldn't swim and the great apprehension on his face spoke of his unholy terror of deep water. 'Is there no way round it?' he stammered anxiously.

'See for yourself. It runs the length of the valley,' said Travers, motioning to the distant horizon where a weak sun reflected dully off the pale ribbon of water.

'Get in the water and we'll hold you up while we swim across,' offered Greenhill.

'No way, you'll drown me the minute my feet leave the bottom,' he said, giving voice to his deepest fears. He agreed to enter the water only once we'd found a spot where he could ford most of it. A long pole was cut and I was designated to reach out to him with it while the other two held me round the waist.

It was painfully slow progress, but finally Mather scrambled in up to his chest then grabbed onto the stick, which I held out to him. Thrashing his legs as we pulled him across the deeper part of the river, he let go of the stick as soon as his feet touched the bottom and then wobbled his way across the moss-covered boulders that lined the riverbed. But he wouldn't accept the helping hand that Greenhill stretched out to him. He was almost across when he slipped, his right leg folded under him and he went headlong into the water.

It was all the invitation Greenhill needed. Darting like a serpent, he seized the gasping Mather round the neck with one arm and dragged the sharp edge of the knife he'd concealed in his other across his quarry's throat. Mather let out a squeal of pain and a gush of red suddenly clouded the clear waters.

But far from subduing him, Greenhill was raised up on Mather's young, bull-like shoulders as he reared up and out of the water, roaring like a wild animal as the blood flowed freely down his shirt. Greenhill tried to ride him down to ground, but Mather kept rising up. 'Come on, help me!' he roared at Travers and me.

Travers grabbed my shirt and shook me out of my stupor. We both ran a few paces and being smaller men came in low and took Mather's legs. That toppled him and Greenhill was able to plunge his blade into his side, but the wounded Scotchman still wouldn't yield. With the frenzied roar of a man fighting for his life, he blindly rammed his bunched fist into my face, bursting open my lip; yet still I held on grimly as I had to Dalton. Greenhill and Travers kept hacking and slashing at him with the axe and knife, trying to land a death blow. The torrent suddenly swirled around my legs and over the rush of water I heard my da roaring,

That's it boy, hang on!

Suddenly, I felt the fearsome strength leave his grip as he stopped struggling, staggered and fell backwards into the water. We briefly came face to face as Greenhill seized him by the neck and plunged his head beneath the surface and held him there. Through the glassy water I watched his stare lose its intensity and, though it may be hard to credit, I saw a peaceful, faraway look in his eye, as though he had caught a glimpse of the realm beyond to which he was now headed. His eyes closed. It was over.

All was quiet, except for our heavy breathing and running water. I looked down. There was blood in the water, just as the moon had foretold.

It took all three of us to haul John Mather's lifeless body out of the water and dump him on the bank. Travers ran his hand across the muscular form and said approvingly, 'There's plenty of good eating in this big fellow.' This time I found his comment neither distasteful nor disturbing as my descent into barbarism continued apace. Instead, I found myself already looking forward to a good feed. I stilled my uneasy conscience with the thought that if it wasn't Mather it would have been me.

Greenhill said casually, 'Right, let's hoist him up.' Once again, he began the grisly task of washing down the body.

Less than a minute later the bickering began over the choice parts, but for the first time I found myself demanding my fair share of the offal.

Totally absorbed by the desire to sate our hunger there was silence while we fed, just the crackle of the fire, the sound of chewing and the odd grunt of satisfaction. Three men had now been served up to me and each time I'd felt less guilty than the time before. A small part of me worried that I was getting the taste for my fellow man because, truthfully, I'd never feasted on anything so good with the piercing sharpness of my hunger completely conquering my earlier misgivings. Finally, my belly full to the brim I glanced over at Greenhill and Travers whose faces were smeared with grease and blood, their eyes wild and bright with the sheer savagery of it all. I knew my visage was no better. This time, to the surprise of my two remaining mates, I put my hands out when they passed the gourd of blood and drank my share.

There was no one between them and me, and I'd need all my strength. No sense in giving them a head start. I heard the high-pitched whine of an insect just before my da spoke. *Needs must, eh? Maybe you're just getting the taste for it. Is there any sin as forbidden as this?*

No.

It wasn't a sin.

Not any more.

I couldn't think like that . . . if I wanted to live.

I wanted to live.

That's the spirit boy, we'll make a man of you yet.

Chapter 12

A Serpent in Eden

AGAIN, THERE WAS A night of feasting followed by a day of rest as we ate our fill of the meat we couldn't cook and carry with us. By now I knew I had the time it took to consume Mather's flesh and maybe another day or two more before they started thinking about their next victim.

They would side with each other against me. Nothing was surer. I knew I'd have to make the next play.

I delayed such drastic action as long as possible, hoping that we would reach safety or that one of the others would do the job for me. I fretted that I should've sided with Mather or taken the axe when it was given me and changed the odds in our favour.

Twenty-one days out of Macquarie Harbour and two days after we killed Mather, Greenhill, Travers and I summitted a big saddle of solid rock, which lay behind a huge mountain we had scaled a few days back. The character of the country changed again and became softer, grassy and more open. It looked much like the back country just out of Hobart where I'd spent my first year or so tending sheep. As we descended into a huge valley we left behind the rugged, mountainous country and the turbulent weather that had dogged us since we'd ventured from the coast.

On the wide, flat plains below we saw mobs of large kangaroos and long-legged emus. We were dying of starvation in a country suddenly teeming with game, but made no move to take them. Rather than waste our days and our valuable energy trying to hunt the local beasts we pushed on towards safety. When the hunger got too bad there was much easier two-legged prey to hand.

I'd come to realise that the orgy of human flesh was a sin too great to be tolerated by the pious men who'd sit in judgement on us in a Christian courtroom. Only one of us would get out of here alive and he'd tailor the truth to his needs – a notion confirmed by Greenhill in short order.

'If we've made it out then it's a good job we served up that damned Scotchman,' he huffed, 'that soft bugger would spill his guts to the first cove we met.'

I immediately took my guard, fearing I'd be seen in the same light, but then nature intervened in a most unexpected way.

We were making our way through a section of long grass when Travers suddenly let out a cry of pain and fell down in the grass. We rushed over just in time to see the back end of a large striped snake disappear into the grass. Though still cold and wet, it was spring in Van Diemen's Land and all manner of creatures were starting to emerge from hibernation.

Travers was writhing on his back, clutching his ankle. 'It burns like hellfire!' he wailed.

'Let me look,' soothed Greenhill. Travers saw me then and not wanting to admit to any pain or weakness tried to stand up, but fell back down onto the soft cushion of grass, his face contorted.

'Lie still,' ordered Greenhill.

'It's nuthin,' insisted Travers, his eyes still fixed on me, his restless tongue darting in and out of his mouth. Greenhill pushed him back and grabbed his ankle causing him to grimace in pain. As he peeled off his boot it was clear he'd been fanged. The skin around the two small puncture wounds was already red and inflamed.

'Did it get me, did it get me?' Travers demanded in a high-pitched voice.

Greenhill, who had his back to Travers, said nothing for a long moment, as though coming to terms with the awful truth, then nodded his head. 'Yeah, the bastard got you good.'

'Was it poison?' Travers demanded.

Greenhill shook his head. 'Don't know, but expect we'll find out by and by.' Greenhill turned around to look his lover in the face. 'I'd best bleed you and suck out the poison, just in case.' Seeing Greenhill's face seemed to have a calming effect on Travers who nodded and lay back.

Using the axe blade he always kept keen, Greenhill made a little nick in Travers's ankle and squeezed the flesh. A thin stream of blood ran down his leg and Greenhill brought his face down and started sucking. Once he'd a mouthful of blood he'd bring it up and spit. He repeated this a few times before wiping his bloody mouth with the back of his hand.

Travers limped on, determined not to hold us back or show any sign of weakness. He knew as well as I that any show of weakness meant death.

Gamely, he kept up with us the next day, refusing to let Greenhill look at his foot and insisting it was all better, though it was obvious the poison was taking effect. His skin was white and waxy, but his face red and flushed. He was burning hot to the touch and the sweat poured off him day and night. Greenhill helped him along during the day and mopped his fevered brow at night. He could do little more.

As I watched him struggle on I knew Travers was gone.

A few men died of snake bites at Macquarie Harbour. For all the pills and potions in his little bag of hope and healing, Dr Spence couldn't save them, just ease their passage.

Being a hard-headed survivor, Greenhill hadn't yet accepted that Travers would die next. I didn't press him on the matter but noted it'd been two days since we finished the last of Mather. It would soon be killing time again and he'd come round to it himself.

Travers took a turn for the worse that night and couldn't rise the next day. Greenhill got him to his feet, but Travers wasn't able to put any weight on his infected foot. A sudden breeze rustled the leaves above us.

The poison's taking effect, he's done for now, noted my da.

'We must push on,' insisted Greenhill.

My da advised, *Help him, get his confidence and put Travers between you and Bob.*

'Come on, I'll help you,' I offered. Greenhill nodded his thanks and in that moment an alliance of sorts was formed. Travers, realising what I was up to, tried to refuse my help, but Greenhill settled him. 'Matthew, I can't carry you on my own.'

We struggled along for the whole day under the weight of him and had to stop frequently to rest. Once or twice I caught Greenhill looking at me, but I avoided his eyes.

That night Travers slipped into a fevered sleep and Greenhill took a look at the wound. I caught the sour smell of putrefying flesh from ten yards. His whole foot had turned black and had swollen to almost double its size. Greenhill just shook his head, despair and desperation etched deeply into his features. I didn't want to be the one who pushed him to reach a decision. He and I would be the last men standing and it was important that he think he was in command.

He'll come round to it by and by, said my da as he departed on the breeze that skirted the treetops.

Greenhill broke the strained silence with a melancholy sigh. 'We can't carry him much further, it's wearing us out.'

'The poison's slowly killing him,' I agreed, slipping comfortably into the conspiracy I saw forming against the stricken Travers. He looked over at his sleeping lover, the terrible struggle within showing clearly in his face.

'Mind him, will you?' he murmured and went off into the night to make peace with himself.

I dozed by the fire, stirred occasionally by Travers's feverish cries. It sounded as though he was being tormented in some far-off realm.

Greenhill returned just after first light and waited until Travers began to stir. We watched as he came round slowly, but was very weak.

'Let's serve him as the rest,' said Greenhill calmly, turning his searching gaze onto me. His night alone had obviously stiffened his resolve.

'What?'

'It's three days since we ate the last of Mather and we're wandering in circles from want of food. If we are ever to reach "the summit of our hope" then we must eat.'

I just nodded, not wanting to appear too keen in case it was a ploy to draw me in and get me off guard.

'He's been a good friend through fair and foul, but . . .' he stopped short, apparently lost for words for once.

'Needs must,' I offered, eager to ensure that I had not misunderstood what he was proposing.

'Yeah,' he said with a rare trace of regret in his voice. 'I won't do it in his sleep,' growled Greenhill, suddenly fierce, 'not before we say our goodbyes.'

'Aye, right,' I conceded. 'Do you want me to do it?' I offered as gently as I could.

His first instinct was to see it as an act of kindness and, briefly, his eyes were tranquil pools of innocence. But they narrowed a moment later as the animal cunning quickly returned. He realised he'd have to give up the axe and not killing Travers himself might be mistaken for weakness. As was his way, he hid his true feelings behind a little speech.

'No, no I should do it, he's my closest friend.'

I cursed silently but nodded, my face impassive. I didn't want to arouse his suspicion.

Travers saw us in conference and sensed something was afoot. 'What's going on?' he asked edgily. His concern turned into outright fear as he saw Greenhill approach with the dreaded axe in his right hand. Greenhill knelt down, helped him sit up, gave him a cool drink of water, mopped his fevered brow with a tenderness I hadn't credited him with and held his hand. There was obviously a deep affection between them.

'Matthew, your foot is poisoned and you won't last much longer.'

Travers's eyes, which had been drooping sleepily, suddenly snapped open and his tongue was stilled for once. He knew what was coming and burst into tears. 'Please don't kill me,' he pleaded in a most sorrowful voice as he choked back the tears.

'We've been mates a good long time, since England, and stuck by each other through thick and thin. We'll get through this. It'll be better in a day or two.'

But the privations Greenhill had endured at sea and during this ordeal in the forest had hardened his heart and inured him from distress. He shook his head and spoke the truth plainly. 'We can't wait and we can't carry you a step further. We have to go on from here alone if we're to have any chance.'

A broken cry of despair escaped from Travers's lips as he heard his fate sealed by his lover. They looked at each other for a long moment as something unspoken passed between them and finally Travers swallowed and nodded.

Without shame, they embraced one last time and Greenhill kissed him full on the mouth. I had always thought of such relationships between men as purely physical, satisfying some bestial need without ever considering that there could be any real tenderness or affection. This parting was as emotional as any I'd seen between a husband and wife or star-crossed lovers. This wretched system of transportation ripped thousands upon thousands of lives and families asunder, with no thought or care as to how they would be put back together again once their justice had been satisfied.

Greenhill laid the sobbing Travers gently on his back, turned his face away with the palm of his left hand, and with very little backswing brought the blunt end of the axe down hard on the side of his head, just above the temple. There was a resounding crack as tempered steel met bone. Such was Travers's delirium and pain that he just stretched his limbs and then expired.

Mercifully, it had been quick and clean.

Greenhill kneeled over the body for a minute or so, eyes closed, head bowed with the bloody axe still clutched in his right fist. Then, without looking up he said in a strong voice, 'I'll see to his body. Gather up some firewood.'

Greenhill was the staunchest man I'd ever met. I'd give him that.

By the time I returned with a large armful of kindling, his pain and grief had been replaced by a cold sense of purpose. He had neatly butchered his lover's body and left his bloody remains for me to bury.

'Dig a hole for him,' he ordered as he rinsed the blood from his hands. His cold tone betrayed the jealous suspicion that now lay in his heart. He resented me for living instead of dying, as I'm sure they'd intended. The shallow grave I started to dig for Travers should've been mine. They'd have jumped me had that serpent not struck.

When I thought back to each man he'd killed, this was how it always began. He'd recite their imagined faults and weaknesses and build up grievances against them until it drove him into a murderous rage. Dalton had been too phlegmatic, Bodenham too melancholic, Mather too choleric and Travers too sick.

As I patted down the mound of earth, the aroma of cooking meat drifted over to me. This time the prospect of feasting on human flesh didn't faze me at all, in fact my stomach grumbled and my mouth watered at the prospect of dining on Travers's choicest cuts. Like any other creature living in nature, I'd changed to suit my circumstances.

My descent was now complete.

I awoke the next morning to find Greenhill crouched by the fire gnawing the gristle off what looked like Travers's thighbone, though it was so blackened by fire it was hard to tell what it was.

Now that the hunger pangs and stomach cramps had abated we looked at each other and realised there was no one between us.

He started trying wear me down straight away, building that righteous anger in preparation for his final kill. 'Just you and me. I wonder who'll bend first?' Greenhill chided, a fierce but playful look on his face, as though he regarded this ordeal not simply as survival, but sport. I knew his game by now. It wasn't a direct threat, so I said nothing.

I knew that so long as he had a full belly I was safe. Although he was a merciless murderer, above all he was a survivor. He needed to conserve his food supply for later and as long as I was alive, my meat was fresh. He'd move me as close to the 'summit of our hope' as his hunger would allow before killing me.

It's time to strike Alec, confirmed my da, a burst of welcome sunshine announcing his arrival. *So far you've got by just by shifting your allegiances and some good fortune, but now it's you or him.*

I've never killed anyone before, never even hit anyone.

That's right, you were bullied.

I don't think I can do it, it's just not in my nature.

These are unusual circumstances and to survive you must learn to kill. Needs must, son, needs must, counselled my da as the clouds returned overhead.

The coward couldn't hide any longer.

There was no one left to hide behind.

Eat or be eaten.

That was the simple choice.

Sensing that I might be becoming more wary, Greenhill came towards me and held out his hand, just as he had to Mather.

But I wasn't fooled by his ruse.

'Come on Alec, I'm offering you my hand,' he implored, 'you and I are going to get out of here alive. We're the strongest, we've proved that.'

As the steaming vapours rose up off the grass my da warned, *Keep your hand in your pocket, boy. If you trust him you'll die.*

I didn't take his hand.

'I promise I won't try and harm you,' he insisted.

Still I refused so he gave a weary sigh and instructed me as if I were a child. 'The notions of Heaven and Hell, God and the Devil, good and evil might frighten boys, but they should hold no fear for men of the world like us. We're survivors, the strongest specimens of nature's greatest creation, though I admit at the start I'd wouldn't have wagered that you'd make it this far. But fair play to you, you've played a clever hand.' That sweet little smile sat on his lips and I felt my anger rise at his condescending manner.

'That's the curse of being a wee man – you always have something to prove,' I responded. Then, for the first time, I snapped back at him, 'So, had you planned to eat me before this?'

I saw a little glimmer of surprise in his eyes, but his lazy drawl didn't give anything away. 'Nah, I just took the weakest without fear or favour. Dalton was strong, but unruly, Brown and Kennelly too old and slow, Bodenham too disturbed, Mather too faint-hearted and Travers too sick.'

His outstretched hand was still there.

Don't take it. Ask the question that's been on your lips for days, urged my da.

'Had the serpent not bitten Travers you would have taken me before him,' I countered boldly. This time I saw a flash of rage light up those green feral eyes, but again he controlled himself and withdrew his hand, saying calmly, 'I see I must earn your trust again. Remember that without me you'd never have got this far. That's why you gave me the axe rather than try to kill me.'

That silver-tongued Devil didn't fool me for a moment. A predator that had just killed and eaten its mate would take a stranger in the blink of an eye.

Why do you keep up this fiction? You mean to feast on my flesh and there's no maybe about it.

For the sport, son, he must have his sport before he kills, explained my da as the morning mists thinned enough for us to begin our day's trekking.

Thereafter we kept our distance, our mutual suspicion overt. Greenhill and I spent the long, cold nights watching each other through the flames of the fire, waiting and willing the other one to close his eyes and doze a moment too long. I resolved that my next sleep would either be a peaceful one after I'd killed Greenhill or the eternal sleep of death after he'd killed me.

Despite our strained relations, we united one last time on the day we saw a thin spiral of smoke rising above the thick green canopy. This was no figment of our imagination. Our enmity was immediately forgotten in the face of danger and we crouched in the bush, peering around fearfully.

'It's the bloody savages,' hissed Greenhill. 'Maybe they're feeling bolder now there's just the two of us.'

'I hope that's a signal and not a cooking fire,' I said.

The fate of that first party of bolters from Macquarie Harbour and the soldiers and constables who'd gone after them but never returned was never far from our minds. I shuddered as I considered that maybe this was how they'd met their end.

An hour later we'd still seen no movement so we crept cautiously towards the source of the smoke. Through a screen of trees and shrubs, we counted sixteen men, women and children sitting around a camp fire eating the carcass of a small furred animal, most likely a wallaby, that they'd recently killed using the long spears that were now propped against a tree, their wicked points red with blood. The skin had been expertly removed and stretched out to dry between two twigs. I counted six male warriors, any of whom could hole us at thirty paces. I'd seen them do it to 'boomers', as they called the large kangaroos here, when I was a shepherd near Hobart. Quite a few white men had also perished on the points of their spears. Fortunately, they were too busy ripping the meat off the bones of their kill to notice us.

The aroma of cooked meat drifted over to our twitching nostrils, almost sending us into a frenzy. My dry mouth filled with spit. We'd finished the last of Travers two days before. Starvation was one of the worst privations of convict life. We knew how it pulled otherwise decent men down and drove them to torment, insanity, murder and even cannibalism.

'I think we should rush them and get that grub,' hissed Greenhill recklessly, that eerie yellow light burning fiercely in his feral eyes.

'They're more afraid of you than you are of them,' I said, recalling something Mordecai Cohen had told me. 'I'm game, but we need to scare the shit out of them,' I insisted.

Greenhill's brow furrowed as I picked up a large white cockatoo feather, recently lost in some treetop skirmish, and stuck it into my wild tangle of hair. I then shoved my hand into the dirt and drew my finger across his face, leaving a thick black smudge.

'If we stick some of these in our hair and blacken our faces up with dirt, they'll run a mile,' I whispered. Greenhill fixed me with his quizzical little smile, unused to taking orders, but nodded his assent.

That's the spirit, boy, growled my da, riding in on a distant rumble of thunder.

'Needs must, Mr Pearce,' hissed Greenhill, using his by now familiar refrain.

Five minutes later our faces were smeared with muck and our hair adorned with feathers. I imagined that even without the disguises we looked more like savages than they did; but we would only get one shot at this and the element of surprise was our only weapon, other than Greenhill's axe and the sun, which remained hidden behind a bank of gilded clouds.

By now we were well acquainted with the weather and its peculiar habits at this latitude. At about four o'clock there was usually one final brief burst of light before the sun dipped behind the trees and disappeared for the day. We moved round to the west so that it would be directly behind us when we charged and lay in the bush on our bellies listening to them talking and laughing in their strange tongue, all the while keeping a close eye on the sun's progress. It had already begun its steep descent and we began to fear that it wouldn't give us any assistance.

'Come on, come on,' urged Greenhill in a terse voice, demanding the very elements bend to his will.

Suddenly, there was a sharp crack as a twig broke underfoot and we jumped as though a gun had gone off. We instinctively flattened ourselves as close to the ground as nature would allow and stiffened, fearing a sharp-eyed lookout had spotted us.

But there were no blood-curdling yells, no massed ranks of warriors bounding towards us, spears raised high, ready to make a deadly strike. Just to the left of us, a tall warrior broke through our leafy screen and came striding towards us from the direction of the camp. We knew them to be masters of their domain, skilled hunters and trackers, able to attack and melt away into the bush, but to our immense relief he was naked, except for a small loincloth and his black mop of wiry hair, and he wasn't carrying a spear. I would've put him at around twenty years, though it was hard to gauge the blacks who seemed to age much better than we white fellows.

My heart almost winded me as it thudded hard against my ribcage and the spit dried in my mouth as he kept coming closer. His dark skin seemed to blend into the long thin shadows of the trees so that he seemed to appear and then disappear like a ghost. It made it hard to judge his distance from us or to know where he would appear next. We now understood why the white settlers were having difficulty subduing the invisible enemy around their newly settled land.

Greenhill's hand snaked silently down to his belt where he kept the axe at all times. I shook my head, but he had it in his right fist and his eyes were locked on the Aborigine who was almost on top of us. Greenhill pushed himself up on his arms and braced himself for a headlong charge. Still he came. Greenhill got up on his haunches. The warrior was barely ten yards away when he stopped, turned, pulled aside his loincloth and pointed his member at a tree. He sent a strong stream of yellow piss arcing outwards, then, once finished, he turned back to the camp without a glance in our direction. We both expressed a huge sigh of relief.

My heart was still thudding in my ears as a sudden warmth spread across my back. The sun, now a molten golden orb, had finally slipped from behind its cover. We were bedazzled by its hard, yellow light as we looked over our shoulders and realised that we only had a short time before another cloud moved in to cover it.

Greenhill seized the moment. 'Now!' he roared at the top of his voice as he rose to his feet, leaving me little choice but to follow him.

'Aahhhrrrgaaa! we screamed in ragged unison as we ran full-tilt towards the gathering, waving our arms like demented idiots. The tall trunks of trees created a ghostly echo which gave greater effect to our din.

The sight of two wild-haired creatures coming screaming out of the sun into their camp caught the Aboriginal clan completely off-guard. The piercing cry of a woman answered our war cry. Fear is like any contagion and once the piccaninnies started wailing, other female voices joined their chorus. Fortunately for us, the blacks are as superstitious as we whites and when faced with a seemingly otherworldly presence, all reason departed and self-preservation became the order of the day. With no thought for their food, weapons or kin they scattered into the trees yelling and shrieking, their brave warriors leading the retreat.

Buoyed by our success and wanting to ensure they didn't return, I pursued them through the camp, my evil cackle nipping at their spindly heels as they crashed away through the trees.

By the time I returned to the camp, Greenhill already had their spears in the fire, points first, to deny me the chance of a weapon. For all his fine words about comradeship, his first thought had been to ensure he continued to hold the only weapon.

We sat in silence as we stripped their carrion clean of any flesh, crunched the small bones and sucked the marrow out of them. But the little nourishment we took was scarcely enough to keep our faculties in motion; indeed it was small reward for such a huge risk.

We moved on before first light, just in case the natives came back with an army, knowing we couldn't risk attempting our ruse a second time. Unless we came across a dead or injured animal, the next meal would be human flesh, his or mine.

Having a larger build and being older than me, I sensed his need would be greater and come sooner, so I decided it was my turn to lead the hunt. I didn't want him luring me into a trap and having the element of surprise. Two warring birds started noisily disputing a nearby branch as my da urged me on, *You lead, let him follow for a change*.

Without warning I took off in the opposite direction across a stretch of waist-high, khaki-coloured grass.

'Where in the hell are you headed man?' he scolded, 'you're going the wrong way.'

I said nothing and kept walking. Direction didn't matter, only survival. If he wanted to kill me, he'd have to catch me.

'D'ya want to play games, eh?' he shouted, his anger finally surfacing. But Greenhill had no choice if he wanted to eat again and started after me, his desperate need writ large across his grimy, careworn face.

'You'll never make it through, you haven't the guts!' he yelled, his voice full of the usual bluster.

He kept it up the whole day, cursing and swearing as I dragged him across some of the roughest country on God's earth, up the steepest hills, down hair-raising ravines and across a fast-flowing river. By the end of the day he was staggering rather than walking and he'd run out of words.

Now I'd made the break I sensed he'd try and take me very soon, so I gave some thought as to how I'd overpower and kill him. It was too much to hope that a snake would bite him too and I wasn't strong enough to dominate him, so dropping a rock on his head or pushing him off a precipice were my only options.

As we sat around the same fire that night, I was constantly on my guard as he'd go off into the bush for a piss and then try and circle round behind me, or I'd close my eyes for a moment then open them to find him on his hands and knees staring at me intently. Realising I'd seen him, he'd quickly lower his gaze and pretend to pour a cup of green peppermint tea, the only sustenance we'd had in three days.

On one occasion I was awoken from a fitful doze by a voice calling my name. There was nothing there, except the wind rustling the treetops and the sleepless Greenhill glaring at me through the flames. The fire crackled and my da whispered, *Watch yourself Alec. To sleep is to court death.*

In the end, on the twenty-second day of October, six days after we killed Travers and thirty-two days out from Macquarie Harbour, I killed the bastard in cold blood. But after all the fear, harsh words, horror and pain that had led up to that moment, there was no duel, no life and death struggle, just a solitary blow like an executioner might deliver.

I simply wore him out in the end.

He pushed hard to try and keep up with me, but finally fell into an exhausted slumber just before first light on the eighth day we were alone. All I had to do was walk up to him, snatch the axe he used as a pillow and smash him over the head, but that's easier said than done when you've never killed a man before. I sat there and watched him as he began to snore softly. My da must've sensed my apprehension because the fire crackled and popped angrily and he was quickly back into me. *He's asleep, now's your chance.*

I can't.

If you let him waken he'll know you'll have to sleep next and when you do he'll show you no mercy.

No.

What are you afraid of? he admonished.

I'm afraid of becoming like Greenhill and Travers.

You're nothing like them, boy, but you have to do this if you ever want to see the green of Ireland and your mammy's poor face again.

Still, I couldn't bring myself to do it, but my da wasn't finished yet. The fire burned more brightly as his voice took on a harsher, crueller edge.

When you shot out of yer mother you were as skinny as a beggar's arm. You were a wee baby and you were always gonna be a wee boy. There's no one to hide behind now. You have to face this like a man and kill him if you want to live.

I'd rather die.

You're weak, you weren't worth coming back for, he jeered.

Don't say that da, I pleaded.

Why not? It's time the truth was spoken. A man needs a son he can be proud of, not some snotty-nosed runt who can't fight back . . .

I'm not like that.

. . . who runs home to his mammy and hides behind the bigger boys.

I'm not like that!

Prove it, or I'll leave you here to die, he challenged as the flames leapt higher.

How?

Kill Greenhill. Get that axe and smash his fucking head in, he roared, his voice now sounding oddly different; but then I'd never heard him shout before.

I can't.

Coward! You fucking coward! he taunted.

Don't go, da.

Do it then. What was that you said to him about wee men always having something to prove? Prove that you're a man, a worthy son. Kill Greenhill and go on living because he'd do it to you in a second.

As my da laid forth and the flames licked the lower branches of the tree we were camped under, I could feel my rage building as I got to my feet. In my mind's eye I saw Greenhill's snide face and cocksure little grin and recalled all his little put-downs: 'Looks like we've come up short', 'Are you sure you're up to it?', 'I'd never have wagered on you getting this far', 'You'll never make it through, you haven't the guts'. Before I knew it I was seized by another of those wild sensations. A red cloud of rage eclipsed all reason, my blood roared loudly in my ears and I felt short of breath. Beside me the inferno had thrown a wide arc of light to where Greenhill lay sleeping.

I marched up to him and pulled the axe from under his head. I swung it high above me and chose my spot. Down it came just below the crown, on the back of his head. I'd learned well from the master. Dimly in the red mist I could hear a scream and a clutching hand easily pushed away.

But the bastard wouldn't die. He moaned once and rolled his eyes, as he sensed me standing over him. I'll admit to a small moment of triumph, though bludgeoning the only man who could guide me out of this accursed wilderness hardly warranted celebration.

'It's not who starts the job, but who finishes it,' I mocked, turning his words back against him.

That's the spirit boy! roared my da approvingly.

But as was his wont, Greenhill had to have the last word. Even with blood spilling down his face, he fixed me with that despicable rotten-toothed grin and laughed defiantly in the face of death. 'Don't go thinking it's over just because you've killed me,' he taunted.

I cut him short by bringing the axe down on his head again with an extraordinary violence I didn't know I possessed. He closed his eyes and his head rolled to one side as he slipped away.

Bob Greenhill was the first man I'd ever killed, or even struck a serious blow at, but I felt none of the horror or shame that would have filled me to overflowing just a month before. Something cold and dark had welled up from the dark region of my soul.

Well done son, I knew you had it in you.

What did he mean, 'Don't go thinking it's over just because you've killed me?' I wondered.

It will become clear in good time, boy, all in good time. The flames settled back down to a companionable flicker.

I didn't give Greenhill's dying words too much weight and by the light of the fire I bled him and stripped his lean cadaver of the head, hands, genitals and feet. I bound his ankles with the rope and hoisted him up, as we'd done with the other four. With no thought in my head other than getting a feed, I slit his stomach and liberated his slick, shiny offal which came tumbling out in a wet, sticky rush. Though he was uneducated, Greenhill had proved an apt tutor in the book of life.

That night I feasted like a king on his heart, liver and a tender slice of thigh, which I washed down with blood. Despite the horror and barbarity of it all, I settled down for a peaceful night's sleep for the first time since we escaped from Sarah Island.

Da?

There was no reply. Nothing stirred out in the darkness.

Da?

I continued calling until I was hoarse. Getting rid of Greenhill was just the half of it. I needed him to see me home.

There was nothing, just a familiar ache in my heart as I realised he'd gone and left me to fend for myself again, as he had once before a long time ago.

Huddled by the fire, which was no more than a pinprick of light in a vast kingdom of darkness, I suddenly felt very small and alone.

Chapter 13

The Summit of Our Hope

I woke up screaming and soaked in a cold sweat, a feeling of absolute terror welling up in my throat. My cries ricocheted around the wooded gully where I'd spent the night and announced my fear to every hill and mountain within cooee. I leapt to my feet, grabbed up the axe and slashed at thin air as I prepared to meet my attackers; but when the miasma cleared from my head I realised it was a dream and I was alone. Only the forest, dark, silent and unmoving, waited for me beyond the swirling vapours. I'd come to hate it almost as much as I'd hated Greenhill.

I sank to my knees as I realised that it was not just my proximity to the fire that had brought back the sick feeling in my stomach and caused the slimy sweat to run off my body. The memories of the lives I'd helped to take brought shame and revulsion flooding into me. The only ones I felt no guilt for were Travers and Greenhill; they'd been the architects, the pitiless instigators of our terror, and I wouldn't waste my sorrow on them.

From that night on the ghosts of the dead started visiting me in my dreams. While I ruled the day, they ruled the nights. I came to realise that's what Greenhill meant when he warned that it wasn't over just because I'd killed him.

As was tradition after every kill, I'd hoped to spend a day feeding and resting, but my rude awakening had unsettled me and I decided to push on.

For breakfast I ate my fill of the surplus meat I had carved off Greenhill's limbs, knowing this would be my last full meal before I reached safety or died. I took what I could carry of Greenhill's flesh, mainly the plump prime meat of the thighs, arms and saddle and reluctantly left the rest behind. I hadn't the inclination or the strength to dig him a grave. He was the one least deserving of a Christian burial, so I left him for the beasts.

I stood up, took a deep breath and ventured forth alone. I had no plan, other than the one Greenhill had devised: to head for Table Mountain, 'the summit of our hope'. Greenhill had pointed out a distant, green-fringed ridge with a distinctly flat top and assured me that the settled districts lay just beyond.

Every stone, every blade of grass seemed hell-bent on slowing my progress. The endless tyranny of green stretched out before me, determined to show me no pity even after all I had endured. The huge distances and the rough nature of the country I'd travelled could be measured by the leather soles of my boots, which were all but worn to nothing. Sharp stones and thorns stuck into my feet, but I soldiered on like Christ carrying his own cross up to Calvary Hill and remembered Dalton prophetic words, 'Is this our Golgotha?'

I sighted the odd wallaby and opossum in the undergrowth, but was too exhausted to give chase. In any event I'd lost the axe, dropped it or left it at one of the camps. In my befuddled state I couldn't recall what I'd done with it.

The days seemed endless but the nights when I fell into an exhausted sleep seemed to pass in a blink of the eye. Each morning the inquiring red eye of the sun peeked at me through the trees and urged me to get up, to keep going. I knew if I allowed myself to lie there too long I'd lose the will to rise.

I got what moisture I could in the mornings by licking the dew that collected in the folds of large, wide leaves and on the tips of the grass. Occasionally, I'd come across a trickle of a stream or catch some run off from the rocks.

Exhaustion, hunger and thirst scrambled my senses and very quickly I'd become disoriented and started to doubt my own judgement. More than once I'd come upon a familiar tree, rock or landmark and realise I'd seen it before. I'd wasted hours walking in a huge circle. I freely confess that in those moments of desolation I sat down and cried like a child and was fearful of death. Every man has limits of hope and faith and I'd already gone far beyond mine.

Now alone, I quickly lost track of the days, but though I slogged on day after day, the blessed summit never seemed to get any nearer; it was seemingly stuck fast to the distant horizon. The 'summit of our hope' had fast become the 'slough of my despond'.

One afternoon, just as the sun had started to turn from gold to bronze, the legions of eucalyptus trees that tore my shins and scraped at my flesh suddenly thinned out. I found myself walking through an open plain of buttongrass that had faded from verdant summer green to a wintry yellow. I didn't dare set too much store by it. This terrain had filled us with false hope before, tricking us into thinking we'd reached the settled districts.

I stopped to peer up at the long ribbons of broken cloud above me that were shot through with gold, crimson and then black as night came in behind them. I spun around in a circle, searching for that flat ridge that Greenhill had pointed out, but the horizon was empty. *Have I wandered off course and got lost? Where the hell am I?* I took some rough bearings and looked down at the rude clumps of grass beneath my ragged boots and realised with a flood of emotion that I was finally standing on it.

I scoured the horizon, hoping to spy a shepherd, a homely shingle-roofed hut with smoke billowing from its chimney, or a flock of sheep – some earthly sign that I'd made it through. But once again, I was disappointed. I fell to my knees, rolled myself into a ball and cried, dredging up weeks of pain, regret and sorrow. I'd played a desperate game of life and death against such fearful odds and lost. This was the end of the journey. I had nothing left in me.

I pulled the long leather strap off the empty bag I'd carried all this way, ever hopeful I'd find food to put in it. It made a makeshift noose. I decided I'd rather hang myself than sit under a tree and wait for death. Once or twice I'd placed my toes on the edge off one of the many panoramas I'd climbed and seriously considered throwing myself to a dramatic but painless death. Three or four days back I'd come upon the smouldering embers of an Aborigine camp fire and fell upon the skin and scraps of their meal. They were about, I knew they were. I called on them to come out and spear me but they never showed themselves.

I dragged myself to my feet and started looking for a low overhanging branch to hold the strap. A strange lightness of spirit filled me as I tested various limbs; I even started whistling. I'd heard it said that cheerfulness is common in people who know death is close. Some inner resolve helps them get past the terrors and calmly face what must come, eventually, to all men.

I was testing a likely branch when a familiar wailing stopped me in my tracks. At first I thought it was just my merry tune, so I stopped whistling and listened more closely. *Was it possible, or was this another of my wild sensations?*

My heart thudded so hard against my sides that I found it hard to breathe, but my legs found new strength as I dropped the strap and almost tumbled downhill towards the noise, stopping to listen before moving closer.

By degrees it got louder.

'This has to be it,' I said aloud, 'either I've made it, or I die.'

Then, up ahead, in a hollow a hundred yards away, I saw the loveliest sight I'd seen in my whole life: the fat woolly backs of a half-dozen black-faced sheep, heads down, nibbling the scrubby grass at their feet.

Greenhill had been spot on.

A great swell of emotion rose up inside of me and I began to sob, a flood of tears streaming unchecked down my face. *Surely now I'd defied God and nature and made it through.* As I crouched on my haunches and took a few moments to compose myself I was seized by a sudden fear. *Have I reached civilisation or are these stray sheep turned feral?* No matter, one of them would make a tasty meal.

I dredged up my last reserves of strength, and with the juices flowing freely in my mouth crept forwards. I got to within twenty yards of them before they sensed my clumsy approach. They looked up, almost as surprised to see me as I was them, and began bleating soft warnings to each other. They grew louder and more anxious as I rushed them headlong, hoping to catch one unawares, but they scattered.

I launched myself headlong at a slow ewe, got a fistful of its wool, but little else. I lay winded on the ground for fully five minutes before I painfully got to my feet, my every muscle and sinew crying out for me just to lie still and accept the inevitable. I attempted two or three other such graceless manoeuvres with the same result until, finally, I happened on another mob with a few young lambs in tow.

I scattered them, but one lamb hesitated momentarily, just long enough for me to throw myself on top of it. It started bleating fearfully, its call taken up by the other sheep in the vicinity, but there was no pity left in my heart. I sat on its back and twisted its neck round and round until it cracked and the beast fell silent.

So overcome was I by the need for nourishment that I buried my face in its soft wool and started ripping at it with my teeth. I quickly found soft skin and then tasted blood, which only fed my frenzy.

I was oblivious to everything, even to the figure who stole up behind me. The first I knew of him was when he pressed a cold, double-barrel into my temple and barked a warning in a tremulous, but strongly accented Irish voice, 'Stay right there ye thieving fucker, or I'll blow yer brains to kingdom come.'

They were the sweetest words I'd ever heard.

Very slowly I raised my hands in surrender, but the gun remained pressed hard to my skull.

'Right, ye wild-looking fucker. Get over on yer back an' let's be havin' a look at ye. Mind and keep them fecking hands where I can see 'em.'

That voice is very familiar, I thought as I rolled over and found myself looking up at a short, fat, red-bearded man wearing a felt hat pressed down on his unruly mop. Even though he had the gun and I was on my back, his hands still trembled.

'Aw, 'tis only yerself Paddy Maguire!' I called out, putting a name to the face.

Hearing his name spoken by some 'wild-looking fucker' dressed in rags, the blood of a lamb smeared across his chops, did nothing to re-assure the man. Instead, it seemed to fill him with a mighty dread and he tightened his grip on the gun and forced the barrel harder into my chest. 'I don't know who or what ye are, but stealing sheep is a hanging offence in these parts.'

'Well, ye'd know all about that, Paddy. You dodged the noose once back in Wicklow and then there was that time we stole them ten sheep from John Bellinger, drove them to New Norfolk and had a rare week with the proceeds.'

There was a long silence, then I felt the pressure on my chest ease as he took half a step backwards and regarded me for a long moment, trying to make out the face behind the wild hair and bloodied beard. His eyes fairly boggled in astonishment and he crossed himself rapidly as he said, 'Jesus, Mary and Joseph and all that's holy! 'Tis Alec Pearce, so it is!'

It's a curious fact that whenever an Irishman invokes the deities his accent gets thicker and he speaks faster than he normally would. I allowed a grin to split my face as he dropped the gun and rushed forwards to help me up, chattering twenty to the dozen.

'Where in the blazes did ye come from? I heard they shipped ye off tae Macquarie Harbour.'

'So they did, but I escaped.'

'Did ye steal a boat?'

'Aye, we did, but we had to leave it and walk.'

'Walk? Through yon forests and over yon mountains?' he said shaking his head incredulously. 'Nah, no one who tried ever lived to tell the tale. Some tried it and were never heard of again.'

'Well, you're looking at the first. When you found me I was searching for a tree to hang myself from,' I said, producing the makeshift noose that I still clutched in my hand.

Looking down at the lamb I'd savaged and then taking in my wasted features, Paddy realised that maybe I was telling the truth. He shook his head again as he lifted up the lamb. 'It's like a wolf has been at it. Come on, let's get you home and cook him up. No sense wasting good meat.'

Paddy lived in a small but sturdy wooden hut a mile or so away, facing north to absorb what little sun there was. He'd chosen straight sturdy timbers, plugged any gaps with clay and double-lined the roof with bark and wooden shingles to keep it weather-tight. He'd fashioned a rough table and a couple of bench chairs using wood and nails, but after months at Macquarie Harbour and then the woods, it was a palace to me. I perched gingerly on one of the chairs, trying to remember when I'd last sat on one.

Paddy lit the fire and the smell of roasting lamb and fresh bread soon filled the hut. As he handed me a plate piled high with bread, gravy and meat, he said, 'I gave you the fat. You're more in need of it than me,' he said, patting his impressive paunch.

As we ate in silence I became aware of Paddy watching me. I looked up at him quizzically and he smiled. 'I was just thinking I don't know what you were eating out there, but I bet you're glad to get your teeth into some decent meat.'

I said nothing and just nodded.

Surprisingly, considering the length of time since I had last eaten, my hunger was sated quite quickly and I began to get stomach pains.

'Ah, 'tis common enough when you've starved a while. Your stomach has shrunk down to nothing, but we'll soon feed you up and it'll come right.' He crossed to a small cupboard and pulled out a bottle of clear liquid. '*Pocin?* A nobbler or two will iron ye out.'

'Where in the world did you get that Paddy?'

'The military. They give me a few bottles and I turn a blind eye while they lift a lamb. After all that salted beef the army feeds them, fresh meat is something of a luxury for those boys.' He relaxed once he'd downed a few, got out his clay pipe and started chortling.

'What's the joke?'

'Alec, I have to confess that when I saw you down on that lamb ripping it apart with your teeth I got a hell of a fright. I thought you were the *bunyip*.'

I frowned at the sound of the strange word. '*Bunyip?*'

Like all the best storytellers, he kept me waiting as he packed baccy into the bowl of his pipe and got it lit. Then, his fleshy bearded face wreathed in smoke, he continued, 'Aye, it's a story told to me by the blackfellows I use as shepherds and drovers. They're a superstitious mob alright. They never travel at night and stick close to the fire. We was driving a flock of sheep to market a few months back when a branch fell on the road and they stopped dead and started jabbering away amongst themselves. They refused to go another foot.' Mimicking their pidgin English and wide-eyed expression Paddy said, 'No go there boss. No good.'

Pausing to take a good suck at his pipe, Paddy blew out a thin jet of smoke and continued, 'It's just a branch, ye silly buggers,' I scolded them. "No boss, it a warning. Bad things over there," they insisted. With that, they lit off into the trees and I had to take the lot to market meself, but came home without a scratch.'

'What's this *bunyip*?'

'It's said to be part man, part beast and is twice the size of a normal man. Covered all over in rough hair, it's got big teeth, sharp claws and is green and brown in colour so it can hide in the trees. It guards the waterholes and lures passers-by to their doom by striking its flat tail on the water.'

As was his way, Paddy's eyes grew wider, his face became more animated and his hands moved quicker than a card sharper's. 'Its screams and cries are enough to melt the courage of the bravest man and its skin is so thick that not even a spear can pierce it, but it's scared of fire.'

'Paddy, tell me you don't believe a word of this,' I scolded.

'Well, not at first, but this is strange country, as you'd well know. It's sorta eerie and preys on yer mind after a while.'

'But you've not seen it.'

Paddy fell silent while he fiddled with his pipe, then after he'd lit it and had a good draw he nodded, as if he'd decided something.

'Well, one night I was coming back late from Jericho when I saw some strange lights in the distance. At first I thought it was a cottage or a camp, but they moved quickly just to my shoulder. I called on whoever was there to show themselves. The horse got right agitated, so I gave it the spur and tried to outrun them, but they kept pace with me. There was two of 'em, both about three feet round, sat about ten feet above the ground. Their colour changed from a pale misty grey to a hazy blue depending from which direction you looked at 'em.'

'What happened?'

'Once they had scared the bejesus out of me they moved off

quickly, faster than any horse could gallop.'

'You weren't under the influence were you now Paddy?' I jibed him.

'As God's my witness,' he said indignantly, running his index finger across his breast in both directions.

'What d'ya think it was?'

Paddy shook his head. 'It was like nothing I'd ever seen. The blacks call them *koorari* in their lingo. They say they're the ghosts of the blacks killed by us whites, the unsettled souls of the dead still roaming the earth, something like our Jack-o'-lanterns.'

'Ach Paddy,' I snorted, 'it's just superstition.'

'Aye, maybe,' he muttered quietly.

To lighten the mood I told him the story of how Greenhill and I rushed the Aborigine camp all blacked up and naked with feathers in our hair. Paddy gurgled like a drain and slapped his knees in delight, but then he leant in closer and lowered his voice to a confidential tone, 'For all the world I thought you was it.' His expression was sombre, but I made light of it by rubbing my hands together over the flames. 'Ah you're safe enough Paddy. I still enjoy a good warm at the fire.'

I didn't tell him about our trials in the forests. A lot of strange things had happened out there and I needed time to ponder them.

He found me some new clothes, burned Greenhill's ragged convict canaries and drew me my first hot bath one in nearly a year.

'God have mercy,' breathed Paddy as he watched my skeletal frame covered in bites, cuts and scratches emerge from the foul waters. 'I'd swear there's as much of you in the bath as there is out of it.'

I sharpened Paddy's cut-throat on a leather strop hanging

off a beam and stood before the sliver of mirror he'd stuck into a crack in the trunk. A grizzly haired, wild-bearded creature greeted me. Little wonder Paddy didn't recognise me. As I scraped the hair off my face to reveal the former Alexander Pearce underneath I examined myself curiously. No horns, hideous fangs or bloodshot staring eyes. I hadn't turned into Paddy's *bunyip*. When I'd finished, there was an ordinary man in the looking glass peering back at me and I decided it was time to make peace with myself.

I'm sorry that I killed and was party to the death of fellow convicts. It was no way to die. But I did what I had to do to stay alive and for no other reason. I'll re-join the community of men I once belonged to, live a normal life and resolve never to speak of it again.

With that, I locked my story in the dark corner of my mind that held my other secrets.

Paddy and I sat around the fire drinking and yarning a while longer, but the grog and the warmth soon made my eyelids droop and he yawned himself.

'Aye you've had some day, Alec. Best get yer head down.'

'Do you know what month it is Paddy and what day? I'm sorry, I've lost count.'

'It's the eighth day of November,' he said patiently as he rolled himself in his blanket. Within a short time Paddy was snoring gently and I started drifting away, my body as weightless as an empty sack, as though all my bones had fallen out of it.

Tortured, twisting shapes started swirling around behind my eyelids, the ghosts of my past trapped in unhappy limbo. At first they all came in turn: Dalton, Bodenham, Mather, Travers and Greenhill stood silently over me, blood dripping down their waxy white skin, sleepless black eyes staring at me with grim expressions fixed to their stiff faces. Then, by and by, they began to create little cameos, such as the one in which Dalton is served up to me as a meal.

In another, I'm being led through a slaughterhouse with carcasses of bloody, freshly killed animal meat hanging on either side of me. My guide stops at a closed door, taps his nose with his finger and tells me that beyond the door is a choice cut of meat only tasted by few men. He opens the door to reveal a single carcass hanging from a hook. As I approach I see by its genitals that it's the body of a man. The cadaver has a face, that of Matthew Travers, the butcher from England who became so again during our journey.

When my ordeal is over and they release me back to sleep there is no sign of guilt on their faces because they know they've been judged and I haven't.

Again Daniel Ruth found himself looking up from Pearce's memoir and shaking his head in wonderment. *What a story! Almost unbelievable!* he mused, even though he believed most of it was true. When published, it would be a sensation in every part of the known world.

By his rough calculations, Alexander Pearce survived forty-nine days in the wilderness, overcoming every obstacle nature put in his way. Daniel smiled wryly as he was struck by a sudden irony. Had Pearce not been a convict and a cannibal he would have been hailed as a hero for surviving such an ordeal and feted throughout the world. Only a man of incredible strength and willpower could have survived such horrors.

As he cast his gaze across the flat grey expanse of the harbour to the towering peaks on the horizon where circles of soft, downy mist sat above them like halos, Daniel examined his feelings more closely. Far from the usual odium and disgust that normally accompanied Pearce's name, he'd begun to feel a grudging respect for the nuggetty wee Irishman who'd refused to die. He was a fighter. He found it curious that Pearce believed it was his father's voice guiding him in the wilderness, but Daniel reasoned that fraught situations did strange things to people. Stories of men lost at sea or in snowstorms who claimed they received guidance from departed family members were legion.

Daniel's musings on the preternatural were interrupted by the more temporal rumbling of his stomach. He couldn't remember the last time he ate or how long he'd been up in the garret. He opened a can of beef stew, heated it in the hot ashes at the edge of the fire and then dug into it with a spoon. He counted the other discarded cans and noted he was eating stew for the seventh night in a row. Ruefully, he recalled instructing the kitchen staff at *Druim Moir* never to serve him the same meal twice, which had taxed the ingenuity of the three chefs that had passed through its kitchen in as many years. Viewed through the prism of Sarah Island, he began to see his many extravagances as faintly ridiculous.

As he chewed on the chunks of rough beef, a deeply confronting thought suddenly entered Daniel's head. *If it came to it, could I eat a piece of a man?* He spat his mouthful of food into the hissing fire and shuddered before rapidly dismissing the notion from his mind. He'd come here well-stocked, over-stocked even, so the question would never arise. Besides, he was all alone on the island so there was no one to eat, even if he *did* feel the inclination. Daniel looked out at the brooding landscape, which had repelled mankind's one and only attempt to conquer it. Despite his strongly-held belief in science and rational thought, there was something unsettling about this place that had caused the ordinary people who were sent here to do terrible things. '. . . It preys on the mind,' as Paddy Maguire had said to Pearce.

'You're talking nonsense Daniel,' he retorted aloud as if words were enough to break the evil spell that he felt was being woven around him and defiantly shovelled another spoonful of stew into his mouth. As he poured himself a tot of warming rum he smiled and mused, *If my mother could see me now* . . .

That stray thought dragged Daniel's mind to Caroline and his parents. He wondered how they were coping in his absence and felt a pang of guilt as he realised he'd been away almost five months but hadn't really given any of them much attention. His parents would have interrogated poor old Miss Lambert by now, but because he'd booked his passage to London under an alias the trail would soon go cold.

Caroline would've taken it very badly. He hadn't confided in the woman everyone expected to be his wife and this would've been a blow to her pride. He looked at the small portrait he kept in his wallet, a girl in the spring of life with all the promise of a long summer ahead. He recalled her leaving Christ's Church on his last Sunday at home. She was widely held to be the most ravishing creature in the whole of Philadelphia and that day even the modest neckline of her navy-blue dress and the tightest of bodices couldn't repress the voluptuous curve of her breasts.

He recalled wistfully how he had brought her into womanhood one sunny Sunday afternoon two summers ago amongst the frill and lace of her bedroom still adorned with girlish clutter. Daniel closed his eyes as he recalled her breathless gasp as he placed his hand between her legs and parted her thighs so he could slide between them and cover her body with his. He felt himself stiffening as he recalled the smell of her freshly-brushed long, blond hair, her full, pouting lips and the soft, silky feel of those breasts.

With a sigh he opened his eyes and reluctantly returned to the grim present. A cold, blue twilight had now stolen over Sarah Island leaving just a peephole of daylight in the western sky. He stood and watched the gathering darkness soften the hard outlines of the prison block and recalled what a former inmate had said about the place. He'd described these men as 'soldiers in a war against tyranny which sought to crush them, fighting a battle they had little chance of winning, but who fought because fighting gave them a taste of the freedom the system denied them.'

Questions crowded his mind. *What lay ahead for Pearce? Did he ever reach 'the summit of our hope?'* He put the photograph of Caroline back in his wallet. It wasn't time to return to her yet but when he did he vowed never to leave her again. This journey had taught him what a cold, cruel place the world could be and he intended make the most of his chances, especially this one. He'd return to Philadelphia in triumph, settle down and be content with his lot.

Chapter 14

Boon Days

Paddy Maguire's Hut, 13 November 1822

IT WAS THREE DAYS before my natural bodily functions resumed. After almost two weeks I had begun to despair of ever restoring my parts to full operation and when they started I thought I would expire with the effort. The pain was even worse than the lash, but after a half hour of writhing in the bush I finally discharged a callous lump the size of a hen's egg. It was, however, a sign that my bodily functions had started to return to normal.

I spent my days at Paddy's resting, feeding myself up and avoiding his questions about what had happened in the wilderness. He was surprised that there was no word of the other men I had escaped with. I explained it away by saying that two had turned back, two more had died along the way, and the rest had drifted apart once starvation took effect and we'd argued about the quickest way out.

After about a week, Paddy said to me, 'It's time you moved on, Alec. Mr Treffit will be here by and by. He'd figure you for a bolter and book a passage to Macquarie Harbour for the pair of us. My brother, Michael, has got a secret hut in the forest where you'll be safe for a while.'

He took me to the edge of the woods and gave me careful directions. Turning to him I held out my hand. 'Thanks Paddy, I owe you my life.'

He shook his head sombrely. 'Nah, you owe the good Lord your life, Alec. How you ever made it through that bloody wilderness I'll never know,' he said searching my face for an answer.

'Thanks anyway,' I said.

He brushed the brim of his hat with his fingertips. '"Death or liberty" as they say. You're one of the few who got liberty. Enjoy it.'

'That I will, every last drop of it,' I said with a grin.

Michael's bolt hole was deep in the forest near Mosquito's Creek, well away from any human activity. It was of sturdy construction, comfortable enough and well-stocked. I planned to rest up for another week and then start out for Hobart. Paddy reckoned it was a bit over one hundred miles as the crow flies.

On my second night there I heard a low whistle out in the woods. Fearing it was redcoats, natives, or maybe some of Paddy's ghostly visitors, I doused my candle, went to the window and peered out into the darkness. There was nothing there except the outlines of trees standing silently in the pale moonlight. I waited for what seemed like an eternity and as my heartbeat slowed to normal I began to wonder if it was a night bird or a creature of some sort. I knew I wouldn't get a wink of sleep until I was sure, so I slipped out the door.

I crouched in the darkness for a good while until I felt the chills starting to numb my legs and the sharp cold begin to settle on me. *Must have been opossums*, I concluded, *or maybe*

Paddy's bunyip. I had just straightened up when I heard a click as a pistol was cocked.

'Stay right there shipmate,' a harsh voice ordered. I picked it as Somerset as it had the same melodic lilt as 'Little' Brown's. A pair of rough hands dashed the axe from my grip and was soon about my throat. Using the full weight of his much heavier body as a lever, he pulled me backwards, drove his knee into the small of my back and shoved me down to the ground. Just as quick he was on top of me. The pale moonlight slanting through the thick canopy gave me only the outline of a hat and a bearded face breathing cold steam. He was joined by a second figure, the one from Somerset with the gun.

'Who are you?' the man on top of me demanded in what I took to be a broad Lancashire accent.

'Alec Pearce, a friend and fellow countryman of Paddy Maguire.'

'Never heard of ya,' challenged Lancashire.

'Probably a spy. Let's shoot him.'

'Nah, a bullet's too quick. Burn 'im alive. He'll spill his guts double-quick.' Being something of an authority on human cruelty, I believed he meant it.

'If he's a spy then let's get rid of him and be gone. His mates might be expecting us,' countered Somerset.

This sudden thought spurred them on and in short order I was on my feet and up against a tree. They took ten paces backwards, pulled two pistols each from their belts, raised and cocked them before I came to my senses. *Surely I hadn't come all this way to die like this!*

'I'm not a spy!' I pleaded.

But my denial was met with harsh laughter. 'Prove it,' roared Lancashire.

Prove it? How do I prove it? I thought frantically. I thrust out my arm, rolled up my sleeve and showed them my tattoo. 'Look, I'm a convict.'

Their stance relaxed a little. 'What does it say?' demanded Somerset.

'102 . . . I'm convict 102.'

'Could have had it done special to fool us,' was the uncharitable reply.

Ignoring the freezing cold night, I pulled off my jacket and shirt and showed them the 'DL' tattoo on my shoulder. 'Look, what spy would have this?'

Though still wary, they came in closer to inspect it. 'Death or liberty, 'eh. I wonder which it's to be?' muttered Somerset.

'Death,' spat Lancashire.

'Liberty,' said I.

'Where did you escape from?'

'Macquarie Harbour, about two months ago.'

They gave a low whistle. 'A harsh billet, I hear,' said Somerset in what sounded like a more sympathetic tone.

'The Isle of Misery was well named,' I agreed.

Sensing his quarry slipping away Lancashire sneered, 'How did you get here then?'

'I walked.'

His eyes widened in disbelief. 'Through those woods? Nah, no one's ever done that.'

'I'm the first then.'

'On your own?'

'Eight of us started, but only I made it out. The rest perished. It was Paddy who found me and looked after me this past week.'

There was a rustling of paper as Somerset produced some

sheets of newspaper from his coat pocket. 'I read something in the *Hobart Gazette* about bolters from Macquarie Harbour. Lucky for you I have it.'

'Or unlucky,' spat Lancashire, still hoping for some sport.

'Let's go inside into the light and settle this once and for all.' Somerset pointed his pistol at me. 'After you Mr Pearce, and if there's anyone in there you'll die with us, be sure of that,' he warned me harshly.

We entered the darkened hut, shoulder to shoulder, the cold steel of Somerset's gun planted in the back of my neck. I lit a candle and held it aloft as he walked me very slowly round the room, poking into every corner to make sure we were alone.

'Stand by the door,' he ordered Lancashire, and unfolding his newspaper he motioned me to sit down. While he pored over it by the light of a candle I took the opportunity to study my captors. Both had the look of wild bush men, being long-haired and heavily bearded, their clothes some way past their best. Somerset's fleshy face looked kindly, fatherly even. If he was a bandit, he didn't much look like one. Lancashire, on the other hand, fitted the mould much better. He was about ten years younger, a shade under six foot, leaner, with a cruel, hard glint in his eyes. The scarred skin around his freckled nose told of an active career with the fists. I also noted he'd lost an inch off his right index finger.

After what seemed like an eternity, Somerset looked up at me and a slow smile cracked his face. 'Looks like you've been telling the truth Alexander Pearce.'

Lancashire, obviously stung, abandoned his post to come over to the table. 'What does it say?' he demanded.

Slowly, grappling with each word, Somerset read out the report: '"Eight men were reported as having absconded from Macquarie Harbour some six weeks ago." They list their names, the last one being Alexander Pearce. Convict 102 is described as being an Irishman, 5 foot 3 inches tall with brown hair, grey eyes and pock-marked skin. Your tattoo saved your life,' he concluded solemnly.

Lancashire gave a low moan, 'You mean we ain't gonna kill him?'

'There's a ten quid reward for his arrest or return,' added Somerset as he folded up his journal.

'Boys, don't turn me in,' I pleaded.

Lancashire shook his head. 'There's no loyalty in "the game", it's just the fortune of war.' I had the feeling they might be bushrangers and now they'd confirmed it. Better that than just evil cut-throats.

'Of course, if you were prepared to join us that might persuade us to let you go free,' cut in Somerset looking at his mate for confirmation.

'Join you?'

'We're a bit short-handed. Three's best in our game.'

I watched Lancashire eye me up and down and his lip curl in dismay as Greenhill had on my first day at the logging. He'd wanted another flash cove in the gang, someone like himself.

'The trouble is finding someone we can trust,' Somerset added.

'Aye, the last lad who tried to dob us in didn't live long enough to collect,' growled Lancashire, angry at my elevation from victim to partner.

Delighting in his own cruel sense of fun, he took a swig from a small bottle he carried in his coat pocket and with the stink of strong rum on his breath recounted the chilling story of how they'd accounted for the rat in their ranks over at Brown Mountain.

'A man willing to turn King's evidence is as rare as hen's teeth and to protect them from retribution the military never include their names in official reports or statements. When one of the soldiers in our pay off brought us the statements made against our names, we discovered that they were just called "the informant" or their name is blacked out.'

'How did you find out who had spoken against you?' I pressed.

He tapped the side of his nose and took another draught, pausing to savour the warmth as it coursed down his gullet.

'By working a corporal known to be "willowy" or easily bent,' recalled Somerset taking up the story. 'It's often said that a shilling in grog buys twenty times its worth in information and the thirsty trooper who sat before us was determined to have his fill, every glass of it. Once we'd sweetened him up enough, the redcoat started blowing off about his great adventures tracking down the notorious bandits Churton and Davis, little knowing his newfound mates were the one and the same!'

Lancashire chuckled as he picked up the threads of the story. 'We worked him patiently and eventually got the name we wanted, then he put his index finger to his lips and blearily tried to recant his confession. "We won't tell another soul," we promised him. 'By the time the corporal awoke the next day, remembered his transgression and galloped over to the informer's house, the man had already been dragged from his bed and was lashed to a tree out on a lonely plain. He kept screaming for someone to save his life, even though he knew by the stunted twisted gums, scrubby grass and fly-blown desolation of the place we'd brought him to that it was out of call of human habitations and there was no one to hear him.'

'Did you kill him?' I asked. After my journey through the

wilderness, death was no stranger to me and I doubted he could shock me.

'By and by,' he said, taking another gulp of the warming spirit, 'but first I sharpened my butchery cleavers in front of him. He shat himself long before I took his nose off with a single swing of the blade,' boasted Lancashire, smacking the edge of his hand into the palm of the other for emphasis. I feigned shock, even though I'd seen and done much worse myself. Thinking he had me going, he leaned closer and added the gruesome details. 'During the summer, out in the back country, those vicious jewelled blowflies and cattle flies need little invitation to swarm and the smell of shit and fresh blood works them up into a right frenzy.' Savouring the memory, he chuckled, 'They were so thick on his face that it looked as if he was wearing some native mask. Next to toothache and a broken leg, I am told this is one of the worst tortures that can be inflicted on any man. Their frenzied noise as they swarm is enough to send the strongest mind screaming mad.

'Breathing through torn nostrils is impossible so every time he tried to inhale through his mouth, it filled with flies. No amount of spitting and head-shaking would get rid of them. Any thoughts he had that darkness would bring him some respite were dashed by the vicious squabbling of the devils and the bark of the tigers in the brush.

'Finally, we decided that the pimp had suffered enough, so I cocked a loaded pistol and levelled it at his heart. By now, the informant was exhausted and had given up on his life. "Don't leave me like this, just finish me off," the bugger pleaded.

'"I'll leave that up to you," I said, "there's a big enough price on our heads without adding cold-blooded murder to it."

'Loosening his bonds a little, I freed his left arm, put the loaded pistol in his coat pocket and told him, "When you've had enough, put an end to it yourself." Shaking his head and chuckling, Lancashire recalled, 'As we saddled up, a strangulated "bastard" was all the gratitude we got.'

'What became of him?' I asked.

Clearly relishing the opportunity to do a bit of peacocking, he threw his hands open, 'Being game coves and true students of human nature, we sat a while in plain view to see if he would use his one shot to get even with his tormentors, but he wasn't giving us any more sport and just hung limply against his bonds, waiting for us to go. We'd gone less than a mile when we heard the crack of a pistol in the distance.'

'Did they find him?'

Somerset shrugged. 'As far as we know he's still tied to that tree, his eyes picked out by birds and the flesh long since stripped from his bones.'

'Ever do anything as bad as that?' Lancashire slurred as the strong spirit started to take effect.

'Nah,' I said, shaking my head and closing the door on any further discussion.

I had been forewarned. He was not a man to cross and I fancied those who did repented too late.

The warning over, they formally introduced themselves. 'Ralph Churton,' said Somerset, placing trust in me by revealing his identity. Lancashire still looked a bit put out, but prompted by Churton he muttered, 'Will Davis.'

We all shook hands solemnly and broke open a bottle of *pocin* Paddy had stashed in the cupboard. 'Liberty and a long life,' was the toast even though this seemed a remote possibility given we were all on the run from the British redcoats. They told me they'd escaped from an army guard on April last while being transported to Hobart on a charge of sheep-stealing. They'd barged aside the redcoats on the bridge over the Ouse River and jumped into its freezing waters still chained together. By some miracle none of the volleys fired at them took effect and they didn't drown.

'Grog and sin, that's my prescription for a long and happy life,' chuckled Davis.

We drank to this, drank to my escape, to Paddy Maguire and to everyone we knew. Amongst the criminal classes there is a great deal of mistrust and bitterness, but also a ready acceptance of new chums – until they prove to be otherwise. It's the nature of our craft. I was safe and warm, had grog and these stout fellows for company. It didn't pay to think too hard about the future, so from now on I resolved to just live for each day. Soon with various liquors singing in my head, I was stupidly befuddled and before I could stop myself, I'd agreed to join them.

Davis decreed that our partnership could only be sealed by the taking of more strong drink and it was a late hour by the time we arrived at a sly grog shop off a by-road run by an ex-convict called James Unsworth, a native of Birmingham and a thoroughly unscrupulous, untrustworthy character. His property was a collection of low-roofed shingle and bark huts. The bar itself was no more than an earthen-floored single room, twenty foot square, with a couple of small windows at one end. The atmosphere was hot, dark and smoky and the smell of strong spirits mingled with the sour odours of unwashed bodies, burning tobacco and hot candle wax.

'I've got a fresh-picked lubra out back by the name of Mary,' whispered Unsworth with a sideways tilt of his head, 'I bought her off her da for a jug of rum,' he boasted with a wink and a chuckle.

'Young, is she?' Davis leered, his voice thick with desire.

'Little more than a girl, but comely enough,' crooned Unsworth. Davis licked his lips. 'Usual price?'

'Two bob,' shot back Unsworth, doubling his price in the face of Davis's urgent need, 'on account of her being young and fresh like,' he added by way of inducement. Davis put his money on the roughly hewn bar and went out back. 'Best get me money's worth then,' he called over his shoulder.

'Go easy, she's got more to see to tonight,' grumbled the landlord.

After a few minutes we could hear a furious pounding and some stifled screams even over the low rumble of voices, a squeezebox playing a jaunty tune and Churton and Unsworth chewing the cud.

'She was a bit feisty when I first got her,' recalled the bar owner, 'clawing and spitting at anyone who came near her. I quietened her down with a few heavy backhanders, starved her until she was too weak to fight back and then broke her in like one of those wild horses they get out in the bush.'

Davis appeared a half-hour later, a rare smile splitting his face. 'That's a good a ride as I've ever had,' he declared loudly. Slamming two bob on the bar, he pointed at me. 'This is Alec Pearce, a mate of old Paddy Maguire's and until recently a guest of His Majesty. I reckon he deserves the next turn.'

It'd been a while since I'd had a good meal and a drink, but even longer since I'd had a woman and it wouldn't do to refuse the hospitality of a new chum. I went out the back, the chatter of voices fading as I closed the back door. After the close, smoky atmosphere inside, the cold, clear night air was bracing. Ahead of me in the gloom was a door leading to the so-called 'dead room', a small annexe with a cot where drunks were left to sleep it off when they passed out. I flipped the latch and the door opened into total darkness. There was a heavy, resigned sigh and a weary creak of timbers as Mary swung her legs off the floor and lay on her back. She had her skirts up over her knees by the time I got on top of her.

I never discovered whether Mary was pretty or not, but I knew she was young by her breasts and flesh, which were still firm to the touch. I unbuttoned her dress, flattened my hands against her soft titties and worked her big nipples between my thumb and index fingers as I got up a good rhythm. Every lubra I ever saw had big, black sow-like teats. Maybe it's a characteristic of their race, but I liked them better than the small, pink little buds you mostly get on white women.

After about ten minutes there was a knock. And after another five minutes came a thump and a high-pitched Midlands whine, 'Don't wear 'er out lad. There's others what's paid their money.'

The next time we went there Mary was gone. She'd lasted less than a month. Some drunk had forgotten to put the latch on the door and she escaped. Unsworth and some of his sporting regulars got their guns and kangaroo dogs and went after her.

It turned out to be the shortest manhunt in the history of this colony. She only went as far as the nearest tree, threw the clothes rope over the topmost branch, tied the other end round her neck, climbed up a few feet and jumped.

They buried her out in the bush.

No one missed her.

No questions were ever asked.
A shit life. No better than a convict's.

I happily went back to being wee Alec, who no one paid much attention to and did what he was told because he wasn't big enough to fight back. During my first year in Hobart I absconded a couple of times and spent a few months roaming the countryside, robbing and stealing – living off the land, so to speak. I knew all the ploys and acquitted myself well. It was just as well because Churton and Davis were a pretty rapid party. We covered a large area of back country from Great Lake in the north to the Derwent in south and from the Ouse east to the Coal River in the west, never spending two nights in the same place. Each day we'd rob a farm, a mail coach, a traveller, a store or a hotel, move on and sleep wherever we landed up when the sun went down. We had watches, money and jewellery stashed under rocks, in caves and in hollowed-out trees right around the area and paid frequent visits to Mr John Mortimer, a fence who used his jewellery business in New Norfolk as cover. There was also a handy network of hut-keepers and farmers, all ex-convicts, who were willing to supply us with food and shelter, fresh horses, and keep us advised of the military's whereabouts, for a consideration of course. Ensuring they were well paid was also an insurance against informers who might be tempted by the £30 they'd collect if they turned us in.

Business went along fine for a time but, as always with the criminal classes, once they get some money in their pocket they get flash. Davis was a deal too fond of the grog and women. His crapulous, disreputable vices were accepted as things of usual course but my instinct told me they'd be our undoing. In any case, I didn't intend to stay long in their company, just long enough to get my puff back and make some easy money.

Things started to go wrong the night we surprised a farmer, his wife and daughter who were sitting quietly at their fire. The Sykes family from Dorset had settled near the River Ouse almost five years before and were known throughout the district for nothing except Christian kindness and fine cheese.

We took anything of value we could find about the place, including the old mare's wedding ring. She cried and said it was her mother's and asked us not to take it. Many bushrangers went by the chivalrous code of Dick Turpin and would've let her keep it, but not these two.

'Old gold is purer and fetches a better price,' barked Davis, repeating something Mortimer had told us.

Mrs Sykes berated us in very harsh language but Davis didn't care. He'd been tugging at a gin bottle he found in a cupboard since we'd arrived and its effect was starting to show; between the grog and the heat of the fire his face was almost the colour of his ginger hair.

I noticed he'd been eyeing off the farmer's daughter who looked to be about seventeen. A right comely little maid she was, tall and stately with long tresses of dark hair that flowed down past her shoulders, a face like a doll and a pert young bosom that we'd all admired. Churton ordered the wife into the kitchen to fix us some grub and prodded her husband outside to look at his horses. Ours were a bit knocked up after many weeks in the saddle. Davis approached the girl and said, 'Let's see what you've got upstairs. Bet there's some trinkets we could sell.'

When she refused to move he pulled her roughly to her feet and scolded her. 'Do as you're told missy, or it'll be the worse for you and your parents.'

She shook off his hand, which lingered on her shoulder a little too long for propriety's sake, and flounced up the stairs, Davis in close pursuit.

Thinking little of it I sat down in a comfy chair and enjoyed a rare warm at the fire as Davis and the girl went from room to room, banging doors and shouting. After a day in the fresh weather the heat made me dozy and before long I felt my eyelids drooping.

A shrill female scream brought me bolt upright. It came again and the mother rushed in from the kitchen, her face the colour of her arms, which were white to the elbows with flour.

'Wait there,' I ordered her, taking the stairs two at a time. I moved down the darkened corridor where sobs now replaced the screams and barged open the door where the noise was coming from. I was greeted by the unedifying sight of Davis with his trousers round his ankles and his pale arse bouncing up and down on top of the daughter. Her skirt and petticoats had been thrust up around her hips, her blouse and bodice ripped down to the waist, and her soft white breasts exposed to the whole world. She was sobbing hysterically, which only seemed to spur Davis on. Hearing the door open he lifted his head and leered at me, 'Wait yer turn, boy.'

'For God's sake man, she's just a girl!'

'She's woman enough, as you can well see,' he grunted, and with that stopped driving at her, stiffened, gave a low groan and fell panting on top of the distraught girl who'd covered her tear-streaked face with both hands. Though I was no saint, I didn't agree with molesting women and I turned from the door as the father and Churton came bounding up the stairs, pistol in hand. 'What in the hell's going on?' he yelled. His face fell when he saw Davis climbing back into his breeches and the de-flowered daughter lying on the pile of bloodied sheets behind him.

'Don't get yerself all fussed, t'were only a bit o' fun,' muttered Davis.

Sykes, momentarily stunned by his daughter's distress, rallied and making a curious mewling sound like an animal went to attack the grinning Davis. 'You bastard! She was keeping herself pure 'til she was wed!' he raged.

I knew that Davis, who always kept his knife and pistol about him, would use either without a second thought. Grabbing the farmer's arm I cautioned him, 'Nothing you can do will restore her virtue, so don't do anything rash and get yourself killed. We'll soon be clear and you'll live through this. Your wife and daughter still need you.'

Still he wrestled with me, but my words had taken effect and his pained, tear-filled gaze met mine. He realised I'd spoken sense. As well I knew, men are capable of surviving the most terrible ordeals.

It was a wild, dark night outside, the sort the Devil might relish. You could smell rain in the wind, the messenger of the coming storm. Frightened sheep bleated somewhere out in the black beyond.

Once we got clear of the house I rounded on Davis. 'You've put our necks in a halter,' I scolded him.

Davis, with the memory of the girl still clear in his mind and her warm musk still on his skin, made light of it. Spreading his arms as if to embrace the gathering storm and the Devil who was riding in on its coat-tails, he sang out, 'Only if they catch up to us.' Letting out a great belly laugh he added, 'You're only jealous because I got the use of that hussy before you.'

'No, I'm worried that every trooper in the colony is going to be looking for us now and the fat reward might tempt some dog to split on us.'

Davis rounded on me, his coal-black eyes shining with pure malice. Pushing his foppish fringe back from his face so I could see his seething rage he said slowly through gritted teeth, 'There's already a reward on our heads, but no trooper's had a sniff of us in the best part of a year.'

I made out the dangerous curve of a blade as Davis slipped it from his belt with a cold little smile.

'Put that away now Will,' demanded Churton.

Ignoring his partner, he jutted out his chin and snarled, 'Want to play knife with me?'

I shook my head.

'Come on, Mr High and Mighty. If you wanna be the boss, come over here and earn the right.'

Still I did nothing. It was an ugly scene all too familiar to me. That terrible lump of fear lodged in your gut like a piece of half-chewed beef, the dry mouth and the cold sweat on your neck. They're the feelings you remember when you face death.

'Come on!' he roared, his terrible wrath matching the storm that was quickly gathering around us.

He's another Greenhill in the making, I thought to myself as I felt that primitive anger stir deep within me again.

But I had no desire to revisit that side of Alexander Pearce so I let my hands fall to my sides in a gesture of surrender.

'I thought not,' he sneered, shoving the knife back in his belt. Then, coming close and pushing his stumpy little finger into my cheek, he added, 'Don't ever cross me again unless you're ready to die.'

'That's it Will, let's be on our way,' said Churton, slapping him on the shoulder in a matey way, but Davis hadn't had his fill yet. As we mounted up he added, 'Who are you anyway Alexander Pearce? Perhaps it is you who is more wanted than us.'

It was an argument I couldn't win, so I bit my lip and put up with Davis's taunts for days after. I'd tolerated much worse.

Fine Merino wool was much in demand in England. Offspring from John Macarthur's now-famous stud in Sydney were brought down here to breed and were fetching a pretty price, so we lifted about hundred head from runs round the Bothwell and Oatlands area, altered the sheep's ear-markings and rested up while they healed. There was a market at New Norfolk in a few weeks where no questions would be asked and we could sell them there for a tidy profit.

Two days before, we did a muster and drove them towards New Norfolk. It was an uncommonly hot day and we decided to let the sheep take their fill of water at a creek beside the road while we went further upstream to bathe in its cool waters.

No sooner had we plunged in than a detachment of redcoats, their bright tunics clearly visible through the trees, happened past. Seeing a mob of sheep roaming loose they decided to investigate. We might have bluffed our way through, but we were all wanted men and it would need just one sharp-eyed trooper to end our spree. We prized our liberty above a few head of sheep, so we submerged and swam to the distant bank where a low hanging ti-tree trailed its branches into the river. We hid in its leafy embrace while the soldiers marched up and down the bank, jabbing at bushes with their bayonets, seeking the owners of the sheep. Fortunately, our horses had wandered off to graze and we'd hidden our clothes and guns up a tree so they found nothing. They did a muster and headed up the road towards the nearest hut.

We high-tailed it to Davis's property near Bothwell, a desolate acreage of stony hills and scrubby grass fit only for sheep. Davis never mentioned that he had a wife and a brood of bare-footed, curly-headed children whose sour, mistrustful expressions and flame-coloured hair were proof enough of their heritage.

We lay low for a week after receiving word that the military was scouring the countryside for the sheep-stealers. Unable to roam freely, we frequented Unsworth's grog shop and found he'd replaced Mary with a new girl, a lusty Norwich lass of mature years by the name of Peg. I introduced myself by thrusting my head between her white, dimpled thighs and diving downwards like a duck to taste the tang of her womanhood.

'Ooohh, you're a saucy one,' Peg squealed. 'Been a while has it?' As time is money in her profession I did not waste words, but continued my debauchery with relish. 'Bit of a wild man, aren't you?' she said, keeping up her narrative as I drove against her matronly buttocks, 'Lost in the forests for weeks, I hear, no men or women for company.' As I jigged up and down and looked at her auburn tresses, I tried to conjure up an image of Teresa, the doxy I'd left behind in Ireland.

Teresa Mary Bernadette . . . she had all the names of the saints but even they couldn't protect her from my lusting. Every time I clapped eyes on her I felt the raging fire that a man will only feel once or twice in his life for a woman. I resolved that I would do whatever I had to do to have her: kidnap, rape, bribery, or all of them together. Bribery worked the best and those carnal desires started me on the life of crime that landed me here.

'Tess, Tess . . .' I whispered, recalling my pet name for her.

'I'll be Tess or your own dear mother for an extra shilling love,' Peg cackled, a foul odour wafting up from her mouth. *A shilling?* I'd not have spent a farthing on such a trollop back in

Monaghan, but there were four men for every woman in this accursed place and she had one of the most precious commodities in the colony between her legs.

My ranging days ended after seven weeks one hot, sticky Saturday afternoon early in January. We were heading for Davis's property after a spell around Oatlands, robbing stores and outlying farms. Davis had hoped to sell a lubra to Unsworth but the girl refused to leave the hut-keeper who was presently her custodian. Truth be told, I found 'blackbirding', as it was known, distasteful and was glad we were on our way.

We stopped and took a rest under a shade tree between Tom's Hill and Glenmore Sugarloaf, not far from Noah Mortimer's land. We'd just settled down when we were startled by a very plummy English voice, 'Stand, you blackguards.'

We leapt up, but by the time we gained our feet we had been fronted by five redcoats with Brown Besses who appeared in a line above the nearest rise about twenty yards ahead. Will Davis, knowing he would face the gravest charges if we were taken, decided on our behalf not to come easy. As he reached down for his pistol there was a sharp crack from one of the muskets followed by a puff of white smoke. Davis let out a cry of pain and staggered back clutching at his shattered right hand as we were wreathed in gun smoke, the sharp smell of burning gunpowder stinging our noses.

'I'm shot!' he cried as blood poured forth from a gaping wound.

'Stand, or the next ball will go right through your fucking head,' called the captain, the curse sounding odd in his refined English accent.

We raised our hands.

The captain, distinguished by his cocked hat and longer red frock-coat, came forward. He was no more than twenty-five, his commission doubtless paid for by a well-heeled father.

'Ralph Churton and William Davis,' he said crisply, 'I arrest you in the name of His Majesty King George.' He looked right at me. 'Who are you?' he demanded.

I tried to stay calm. 'Paddy Maguire, sir,' I shot back without hesitation.

'And what's your business here?'

'I'm a shepherd hereabouts in the employ of Mr Thomas Tiffet.'

As he'd been trained, he searched my face for tell-tale signs of a lie. I thought I was home free until he gave a scornful snort. 'A likely tale,' he mocked. 'We'll have a look at the outstanding warrants back at barracks.'

Damnation! I knew I was sunk. This was not a chance encounter, but a carefully laid ambush. The redcoats knew Churton and Davis would be present. I was an unexpected bonus. Some pimping bastard had given music to the redcoats and collected thirty quid on our account. May the Devil take his black heart.

The young captain interviewed me back at the Jericho barracks. When he entered the room holding a scroll of paper my heart sank. *Damn his officious ways.* Often warrants are forgotten or mislaid, but not mine. Moving his eyes from the description given on it back to me, he rolled it back up in one crisp action.

'The description in the warrant confirms you are Alexander Pearce, Convict 102 late of Macquarie Harbour.'

'Surely sir, you're mistaken . . .' I stammered.

'That's enough nonsense Pearce. I mean to get the truth out of you. It says here that you escaped with seven other convicts. What became of them?'

I fell silent as I realised that I'd come to a crossroads. *You can either be tried as a bushranger and sheep thief and most likely hang alongside Churton and Davis, or take a gamble*, I told myself. I decided on a very risky strategy, very risky indeed, as you get no second chances in this game.

'Two turned back to Macquarie Harbour,' I ventured, stalling for time.

'What of the other five?' he snapped. I hesitated as I tried to summon up all my courage. My blood was coursing through my body and a little knot of worry had buried itself deep in my guts like a closed fist. *Come on, come on! You've taken enough big risks to get this far, hold your nerve. A faint heart will get you hanged.* I'd made peace with myself and put my descent into barbarism to the back of my mind where I hoped it would never again see the light of day, but . . .

'Come on man, speak up,' spat the captain impatiently. I threw up my hands in a gesture of submission and allowed the tears to roll down my face.

My sudden display of emotion caught the captain on the hop. 'What in God's name is the matter with you man?' he demanded, his tone now more puzzled than angry.

Wiping away the tears and snot with the back of my hand, my heart hammered violently as I heard myself say, 'I can't live with what I've done . . .'

The captain fell silent and allowed me a moment to compose myself. Then, bringing my tearful gaze level with his, I confessed to him as though he were a priest.

'I regret to inform you captain that I killed and ate them.' With that I sat back and watched as the young soldier's face turned a deathly white before my very eyes.

'What in the universe do you mean?' he stormed, clearly flustered by this unexpected admission. 'This had better not be some joke.'

'It's no joke, I assure you, sir,' I sniffed, wiping my eyes with my sleeve and savouring the young upstart's discomfort and distress.

Three days later I was gazing up at the craggy, inscrutable face of Table Mountain that loomed over Hobart like a censorious guardian. I'd hoped to see it a free man rather than in chains. An involuntary shudder passed through me as I recalled the grim, nameless monoliths we'd encountered during our terrible transit.

Though it was home to only some 12,000 inhabitants, Hobart had the makings of a proper provincial city. Fine brick and sandstone buildings had begun to replace some of the original timber dwellings and a few of the main thoroughfares had gutters laid. As we made our way through the familiar streets where I'd whiled away the first year and a half of my sentence, we passed my old drinking haunt, the Hope & Anchor, which shone out like a beacon on a cold, rainy Hobart night, the warm radiance of its bar-room window advertising itself to passers-by. We didn't nip in there nor the Waterloo or the Whalers' Return down on the harbour for an ale and a hearty feed of meat and potato stew, the mere thought of which had sustained me during many a long day in the wilderness. Instead, we continued out to the eastern outskirts where the gaol was located.

Churton, Davis and I were marched up to the stout, studded gates where some cruel wag had installed a door-knocker in the shape of a lion's head – the symbol not, as you might expect, of retribution but of Bacchus, the Roman God of wine and revelry. My heart sank as under the vigilant gaze of the two watchtowers the tall gates swung open and accepted us into their sweeping embrace. As we were prodded over the threshold, the tall buildings of the penitentiary shaded the sun that had warmed us all the way along Macquarie Street. We had passed, once more, into the realm of perpetual gloom.

Chapter 15

The interview

Hobart gaol, 27 January 1823

ONCE INSIDE THE GATES, I was separated from Churton and Davis without explanation and locked in a dank cell in a different part of the prison. I knew by the curious reception I received from gaolers and fellow convicts alike that the rumours of my misdeeds had marched here with me in even time. It was here, while awaiting my fate, that I first met Governor John Bisdee, though the title was a bit grand for a mere gaoler.

John Bisdee was a decent, God-fearing Christian man, sympathetic to the plight of the unfortunate prisoners in his charge. He'd seen men of all classes and character pass through this gaol and accompanied a good many to the gallows. A kindly word and a sympathetic ear went a long way in a place like this. Consequently, there was very little strife amongst the prisoners and few escapes. I think he felt sorry for me because everyone else, even the other lags, had shunned me as though I had some sort of contagion. I also think that like all true men of God, he refused to believe that any man was beyond redemption. I was a challenge, a lost soul who he'd bring back to Christianity.

On the Saturday morning, two weeks after my arrest, Bisdee came down to the cells to see me. 'The Reverend Robert Knopwood has requested your presence over the road at the Supreme Court.'

'What for?'

'The confession you made when you were first arrested has come to the attention of the lieutenant-governor and he's requested a report.'

'What's he like?'

Bisdee, who soon revealed himself to be a source for all manner of prison rumour and whispers, chuckled, 'Oh, old Bobby's a decent-enough sort, firm but fair. I've heard some of the colony's most influential gentlemen say he's a charming fellow with a ready wit while others swear that he's a drunken womaniser.' Lowering his voice, he told me Knopwood's dark secret, which every man, regardless of his vocation, has hidden away somewhere: 'He has a young orphan girl of consenting age in his charge, and a comely little miss she is.'

'And him a man of the cloth,' I huffed in mock horror.

Bisdee snorted, 'He might be a man of God but he never spared the lash when he was the Hobart magistrate. Mind you, he's only done bits and pieces these past few years on account of his stones.'

'His stones?' I chorused.

Bisdee chortled. 'Aye, his bladder stones. I hear that when they get bad he has to call out Dr Brewster who sticks a *bougie*, which is some sort of a rod, up his hole just so he can relieve himself.' Bisdee chuckled again, 'The procedure makes him somewhat ill-tempered.'

A short while later I was squired along Campbell Street in fetters by two armed redcoats. The Hobart courthouse was a square, two-storey sandstone building with wide sash windows and fancy stone cornices across the roof in the popular Georgian style. A handsome flight of stone stairs led up to a pair of stout double-doors.

I was shown into a wood-panelled courtroom with high cathedral ceilings and an imposing air of grandeur and gravitas as befitting a palace of justice. I was made to sit on a bench near the front and wait for Knopwood along with another man. He didn't bother to introduce himself to a mere convict, though I saw by the faded swallow tattoo on his hand and his hard countenance that he'd been a 'government man' himself. He'd served his time, got himself into good employ, and tried to leave his past behind him.

Knopwood arrived late at the courthouse, stooped, deathly pale and irritable. His blue-veined hands clutched onto his carved walking stick, time had blurred his features, and his pink scalp was only sparsely populated by grey hair; he looked much older than his sixty years.

But though the reverend's body might have aged, his piercing blue eyes served notice that his keen mind had lost none of its edge.

'Mr Wells, what brings you here?' he snapped, addressing the man next to me. I racked my brain: *Where have I heard that name before?*

Bowing solicitously, Wells explained his unexpected presence with smooth diplomacy, 'The lieutenant-governor is most anxious to receive a report of the prisoner's testimony.'

From the sour look on his face, Knopwood obviously felt he was being undermined, despite Wells' seemingly innocent explanation.

He was right to be wary. Thomas Wells, I now recalled, was the author of a racy little pamphlet entitled *Michael Howe: The Last and the Worst of the Bush Rangers of Van Diemen's Land*. It had sold quite well and earned Wells a modest amount of celebrity. Doubtless, he was hoping to use my story to further his literary ambitions.

'Tell Colonel Sorell I'll take the statement and furnish him with a copy,' insisted Knopwood.

'Reverend, the lieutenant-governor rather hoped to see it today,' retorted Wells, restoring Sorell to his rightful mantle in a pointed attempt to justify his presence and remind the clergyman who held the higher rank.

The slight was not lost on Knopwood whose ire rose at Wells' obstinacy. 'Today? Impossible. I have a sermon to prepare for tomorrow's service,' he barked.

'Then permit me to take some notes and ease your burden.'

'Mr Wells, taking a legal deposition is a skilled business, which may only be carried out by an officer of the court.' Then, seeing a chance to throw a well-aimed dart at Wells and the liberal attitudes that he believed were undermining convict discipline, he added, 'I'm afraid that's something your past history precludes you from ever becoming regardless of Governor Macquarie's opinions about the rehabilitation of the convict classes.'

Wells wisely refused to be drawn into such treacherous waters and stuck to his brief. 'Reverend, the lieutenant-governor was insistent that I return with notes for him this afternoon. Am I to tell him that you are declining his request?'

The colour rose in Knopwood's cheeks. He outranked Wells but not Sorell. Drawing in a great breath, he examined the floor for a moment then, having arrived at a solution that would allow him to grant the governor's request and still save face, the reverend sighed and nodded at Wells. 'Very well, you may sit in on the interview but you are not permitted to ask questions or pass comment. Please inform the lieutenant-governor that I will ensure he gets a copy of the deposition and a qualified legal opinion so that he might be in possession of *all* the facts.' He'd managed to satisfy the official request and sideswipe Wells in the same breath.

'As you wish Reverend,' said Wells, the lightness of his tone indicating he was claiming a minor victory.

I watched on amused. This petty exchange was so typical of colonial society, which is naught but a thin facsimile of England with its myriad titles, pecking orders and empire-builders who work tirelessly to create their own little kingdoms so that they might reign supreme in some small corner of God's earth.

The battle-lines drawn, the interview began.

Knopwood sat down gingerly, a small grimace of pain tightening his thin lips.

'I trust you're not poorly Reverend?' asked Wells, his features clouding with concern.

'I'm fine thank you, Mr Wells,' replied Knopwood testily. 'Please, let us proceed.' After parking a pair of pince-nez glasses on the end of his soft snub nose and perusing a sheaf of notes for a moment, he cleared his throat and finally acknowledged my presence.

'Alexander Pearce, convict 102,' he began, peering over at Wells to check that his scribbling nib was faithfully recording the information. 'Now Pearce, according to the officers who arrested you near Jericho on 11 January, you have made some sensational claims about events that transpired between the time you escaped from Macquarie Harbour on the twentieth day of September last and arriving in the settled districts in early

November. I refer specifically to your confession that you killed and ate the fellow members of your escape party.' The weight of incredulity he placed on those final words made it clear that he didn't believe my yarn.

'Yes sir,' I replied.

It was a very hot day at the end of a long Hobart summer and the atmosphere in the airless, empty courtroom was stifling. Knopwood produced a white hanky, which I noted was made of silk. *We all have our vices, Reverend,* I mused, conjuring up an image of the fresh-faced, full-bosomed orphan girl waiting by the window for his return. I don't know whether it was the heat, the unexpected presence of Wells, his bladder stones, or that he found my confession disturbing, but Knopwood suddenly became very agitated.

'Pearce, tell me what happened.'

'We escaped from Macquarie Harbour on the twentieth of September last by overpowering our overseer, Corporal Logan, and stealing the whaleboat that was used to transport us. We proceeded to Coal Head where another of our number, Robert Greenhill, was working. On coming ashore we raided the pilot's hut and stole ten pounds of bread and six pounds of salt beef. We did not damp the warning fires properly and the commandant was warned that we were on our way to Hell's Gates . . .'

'Hell's Gates?' exclaimed Knopwood, alarm and confusion in his voice.

'It's what the convicts call the entrance to Macquarie Harbour,' interjected Wells. The reverend, feeling his authority again being challenged, rounded on him, a bright red flush colouring his normally pallid complexion. 'Mr Wells,' he snapped, 'I would remind you that I am conducting this interview and I only wish to hear from the prisoner.' Turning back to me, he ordered, 'Proceed.'

'The convicts on shore managed to light the fires and shortly after we saw a signal being sent from Sarah Island to the troopers at the pilot's cottage. We decided not to brave the gauntlet of lead that would surely await us there and instead went ashore and travelled across country.'

The reverend held up his hand to signal he needed some clarification. 'But it was your original intention to take to the open sea?'

'Yes sir. We hoped to make our way to Timor or Batavia.'

Knopwood shook his head, though whether it was due to the stupidity of our plot or its audacity, he didn't say. Pressing his silk hanky to his nose, he waved his hand for me to continue.

'We headed inland using nothing but the sun and the big mountains as our compass, pushed through the densest forests I have ever seen, forded wide rivers and traversed tall mountains for a week before we ran out of food.' I paused and Knopwood hurried me on with an impatient wave of his hand.

'We tried to capture some of the local wildlife, but they were too quick and stealthy. Robert Greenhill, our leader and a former mariner, said that in such situations the "custom of the sea" is enacted, meaning one of the party is eaten so that the others might have a chance of survival.'

Impatient to get to the heart of the matter, Knopwood asked, 'Who was the first to die?'

'Dalton, sir.'

'And how was that decision arrived at?'

'Greenhill told us he'd volunteered to be a scourger at Macquarie Harbour so that he might have better rations and lighter duties and that he should be the first one to die on account of his treachery.'

'You all agreed?'

'We were starving, sir. We had even roasted our kangaroo coats and eaten them and were getting weaker by the day. We were also afraid of Greenhill and Travers.'

'How so?'

'They were together . . .'

The good reverend's sharp ear missed nothing. 'Together?'

'They were close, in all ways, and we feared if we refused to take Dalton, they might have turned on the rest of us.'

'So you are telling me that Greenhill and Travers were the instigators of this murderous act.'

'Yes sir.'

'Dalton was your friend, wasn't he?'

I frowned for theatrical effect, and having carefully laid the ground, told my first lie. Dead men tell no secrets. 'I met him on the deck of the *Duke of York* that brought us from Hobart to Macquarie Harbour and I cut the Queen's English with him on occasion afterwards as we were assigned to the same work gang, but we were not really friends as such.'

'Tell me how you killed Dalton,' asked Knopwood, laying a trap with his carefully chosen words, but I saw him coming.

'It happened while I was away collecting firewood. I heard a terrible scream coming from the direction of our camp. By the time I'd returned Dalton had been killed by several blows to the head with the axe.'

'Who administered the fatal blows?' pressed the reverend.

'I was later told by those who witnessed it that it was Greenhill, sir.'

'Did you eat him?'

'Not right away. Most of us were too shocked at the murder and did not partake. Only Greenhill and Travers ate Dalton's flesh on the first night.'

'What did they eat first?' asked Knopwood, unable to repress his fascination for the gruesome details.

'His heart and kidneys.'

'Did you eat any part of him?'

'The next morning Greenhill forced us to partake of his flesh, saying that everyone must be implicated in the deed so that no one would confess if we were caught.'

'Who was killed next?'

'Bodenham. Brown and Kennelly being older and fearing they might be next decided to return to Macquarie Harbour and face punishment. I don't know what became of them.' I searched Knopwood's inscrutable face for a reaction or flicker of emotion, but found nothing. His years at the bench had taught him well. He signalled me to continue even though Wells was struggling to keep up with the sprawling narrative.

'How was he killed?'

'We drew lots this time and he accepted his fate calmly. He asked for a moment to make his peace with God and as he bowed his head Greenhill hit him with the axe.'

'You witnessed this?'

'Yes.'

'You partook of his flesh?'

'We all did, again at Greenhill's insistence.'

'This Greenhill chap seems to have had some strange hold over you all,' probed Knopwood.

'It was the axe. We had no other weapons and it became the symbol of his tyranny. Also, he was the only navigator amongst us and we knew that without him we'd wander in ever-decreasing circles until we perished. While he was alive there was always the chance we'd reach the settled districts before we needed to kill again.' I thought I detected a slight shudder pass through the reverend as he pondered this. But perhaps it was only his stones paining him.

'What became of the others?' he continued.

'As we pushed on towards civilisation, our situation became direr and the others were taken one by one. Mather was next to go, then Travers after a snake bit him on the foot. Greenhill and I carried him for some days but when his foot turned black we knew death was near and finished him off.'

Knopwood's expression remained stony, even in the face of the mounting horrors.

I continued. 'That left just Greenhill and me. Despite declaring he was my friend and swearing he'd never harm me, he tried to take me on numerous occasions.'

Again, pausing to mop his face which was now flushed, Knopwood prodded me towards the end of my story. 'So you prevailed in the end.'

'I did sir. We remained without sleep for three days until, finally, he charged me and I had no choice but to defend myself. I killed him with his axe. Shortly afterwards I reached the settled districts where I was captured by Churton and Davis who brought me along with them.' I thought I'd best keep old Paddy Maguire out of it.

'Is that your testimony?'

'It is, sir.'

'And do you swear by Almighty God that it is a full and true account of what happened?'

'I do sir,' I said crossing myself for good measure, a gesture that caused Knopwood to purse his thin lips.

'You do realise Brown and Kennelly made it back to Macquarie Harbour?' Knopwood peered closely at me, eager to see if my face betrayed me. Even though I was an accomplished liar, I was able to shake my head truthfully.

'Is there anything you wish to add in light of this information?' he cautioned me.

I shook my head again, feigning indifference, though my heart was beating out a wild tattoo in my ribcage. *What if they'd concocted a story to clear themselves and damn the rest of us?* Whatever his physical frailties, Knopwood was a skilled interrogator.

He made me wait a long minute in that hot, airless room before again pursing his lips. 'Neither mentioned any such gory deeds before they died of exhaustion. How do you account for that?'

'I can't say, sir. Maybe, as they were party to the death of Dalton, they were afraid they might be tried and hanged in the event they survived.'

Knopwood fixed me with gimlet eyes as he weighed up my answer. A bead of sweat appeared on his brow and the reverend again mopped it up with a shaky hand.

'Where exactly did all these killings take place?'

'I couldn't rightly say, sir. We had no compass and as far as I know the area between Macquarie Harbour and the settled districts around Jericho where we emerged has never been charted and only a few of the landmarks have been named. The best I can say is that the bodies rest somewhere in that general area.'

'Could you find them again?'

'I don't believe I could, sir.'

Knopwood opened his mouth, but then thought the better of it. He looked down at his feet and ruminated for a long moment before speaking. The vast oak-panelled room was silent except for the scratching of Wells' pen.

'You can see my difficulty, can't you Pearce?' he said loudly, as much for Wells' benefit as mine. 'Your record shows that you are a seasoned liar and thief. You appear out of thin air with this diabolic tale of foul play and cannibalism that would put the bard himself in the shade and there is not a scrap of evidence to support it.'

'Except that there are five convicts unaccounted for,' interjected Wells. He received a most poisonous, slit-eyed stare from the good reverend and fell silent again.

Watching the two men during my confession, it was obvious Knopwood didn't believe my tale and Wells clearly did. Without doing Wells the courtesy of asking him whether he had any questions, the reverend stood with some difficulty, leaning heavily on his stick. His mouth twisted into a tight grimace and he said slightly breathlessly, 'That will do for now, Pearce.' Turning to Wells, regarding with some distaste his ink-stained fingers, he added pointedly, 'Bid the lieutenant-governor a good day. His Excellency can rest assured he will have my legal opinion within the week.'

With that, Knopwood hurried back to his mansion up on the headland at Battery Point where he would recline on his private commode, or 'seat of ease' as it was known, to impatiently await the arrival of the good doctor and his faithful *bougie*.

Days and weeks passed, but no one summoned me to court to answer for my crimes. Finally, Bisdee put me out of my misery early in April. Late one night he came to my cell door, his world-weary face cast in a sinister light by the yellow, foul-smelling oil lamp he held aloft.

'You're in the clear.'

'Really?' I said feigning disbelief.

'I never jest about matters of life and death, not in my line of work,' he retorted; it was the first edge of annoyance I'd ever heard in his voice.

Startled by this news I pressed him further. 'How did you come by this information?'

Bisdee paused while he fixed himself a pipe and only once he had the smoke billowing about him did he continue. 'I was present while a panel of eminent gentleman discussed your case. There were just three present: the Colonial Surgeon, Dr James Scott, Reverend Knopwood and myself. Given the controversial nature of your confession, which is already the talk of the colony, Knopwood thought it prudent to take soundings from other senior members of the administration.'

'What was said?' I asked and closed my eyes, trying to picture the scene as Bisdee narrated it.

'When I entered the room Knopwood and Scott were midway through a circular and very acrimonious debate that had been raging between them for some time.'

'Scott? I don't think I know him,' I murmured, so Bisdee drew a picture with words for me.

'Large-boned, rambunctious fellow with rosy cheeks and a full head of unruly fair hair. The surgeon is on the wrong side of forty, portly and unattractive both corporally and in character. His fading prospects of matrimony in England have dwindled even further here where the belles can have their pick of suitors. The crushing regret that he would leave no heirs, nor found a dynasty, has unleased an acerbic wit which he hones on those around him. Regrettably for Knopwood, their respective professions bring them into regular contact. As I took my chair Knopwood was booming at Scott, "Science cannot explain everything, you know."

'"Neither can God, Reverend, otherwise why are we all

billeted in this godforsaken place?" shot back the surgeon. As might be expected, the man of God and the man of science don't see eye to eye on temporal matters.

'Not wishing to be distracted from the task at hand, Knopwood ended the debate by taking up the papers before him and shuffled them noisily to bring the meeting to order. "Let's turn our minds to the matter of convict 102, Alexander Pearce. Having read the statements from the arresting officer and Pearce's own account, is it your opinion that he butchered and ate his fellow escapees in the manner he described to me?"

'"Yes, it is," said the surgeon, without hesitation.

'"Well, I'm afraid I have to demure, Doctor. I found it a somewhat fanciful tale," retorted Knopwood, "he's probably covering for his five merry mates who are most likely roaming the backwoods as we speak."

'They both turned and looked at me. It seemed I held the casting vote, but Knopwood, wise to the ways of government, the law and the world, didn't intend me to be the sole arbiter. He wanted a unanimous vote, so no blame could be later attached to him if the decision was challenged. Nonetheless, I had my say.

'"Perhaps if he'd confessed to eating one man out of terrible desperation I would be more inclined to believe it, but five men? His tale brings to mind the vampires of ancient Greece. What would have possessed him to eat five men?"

'"The Devil perhaps?" ventured Surgeon Scott mischievously, "I've heard convicts say that there's a dark unsettling atmosphere in those forests and it's inciting the violent behaviour at Macquarie Harbour."

'"Stuff and nonsense!" retorted Knopwood.

'Scott, showing off his education and reading barked, "Was it not Saint Augustine who told us that angels and demons walk the earth and sometimes inhabit a single soul? Perhaps Pearce is such a soul."

'Knopwood exhaled wearily, "Indeed, it was Saint Augustine, Doctor, and as a man of the cloth I understand only too well the struggle between good and evil for possession of men's souls but I can summon neither to testify to that in a court of law. If possession by the Devil were ever to be a valid defence, the entire English legal system would collapse in a heap. I don't think Pearce is possessed by anything other than a penchant for tall tales, which men of science would do well not to credit."

'That barb caused Scott to puff up in indignation, but it was a moot point as neither could prove their position. The reverend and the surgeon glared at each other, their mutual antagonism so great that they failed to realise that each was now arguing the other's point. But the surgeon wouldn't be outdone. In his booming baritone he said, "My dear reverend, so long as the convicts are content to eat each other we should not worry too much, but if their palates crave finer cuts then perhaps we should take a keener interest."

'Scott's tomfoolery drew a shrill appeal from Knopwood who made clear his irritation. "Gentlemen, please. I have a report to complete for the lieutenant-governor and I don't think a wild, preternatural tale is what his Excellency wishes to hear."

'Seeking to steer the conversation back to the issue at hand, I asked Scott, "As a medical man, what do you make of Pearce's claim of cannibalism?"

'"I can't say I know much about it," he said to me, "but I've met several missionary types who have encountered cannibal tribes in New Zealand and the Pacific Islands. They observed that the practice is usually linked to various tribal ceremonies, customs and rituals of war such as eating one's slain enemies.

One Pacific tribe is even known to eat their dead." A shocked silence descended on the panel and Knopwood, his weakened constitution close to revolt, moaned and placed his handkerchief to his mouth. "For God's sake man," he rasped into his lace gag, but Scott ignored his distress and continued unabashed in the same matter-of-fact tone.

'"They also observed that a small number of cannibals actually came to savour the taste of human flesh."

'My ears pricked up at this information. "Is it possible that men can acquire a taste for human flesh?" I asked. Scott, delighted to show off his medical experience, started to wave his hands around in excitement. "Any man who has spent time at sea knows that rodents will gnaw through steel plates to gain entry to the 'dead room' and once they've devoured the cadavers will turn on each other in a frenzy of bloodlust."

'Knopwood, now thoroughly bored of the surgeon's grandiosity and the macabre nature of the discussion, cut him off in mid flow. "Do you mean to tell me that you regard humans as having the same characteristics as rodents?"

'Scott squirmed in his chair, realising that he'd strayed beyond the safe boundaries of accepted wisdom and that outside the medical profession such notions were akin to heresy. In trying to salvage the situation, he only dug a deeper hole for himself. "No . . . no. But, ehm . . . by studying them we might learn something about our own behaviour," he stammered.

'"Science certainly has some very strange notions," chided Knopwood with a note of triumph in his voice and turned away from Scott whose face had become an interesting shade of puce with the effort of suppressing his rage. "God gives men good blood or bad blood, it's as simple as that Doctor," cautioned Knopwood. "Science, whatever that is, will only conclude what we already know: that God created the earth and all the characters who inhabit it."

'Knopwood stared hard at the surgeon, daring him to challenge the accepted order of things publicly. Science and blasphemy had always trod a very fine line and whatever his private views, Scott knew that it would never do for the colonial surgeon to doubt the existence of God.

'I asked, "Is it possible Pearce ate the fellows he escaped with?"

'Knopwood shook his head. "Unlikely. His record indicates that he's a scallywag with a string of petty criminal convictions to his name, but has no pretensions to becoming a murdering cannibal. Also, it is well-known that white men do not exhibit the same savage tendencies as our black brethren and would it really do to suggest otherwise?"

'Finally, there was a confluence of opinions predicated on self-preservation and mutual self-interest, the reverend credited with bringing the two streams of thought together. "Other than the dubious currency of his word, what evidence is there that Pearce actually performed these macabre deeds?" he asked.

'"None," admitted the surgeon, a scowl creasing his brow, "but I still think the bastard did partake and he was in it more than he admitted."

'"Candidly gentlemen, to make the charge of murder stick we need a body. If we hang him on the strength of his confession and our collective abhorrence of what we believe he might have done and then his comrades later re-appear from the bush, bedraggled and starved, we may find ourselves climbing the gallows steps," cautioned Knopwood.

'"The reverend has a point," I quickly agreed, happy to defer to Knopwood's considerable experience as chief magistrate. "I must confess that the dubious honour of being the first prison governor in New Holland to be hanged on his own gallows holds little appeal for me."

'The surgeon, also unwilling to risk his neck on a hunch, put his reservations aside and glumly nodded his assent to a common agreement based on jurisprudence rather than wild speculation.

'"Then, whatever our private feelings on the matter, we cannot legally find him guilty," concluded Knopwood smoothly. Hearing no dissenting voices and sensing a consensus close at hand, he pressed on. "So, how do we explain Pearce's sudden confession to the lieutenant-governor?"

'Feeling the discussion swinging back towards his field of expertise, Scott laid his huge palms flat on the desk and used them to lever his large frame into an upright position. "Delirium," he declared imperiously, his medical experience dovetailing at last with the reverend's legal expertise.

'"That's it," I cried, gratefully seizing the medic's simple, catch-all explanation with both hands.

'Knopwood paused as he peered out of the window to the ghostly outline of the scaffold waiting patiently to be put to work. But he knew Alexander Pearce wouldn't be treading its boards, not next Monday at any rate. Turning away from the window, he neatly completed the doctor's line of thought. "It's a simple case of a convict becoming unhinged during a long and difficult transit through the wilderness. Isolation, hunger, cold and disorientation are known to do strange things to the mind. Why else would he confess to committing murders that could never be proven?"

'"Undoubtedly," confirmed the surgeon, vigorously nodding his assent.

'"And whether we believe he's a fantasist or a cannibal, we

can at least agree that Macquarie Harbour is the best place for him. His condition is nothing that a spell in heavy irons and rigorous adherence to the Protestant work ethic won't fix," I added.

'"Especially a troublesome Irish Catholic," observed the surgeon dryly.

'Knopwood ignored the medic's flippant remark and nib poised over his paper said in a firm tone, "So we're all agreed, then?"

'"Aye," said Surgeon Scott.

'"Aye," said I.

'"Good, a unanimous verdict,' sighed Knopwood, grateful to have concluded this tricky matter satisfactorily.'

Crossing himself Bisdee added, 'You've the luck of the Devil Alec and no mistake.'

I nodded, but gave no weight to his words. Luck had nothing to do with it. I'd played what is known amongst card sharpers as a 'double blind'. They could've hanged me easily for highway robbery and sheep-stealing, but then I admitted to something much worse. In their haste to investigate the more shocking allegation of cannibalism, they'd overlooked the other charges. 'A lie well stuck to is as good as the truth,' as the old proverb goes.

No such doubts foreshadowed the verdicts against Churton and Davis. The jury returned a unanimous 'guilty' verdict when both appeared in court on 27 February 1823, charged with highway robbery, stealing five-hundred sheep and Davis having unlawful carnal knowledge of the farmer's daughter. Chief Justice Pedder had no hesitation in donning the black cap.

Six weeks later, on Monday 14 April, they went to their

deaths just after first light. From my cell window on the upper floor, which afforded me a view of Macquarie Street, I watched throngs of people arriving to witness the spectacle. It was supposed to be a deterrent to other would-be transgressors but instead it had become a theatre of the macabre. For many of the wretched creatures being hanged, their execution day offered a rare moment of public sympathy and a chance to repent, but for others like Churton and Davis, who chose to go out like martyred heroes, it offered a stage where they might perform.

I heard them shuffling down the gloomy passageways for the last time. Even on Judgement Day they ignored the entreaties of the portly Reverend Conolly, who was struggling to keep step with them, still urging them to make peace with God before they faced Judgement.

Some die flash, some die weeping, but those boys died shouting. Churton roared out, 'We've no need of your God where we're going! We've lived the life and now we're Hell-bound!'

'It's the fortune of war!' yelled Davis.

The other prisoners cheered loudly as they passed by. I raised a hand in salute as I caught a brief glimpse of them as they flitted in and out of the shadows, at the point of a bayonet. 'Live long Alec,' called Churton in a strong voice, each word booming down the passageways like bullets out of a gun. Though I couldn't see the gallows from my cell I could still hear everything clearly. Even as the church clock struck nine o'clock the two of them were still determined to 'die hard', as we say in criminal cant, or without showing remorse, as ordinary folk would say. The law dictates that the hangman must wait until the last chime has gone before pulling the lever, just in case our troubled lieutenant-governor felt moved to reprieve them, though given the recent scandalous court case surrounding his marital arrangements, this seemed extremely unlikely.

In 1817 Sorell succeeded Lieutenant-Colonel Thomas Davey, or 'Mad Tom' as he was dubbed by the convict class, as lieutenant-governor of Van Diemen's Land. He arrived at Sydney accompanied by four children and a woman he introduced as his wife to Governor and Mrs Macquarie. However, the Macquaries knew her not as Mrs Sorell but Mrs Louisa Kent, wife of Lieutenant William Kent of Cape Town whose acquaintance they had made some years previously. Evidently, Sorell had used his prerogative as an English gentleman to leave his real wife, Harriet, and their seven children behind in England.

Sorell and Louisa lived together in Hobart and in company Sorell referred to Mrs Kent as 'my wife', which was surely a denigration of just about every commandment in the Holy Bible. The scandal came to a head when the London *Times* reported that the unsuspecting Lieutenant Kent had returned from South Africa to discover he'd been cuckolded and sought redress in court.

Sorell, unable to travel to London to defend his good name, was forced to follow the progress of his own trial in the newspapers, along with the rest of the colony. He was found guilty in his absence of indulging in 'criminal conversation' with Mrs Kent, as the judge so colourfully put it. The Colonial Office ordered him to pay Lieutenant Kent £3000 by way of reparation, an enormous sum for a man whose yearly stipend was only £800. It also added insult to injury by seeming to put a monetary value on Mrs Kent's virtue.

The verdict was also grist to the Hobart capitalists whose attempts to corner lucrative new markets had been thwarted by Sorell. They instigated a humiliating investigation into his 'moral character', which revealed that his real wife and children had ended up in the poorhouse in England. This rendered his position untenable and resulted in his recent recall to London.

His Excellency was evidently not in a forgiving mood because after only five merry chimes they pulled the lever, thereby ending Churton and Davis's noisy bravado with an awful crash.

I imagined that like Allen, Hudson and Oates they'd dropped out of sight and danced on air for a few moments before they dangled.

An awful hush came over the crowd.

It was done. The message that a reign of rape and plunder earns but one reward had been duly dispatched to the public. I could hear the crowd dispersing quietly, but I knew their respect for the recently departed would only last until they reached the nearest tavern.

They would all be back again next Monday, execution day in Hobart.

Some hours later Bisdee came down to see me in the cells, a mix of wonder and bemusement writ large across his sombre face.

'Was it clean?' I asked.

He nodded. 'Old Solomon is very thorough.'

He gave me a penetrating stare, as though trying to discern what lay on the inside of me. At last he spoke. 'By rights, you should've been out there kicking the clouds with them.'

To draw attention from the blind that had saved my neck I gave them a tit-bit. As no further retribution could be visited on Davis or Churton, I didn't judge it a betrayal to tell Bisdee about the informant they'd murdered.

He returned a week later with news that a patrol had found

the man's skeleton still tied to the tree. I nodded but Bisdee still stood there. He had more to tell.

'It seems there's still a ten-quid reward for information leading to his whereabouts.'

I shook my head. 'Money's no good to me in Macquarie Harbour. See that it's paid in the name of Private Alexander Dalton late of the 64th Regiment of Foot. He'll have a grieving mother somewhere in Ireland. The army will know where to send it.' *Not quite the Biblical twelve pieces of silver, but I'd owed Dalton my life and taken his instead.*

Bisdee nodded, unsure what to make of my generous gesture. Maybe he was wondering whether cannibals are still capable of normal feelings.

Chapter 16

A Return to Hell

Hell's Gates, Macquarie Harbour, 26 May 1823

IT WAS MY FATE to be returned to Macquarie Harbour. I felt a distinct sense of *déjà vu* as I slipped through Hell's Gates again, this time on calmer waters with the pilot ship *Waterloo*, commanded by the pilot, James Lucas, pulling us through on a line.

I was greeted on the jetty by Commandant Cuthbertson in full military dress clutching the infamous Black Book, his trademark sneer spread across his face. When a man has been pushed beyond his limits, terrified out of his wits, stared down death and much worse, it alters his character. He no longer fears the things he once feared or their vengeance.

'Mr Pearce, you have a rare talent for escaping punishment,' he chided. 'First, you took advantage of the lieutenant-governor's amnesty and now, despite confessing to murdering and eating your comrades, you again escape sanction.'

I kept my head down and said nothing.

'Truth be told, I didn't think you had it in you.'

'Appearances can be deceptive. It's not what a man says,

but what he does that counts,' I muttered.

'I doubt we'll ever know what you did out there,' he countered smoothly.

I shrugged, 'I made a full confession to Reverend Knopwood.' I caught the sly look in his eye and thought to myself, *The bastard's got something up his sleeve.*

'If it's any consolation, I believe you,' Cuthbertson confided.

'Why?'

'Because of what Brown and Kennelly brought back with them.'

I looked up and noting the glimmer of curiosity in my eyes he taunted me further. 'Don't you want to know what they brought back with them?'

I shrugged, but Cuthbertson was determined to have his sport. Taking a few steps closer, he smirked and said, 'Brown carried half a pound of flesh all the way back with him in his trouser pocket. Just before he died, he declared that it was a piece of Dalton.'

'Could've been a piece of an animal.'

'Could've been,' admitted Cuthbertson before delivering the *coup de grâce*, 'except that Dr Spence identified it as belonging to the upper arm of a man. The lump of flesh which, as you might imagine stank to high heaven, still had a strip of skin attached to it bearing a pockmark like the ones on your face.'

I regarded him coolly. 'Maybe you should've investigated the matter yourself.'

'Maybe I should.'

'Go on, fill your boots, but without the bodies, you'll never get a murder charge past a judge,' I shot back defiantly.

Cuthbertson knew I was right, though his cruel sneer would never allow me the satisfaction of seeing him concede even a single point.

'Why didn't you tell Knopwood?' I challenged him.

'Because the old fool had already handed down his judgement and if I'd cut across him I'll be stuck here 'til doomsday.' He stared me out, curling up his top lip like a snake before it strikes. 'What you did isn't natural,' he hissed.

'Oh, but it was,' I admonished him. 'Survival is the most natural thing in the world. When pressed, a man will cling to life with every inch of his being.' Pushing myself up on my toes, so I could look Cuthbertson straight in the eye, I delivered my parting shot. 'He'll do anything to survive . . . anything.'

We looked at each other hard for a long moment. I was determined not to yield as I had so often before. In those flinty grey eyes I saw the faintest glimmer of surprise at my insolence, but he broke the spell by glancing down at the Black Book and giving a cruel little chuckle. 'Poor old Bobby. In his haste he forgot to punish you for absconding from a penal colony. It would never do if you were allowed to escape punishment. It might set a bad example. The tariff for bush travelling is a 'canary' and six months in irons, the first on Grummet Island. That ought to balance the books.' With that he leaned in so close I caught the spicy scent of dark rum on his breath. 'Watch yourself Mr Pearce,' he growled.

I was taken directly to the 'iron triangle' where I copped a 'canary' from John Flynn, the most that could be given in one serve.

Then my shattered back and I were transferred to Grummet Island, the address at which all turbulent and permanently bad characters worthy of the moniker the 'out and outers' resided.

Like Sarah Island it had been named by Captain James Kelly. In nautical terms a grummet was a small metal ring set into a sail, but was also cant for a quim. Given its oval shape and the long split that ran across one side of the island, I could see that it could be taken either way. Naturally, we convicts favoured the latter interpretation, speculating that perhaps it reminded Captain Kelly of Sarah's quim and joking that it was 'a cunt of a place to be sent to'. From all I'd seen and heard, they weren't wrong.

Once ashore, my back was cleaned by the new surgeon, Henry Crockett, recently arrived to work in the hospital and help Dr Spence. I was then put in heavy irons. I had to drag around an ankle bracelet weighing some fifty pounds like those wretched souls we saw the first day we arrived. All but four of the forty men on Grummet Island were similarly attired.

Not for nothing was this known as the 'small island'. Just forty yards long and eight wide, it commanded no more than an acre of ground and was little more than a rock, rising just fifty feet above the level of the sea. In bad weather, when ferocious gales blew in from the north-west, the surf often broke over it with such violence that the water almost covered the summit where all its inhabitants were forced to seek shelter in the hospital and gaol-house. Like Sarah Island it had been stripped of all vegetation, the trees being used to construct the buildings. The ground was covered in weeds and rank grass, and where there was any soil a few stunted, persistent shrubs struggled to grow.

The routine, rations and living conditions were also harsher on Grummet Island, its inhabitants forced to survive on half-rations of only one and a quarter pounds of bread per day washed down with water only. There was no salted meat or vegetables.

I quickly discovered that my terrible reputation had preceded me: mud sticks whether the charge is proven or not. I was an object of lurid fascination to be stared at and commented upon, but I also quickly noted that no one would meet my gaze, perhaps for fear of what they would see there. Men, who'd previously paid me scant regard, looked at me with a new respect. No white man had ever made it alive through this hostile country. I'd risked all and survived while fifteen others had perished. One gaping convict even shook my hand and told me that I'd 'prised open Hell's Gates'. For once, the wee man had done what big men couldn't and I was now considered to be as big as any of them. It was powerful knowledge, something unspoken, instinctive, which the other convicts, who knew every subtle nuance, picked up on. They sensed it in my walk and could see it written across my face and in my eyes, as though I carried a sign around my neck.

As usual our days began with a pint and a half of skilly, the hasty pudding composed of flour, water and salt. The unruly souls not allotted work on Sarah Island were ordered to row to a place of work, which was varied often and without warning to prevent the hatching of escape plots. To further frustrate our scheme of carrying off boats, we were transported in light whaleboats, not robust enough for the open seas, with two soldiers as a guard to discourage any who might try.

Our labours over, we pulled ourselves back to our cheerless home, often in bad weather. There was no landing stage on the island, so five yards from shore we were ordered over the side. Up to our middles in water, we had to wade back to shore dragging our heavy irons over boulders and through soft sand. Having no change of clothes, we spent the nights in wet clothing shivering on the rocky floors of our rough stone cells, which made the punishment doubly worse.

These 'cells' were just fissures in the base of the rock close to the shoreline, created by those great architects of nature, the wind and waves. Using primitive digging tools the prisoners had enlarged them over time, their names, dates, dreams and fears all carved into their stone walls.

These crude apartments already boasted a short but bloody history known and feared by the entire convict population. There was a dark recess on the southern side of the islet known as 'Murderer's Cave' on account of the men who'd been murdered and thrown into it. A jib in the guts was how they settled arguments here. Spatters of blood could still be seen on the rocks where some poor unfortunate recently met his fate.

Those turbulent characters deemed too dangerous to ever be returned to Sarah Island kept their distance from we temporary residents and with their long hair, Biblical beards and ragged clothes they resembled a colony of hermits.

I noted that one of them had taken a strange interest in me. I'd catch him watching me when I was eating or having a brief warm at the fire and often he'd follow me whenever I wandered across the rocks, always careful to keep a good distance between us.

I asked George Lacey, a long-term resident described as a 'constant stimulus to bad spirits', who he was.

'Oh him,' he said casually, raising his thick eyebrows, 'that's Jack Barclay, or "Jack the Lad" as we call him. He absconded into the woods with two others just after you left but returned alone four weeks later half-dead from thirst and starvation and hasn't spoken barely a word since, just sits around staring into space. You'll hear his screams at night as though he's battling with some unspeakable demons.'

It sounded familiar. I nodded grimly and pressed further, 'What became of the other two?'

'They searched, but found no trace of them.'

'Has he said anything at all?'

'Oh, he peers through his hands, shrugs his shoulders, cocks his head as if listening to something, but that's about it. Dr Spence said the strain of hunger, thirst, fear and isolation of the senses sends many men out of their minds. Most likely they wandered off and the blacks got 'em.'

I nodded and noted that he didn't ask me what became of my mates, but that's convict etiquette. You never ask another man's name or business, you wait 'til you're told.

There had been few serious escape attempts since my return. Cuthbertson had stopped all the crapulous old practices like freebooting, and any stores or materials that might aid an escape were strictly controlled in an accounting ledger, which he personally checked at the end of each week to ensure they tallied. For this reason water and wood to the 'small island' were also strictly rationed. We never held more than two days' supply of water at a time in case of a revolt. In such an event the commandant could cut the supply, forcing the rebels to quickly surrender or perish. Only the worst wood was sent here because it didn't float. If it had that quality, it would have been made into rafts.

But there exists such a degree of careless desperation that they built all manner of craft from the most unlikely of materials. During my month here the three men whose onerous task it was to empty the privy pots lashed them together to make a raft and took to the open sea. Not surprisingly, their cumbersome craft broke up and all hands were lost.

A second party, who constructed a raft from two water casks, a night tub, and a small portion of a water closet, also met a similar fate. To deter further escape attempts the water casks were set into rock and the night vessels were made instead from iron tar barrels, cut through the middle.

There were so many shambolic escape attempts because it was deemed too dangerous to post a military guard on Grummet Island so we were left under the sole control of overseers of our own class. One of the well-conducted prisoners, a tyrant known as Constable Rex, aided by Constable Grew, reported any misconduct and guarded us, their reward being better rations and a room in the gaol-house. As on Sarah Island, physical punishment was the principal method of control, though it had a more medieval character here.

Bolters or those meriting special punishment were crammed into narrow, windowless solitary confinement cells barely as long as a grave and with a roof so low that the prisoner could not stretch out or sit up. Such was the intense feeling of discomfort and near suffocation that men could be imprisoned there for a maximum of two days at a time – long enough to unhinge the minds of some. I'd also heard it said that there was a water pit in the bowels of Grummet Island. Left naked and in the dark, the only sound they could hear was rushing water as the tide came in and they spent the entire stretch in constant fear of drowning.

These innovations were a perversion of one of Jeremy Bentham's theories that deprivation of the senses was a more effective deterrent than physical punishment, except here they used it *as well as* physical punishment.

For more persistent offenders for whom the lash and the isolation no longer held any fears, there was a lower circle of damnation. Grummet Island housed a torture chamber of medieval pedigree where all manner of torments were inflicted upon poor convicts by our deranged and syphilitic commandant who continued to dose himself with mercury and romp with his whore. We discovered this the day Cuthbertson visited the island in a foul mood. It had been reported to him that morning that the first crop planted on Sarah Island – wheat and potatoes – had failed. This was another cruel setback on top of the discovery that the surface coal deposits that promised a rich yield were of such a low grade that they couldn't even be used to fuel the island's fires in winter. His plan to make the colony self-sufficient in basic food items was coming apart.

If we Irish know anything, it's potatoes. The heavy soil had retained so much moisture during the persistently wet winter that all the promising green shoots that poked through the ground during the first few months turned black and rotted in the ground. Cuthbertson would now have to ask Sorell for additional wheat supplies and buy potatoes from the pilot, James Lucas, who had managed to grow them successfully on the lighter, better-drained soil out at the heads, which only added to his chaff.

He disliked the ambitious pilot who seemed to prosper in his every endeavour while his own floundered. Lucas had also started harvesting whales for their oil using his pilot boat and crew to catch them, and the supply ships to send his ever-growing harvest back to Hobart.

Cuthbertson's as yet unnamed ship was his last great hope. I had often seen him gazing at the half-completed vessel with a far-away look in his eye. I noted as I came into Sarah Island that the hull was now enclosed and the deck was being laid. Cuthbertson wanted it launched before Christmas, the second anniversary of the island's foundation. Surely that would earn him a promotion he so craved and a posting away from this sink.

Cuthbertson's mood was as dark and unpredictable as the skies over the harbour and as was his wont he ordered six residents, including me, to accompany him on his tour. It was mostly a routine inspection of the hospital, the books and the stores, but when we entered the gaol-house we were shown through an unfamiliar doorway and the reason for our presence became clear.

By the light of flaming torches we followed a natural path into one of the many caverns that honeycombed this rock. Cuthbertson had furnished it with a small collection of medieval devices manufactured on Sarah Island to his precise specifications.

He was a bastard of a man and that's the best that can be said of him, but he knew that the best method of controlling the 'out and outers' was by terror, namely the gag, the cradle and the globe. I recalled Mordecai Cohen telling me that the word 'torture' is taken from the French word *torquere*, which means to twist, and how it had taxed the perverted ingenuity of man for centuries.

The cavern consisted of three small caves, one leading through to the other. Like some circus of the bizarre we watched by the light of the torch as a naked man in the first room writhed about on the floor with a gag of wood shoved halfway down his throat, held in place by a black leather strap. As we climbed over loose scree into the next cavern, we saw another convict who'd been rolled into a ball and imprisoned in a spherical-shaped metal girdle that could be progressively tightened at the discretion of his torturers.

In the last room was Cuthbertson's *pièce de résistance,* the so-called 'Judas Cradle'. A naked man, who I recognised as Joseph Armstrong, a persistent escapee and long-time resident on the rock, was balanced on the apex of a wooden pyramid with the help of two ropes suspended from hooks driven into the roof. Knotted muscles stood out on his arms, which trembled with fatigue, and sweat drenched his body from head to toe. Soon, he would tire and lose his balance, which would result in a painful 'maritime entry', as any invasion of the back passage was known, seafarers being none too fussy where they found their pleasure.

'With some men, the body and the spirit must be broken before they come to heel,' was the only explanation offered. Cuthbertson still had the inquisitor's zeal and his sadism, checked by school and his strict Protestant upbringing, had been liberated by the military, Spain and Macquarie Harbour. They allowed him to indulge those 'unnatural tastes' remarked upon in his military record, which out of the reach of courts and judges could be justified as 'necessary rigour'. This little palace of pain would have gladdened the heart of the late Marquis de Sade.

As I watched Cuthbertson end his tour of inspection and step back into the whaleboat, an unfamiliar voice from behind me said, 'Nothing will ever prosper in this accursed place.'

I turned around and saw 'Jack the Lad'. I looked at him questioningly, but he just stared back at me in his usual blank way. *Had he spoken or had I imagined it?* The ghosts of my past had stopped visiting me at night but the old terrors that had afflicted this colony from the beginning flared up again.

A week or so after Cuthbertson's visit, we were woken by the bell one grey Tuesday morning. But instead of its usual sleepy hollow tone, the bell clanged more loudly and urgently, immediately alerting us that something was wrong.

We rushed outside to discover the short dumpy silhouette of Mr Shaunessey, who looked after the hospital, up on the summit ringing the bell frantically. Next to him was a flaming pyre which, aided by the heavy rain, was sending a curling black spiral into the lightening sky. Someone had been killed.

From my vantage point overlooking the sandy cove where

the boats landed, I could make out the familiar overweight frame of Constable Rex lying face down in the shallows of the inlet, small white-crested waves breaking over his back. There was a half-circle of scuffed sand around him and footprints leading up the beach where his nine murderers sat silently above the high-tide mark. Some had their heads bowed and the sound of soft sobbing carried over to us on the breeze. I recognised them all: William Jenkins, James Kirk, Samuel Measures, John McGuire, John McMillan, James Reid, John Ward and John Williams. I also picked out George Lacey's big woolly black head amongst them.

They were awaiting the arrival of the whaleboat full of soldiers, which was already halfway across the channel from Sarah Island, their bright red tunics the only splash of colour in this bleak picture of human folly. Over the sound of the wind and breaking waves, Sergeant Waddy's booming Welsh baritone urgently called, 'Pull boys, pull, pull!' Two riflemen were crouched at the bow, guns at the ready.

'They'll be as dead as mutton a month from now, nothing's surer,' said a voice behind me. I whipped around to find 'Jack the Lad' at my shoulder. *He spoke. I wasn't hearing things.*

Glancing around casually to ensure that no one else was within earshot he continued, 'While you were sleeping they tried to get away on a raft.'

'Where did they get it from?'

'Oh, they've been building it on the quiet for the past few months from scavenged driftwood and kept it hidden down at Murderer's Cave. No one goes near there lest they be killed.' He saw the question forming on my lips and showed me a row of rotting, baccy-stained teeth, 'Oh, I see everything. No one pays Jack no heed. I'm mad, you know,' he chortled, pulling a theatrical face and tapping his scabrous forehead with a dirty finger.

'Where were they headed?'

'They had great plans, oh yes. They intended to sail it to Sarah Island, use the element of surprise to overpower the military guards and liberate all the prisoners. Then, crewed by fellow convicts, they would take to the open sea in the supply ship that docked yesterday.'

'What happened?'

'The first part of it went alright. They overpowered the cooks, Cock and Henley, the hutkeeper, Shaunessey, and Constables Grew and Rex and left them tied up on the beach. But the raft wouldn't support the lot of them and broke up in the choppy waters, forcing them to swim back to the island. After spending the night huddled on the shore they were confronted at first light by Rex who freed himself and made his way down to the beach. He ranted, threatened them with all manner of terrible punishment and ordered them to surrender.

'One of them, I couldn't see who, Lacey I think, shouted back that they'd never come to heel for the likes of him and he'd rather stand on the gallows than serve his like. His stirring words seemed to get some of them riled up and they knocked Rex down, dragged him to the shore, and though he pleaded very hard to be spared they pushed him under the water and held him down 'til he drowned in plain view of the other captives.'

'Christ,' was all I could muster. Even by the standards of Macquarie Harbour, this was serious. We stood and watched in silence as the redcoats beached the whaleboat and ran across the sand, rifles waving in front of them as they shouted for Rex's murderers to stand though they remained sitting quietly in the sand. They formed a ring of red around them while Sergeant

Waddy lumbered down to the shoreline, slowing to a walk when he realised that Rex was long past help and a minute more or less wouldn't make any difference to him now.

'You were out there and you heard it too didn't you,' said Jack flatly.

'It?'

'The voice.'

A chill raised every hair on my body as I realised that it hadn't been a figment of my wayward imagination. Nevertheless I shook my head.

'Is that why you confessed, to get free of it?' he pressed.

Still I said nothing, and in a steadily rising voice, the fear in it palpable, he warned, 'It'll never let you be! It'll drive you back out there to do its terrible bidding.'

Though I felt the shock of his words tingle every nerve in my body, I kept my face straight and replied evenly, 'What voice? I never heard any voices.'

Jack didn't argue, he just held me in his searching stare for a moment or so, nodded, and then turned on his heel. I'd got free of the forest and the voice of my dead da and I didn't want to hear of them ever again. I wasn't even tempted to ask him what became of the two men he escaped with. I knew already. It was a burden he'd have to bear.

The remainder of my thirty days on Grummet Island passed, mercifully, without further incident. Each evening I'd scratch a mark on the wall of my cell and put a line through them when I had a row of five; I now had six groups. Sure enough, the grizzled Sergeant Waddy came ashore and called out, 'Alexander Pearce, convict 102, to the boat. You've got a return ticket!'

I was stationed at the bow facing the little island as the crew stroked me back to Sarah Island. 'Bet you're glad to be off that cold little chip of rock,' boomed Waddy in his cheery Welsh baritone. *Too bloody right*, I thought. Compared to Grummet, Sarah Island was a luxury resort.

As we pulled away from the shady overhang of the sea cliffs into the open waters, I saw someone standing up above, watching. Though his outline was black against the sun I knew it was Jack Barclay.

Chapter 17

Bloodlust

THERE WAS NO MORE than the usual amount of turbulence you'd expect in a bastard of a place like this, except two of Constable Rex's murderers, Lacey and Ward, were found to have cut through their shackles with a little saw that had been smuggled into the brig. There were said to be as many as fifteen men ready to help them break out, but the plot was foiled and the accused shipped out to Hobart and hanged for murder, adding further lustre to Macquarie Harbour's horrid celebrity.

After my grim little cameo on Grummet Island I was put back on the logging under the supervision of Constable Logan who had not forgotten the circumstances of our last meeting. 'Ye're back, ye wee fucker, as I knew you would,' he hissed.

'Nice to see you again Constable Logan,' I said cheerily, giving him a little knuckled salute like mariners do their captain.

Knowing I was alone with no Dalton or Greenhill to protect me, he gave me a barge in the back, nearly sending me into the freezing water. 'Try anything on my watch and I'll finish ya,' he menaced. Logan pushed his grizzled face close into mine to make the point, but he didn't find the old Pearce there. I felt none of the old terrors, just a flat calm. Instead it was Logan who pulled back, seemingly startled. I don't know what he saw in my eyes, but his parting shot lacked the bluster of old. 'That's your cards marked,' he said rather lamely.

The moment was not lost on the rest of the crew who noted Logan's hesitation. I'd heard it said that I'd butchered and eaten five of my fellow prisoners single-handedly, a yarn that always floundered on the fact that no bodies had been found and I was never charged. It better suited people to believe that my mates were running free as it kept their own precious dreams of escape alive.

The first time I took up the axe a slight tremor ran through the ranks of my fellow loggers, but they needn't have worried. I'd had no desire to partake of human flesh since I'd done for Greenhill, yet my air of mysteriousness made people wary of me. I also noted the surprise in people's eyes when they first met me. I suppose they were expecting a giant not a dwarf, but the scuttlebutt had been repeated so often that it'd taken on the substance of fact and I grew a foot before their very eyes. For a wee man in a place like this, it was a useful insurance policy.

That night in the barracks, curious to test the limits of my new status, I boldly pushed my way to the front and the crowd parted to let me sit by the fire. Even the hard men said nothing. Later, as we lay down to sleep, I found I had enough room for three men. No one was keen to sleep close by me in case I decided on a midnight feast – though they did their best to discourage it. My dinner plate was piled as high as the hard men's, confirming that I'd joined the Aceldama of horrid Sarah Island celebrity.

When it was my turn to wield the axe in the logging crew I

was often partnered with Thomas Cox, a young lad of twenty-three from Shropshire. He seemed a quiet, pleasant-enough sort. He had a head full of blond ringlets such as you'd see on a girl, a slim figure and a handsome, hairless face. I'd heard that he'd been used as a Molly by some of the beasts who were still free to sate their unnatural appetites without hindrance.

At first I assumed he stuck close by me in the evenings because he imagined I might protect him from the abusers, but he seemed fascinated by my transit through Hell. He asked all manner of questions about the nature of the terrain we'd crossed, the direction we'd taken and how many days we'd been out there, but always steered clear of asking what we ate.

One day I said in jest, 'Why all the questions? You planning to make a break for it?'

He went quiet and looked around him. 'What if I was?'

'Then I'd save you the bother by telling you it's a fool's earn.'

He gasped and a cloud passed over his finely appointed features. 'Why do you say that?'

'It's the truth.'

'But you made it through, you proved it could be done.'

'Aye, but I paid a high price for my freedom. Given time back, it's a price I'd never have paid,' I said mysteriously.

'What price was that?'

'When Cuthbertson told you the forest is the prison, he told you true. There's no escaping it, ever.' My riddles were as elusive as a fistful of fog and try as he might, Cox couldn't grasp their meaning.

'So you wouldn't try again?' he pressed.

'No way, boy. I'll see out my time here.'

The Shropshire lad looked a little crestfallen, as though I'd dashed all his dreams, but I didn't want to fill him up with false hope. I nodded at a strongly built man who stood with his back to one of the huts, gazing out to sea. 'If you want out, speak to him. He's the boy.'

'Who is he?'

'Matthew Brady. This place won't hold him.'

Brady was the cock that had arrived to replace Greenhill in my absence. A stocky six-footer from Manchester, he'd already racked up 350 lashes in less than three years for a variety of offences including insubordination and attempting to abscond. An unearthly calm radiated from his striking blue eyes even when all around him was chaos. He was very sure of himself, and with the stature of a prize-fighter he had every reason to be. He never squared his shoulders or took his guard when approached, as most other men do. He just stood his ground with his hands in the pockets of his over-large canary breeches, his eyes narrowed and his bottom lip twisted into a sneer as though he knew something we didn't. Even though he'd worked as a groom back in the Old Dart, Brady could read and write well enough to forge his master's signature on a cheque made out to his own good self. He was spared the rope and sent here instead.

He seemed to know that Cox was planning to make a break for it. One evening as we sat eating our dinner Brady came over. There was no preamble. 'I hear you're away.' It was more of a statement than a question, but Cox nodded anyway. He must have assumed that we were going off together because he gave Cox a queer look as if to say, *Do you know what you're doing*? but never opened his trap. It didn't pay to concern yourself with the fate of your fellow man on Sarah Island. It was every man for himself.

Brady's sudden interest told me he was hatching an escape plan of his own and was impatient for Cox to be out of the way.

Plots were a way of life here. Never a day went by that we didn't hear tell of some great scheme to liberate us, but like Lacey's they were mostly badly organised and ended in failure and death. I would later look back on this moment and realise that my suspicions about Brady were well-founded, though I could never have guessed the scale of his plans.

Brady ambled away without asking if he could join us, or indicating when he might go himself. He'd go in his own good time, no doubt about that. You could see it in his cocksure stride; it was death or liberty for that boy.

Brady's lack of interest seemed to deflate Cox who said no more about escaping.

Though it seems strange to say it, I found some measure of peace on Sarah Island over the next four or five months. The nocturnal visitations had stopped and I seemed to have outlived my terrors, or so I thought. I felt oddly grateful to be back amongst an ordinary community of men, 'ordinary' compared to recent company. The hubris, the cruelty, the floggings, the starvation, the cold, the unrelenting labour – everything that had prompted me to leave in the first place paled next to the terrible alternative: escape. I tried not to think of the past too much, but in a quiet moment I'd sometimes look out across the still harbour to those forbidding peaks dressed in sullen green and remind myself that however bad life was here, it was infinitely preferable to the living, waking terror of being out there.

Little did I know that my oasis of calm was about to be destroyed. The first inkling should have been the conversation I overheard between Sergeant Waddy and Private O'Donnell at muster one morning.

'That idiot did for himself over on the small island last night,' remarked Waddy.

'What's that?'

'Jack the Lad. Jumped off the cliff. Shaunessey found what was left of him on the beach this morning.'

Another tragic tale in the saga of Macquarie Harbour. The weight of the terrible knowledge Jack carried within him was evidently too much to bear in the end.

It should have been a warning,

I didn't see it coming.

We never do.

We were so far away from Ireland that even the order of the seasons was arse-about-face and the temperature had warmed up considerably as we approached Christmas. The sixteenth day of November was particularly hot and we'd all taken off our shirts while we worked. The harbour like the sky had turned a deep blue and a plunge into the water with the logs was a welcome relief. Even Logan seemed quite contented, smoking his pipe, a mug of strong brew in his hand.

As the sun started to dip behind the trees Logan called time. We gathered up the tools and put them into the boat, but when I went back to get my shirt it was gone. I'd left it on a stump near the first trees we'd cut that day. Everyone else had theirs, either on their backs or in their hands.

'Did any of you pick up my shirt?' I asked. No one spoke, dropping their eyes and leaving me to my fate. We all knew a 'dozen' was the tariff for missing slops. I grabbed the nearest man, a Cornishman by the name of Fulton, and whipped him around.

'What's all this?' he protested.

'Shut up,' I boomed and such was my reputation that he sullenly succumbed. 'I've burned an AP into the reverse-side of my collar. If any of you have got it, speak now because every man jack will be checked before he gets in that boat.' I lifted his collar and found nothing. I worked my way through the ranks, but to no avail.

'Well, well,' rumbled a familiar, mocking voice. I turned around and found Logan leaning against a tree behind me. 'Where's your shirt Pearce?'

He had me cold and he knew it.

'Lost,' I conceded.

His jagged-edged grin reminded me of a can opened with a knife. 'Lost?' he teased, 'perhaps you ate it. I've heard it said you've strange tastes.' Logan paused a moment, and realising his dart hadn't taken effect, tried again. 'Ah well, it'll cost you a bob,' he lamented.

'But the tariff is a dozen,' I protested.

'The extra dozen is for checking me.'

'I've said nothing . . .'

'Oh, but you still owe me. I copped a bull because of you. If you say anything more I'll see you get a canary. Now, get in that fucking boat.'

The Pearce of old would've taken it, but not any more. I bunched my fists and went right at him. 'Bugger you Logan. I'm not taking a single stroke on your account.'

Logan started to back off. 'Lay a hand on me and I'll see you spend the rest of your days on Grummet Island,' he warned.

I didn't hear him. My blood was up and I rammed my first into his soft gut, which took the wind out of him and forced him down on one knee. My second punch found the point of his nose and the third his mouth. The blood started to flow as I put the boot into him.

Suddenly, Cox was beside me stomping Logan's head and back. 'Get back in that boat!' I roared, pushing him backwards with a strength that surprised me.

'Too late for that,' he called, his face flushed with youthful exuberance, 'I'm in it now,' and brought his heel down hard on the cowering constable's back for emphasis.

The six others, certain that my bloodlust had returned, lost themselves in the surrounding woods, leaving the empty whaleboat bobbing invitingly on the gentle waves that lapped onto the shore. Cox glanced at me as I picked up a discarded shirt and slipped it on. 'Forget the boat, we'll go on foot,' I shouted.

'Why? It'll be easier,' moaned Cox.

I whipped round on him. 'With only two in the boat we'd never make it past the heads. By the time we get there they'll be lining up to take pot-shots. Supposing, by some miracle, we did make it to the open sea, do you know the way to Timor or Java? Can you navigate by the stars?'

Cox lowered his eyes. 'Right, let's get on.'.

With me still wearing heavy irons, I had to do a strange duck-waddle into the trees. Once we were clear of the camp we stopped and I used the blunt end of the small hand axe I'd kept to 'oval' or bend the ring of my ankle-fetters and slip them over my heel. Now able to move faster, we concentrated on putting some distance between ourselves and the pursing pack that would surely come after us.

As we headed inland into the dense coastal rainforest, I kept my eye on the position of the sun through the thick green canopy above. It was sinking on my right, Logan was behind us, so straight ahead would take us to the coast.

'Why are we going this way?'

'We're heading to the coast.'

'Why not go north-east as you did before?'

'They'll expect that, and this time they'll come with trackers and kangaroo dogs.'

'Where are we headed?'

'Port Dalrymple.'

'Why there?'

I felt the first prickle of irritation at his incessant questioning. 'We'll get a boat there. Now shut up and save your strength for tramping,' I scolded him.

That night as we chewed on a little mouldy bread that Cox had brought with him, the reality of our situation became clear. 'We've hardly enough food to last another day,' I told him, 'we'll have to find some tomorrow or we'll be in dead trouble.'

Cox, who had a naturally sunny disposition, seemed unperturbed and produced a small packet from his pocket. 'I've got a fish hook, some line, rope, rag and tinder I've been saving. We'll be alright.'

The night chills closed in, forcing us to lie down and curl up close together for warmth as it was too risky to set a fire. There was a stillness about the woods, but it wasn't a peaceful feeling. It was the sort of uneasy silence that prefigured something bad was about to happen.

I spared Logan a cursory thought. I wondered what story he'd concoct for Cuthbertson. The same man had escaped from him twice in just over a year. He'd surely cop a 'canary' this time.

*

On the afternoon of our second day we heard shots, three bangs that ripped through the unearthly quiet of the forests like cannon fire. As we flattened ourselves on the ground my first thought was that the redcoats must be in hot pursuit of us. We lay there, our ears, eyes and every sinew straining to see or hear where the shots were coming from.

A short while later there was a second volley that sounded much closer, but this time we heard familiar voices laughing and joking, Dr Spence's distinctive Highland burr to the fore. I turned to Cox, relief written large across my face and whispered, 'It's not soldiers, it's an officers' hunting party. They go out on their days off to bag fresh meat.'

We crept closer to the source of the noise and from our leafy keep spied Dr Spence, Captain James Lucas and John Douglas, Cuthbertson's secretary and clerk, standing bunched together in a clearing. They were on the trail of something and Lucas pointed to a thick copse just ahead of them. Spence took a large satchel off his shoulder and laid it on the ground.

'There!' cried Lucas, spotting a movement in the undergrowth, and they ran off after it like excited children. Spence half-turned and called back to Douglas, 'Mark this spot. We'll come back for the bag later.'

'Right you are Doctor,' said Douglas dutifully.

He then turned around and seemed to look right at the spot where we were crouched, nodded down at the doctor's bag, then went off after Lucas and Spence. Questions crowded my mind, *Had he seen us? Was he telling us to take the bag? Douglas himself was a convict. Was he helping us or was it a trap?* I could feel Cox's eyes boring into me, waiting for me to speak. 'What'll we do?' he said finally.

'Wait,' I said. A half-hour later we heard distant gunshots, shouts and the sound of bodies crashing through trees. I took the chance to dart out, retrieve the bag and move Cox off in the opposite direction. Once we'd put some distance between us we stopped to examine the contents of our gift bag. In it were a good-sized slab of salted pork and two loaves of yesterday's bread that already had the sour whiff of mould about them.

'Our first bit of good luck,' said Cox cheerfully as he prepared us a good feed, cutting up and laying everything out nicely on flat green leaves just as a woman would do.

'We'll need a hell of a lot more than that,' I grumped. His boyish enthusiasm was beginning to irritate me. He had no idea of the perils that lay ahead of us. I should've taken the 'dozen' for my lost shirt and had done with. I brooded on this and started to resent him. He was young, untutored in the ways of survival in the bush, and now expected me to carry him to safety as a parent would a child. The shine had come off our new-found freedom very quickly.

By the end of the next day, our third on the run, we were confident that there were no pursuers and we could leave the cover of the thick forest. In the late afternoon we emerged on the eastern bank of the harbour. Its salty tang hit me at the back of the throat before I even saw it. On the shore opposite us and a little to the north, we could make out the distinctive horn of Liberty Point, which was regarded by mariners as the halfway point between Sarah Island and Hell's Gates. It was a clear, calm spring day on the harbour and the sun reflected off its flat surface, giving it a dreamy, silvery look. For once the peaks, ridges and thick forests that surrounded it on all sides looked almost benign.

We'd been sitting on a small beach by the water a while,

warming ourselves in the sun, when Cox produced his line and hook from his pocket. He dug around in the soft soil for a worm, stuck it on the end of his hook, cast it into the still waters and blow me over if he didn't snag two of those large, spotted trout-like fish I'd seen in the harbour the first day I'd arrived. As he expertly gutted them he chattered excitedly. 'You see? We'll be right. We'll make it through.'

I just nodded soberly.

Cox produced the tinder and a rag, but I stopped him dead. 'It's still too risky. Even a smudge of smoke could be spotted from Sarah Island or Lucas's cottage. We'll have to eat them raw like them Japanners do.'

Cox looked at the fish then back at me. 'Do they?'

'Oh aye, they prefer it that way, least that's what Bob Greenhill told me.' I regretted mentioning his name in these circumstances. Cox sliced the fish into thin slivers and we ate it with some bread to help it go down, our keen hunger overcoming any feelings of revulsion. I nodded, 'It's not bad.'

Cox who had been quiet awhile said, 'Greenhill, he was one of the coves you went off with last time, wasn't he?'

I nodded but stayed silent, offering him no encouragement to continue.

'What does human flesh taste like?' he persisted.

I kept my head down, not wanting to revisit that chapter of my past.

'Like any other meat,' I said after a while.

He took the hint and let it drop, but I felt the dark shadow of the past pass across my mind. The steady, high-pitched rhythm of the cicadas suddenly increased and then he spoke.

Tasted good didn't it? I know you haven't forgotten.

Da! His voice was back in my head. The terrors clutched

at my fluttering heart and set it off racing. Cox looked at me strangely as my face betrayed the turbulence I felt within. 'Are you right Alec?'

I took a deep breath, nodded and clutched at my stomach theatrically. 'Aye . . . me guts just tightened up a bit. Must be that fish.' This gave me an excuse to leave him and sit in the forest. Even though it was still balmy, cold sweat soaked my shirt. *What next?* I wondered.

You know what's next, my da's voice mocked me.

No, no, not this time.

In another few days you'll be out of food.

I can't . . .

You can and you will if you want to see the green of Ireland and see your poor mammy's face again. The cicadas resumed their steady measure.

We began following the shoreline of Macquarie Harbour, the sparser vegetation and the knowledge that we had food enough for the next four days allowing us to move quicker. As we trekked it struck me that Cox, who walked a few yards in front of me, was a comely young lad; with his slim hips and curly blond hair he looked as shapely as a lass from behind. I felt the heat and that terrible aching spread up from my boots to my loins and realised with a jolt that I was harbouring lustful thoughts about him. I pushed such thoughts aside with a determined effort, but I couldn't stop looking and my lecherous thoughts kept returning with a renewed vigour. The sweet smell of pine drifted in from the thicket.

D'ya like the look of that? teased my da. *It's been a while since you lay with a woman.*

That harlot Peg had been the last, almost a year ago, but I'd never been with a man. I was a slave to my baptism. From a young age it was drummed into us that buggery and masturbation were abominations and mortal sins. Because we set such great store by this, we Irish tended to be much less inclined to such perversions as many of the other prisoners. One of the reasons Cox was keen to escape Sarah Island was because he'd been used as a Molly.

It wouldn't be the first time for him, would it now? reasoned my da.

I can't.

You can and you will. Learn to take your pleasures where you find them.

Da, why are you talking like this? I pleaded, but only the birds and the rustling leaves answered me.

I lay awake as the battle between my conscience and my secret desires twisted and turned in my head. Finally breaking, that night I jumped him as he lay on the ground facing away from me, fast asleep. When I groped him, he woke with a start and tried to struggle. 'Alec, what are you doing?' he called out in alarm.

Without reply I rolled him on his stomach, pushed his arm up his back, and keeping my weight on his upper body loosened his breeches and pulled them down over his dainty hips. Forcing his legs apart with my knee I straddled him and pushed myself inside him. Once penetrated, Cox realised there was no point resisting and let me have my way. For a minute or two I drove myself against the soft pillows of his buttocks until I spilled inside him. In the dreadful silence that followed, Cox rolled away, pulled up his breeches, curled up and went back to sleep. Regardless of what had just happened, the cold and the lack of fire forced us to huddle together for warmth. In such situations, survival must come before anything. I'd learned that lesson well on my last foray to freedom.

*

The following day we proceeded in silence, the events of the previous night not mentioned. Cox didn't like being used but he was now in my former position: he depended on me, as I did Greenhill.

The voice inside me was growing stronger. It had started as a whisper when we'd killed Dalton, but seemed to thrive on blood and chaos and had got steadily louder and more demanding. I'd never committed buggery, yet now I was using Cox. What next?

The voice responded immediately, but this time it was not the voice of my da and it no longer signalled its presence discreetly. Instead, a hoarse, brutal bark, a primitive sound, took over. It made my hair stand on end.

Kill him!

Kill him!

KILL HIM!

I started shaking as the roaring reached a crescendo in my ears. *No, no!* I pleaded, but like a torrent rushing into an empty vessel it quickly filled my soul. I had violated Cox's body and now I was sizing him up as my next meal. He was walking just ahead, oblivious to the murderous intentions that were rapidly overtaking me. As I looked at his muscular arms and legs, my mouth watered as the memory of the taste of the tender pink meat just beneath the skin came flooding back to me. *What madness is this?* I scolded.

Yet again I experienced a tingling sensation in my face and a heaviness in my limbs, which was compensated for by a sharpness of vision. It was like looking down a spyglass edged with red. Everything appeared to me in much greater detail, even the fluttering insects who I could've plucked out of the air now their clever little patterns had slowed down to nothing. It was as though I'd been ripped out of my skin and something from Hell had moved in.

I was getting ready to kill again.

With a huge effort of will I turned off into the brush, my hands quaking as I pushed aside the thick foliage and fought to quell the terrible storm that raged within me.

'Where are you going?' *Where are you going?* demanded both the rough voice and Cox in unison, their accusing tones creating a strange echo in my head. I burrowed deeper into the thick, green scrub in a desperate bid to put some distance between us lest I act on the powerful impulse that now gripped my senses. My whole body shaking, sweat dripping from me, I collapsed onto the rough ground and sank my head between my knees. *God in Heaven . . . what madness had come over me to imagine that my father could speak to me from beyond the grave? The voice that had just echoed in my head had come straight from the charnel house, the very Pit itself.* I groaned in abject terror and shame. *How easy it had been to delve into the tender parts of my soul and cruelly assume the voice of the missing father I'd mourned all my life!*

Who are you?

You know who I am, insisted the primitive growl.

If this were a nightmare I would've forced myself awake at once. But this was no dream. It was a journey to the furthest antipodes of the human soul where our basest instincts wait in the shadows to be summoned forth.

Gradually the turmoil subsided and I shakily returned to the path. Cox was obediently waiting, just as I'd imagined. 'Something you ate?' he asked with genuine concern.

Something you almost ate, chuckled the voice wickedly.

I knew I had merely forestalled the inevitable. Powerful and relentless, the hunger pursued me like a wild beast without respite. I might resist it for hours, even days, but it would eventually overwhelm my reason with its desperate desire to be satisfied.

In the small hours, when my will was at its lowest, I awoke and again surrendered to temptation and buggered Cox not for my pleasure, but because the voice wanted to show me who was boss. It had a hold of me now and made me do its bidding.

I killed Thomas Cox the very next day.

The twenty-first day of November, our fifth out from Sarah Island, started quietly enough. As usual, we headed out at first light and skirted the harbour as we kept moving north-west. I reckoned we'd reach the coast where Hell's Gates meets the Southern Ocean by the day's end. To avoid being seen by the redcoats stationed at the pilot's cottage, we'd have to cut inland through the low scrub and sparse stands of ti-tree.

Once clear of the heads, we'd be faced with an endless vista of sand and dunes on one side and thick, green forest on the other. *How would we survive after the food ran out? Could we scavenge enough shellfish and catch enough fish or would I have to take Cox?* I didn't even know the distance to Port Dalrymple. The question nettled me all day: *Should we push ahead or give ourselves up? How long could I resist the voice?*

In the late morning we came to the King's River. As the Gordon River fed the harbour in the south, the King's River fed it in the north. There was a wide, sandy delta where river met sea. I waded in up to my knees to test its strength and though the undertow was still strong, the high tide mark on the bank indicated that the levels had dropped considerably since springtime when the melting snows turned it into a raging torrent.

I looked back at Cox who'd held back on the shore. Irritated by his reluctance I called back to him, 'What's the matter? Get in here.' Cox just stood rooted to the spot, forcing me to go back for him.

'I can't swim,' he admitted shamefacedly.

'What?' I exploded, 'There's a hundred fucking rivers between here and Port Dalrymple. How in the hell are you going to get over them?'

'I thought we were going overland, the way you went before.'

I shook my head vehemently and jabbed my finger at the wall of vegetation that bounded us on all sides. 'I'm not going back in there again.'

'Why not? You made it through once before.'

'You have no idea what's in there.'

'What d'ya mean?'

I couldn't tell him, I couldn't tell anyone. Who'd believe me? Knopwood didn't.

'I wish I'd taken the lash and never embarked on this foolish mission,' I confessed, finally giving voice to my secret thoughts.

'What d'ya mean?' whined Cox, obviously wounded.

'This is a fool's earn. I should have seen my time out at Macquarie Harbour.'

But I was not the only one with secrets. 'I wish I'd never taken your bloody shirt.'

'What?'

'I'm sorry, but I wanted you to come with me. I knew I couldn't make it alone.'

I was speechless with rage. He'd behaved like some petulant child who steals another's toy with no earthly idea of the consequences.

'You stupid bastard!' I roared, 'Have you any idea what you've done?'

I felt the self-righteous anger building up inside of me, as it did the day I killed Greenhill, and knew that this time I wouldn't be able to stop it. In my mind's eye I again saw him lying on the ground, his face covered in blood, nettling me to the last with a sarcastic laugh and his riddle, 'Don't go thinking it's over just because you've killed me.' I now understood the import of his words as I realised with a violent jolt that I'd become just like Greenhill. The voice cackled.

Now you've got it, Mr Pearce. You're him now in all but name.

Cox just gaped at me, a bewildered expression on his face, as I pulled out my axe and advanced on him. The red mist had descended and the voice was screaming in my ears as I drew back the axe: *Kill him! He deserves it for what he did to you! Kill! Kill! KILL!*

Only when he realised that I meant to strike him did he finally react. He threw up his hands, grasped onto my swinging arm, twisted it round, pushed it back against the joint and pulled the axe off me with surprising strength. Suddenly we were toe to toe, ready to fight to the death. He was a young, strong bull like Mather but as he lifted the cudgel to strike at me I doubted Cox had the stomach for murder.

'Come on then ya cove!' I yelled, my pride stung by the way he'd disarmed me so easily. But Cox didn't want to fight and threw down the axe as I'd done when confronted by Greenhill, unable or as yet unwilling to do what I should've done, what Cox should've done: kill his tormentor.

'Alec, I don't want to fight you,' he pleaded, 'what's the matter with you?'

What indeed? mocked my shadowy companion.

I had no such reservations. Not any more.

I bent down, scooped up the axe, ran forwards and delivered Cox a full-blooded blow on the top of the head. I again heard that sickening hollow crack and pop as heavy metal met skin and bone and Cox went down in a heap. I hit him twice more in the head, great round-armed blows that jarred my wrist with their force.

I recoiled when I saw the blood spurting and the rage left me almost as quickly as it had come. *No, not again. I can't go through this again.* Confused and afraid, I dropped the axe and started to ford the river.

I hadn't got past my knees when Cox started wailing. I tried to go on but his piteous cries spoke to the last vestige of humanity in me. I couldn't just leave him lying there grievously wounded, so I staggered back to the clearing where dark blood running freely from a hole in his head puddled in the sand.

'For God's sake Alec, just finish it,' he moaned in pain.

I stood rooted to the spot, numbed by the terrible thing I'd done. Greenhill was an evil bastard. Killing him was a service to humanity, but Thomas Cox was just a lost boy on the far side of the world.

'For pity's sake make it easy on me,' he sobbed.

I obliged him with a well-aimed blow to the side of the head that jarred my wrist. I crumpled into a heap on the sand next to him and cried. The voice, as it always did after exhorting me to do terrible things, left me alone with the terrible consequences. Spent by the ordeal I just lay there looking at Cox. By and by the shadows crept over him like a shroud and then the darkness gathered him up in its gentle caress.

With a great effort of will I forced my mind to leave the terrible present and think ahead. Survival had to be my only consideration. Cox was dead, no amount of tears would change this, and Port Dalrymple was a fair distance away.

Needs must Mr Pearce, said my invisible companion, confirming my thoughts.

I sprang to my feet and looked around for the shape, the figure in the trees that I always expected to see but never did. Bending my knees so I was properly braced, I roared at the water, trees and sky, 'Fuck off, you black-hearted bastard and leave me be! D'ya hear? Fuck off!' Had anyone seen me I'd have been sent to Bedlam right away, but I didn't care.

I collapsed onto the sand, my eyes streaming with tears and my throat raw with the exertion of my screams.

The night chills forced me to build a fire. *Is that wise, you might be seen?* scolded the voice.

I don't fucken care any more.

I dragged Cox close to the fire so I could see what I was doing. Just as I'd done with Greenhill, I stripped him and removed his damaged head, hands and privates. I washed and cleaned his body and suspended the trunk from the branch of a tree. Then I cut the body in half, took out the offal, carved off all the choicest cuts and cooked them. I dressed myself in his clothes, which were much better than mine, used my old shirt as a swag and put the food in it. I selected some of Cox's succulent thigh and had it for dinner along with his liver.

I awoke just before first light as was my habit. I'd left a portion of Cox's thigh for breakfast but wasn't very hungry so I ate some bread and stuffed the flesh in my pocket for later. I looked at the bloodied knife and axe and decided to leave them behind.

As I again headed across the strip of beach towards the King's River, my feet were light but I felt heavy with remorse. I'd killed the others out of necessity but I'd killed Cox while I still had a full belly. Again the question nagged at me, *Should I give myself up or go on?* The answer came to me as I splashed across the river but I was not its author.

I was halfway across, up to my waist in water, when another voice spoke to me, but to my heart this time, not to my head. An overwhelming feeling of guilt, shame and remorse flooded through me and I knew with a crushing certainty that I must return to Macquarie Harbour and face the consequences of my deeds. Overcome with relief and gratitude that my anguish was finally over, I fell to my knees and wept uncontrollably. Quite simply, my heart had failed me. I thought of those poor devils Allen, Hudson and Oates, and imagined they'd experienced this same torment and profound regret. I finally understood why they'd wanted to die.

My first act of atonement was to open my swag, pick out all of Cox's flesh and throw it into the bushes. The fish, bread and meat I put in the pockets of my coat and re-traced my footsteps.

Where are you going? Don't you want to be free? demanded my unseen tormentor. I didn't answer.

You've always been weak, a great disappointment to your da. I kept walking.

You'll never see Ireland, it bit back. Still, my step didn't falter.

Once I'd reached the harbour I decided to rest and started to doze.

Some time later I was woken by what sounded like gently fluttering wings. Through half-opened slits I noted the sun had turned from white to gold and had started slipping down the sky. As I wiped the sleep from my eyes and brought them into focus I saw a ship, its sails puffed out by the wind as she plied the well-worn route between Hell's Gates and Sarah Island. Though silhouetted by the sun I recognised the shape of its keel. It was the pilot schooner *Waterloo* in the charge of Captain James Lucas.

Realising it would be past me in a trice I impulsively pulled out the tinder and rag from my pocket and quickly lit the dry brush.

What are you doing? demanded the voice.
Ending my torment.
They'll hang you.
But at least I'll be rid of you.
You'll never be rid of me, it cautioned.
See you in Hell.

I fanned the angry red sparks, fed them with dry grass and twigs and watched them quickly blossom into flames. Once I was sure the fire had caught hold, I poured some water over the blaze which sent a plume of black smoke into the sky. I stood on the shore shouting at the top of my voice and waving my arms. I could make out little figures on deck looking and pointing as the sails were trimmed and the *Waterloo* slowed in the water. By and by, a small, six-oared whaleboat was hoisted over the side and began to pull towards shore. The boat ran aground in the little cove where I'd been waiting and four men jumped out of it. Two, I didn't know but one was Captain Lucas who I'd seen hunting in the woods a few days ago; the other was William Evans, a tall fair-haired convict from Devon. He'd thrown in his lot with the authorities in return for an easier life.

'What's your name?' demanded Lucas. Before I got leave to say anything Evans blurted out, 'That's Pearce, Alexander Pearce, absconded from Macquarie Harbour a week since!'

Lucas's eyes widened. He certainly knew of me, probably through the gossip he'd heard at Sarah Island.

'Where's Thomas Cox?' demanded Lucas. His face clouded

as his sharp eyes went to the bulge in my pocket where I suddenly recalled I still had the piece of flesh I'd intended to eat for breakfast.

'Hold him!' called Lucas sharply. Instantly, the two roughhouse sailors wrestled my arms behind my back and Captain Lucas pulled the lump of thigh from my pocket and weighed it in his palm. 'What in God's name is this?'

'It's a piece of Cox,' I heard myself say, determined that this time there would be no tricky business, no double blinds, just a straight trot.

'Christ almighty!' yelled Lucas, dropping it as if it were burning coals. The others stared down at the greyish lump with a mixture of curiosity, horror and disgust. Lucas, who could barely look at it, gaped at me in disbelief, his mind in a whirl. He tried to speak but the terrors had stolen his voice. Clearing his throat and attempting to bring his thoughts to some sort of order, he croaked, 'What part of Cox is that?'

'His thigh.'

'Is the body hereabouts?' Lucas enquired almost fearfully. I had to tell him because without a body there was no proof and I'd be sent back to Sarah Island.

Before I could answer, a voice shouted, 'Captain Lucas!' One of his men was waving at us from further up the beach and pointing at something.

In the cold light of day Cox's cadaver shocked even me. I could scarcely believe I'd done this. He was suspended upside down, his head, hands, feet and genitals torn off. His trunk had been crudely split down the middle, his entrails strewn across the sand and the choicest cuts of flesh crudely hacked off. Thousands of shiny black bush flies swarmed every inch of Cox's body, their low, contented hum changing to an angry, high-pitched buzzing as we disturbed them. Though inured to the hardships of the seas, those jack tars had never seen the like of it and vomited copiously onto the sand. Finally, tears in their eyes, faces red with the exertion, they staggered to their feet.

The two roughnecks grabbed me by the collar and threatened to kill me there and then. I did nothing to stop them.

'If we was left alone I'd do for you meself,' said one.

'You'd be doing me a favour,' I said calmly.

Captain Lucas, still a bit green at the gills, restored order with a sharp command. 'Stop that at once and gather up the pieces of the body.'

I stood and watched while they cut Cox down and rooted about for his missing parts, which would doubtless be used in evidence against me later. Noticeably, Lucas stood back and let his men do the dirty work, declining to touch the body himself.

'Have you located his head and hands?' he demanded thickly. Eventually they found Cox's head under a log; it was covered in angrily buzzing insects which had already insinuated themselves into every cavity.

A glint in the sand caught Lucas's sharp eye. Spotting the axe and knife that I'd carelessly tossed aside, Lucas went over and gingerly picked up the blood-smeared instruments of death. Without another word he put them in a canvas bag he carried around his middle. Finally, they wrapped Cox's remains in a canvas sheet and roughly pushed me down the sand towards the whaleboat. All the while they looked about them fearfully as though expecting some unearthly creature to emerge from the woods and grab them.

*

No sooner had I been dragged onto the deck of the *Waterloo* than the watch roared out in the military tone that mariners use, even when they're not in the Royal Navy: 'Vessel approaching off starboard Capt'n!'

I looked out across the flat grey water and saw one of the twelve-oared whaleboats moving rapidly towards us from the direction of Sarah Island. Even from half a mile I could make out the distinctive red tunics. They must have spotted the smoke from my fire and come out to investigate.

Cuthbertson. Good.

Accompanied by Trooper O'Donnell and Sergeant Waddy, the commandant swept aboard, clutching the Black Book to his breast like a missionary would a Bible. His face like thunder, he immediately went into whispered conference with Lucas and I watched his expression change from dark displeasure to disgust.

He commandeered Lucas's cabin and once he'd swept the nautical charts, books and other clutter off the small desk and opened the Black Book I was brought in to him. The cramped, low-ceilinged cabin, lit only by a faint glow that struggled through a narrow porthole, smelt of decent-quality foreign baccy, testament to Lucas's growing prosperity. Barely big enough for the two of us, the redcoats were forced to stand at the open door while Cuthbertson eyed me with a mix of curiosity and open loathing.

'Tell me Pearce, did you do it? Did you kill Cox?'

'He did it, he told me he did!' shouted Lucas from the corridor.

'I want to hear it from his own lips,' scolded Cuthbertson his roguish features creasing in annoyance.

'Yes, and I'm willing to die for it,' I replied.

'Why in God's name did you do it, man?' he thundered. I shook my head and shut myself off from his questions, which became more urgent and insistent. He couldn't, wouldn't understand.

'Have you nothing to say for yourself?'

'I'll tell no man until I know I'm going to suffer.' With that I lowered my head and refused to say another word.

Seeing that he would get no more from me, Cuthbertson slammed the Black Book shut and shot to his feet, his red face fizzing with rage. He wasn't used to being openly defied. He looked daggers at me and growled, 'Oh, you'll suffer alright. I'll see to that personally.'

'He's told us nothing,' moaned Lucas, hovering awkwardly on the threshold of his own cabin.

'Who cares?' snapped Cuthbertson, 'he's given us cause enough to send him back to Hobart where they'll stretch his neck this time.'

'Do you intend to enship him from the settlement?'

'No, we're best rid of him. He's the only one to escape twice and is practically a folk hero,' spat Cuthbertson. 'Proceed directly to Hobart, Captain.'

'Hobart,' echoed Lucas, his voice filled with dismay as he contemplated the loss of at least four precious weeks. 'I have whale oil to be shipped,' he protested.

'That's an order Mr Lucas,' snapped Cuthbertson, his twisted smile savouring Lucas's distress. 'As an Englishman, you surely understand your personal interests must come second to those of His Majesty.'

Once the name of the King had been invoked, Lucas fell silent. The issue settled, the commandant motioned impatiently for O'Donnell and Waddy. As we crossed in the corridor, the big sergeant Waddy shook his head at me sorrowfully but kept his walrus moustache tightly knitted. Even this most forgiving of Welsh Methodists now considered me beyond redemption.

A bewildered Lucas, who had now been pushed back into his office by the crush of bodies in the narrow passageway, beseeched Cuthbertson, 'Won't you at least leave me an escort?'

'They're more needed on Sarah Island, Captain. Take Pearce back to Hobart and see he's charged with murder. Next time I hear of him he better be dead,' he warned, little caring that I was standing right next to him.

'Commandant Cuthertson . . .' protested Lucas, flapping his hands like flightless birds.

'That's right, Captain . . . Commandant.' And with that he disappeared up the ladder and out of sight.

Lucas looked at me fearfully. He'd seen Cox's slaughtered body and was afraid he'd end up the same way. 'Stow him in the brig, chain him to a bulkhead and post an armed guard outside the door until we dock!' he yelled shrilly. Two of his ex-convict crewmen pointed their loaded flintlocks at me. I didn't resist.

Through my tiny barred window I watched the *Waterloo* weigh anchor and shortly afterwards pop through the heads like a cork out of a bottle. Gradually, Hell's Gates receded into the distance, their sinister outline shrouded by scarves of grey sea mist. I asked Almighty God to take my life before he would return me there again.

Daniel Ruth snapped the heavy leather-bound ledger shut and let his astonishment escape with a long exhalation. Pearce's tale had just got even more extraordinary.

During Pearce's first journey through the wilderness Daniel

had been appalled at how they'd preyed on each other, but he'd nevertheless felt a grudging respect for Pearce who'd defied the odds to survive. This time Pearce had turned predator and Daniel wasn't so sure of him any more. Questions ricocheted around in his head: *Why had Pearce given himself up again? Was it another trick or was his conscience really troubling him? What of this voice; if it wasn't his father's then whose was it? Was there a voice at all, or was it just some grand delusion?* It was all turning into an extravagant mystery.

Having broken his deep concentration, Daniel became aware of his heavy eyelids and dull headache. He'd been sitting in the room too long. Stretching his cold, cramped joints, he went downstairs and snatched in a reviving lungful of cold, clean harbour air. He walked down the overgrown path to the western tip of the island where he saw the remains of a jetty, its split, jagged stumps sticking out of the water like a row of rotten teeth. Facing north he peered at the mountain peaks and shuddered at the thought of spending a month slogging through that savage forest exhausted, starving and in constant fear for your life. To have escaped once and survived was a great feat, but twice, well almost, was unbelievable.

Daniel brushed his hand across the stubbly beard that now covered his face. It hadn't seen a blade since he left Hobart almost two months ago and stopped performing his other usual daily ablutions such as hair-brushing, washing and changing his clothes.

His actor friends back in Philadelphia often appeared sporting odd-looking beards or moustaches, limping, carrying canes and affecting strange accents and mannerisms. By 'getting into character', as they called it, they believed they could better empathise with the role they'd be portraying on stage. He'd always mocked them, calling them 'bohemians' and 'rakes' but now it occurred to him that he was doing the same. 'I'll never be like Alexander Pearce,' he scoffed.

Thinking of Pearce, Daniel was anxious to get back to his memoir. He gathered up some dry twigs, branches and driftwood for the night ahead and trudged back up the hill to the penitentiary, superstitiously stopping at the bog near the top of the rise to check that all the footprints were his. 'This place is getting to you, Daniel,' he chided himself. But beneath his self-depreciating humour something had begun to trouble him.

He'd awoken that morning to find his eyes inexplicably full of tears. He recalled a similar streak of melancholy when he'd entered puberty, but it had passed as he'd come into manhood and his wealth, good looks and intelligence gave him little cause to be gloomy. Yet now, in this place, he felt those same feelings stirring in him again.

Daniel felt a terrible sense of isolation from everything he'd once known, as if his past belonged to another life in another time. The strangeness of his surroundings had drawn him away from the familiar world where reason prevailed and there were certainties he could count on. This remote corner of civilisation wasn't governed by the rules he knew but ones written long before. It was an inexplicable feeling, some long-forgotten tribal instinct dredged up from the pit of his soul, but an uncomfortable one nonetheless.

Chapter 18

Demon of the Chicane

Hobart gaol, December 1823

Despite my confessions to Lucas and Cuthbertson and the weight of evidence against me, the wheels of justice ground exceedingly slowly all through December. There was nothing I could do but wait as the 'Demon of the Chicane', as Jeremy Bentham described the British legal system, ground to its inevitable conclusion.

I was restored to my former cell where Bisdee continued to visit me, bringing his curious mix of Christian charity and appalled fascination. He let it slip that Knopwood was on the rack for not having brought charges against me the first time I'd escaped. 'Poor old Bobby is spending the hot part of the year, when he'd normally be resting and attending Yuletide *soirées*, interviewing Captain Lucas and his men and sifting the evidence against you, at the express insistence of the lieutenant-governor. By all accounts his stones are driving him to distraction and Dr Brewster has been in close attendance with his trusty rod.'

I managed a rare smile, but Bisdee left me with a sombre

thought. 'I can't say it bodes well for you, Alec. This time they have a body, witnesses and your confession.'

I nodded. He opened his mouth, as if to ask me something else, then thought the better of it. But I knew Bisdee. He'd be back. I was an itch he had to scratch.

As my daily exercise consisted of being hooded, chained and dragged around the cobbled yard for an hour, the Sabbath ritual offered me the only break in my dreary routine. It began at noon on Saturday when work was stopped. Rain or shine, we were marched into the prison yard, ordered to strip, doused with cold water, made to rub ourselves all over with strong-smelling carbolic soap and then put on a clean uniform so we would be presentable in church the following day.

A truly wondrous construction, the penitentiary chapel held five hundred convicts on two sections of tiered bench seats that rose upwards on either side of the pulpit like a theatre. We convicts entered by the southern doors and occupied the seats at that end while the public came in from Brisbane Street and sat in the pews that were rented at a cost of £1 per year. A screen separated us since there'd been complaints that the convicts leered at the young ladies opposite.

In their infinite wisdom, the prison authorities had ordered the architects to build thirty-six solitary confinement and punishment cells, known as the 'dust hole', beneath the chapel floor. Each one measured five-and-a-half feet long and only twenty-seven inches high, not quite the length of a grave. Sometimes two to three men were stuffed into a single cell during a weekend with only a thin blanket for warmth. The cold, the darkness, the sense that the walls and ceiling were closing in, the proximity to fellow prisoners, and the overwhelming stench of vomit, piss and excrement were too much for most men. At various times of the day and night they would become panicked. To our amusement, and to the distress of the great and the good, their piteous moaning and wailing often rose up from beneath the congregation's feet during the Sunday sermon while the Reverend Knopwood exulted God and his infinite forgiveness.

One day early in February, Bisdee came to see me in a lather. He was unable to stop himself blurting out his shocking news before he'd even opened my cell door. 'Cuthbertson's dead!' he exclaimed, his words echoing around my stone vault.

It was enough to bring me bolt upright in my cot. 'What?'

'Word reached the lieutenant-governor a couple of days ago,' he exclaimed. Bisdee's expression was a bewildered mixture of excitement and earnestness, having heard many tales of the late commandant's wanton cruelty. I couldn't quell my emotions any longer and started laughing loudly. This merry tune was seldom heard at this wretched address, other than to announce the first bloom of madness. My mocking call was soon taken up by other hyenas, always game for some distraction, and we chased the ghouls and ghosts out of every shadowy corner.

'Tell me all,' I demanded, pulling my rough wool blanket around me and settling in for a good yarn.

'Three days before Yuletide, a storm blew up in the harbour and the *Governor Sorell*, the first schooner to be completed at Sarah Island, broke from her anchor and began to drift without sail or rudder. Fearing she might be dashed on the rocks at Rum Point, Cuthbertson launched a whaleboat to tow her clear, but it stove in her bow as she came alongside, forcing the men to clamber aboard the ship. He sent another two whaleboats to assist and took to sea himself.'

'That boat was to Cuthbertson what the ark was to Noah, his pride and joy and his salvation,' I added.

'The surf was mountainous close to the heads and even Cuthbertson could see that he had no choice but to let her drift until the storm had abated. After taking on board the men from the stricken boat, he ordered everyone to return to Sarah Island. The first boat made good headway but the commandant's boat, newly built and untried in rough conditions, fell behind as a fresh squall and thick fog came blowing in across the harbour. His coxswain, Anderson, I think his name was, advised him to put for shore.'

'The best coxswain in the place and a sailor to boot, but I'd wager that fool had his say and every word of it,' I muttered.

Bisdee nodded, 'Cuthbertson went against Anderson's advice and ordered him to turn the boat about and head for shelter in the Gordon River. As Anderson predicted, the boat soon filled with water and turned over. Of the eleven men in the boat, five were lost before the rest struck out for the schooner, which was still within reach. The commandant complained of feeling cold and another crewman tried to help him along, but neither reached the schooner.

'The first whaleboat returned safely to Sarah Island and raised the alarm. More boats with supplies were sent out and they searched the shores until dark. At first light they found the survivors from Cuthbertson's whaleboat on the schooner and received the news that the Commandant had not been seen since the previous evening. Though they issued a reward of ten pounds and every boat on the island searched the harbour, they couldn't find him.'

'Was his body ever seen?'

'Aye, he was finally washed up on a deserted shore some

weeks later in a terrible state of decomposition. The next brig that arrived from Hobart brought a lead and cedar coffin and removed his remains. This morning, I attended a memorial service where a monument, paid for by the government, was erected to his memory, bearing a long account of his virtues.'

'Aye, but no mention of the many men who lost their lives on his account.'

Bisdee ignored my bitter words and continued, 'The lieutenant-governor read the lesson and announced that in recognition of his sterling service to the Crown in the most trying of circumstances his promotion to captain had been gazetted.'

I laughed ironically as I recognised the futility and cynical intent behind the honour. 'They only did it because it cost them nothing. Dead men draw no salaries and claim no gratuities.'

Some would mourn the passing of a great man and others might consider it a sign of the Almighty's displeasure at his unnecessarily harsh oppression of his fellows. Either way, Cuthbertson had passed through Hell's Gates before me and would doubtless have a good blaze going by the time I arrived.

Bisdee eyed me and I sensed he had something of import to say. 'Lieutenant Cuthbertson has settled his account with God, but what about you?'

I shook my head but he pressed on. 'Alec, you're facing grievous charges and you won't escape the rope this time.'

'I told Knopwood everything and he wouldn't believe me,' I protested.

'Not everything,' he said, lowering his voice theatrically, 'you've never told anyone the secrets of your heart.'

'What secrets would they be, John?'

'What drove you to do it, Alec? You're no savage, there's something else to it.'

'The voice.'

'What voice?'

I shook my head. 'I don't know who it belonged to. At first it took on the guise of my late father and helped me survive the forest and the bloodlusting that went on during my first escape. But when I went off with Cox it spoke to me again.'

'Was it the same voice, Alec?'

'No, it was a different, rougher voice and it goaded me until I killed him.'

I looked up but Bisdee had gone. I could hear the rumble of his retreating feet on the flagstones fading into the distance.

He came back some hours later, his strained expression testament to his restless state of mind. This time I noted he didn't come right up to the bars of my cell but stayed a few paces back. He was clearly troubled and quickly spoke his mind.

'Alec, I fear that you are slave to some terrible force.'

'What do you mean?'

'I believe you are in the commission of the Devil.'

'The Devil?' I exclaimed. The days of witch hunts and inquisitions had been over for the best part of a hundred years. But what other explanation could there be? I pictured the stricken face of William Allen who'd confessed to cannibalism because, in his words, 'The Devil wouldn't let me rest, night or day'. I remembered Hudson and Oates who preferred to go to the gallows and 'Jack the Lad' who'd taken his own life.

'I can't live with what I've done or the fear I might do it again,' I confessed.

'Are you ready to die?'

I nodded.

'Pray with me, Alec,' he said and got down on his knees.

I had my audience with the lieutenant-governor the very next day and shortly afterwards was again summoned by two redcoats to an interview with Knopwood at the courthouse, this time with John Bisdee in attendance. Perhaps it was his stones, the extra work I had caused him, or merely the strong summer light that illuminated the normally gloomy atmosphere, but Knopwood looked paler and frailer than the last time I'd seen him. He eyed me warily as I entered, his expression a mixture of curiosity and contempt, though I sensed some trepidation in him too. I further noted two armed soldiers stationed at the door in case I jumped on him; fat chance of that, there was more meat on a fiddler's cat. Wells wasn't present this time, Bisdee had been called as a witness instead.

Knopwood left me standing there a few minutes while he scanned the papers before him, drew a sharp breath, lifted his tired, red-rimmed eyes and studied me closely. He came straight to the point. 'Frankly, Pearce, I don't know what to make of all this.'

'I cut off Cox's flesh to support me on my intended journey to Port Dalrymple,' I said simply.

The reverend shook his grey, balding head. 'Why would a white Christian man resort to such terrible barbarity?'

'No man can tell what he will do when driven by hunger,' I insisted.

Knopwood shuffled his papers then spread his hands in a gesture of bewilderment. 'Hunger? According to Captain Lucas you had bread, pork and fish in your swag when you were taken.'

He continued to harangue me, but I shook my head. *Not that hunger, you old fool.* Wanting to put an end to Knopwood's needling, yet having no rational explanation to offer him, I blurted out, 'I prefer the taste of human flesh to chicken or pork.'

'What in the hell are you talking about?' thundered Knopwood bringing the redcoats to attention. He had doubtless recalled what his nemesis, Surgeon Scott, had argued the last time they'd discussed me.

'Bloodlust, Reverend. A state of being where a man would rather consume the flesh of his fellow man than that of an animal.'

His hand shook as he noted down my words and I sensed the guards tightening their grip on their muskets.

'What's got into you, man?' he shouted.

I raised my voice in response, 'You're a minister in God's church. You should know better than anyone what causes men to do evil!' Time seemed to stand still as soon as the words had left my mouth.

Knopwood sat frozen, his mouth agape. In the small window of silence I told myself, *It's done. I've sealed my fate.*

Then, as the world started to turn again, a vivid blush rose in the good reverend's face and he let out a roar that smartly stiffened the backbones of the guards. Knopwood's usual calm authority had been rocked to its very foundations. The bunched veins at his temples pulsed furiously and his eyes flashed. 'Guards! Remove him at once!'

But though he tried to give the impression of authority, his shaking hand had already betrayed his fear. Underneath those saintly robes and the trappings of high office, he was as fearful and superstitious as the rest of us of the things that lurk in the shadows.

*

None of what I said to Bisdee or Knopwood was repeated at my trial, such as it was, which followed a month or so later on 27 February 1824. Indeed, no mention was made of the killings that took place during my first escape, only the murder of Cox. Bisdee had been sworn to silence and at Knopwood's strict insistence, only charges that could be proved by physical evidence and witnesses were to be spoken of.

As might be imagined, the courthouse was packed. Chief Justice Pedder urged the jury not to let rumour or innuendo interfere with their sense of honour and justice and to judge me only on the facts presented.

The charges were then read out and the jury, which consisted of seven serving military officers, peered at me incredulously as though they could scarcely believe that such a small man could've committed the atrocities detailed. The newly sworn in attorney-general, the tall and elegant Tice Gellibrand, again reminded the jury in his refined English tone of their solemn duty. 'Put out of your mind everything you've heard. The confessions made by the prisoner, though inconsistent in some respects, will, when coupled with all the facts, merit the most serious attention,' he assured them.

What followed was a long narrative in which my confessions to Lucas, Cuthbertson and Knopwood were read out in full for the benefit for the jury. Then, in support of my statements, a series of witnesses were called. Captain Lucas, William Evans and Thomas Smith, the coxswain on Cuthbertson's whaleboat, all detailed the barbarous scene they'd found at the King's River and what I'd said in its aftermath.

After informing the chief justice that the prosecution rested, the attorney-general sat down, obviously pleased with himself. He'd managed to steer the evidence away from the wild talk and speculation that had swept the colony about the cruelty at Macquarie Harbour which caused men to lose possession of their minds and commit the most terrible crimes.

Chief Justice Pedder leaned forward and addressed the jury. 'Having heard all the evidence, I ask you now to retire and consider if the charge against the accused has been proven and if the charge should be manslaughter rather than murder because the deceased, Thomas Cox, and the accused rowed before the killing took place. Furthermore, you must be satisfied that the weapons recovered had caused the death of Thomas Cox.'

Clearly under the strictest instruction to secure a guilty verdict at any cost, Gellibrand paled visibly when he heard the chief justice's words, which suddenly seemed to hold out some hope of mercy to me.

Yet this hope was short-lived. I could see the grim verdict written all across the poker faces of the returning jury as they returned to their still warm seats well within an hour.

'Foreman of the jury, have you reached a verdict upon which you are all agreed?' said Pedder with due gravitas.

'We have, Your Honour.'

'In the matter of the murder of Thomas Cox by Alexander Pearce on the twenty-first day of November last, do you find the defendant guilty or not guilty?'

'Guilty, Your Honour.' Though these were the only words the foreman spoke, I could see from their faces that my previous conduct, though not mentioned, and the fact I'd feasted on Cox's flesh, had weighed heavily on their minds.

The legal profession has always had a fine sense of theatre. A calico screen was unfurled in front of the judge while he considered the appropriate sentence. Then, after a respectable pause of two or three minutes – though I doubt it took him half a minute to arrive at his decision – they rolled back the screen to reveal Pedder sitting with a black cloth on top of his wig. There was a gasp from the packed court and even though it came as no surprise to me, I still shivered at the sign of death.

Looking as though he'd sucked on a lemon, Judge Pedder formally handed down his judgement in his gravest voice, 'Alexander Pearce, you will hereby be taken from this place to the gaol and thence to the place of execution, to be hanged by the neck 'til you are dead. Afterwards, your body is to be delivered to the surgeons for dissection. Prepare yourself to appear before the highest tribunal from where mercy may be obtained.' With that his Lordship rose and retired to his chambers for lunch.

Still they wouldn't put me out of my misery. I sat in Hobart gaol for months writing my story and awaiting execution while letters, orders and petitions crossed the oceans between my respective masters in London, Sydney and Hobart as they sought affirmation of the sentence on the cannibal convict.

In the meantime, more dramatic news from Macquarie Harbour reached me via my usual source, Bisdee. He arrived at the door of my cell saying that Matthew Brady had escaped.

'I bloody knew there would be no holding that boy,' I mused, 'how did he get away?'

'About four weeks ago he was working at the vegetable gardens on Sarah Island when he and thirteen others tried to commandeer Commandant Wright's boat with the man and some of his officers still in it. When the rowers brought it out of their reach and raised the alarm, they took to an empty whaleboat, braved the gauntlet of lead at the heads without loss and headed out to sea.'

'What became of them? Did they make it?'

Bisdee held up his hand to signal that he still had more to tell. 'They made their way back round the Cape to the Derwent River. Once ashore they robbed a settler of guns and provisions and set up a headquarters in the bush. Brady said he intended to return with his "Army of Light" to free the prisoners at Macquarie Harbour.'

The hopeful anticipation of Brady's return had given him hero status in the eyes of the convicts. 'When Brady gets here, we'll put your head on a pole!' they taunted the overseers and redcoats who now lived in fear of that day.

'Matthew Brady, he's the boy!' I announced with a loud yell that ricocheted off the stone walls and into every cell. My racket spurred on the other inmates and the redcoats came to see what the commotion was.

'Fucken shut up,' snarled Private Marsh, a red-haired, freckled Liverpudlian whose temper was quick to rise. It was the Irish in him and I'd heard it said that there were more Irish in Liverpool than anywhere in Ireland, except Dublin. I goaded him further with laughter and a shout of, 'He's a credit to Ireland, so he is!' In return, Marsh thrust his rifle through the bars of my cage and gave me the wooden butt to chew. He put my front tooth through my lip and blood poured from my mouth as I picked myself up off the flagstones. I curled my tongue round the wound and made sucking noises. 'Careful boys, I'm gettin' the taste again.' Even with the bars and their loaded muskets between us they still looked afraid. They'd been listening to too much prison scuttlebutt.

Finally, the day of reckoning came. Bisdee brought the news one Friday that I would hang on the following Monday, 19 July, which now brings our story full circle.

Death awaits me on the morrow.

Chapter 19

Envoi

Hobart gaol, 19 July 1824

MY LAST DAY ON earth.

They had no need to wake me at five o'clock. I hadn't slept. Rest is the furthest thing from your mind when eternal sleep awaits you. From my vantage point at my barred window I watched dawn break across Hobart's rain-slicked rooftops and then the bright golden sunrise chase the shadows back down into the vaults and cellars. *Never had the world seemed so full of wonder.*

When I finally pulled my eyes away from the window I found Conolly already seated opposite, keen to start the ritual of death. I was first given confession, sacramental absolution and then Holy Communion.

'Have you anything more to tell me, Alec?' he asked.

'No.'

'You're sure now?'

'Aye.'

Because he also hailed from county Monaghan, he assumed

I would meekly surrender to him the secrets of my soul. Despite being of opposite faiths, Conolly and Knopwood were close, which was not approved of by all in Hobarton. I had a notion that Knopwood had told Conolly about both my confessions. Believing I had more to tell, he almost reluctantly stood aside as Bisdee arrived with my last meal. We exchanged a guilty glance. I know Bisdee was worried that I hadn't confessed everything to Conolly.

'I'll leave you in peace now, but I'll be with you every step of the way, my son.'

'Except for the last few, 'eh Father.'

'Eh, aye,' he stammered as he surrendered the small piece of floor beside my bunk to the governor holding a steaming plate.

'That smells grand, bring it on,' I declared, rubbing my hands.

Bisdee offered me a good tot of rum and a vial of laudanum to wash down my ham, eggs, bread and dripping.

'It'll make it easier to bear,' he confided.

I shook my head. 'I don't deserve an easy passage. I'll pay for my sins in full.'

'You will, when you meet God.'

'If I meet God.'

'We will all be judged by the highest power in Heaven,' he insisted.

Bisdee was right. Whether or not we believe in God, we all fear what awaits us in the dark vale beyond this life. Take the God-fearing, Christian men who work in the gaol. When they cut down the bodies of executed men they wrap them in chains before placing them in coffins to ensure they don't rise from the grave to seek vengeance against their persecutors. In the business of death superstitions don't die as easily as mortal men.

*

My breath quickens as I hear the big front gates creak open and the clamour of the idle and curious get louder as they pour into the courtyard. Presently, Conolly will come for me accompanied by the hanging party and I will be taken away to die. I know exactly how it will go. I have rehearsed it endlessly since Friday last, and when it comes to it I don't expect it will be much different.

Bent almost double I will be taken in chains down a badly lit, narrow tunnel that leads to the gallows. I learned from Bisdee that the gaol, the courthouse, the Anglican church and the Hope & Anchor public house are all connected by a network of subterranean escape tunnels, neatly representing sin, justice, punishment and redemption, the four corners of human existence. My chains will run smoothly along the grooves already worn deep into the sandstone walls by the friction of men being brought up and down these passageways each day.

At the end of the tunnel I will be ordered to wait at the bottom of the stairs that led up to the scaffold. I will bend my knees and lean back, the small of my back fitting neatly into the recess where many other backs have anxiously waited before meeting their fate. Sharp, white daylight will flood into the tunnel as a trapdoor above me is opened. I'll get a poke in the ribs with a watch stick and a callous voice will order me to 'fucking get up there!'

I'll come up onto the wooden platform, blinking into the bright light, and when my eyes adjust I'll be standing before a noisy, agitated crowd of bobbing heads in the small courtyard. The sensational newspaper reports have provoked widespread interest in my case and no doubt there will be a deep-throated roar when they recognise my slight figure.

Just before a hanging it is customary for the priest, the prison governor, the hangman and the condemned to meet backstage like actors before a performance, shake hands and wish each other luck – though 'break a neck' may have been a more appropriate salutation.

Firstly, Conolly will offer me his small, but surprisingly strong hand, his face a creased mask of genuine sympathy. 'God be with you, Alec. I'll see everything is taken care of . . . afterwards.' Once I've dropped through the hatch I'll be left to hang for an hour while they repair to the pub for a drink. It's customary to take strong drink after taking a life. When they return Surgeon Scott, whisky misting his breath, will go beneath the gallows to check for signs of life, declare me dead, and then Conolly will complete the last rites. He will then administer conditional extreme unction, the sacrament reserved for the sick and dying. As no one knows exactly when the soul leaves the body, this will help my spirit on its onward passage to God. The Holy Romans take every care to ensure your soul is delivered up to heaven, especially those in dire need of repair.

Then Bisdee will clasp my hand warmly and pat me on the shoulder. There will be genuine feeling in his voice when he'll say, 'Goodbye Alec.'

'You're a decent man John, and long may you prosper,' I'll reply. He'll hold onto my hand, draw me close and whisper, 'It's not too late.' And I'll nod my head.

Finally, I'll come face to face again with my executioner, Solomon Blay, though this time he'll look much more sinister, a vision of death itself. As demanded by tradition, he'll have blackened his face with burnt cork and mud so the family and friends of executed felons who might be seeking vengeance won't recognise him. We'll shake hands and he will wish me good luck in the afterlife. I'll tell him that I bear him no grudge; he wasn't the one who decided my fate, just the instrument ensuring my dispatch.

I'll look up at the noose swaying patiently in the breeze and bring to mind another piece of gallows folklore told to me by Solomon as he measured me up last Friday. While waxing about the sort of rope he favoured and its careful preparation, he told me there are thirteen knots in a hangman's noose, twelve for the jury and one for the judge. I don't know whether it's true, but it's a great yarn nevertheless.

I turn to the side and nod to the four men I'll be hanged with. All I know of them is that three have Irish names. As usual, their expressions range from boredom to fear-stricken. They wait patiently knowing they aren't the main attraction.

I'll wager down at the front of the gallows the gentlemen of the press will be well-represented. Some clever scribe has dubbed my story 'a thrilling tale of incredible barbarity', which has fired imaginations throughout the colony and far beyond it. While they scribble their impressions, their artists will be sketching away. I must remember to give them my best side, such as it is. Out beyond them will be the massed ranks of ordinary people, chattering excitedly. I wonder if they realise that it could be any one of them up here with me had they taken a walk in those woods.

Conolly will step forward to address the crowd on my behalf and they'll quickly quieten down. In his rumbling baritone he will tell them, 'This man stands before you condemned at the awful entrance to eternity on which he was placed and is desirous to make the most public acknowledgement of his guilt in order to humble himself as much as possible in the sight of God and Man.' He will relate brief details of my misdeeds. Then he'll pause and look around the faces to ensure he has their full attention before delivering the moral of my sad tale. Taking a deep breath he'll say what he always says, 'Each Monday, here in this prison yard, we see the justice of Providence bring to light the dark deeds of death and how frequently do we see it verified what it says in the book of Genesis.'

Scanning the chastised faces of those below, he'll gesture towards me before continuing, 'This man has done wrong, but has shown remorse for his terrible deeds, confessed his sins to God and is more willing to die than to live. I ask all persons present to take a moment to offer up their prayers and beg the Almighty to have mercy upon his soul before whom he shall shortly stand to receive Judgement.'

During my final minute's grace I'll look over at John Bisdee, head bowed, deep in prayer. I know it pains him deeply that I could never bring myself to tell him everything that happened in those woods, but there was no slight intended. Quite the contrary, he's always been a loyal and decent friend and I wanted to shield him from the terrible truth. I gave up my last gold sovereign to ensure my ledger and the following letter will be given to him. They will satisfy his every curiosity.

18 July 1824

Dear John,

On maps of Van Diemen's Land the simple notation 'unknown' is used to describe the western coastline and wilderness around Macquarie Harbour. This is true in more ways than the man who wrote it could ever know. It might sound fantastical or the last refuge of a guilty conscience but a strange, malevolent spirit lurks in those ancient forests infecting the souls of the unwary with its terrible hunger. I believe it to be the Devil. I cannot think of any other explanation.

The name Alexander Pearce may live on forever in infamy, but others will follow my torturous path from Macquarie Harbour to the gallows.

It only remains for me to thank you for all the kindness and consideration you showed me during my time in gaol and to wish you a long and prosperous life.

Your friend,
Alexander Pearce

These words will chill John Bisdee to the bone. He'll agonise about giving the letter to Reverend Knopwood or to the lieutenant-governor, knowing they'll probably dismiss it as the ramblings of a cannibal awaiting death. So if Bisdee has the sense he was born with, he'll cast it into the big, pot-bellied stove in his office and watch it shrivel into soot.

If only everything could be so easily erased.

Conolly will bow his head, and after a short, respectful silence will step aside. I'll glance one last time over my shoulder at the craggy face of Table Mountain that broods behind the thick vapours. Old Solomon Blay has done this a hundred times and will wait patiently for me to face him. He'll give me a reassuring nod, 'Lower your head.'

Just before the hood goes over my head, I'll pick out Reverend Knopwood and our new lieutenant-governor, Colonel George Arthur, in the impressive gallery of faces that will doubtless gather to witness my dispatch. Both will be fidgeting, anxious for Old Solomon to be done with his work.

I'll feel a light touch on my shoulder as Old Solomon moves

the knot round to the side of my neck and positions it just beneath my ear so that when that three-quarter-inch manila hemp rope he waxed lyrical about brings me to a juddering halt in mid-air, my neck will snap like a dry twig.

I'll step onto the trapdoor, which will creak ominously as it takes my full weight.

A hush will descend over the crowd as they sense the moment approaching.

I'll close my eyes.

When the nine o'clock bell tolls for me, the rough circle of hemp will tighten around my throat. As I count its sweet chimes and Conolly reads the execution prayer I'll reflect that the avenues to death are numerous and strange and none more so than my own. When he reaches the passage, 'he that sheddeth man's blood by man shall his blood be shed', Solomon will pull down hard on the lever and I will fall from this life into the next where all of life's great mysteries will be revealed to me. Yet, the question at the heart of this tale remains unanswered.

Does the Devil really exist? Can any man who suffered the tyranny of Macquarie Harbour say that he does not?

And what of God? Misfortune was my god.

I hear the footsteps of the hanging party on the flagstones. The hour of my liberation is now at hand. My tale is at an end. Envoi.

Alexander Pearce
Hobart Gaol, 19 July 1824

Chapter 20

Needs Must . . .

Sarah Island, 18 June 1851

Daniel Ruth looked up from the yellowing pages. 'Pearce actually believed he was possessed by the Devil,' he exclaimed out loud, his voice echoing through the deserted rooms beyond. He stood up, stretched his stiff limbs and spoke aloud again, finding his anger suddenly roused, 'I can't believe Pearce survived all the cruelty of Macquarie Harbour and the terrible ravages of the wilderness to allow a couple of Christian do-gooders to convince him that he was possessed by the Devil, to repent his sins and go meekly to his death!' Feeling a fire in his chest, he pictured himself back in America standing before a packed auditorium, rapt by his tale. Rehearsing the moment he now felt sure was near, he waved his arms like an orator and thundered, 'God and the Devil are just superstitions, figments of overwrought religious imaginations!'

Daniel paced the room as he started to formulate his strategy. He'd use his own words and modern science to prove Pearce wasn't a cannibal or possessed by the Devil; he was just a petty criminal embittered and pushed to extremes by a cruel system of justice, unduly influenced by men of strong religion and a victim of greed. Henry Crockett had lied to William Cobb Hurry, the Calcutta agent who sold Pearce's skull to Dr Morton. The Assistant Colonial Surgeon who had who tended Pearce at the hospital on Grummet Island and later dissected his body after his execution was well acquainted with Pearce's story, yet told Hurry that Pearce lived in the woods and lured convicts into the forest like one of Lord Byron's vampires. It was what Pearce feared he would become and why he'd bravely chosen the rope, but Crockett had spun a yarn to get a better price. Bisdee had been well-meaning, but his strong religious conviction had convinced Pearce that he was possessed by the Devil, a fear reinforced by Father Conolly.

The little Irishman had certainly eaten human flesh, as had other convicts at Macquarie Harbour, but out of necessity, not to satisfy some wanton bloodlust. Daniel believed that the physical dimensions and capacity of a skull could be used to determine racial type, but not behaviour, intelligence or character traits. As Pearce's story revealed, circumstances, surroundings and upbringing were all factors and a Caucasian was as capable of being a cannibal as a mulatto or Negroid. Daniel realised his conclusions would undermine the theories of his mentor, Doctor Morton, but was determined to publish his findings. He felt he'd earned the right and that it was a perfect example of how science would benefit modern society by replacing superstition and fading Biblical motifs with rational patterns of thought and explanations based on facts.

A loud shout from outside interrupted his musings. 'Ahoy there!'

Daniel popped his head out of the window and was surprised

to see the distinctive black hull of the *Isabella* discreetly riding at anchor at the secluded northern end of Sarah Island. It had arrived earlier than he'd calculated, but was a welcome sight. He'd been on Sarah Island for a little over two weeks, but already felt this island's strange influence invading his thoughts and dreams. He was ready to leave.

Heading down to the shore, he greeted the captain with, 'You've made very good time sir.'

'We were pushed along by a following wind after we rounded the Cape and for once there was no froth at Hell's Gates.'

'Excellent.'

The captain cast a knowing eye to the sky. Like a cat he knew every angle of the sun and where he should be situated at any given hour of the day. 'There's storms brewing to the east and I want to be back round the Cape before those Roaring Forties start blowing,' he rumbled. 'The tide is high and the wind set fair, so we'll leave at first light tomorrow with or without you. We don't want to get trapped here.'

'Suits me, let's get started.'

Daniel walked them across the island, pointing out bricks with signature convict thumbprints and blocks of stones with convict arrows etched into them, rusting metal tools, old boots, the poles from the 'bloody triangle', discarded 'canaries', chains and shackles – everything he'd need to give the great American public an authentic flavour of Macquarie Harbour's convict past.

'That's it?' exclaimed Byrne incredulously.

'That's it.'

'What in the hell d'ya want with all this old junk and rubble?'

'Not junk captain,' Daniel corrected him, 'relics from our

inglorious past that will help change the course of human history,' he added with a flourish.

'Whatever you say,' muttered Byrne, brow still deeply furrowed.

Daniel captured five final images of the brooding landscapes of Sarah Island and its convict remnants. He planned to use them to support his talks and illustrate Pearce's journal when it was published. As the camera clicked, Daniel noted the storm clouds building up in the heavens, just as the captain had predicted.

The light had faded to a dull bronze by the time Byrne's men had finished loading and Daniel had captured all the images he needed. The crew started building a fire and brought ashore food, grog and a little squeezebox to help them while away the night.

Daniel returned to the penitentiary's weathered battlements to spend the last night finishing Pearce's journal. There would be plenty of time for sleep on the return leg to Hobart.

By the light of a candle, the gentle wheeze of the sailors' squeezebox in the background, Daniel opened the final sections of Pearce's journal. To his disappointment, there was nothing more of apparent interest. Pearce's prophecy that 'others will follow my torturous path from Macquarie Harbour to the gallows' had proved uncannily accurate. Daniel's finger traced down the list of names before him:

George Craggs murdered by Thomas Peacock, 13 December 1824.
James Richardson murdered by Morgan Edwards, 13 September 1825.
John Onley murdered by Samuel Higgins and George Driver,

30 November 1827.

Thomas Stoppford murdered by John Salmon, 8 August 1828.

James Jones murdered by John Mayo, 18 August 1829.

Richard Cozier murdered by John Crockshott, 16 January 1832.

But murder wasn't the worst of it. There were several more pages containing articles neatly clipped from the local newspapers, the *Hobart Gazette* and the *Hobart Town Courier*. Daniel guessed the press articles were added by Pearce's gaoler and confidant, John Bisdee, who had the journal in his possession for years before returning it to Sarah Island.

He flicked through the first article dated December 1824, less than six months after Pearce was hanged. It concerned the flight of four prisoners from Macquarie Harbour. Three had returned to the settlement and surrendered. They claimed that the fourth member of their party had died of exhaustion. Commandant Wright didn't believe their story. A search made along the route they'd travelled found bloodstained clothes belonging to the missing man, but no body. The remains of a fire and three bloody sticks, shreds of flesh stuck to their points, were found buried in the ground nearby. Although foul play was strongly suspected there was not enough evidence to lay charges.

The second article was dated March 1825 and concerned the escape of ten convicts. One returned a month later, claiming he'd fled when the others started drawing lots to decide who they would butcher for food.

There were other articles in a similar vein but the headline and prologue from a story published in the *Hobart Town Courier* on 13 August 1831 immediately caught his eye.

HORRIBLE NARRATIVE

Those readers whose feelings are unequal to the perusal of the horrible are advised to pass over the ensuing paragraph.

We announced last week that we should in this day's publication, insert the humiliating statement and confession of the two runaways from Macquarie Harbour, Edward Broughton and Mathew Macavoy, requested to be made public after their death.

Broughton's statement was read in the press room by his own desire whilst the executioner was pinioning his arms and adjusting the rope.

According to the statement given by this wretched man, he was now twenty-eight years of age and had been sentenced to death for robbery in England under aggravated circumstances at the age of eighteen. He had more than once endeavoured to rob his own mother, his horrible conduct breaking his father's heart and sending him to his grave. The youth was confined two years in Guildford gaol.

On his transportation to this colony, he had scarcely landed in Hobart Town when he commenced his robberies. He was at last apprehended for an outrage he committed at Sandy Bar, then tried and transported to Macquarie Harbour.

The party of runaways from Macquarie Harbour, of which Broughton was one, consisted originally of five men: Richard Hutchinson, Patrick Fagan, William Coventry and the two malefactors, Broughton and Macavoy who suffered on the gallows on Friday. These men were at one of the outstations at Macquarie Harbour and in the charge of one constable.

This constable, Broughton declared, had shown him many personal kindnesses yet nonetheless he joined with his *companions and robbed the man of every article he had, leaving him not a loaf of bread to subsist on.*

One would have thought that these five men, thus embarked on a most perilous journey, would have been knit together in one interest for their common safety, yet the very contrary was the case as the sequel proved. They viewed each other with the most murderous feeling, jealous of the possession of the only axe they carried lest one should drive it into the head of another. The demon of evil had possession and walked in the midst of them. Every principle, every feeling of humanity was dead amongst them.

As soon as their provisions were exhausted, the others agreed among themselves to kill Hutchinson and eat his body. They drew lots for who should be the one to drive the axe into his head. The lot fell on Broughton who carried it to execution. They cut the body in pieces and took it with them with the exception of the hands, feet, head and intestines. They ate heartily of it, as Broughton told it.

When all the flesh was consumed, a general alarm seized the party. Who would be next? None among them dared to shut his eyes or doze for a moment for fear of being sacrificed unawares. Under these dreadful circumstances, Broughton and Fagan made an agreement that while one slept the other would keep watch.

Broughton's statement continues in his own words: 'The next to be murdered was Coventry, the old man. While he was out cutting wood one night we agreed to kill him. Macavoy and Fagan wanted to draw lots to determine who should kill him but I said no, I'd already killed my man. Fagan struck him the first blow. Coventry saw it coming and called out for mercy. The first blow did not kill him so Macavoy and myself finished him off and cut him to pieces. We ate greedily of the flesh, not sparing any, as though we expected to come across a bullock the following day. I carried the axe by day and laid it under my head at night.

'*One evening Macavoy bid me come with him to set some snares to try and catch kangaroo. We left Fagan by the fire, and when we'd gone three hundred yards, he asked me to sit down. I had the axe over my shoulder, and I was afraid he wanted to kill me for he was stronger than I. So I threw the axe aside, but further from him than from me, for fear that he'd try and snatch it. But he wanted me to kill Fagan, that he might not be evidence against us. I would not agree to it, saying that I could not trust my life in his hands and we returned to the fire.*

'*When we got back Fagan was warming himself by the fire. "Have you put any snares down, Ned?" he asked me. I said no, there are snares enough, if you did but know it. I sat beside him. Macavoy was beyond me on my right, Fagan on my left. I wanted to tell Fagan what had passed but could not as Macavoy was sitting with his axe close by, looking at us.*

'*I lay down and had begun to doze when I heard Fagan scream out. I leapt to my feet in a dreadful fright and saw Fagan sprawled on his back with a horrible cut in his head, the blood pouring from it. Macavoy was standing over him with the axe in his hand. "You murdering rascal, you b____y dog!" I yelled, "What have you done?" He said, "This will save our lives," and struck him another blow. Fagan could only groan. Macavoy cut his throat with a razor, through the windpipe. We then stripped off his clothes and cut the body in pieces and roasted it. We roasted all of it as it was lighter to carry and would keep longer, and would not be so easily discovered.*

'About four days after that we gave ourselves up at Maguire's Marsh. Two days earlier we'd come across a kangaroo that had been killed by wild dogs. We got the kangaroo and threw away the remainder of Fagan's body. I wish this to be made public after my death.'

Edward Broughton
Witnessed by John Bisdee

Daniel shook his head as his eyes scanned the florid prose and picked out the phrase, 'The demon of evil had possession and walked in the midst of them.'

'God, the Devil, good and evil? What ruinous notions the Old Testament put in people's heads!' he muttered to himself.

A sudden increase in background noise prompted him to lift his head from the pages. Dead leaves rattled out a warning on the glass: *storm coming soon.* The high-pitched squeal of the squeezebox had been drowned out by a rush of air stirring the surrounding trees and whistling through the penitentiary, extinguishing his candle. He rubbed his tired eyes and peered at his fob watch. It was after midnight. He glanced down at the shore, illuminated by white moonlight, and saw larger waves now breaking against the beach. He moved to a less exposed position away from the rattling window, weighed down the precious pages of Pearce's manuscript with loose lumps of masonry, and settled down to read the final selection.

It was an extract from the Select Committee Report on Transportation held in London 1838 at which former surgeon at Macquarie Harbour, Dr John Barnes, gave evidence. Dr Barnes was examined by the chairman, Sir William Molesworth MP, and other members of the committee. Daniel made a note in his journal to try and track down Dr Barnes in London on his return.

MOLESWORTH: *Have you a return of the number of convicts who absconded from 3 January 1822 to 16 May 1827?*

BARNES: *Yes, which I copied from the black books of the settlement. From that return it appears that out of the 116 who absconded, 75 are supposed to have perished in the woods, one was murdered for murdering and eating his companion, eight are known to have been murdered by their companions, six of whom were eaten, two were shot by the military, 24 escaped, 13 were hanged for bushranging and two for murder, making 101 out of 116 who came to an untimely fate.*

LORD HOWICK: *What is the authority for supposing that 75 perished in the woods?*

BARNES: *They were never heard of again, though some skeletons were found.*

HOWICK: *Do you suppose that none of those who are put down as having perished in the woods were taken off by boats?*

BARNES: *No boats visit that part of the coast; it is not a whaling nor a sealing situation, and the only bay to which they could go and the only entrance to the harbour was guarded by the soldiers. No boat could enter the settlement without the knowledge of the commanding officer.*

SIR CHARLES LEMON: *Is there such frequent communication with the natives as to enable you to ascertain whether some of the people are not with these tribes?*

BARNES: *I believe that at the present moment there is not a native in the island. I understand that the natives have been either destroyed or captured.*

LEMON: *Then the convicts generally believed that they had escaped in some way?*

BARNES: *Yes, they did; and there were constantly rumours coming by fresh batches of convicts that such and such a party of men who had left the settlement at such a time had made their escape from Launceston or Hobart Town, or some place that the ships visit, but the impression of the commanding officer and others who had an opportunity to examine the matter very closely was that very few if any did make their escape; they could not possibly get through the woods without perishing, except in the case of Pearce, who got through the woods and reached the settled part of the country by sacrificing six[2] of his companions, upon who he lived.*

There was a flash like lightning and Daniel saw someone pushing through thick green foliage. His breathing was heavy and ragged. A hand, which he recognised as his own, pulled back a branch to reveal a man with his back to him. A large patch of

---

2 Pearce was only party to killing five of his seven fellow travellers. Brown and Kennelly returned to Sarah Island where they died shortly afterwards.

sweat had formed an oval at the centre of the man's shirt, the size of a target. He saw his hand go to his belt, pull out an axe, then advance right up to him. The axe was raised as the heavy breathing reached a crescendo.

Knowing he was about to smash the axe into the man's back, Daniel came bolt upright, forced his eyes open and realised that his heart was beating wildly. Hot sweat was pouring down his neck and soaking through the front of his shirt. Fear had stolen into his heart like an unwelcome intruder.

'A dream . . . it was just a dream,' he breathed, trying to still his panic.

As Daniel chased the phantoms of sleep from his mind, he pulled opened a window and welcomed the cold, bracing blast that blew in off the misty harbour.

Somewhere in the small hours he was awoken again with a start by a terrific banging and shouting. A squall had kicked up. Rain drummed against the windows and he could hear men running around and shouting below. After ensuring that his precious papers were wrapped up in a piece of oilskin and safely stowed in a nook in the wall, which he blocked up with heavy stones, Daniel took the stairs two at a time.

He arrived at the jetty to find Captain James Byrne and his crew desperately fighting to hold onto the *Isabella*'s mooring ropes, which were threatening to uproot the pillars of the jetty. 'We must hold her!' Captain Byrne shouted. Daniel's numbed hands grabbed onto the thick mooring rope as the squalling wind and lashing rain gave them a taste of what Pearce and those other poor devils had endured most days of the year.

He was just thinking what a good climax the storm would make to the foreword of his forthcoming book when the wooden planks beneath his feet were torn asunder with an alarming crunch. Daniel was dragged off his feet as the *Isabella* lurched to starboard, uprooting the mooring posts as easily as a row of rotten teeth.

Out in the coal-black waters, framed by the silver spotlight of the moon, the hull of the *Isabella* pitched and rolled from side to side. It reminded him of the frightened wild stallions he'd seen captured on the wide dusty plains of Arizona. They hung desperately onto the ship's mooring ropes but the sea is not as easily tamed as the spirit of a wild horse. Such was the force of the gale that the hastily abandoned squeezebox rolled past them, end on end, scoring a discordant accompaniment to their travails.

'Let her go or she'll take you with her!' screamed Captain Byrne. Daniel felt a sharp, burning pain as the thick mooring rope rasped his palms, taking the skin clean off them. Michael Isaacs, one of the ship's hands, wasn't quick enough. With one violent motion the rope cracked like a whip and the pale figure disappeared like a rabbit in an illusionist's trick.

'Michael!' howled a lone voice as they frantically scanned the foaming waters for some sign of his outstretched arms or a bobbing head, but there was nothing. The dark harbour waters had dragged him under.

Soaked by the rising waves and whipped by the mighty gale, the fear of exposure forced them up onto higher ground where they shivered in the darkness and listened to the crunch of splintering timbers as the *Isabella* was torn apart.

'This bastard place is cursed!' spat Byrne.

At that moment no one, not even Daniel, cared to disagree. Byrne's oath brought to mind the words of David Burn, who had accompanied Sir John Franklin, the polar explorer and then lieutenant governor of Van Diemen's Land, on an expedition to this desolate coast: 'Unblessed by man, accurst by God.'

The wind dropped as suddenly as it had risen and at the first light of dawn all their worst fears were confirmed.

There was no sign of Michael's body but the wreck of the *Isabella* was sitting in around fifteen feet of water. She'd been dashed against Badger Rock, where the daily floggings had taken place and Allen, Hudson and Oates had been hanged, and holed beneath the waterline. No amount of bailing would ever make her seaworthy again.

After reciting every seafarer's oath, Byrne ordered his two strongest swimmers, Bridges and Lewis, to strip off their clothes. They took to the waters, swearing and cursing as the chilly waters nipped at them. They came back quickly holding a small bundle above the ruinous waters, which contained everything of use they could salvage from the stricken ship.

'Damn and bugger it,' seethed Byrne.

All that was recovered was a small quantity of bread, salted beef and a knife.

'She's badly holed and completely flooded below decks,' Bridges confirmed. 'The water ruined nearly all the food, the muskets and powder. This is all we could find.'

'So Captain Byrne, what do we do now?' wondered Daniel.

Byrne paused a moment while he composed himself. 'The only thing we can do: make ourselves a raft, paddle to the furthermost shore, bear west and walk back to the heads, and wait for a passing ship to put into the harbour.'

'Even counting his supplies we've only enough for five days, a week at the most,' warned Lewis.

Daniel opened his mouth to ask what happens after that, but stopped himself as he felt a cold prickle creep across his scalp.

He already knew the answer.

A scream leapt from of the pit of his stomach and jammed in the back his throat. He reeled backwards, his hands frantically windmilling as he tried to regain his balance on the downward slope.

Pitching and rolling on the soft ground the young American ended up on his knees, face buried in the ground. He let out a high-pitched wail as the significance of the press cuttings in Pearce's memoir suddenly became clear. A sense of absurdity and disbelief blurred Daniel's normally clear thoughts as he realised he was somehow being written into the last chapter of the story he'd just read. It was being authored before his very eyes. *How is this possible?* he thought fearfully, his chest heaving as he struggled for air. He felt as though he were in a dream, unable to grasp the terrible reality still floating above him. Sensing his grip on reality slipping away, he lifted his face to the heavens and covered his eyes. *What's happening to me?* He suddenly caught the strong aroma of wild mint, as he had on the first day he arrived. Then he heard the voice.

You know what's happening.

Who's that?

You know very well who I am, it taunted him.

My God, it's been here all the time, watching me.

Thick, choking vomit forced its way out of Daniel's mouth and nose in a violent rush as fear clutched at his chest. The dots finally joined up before his eyes. The face was the Devil's.

'What's wrong with you, man?' shouted Byrne, but Daniel, his mind reeling, didn't hear him. It had occurred to him that whatever had taken possession of Pearce had let him go very easily after he killed Cox, but as he now heard those awful words: 'You'll never be free of me' echo round his head, he finally understood their import. Pearce's skull, which he'd held that night at Dr Morton's, had somehow become imbued with the evil of Macquarie Harbour and drawn him back here to continue its terrible legacy. Somehow the past had come tumbling into the present.

This wasn't some old curse that had lost the power to scare. It was very real and very frightening. Feeling damp patches of sweat break out all over his body he told himself *it's ridiculous, it's impossible . . . isn't it?* Yet, the very things he'd denounced as 'superstition' and 'nonsense' were taking form in front of his eyes. Daniel had given up the notion of good and evil in favour of science, but in a stunning moment of revelation he saw that it could no more fathom the mysteries of the universe than religion ever could.

He didn't even notice the roughneck crew of the *Isabella* looking down at him with varying degrees of disgust. Not having read Pearce's account themselves and still unaware of the terrible predicament facing them, they took him for a soft-handed, toff unused to danger, hardships and the unknown.

'On your feet sir,' said Captain Byrne, the scorn clear in his voice. 'I caution you, when we reach safety I'll still want paying for the whole trip.' The young American just nodded. *Money is the least of their problems, if they but knew it* he thought, but was wise enough to keep it hidden in the shadow behind his easy smile.

As the mariner led his men down to the shore to scavenge for driftwood, Daniel looked around the harbour fearfully as the white fog rose up off the grey waters to reveal the forest awaiting them, dense, green and secretive. A spear of regret lanced his chest as he had a sudden premonition that he'd never see Caroline again. *Should he leave her a letter? He'd promised Dr Morton discretion.* The dull ache in his heart told him that he must.

He raced back up the stone stairs and taking his seat at the table began to write:

Sarah Island, Van Diemen's Land, 19 June 1851

My dearest Caroline,

I beg your forgiveness for not explaining myself fully before I so abruptly left Philadelphia, but I was sworn to secrecy and honour-bound to keep my silence. I came to this strange faraway place, which you will not easily find on any map, because I saw the chance to make my fortune and reputation. It would have secured a wonderful future for us and the many children I feel sure we would have had. I have come to realise too late that I was foolish, ignorant of the world and the good fortune and opportunities my birthright has afforded me. There are many people on this earth on whom good fortune never smiles.

I love you above everything and was so looking forward to returning to you and the wonderful life we had planned together before misfortune overtook me, the details of which I will spare you. If you receive this letter you must assume I have been lost. Don't mourn me too long. Continue your life with the assurance that I only wish you love and happiness. I ask only that you spare me a thought each thirteenth day of September. That was the day I saw you emerge from the shadow of the Upper Quad Gate at the university and walk towards me down the avenue of maples on a carpet of crimson and gold leaves. Your eyes were an impossible blue and your hair the colour of ripe corn. That image will live in my memory for as long as I draw breath.

I will love you always.
Daniel

As his pen stopped scratching and ink began pooling on the paper, Daniel found his face was wet with tears and there was a terrible churning in his guts. He'd finally allowed his heart to speak freely, too late perhaps, but better late than never. As the pen fell from his fingers he thought it strange that a man who'd spent his one-score-and-three caring only for sensual pleasures should think of fidelity at the last. This mysterious land had humbled him just as it had Alexander Pearce.

'Come on Mr Ruth, let's be away!' came an impatient shout from below. After securely wrapping Caroline's letter, Pearce's memoir and his own journal in an oilskin and stowing them in his knapsack, Daniel went downstairs and helped Byrne and his men shove the ungainly craft they'd fashioned from driftwood and barrels into the water.

Once they'd gained the far shore, Daniel held back as the mariners plunged into the forest. Given that he was the only outsider and the most expendable, he decided not to disclose what he'd discovered in the penitentiary. Instead, he slipped his axe into the belt of his breeches with the uneasy feeling that he was going to need it. Through reading his chronicle, Daniel had seen things from Pearce's perspective. Although he was sorry for the way the convicts had been treated and admired the little

Irishman's pluck, he'd been appalled by his brutality. But now he began to see that mankind, for all his pretensions and supposed love of God, was no different from the primitives who'd travelled in the night of the first ages.

Daniel parted the springy, green vegetation that fringed the shoreline and stepped into the forest, just as Pearce had done nearly thirty years before him. As he watched the brush close behind him, the little Irishman's words flashed through his mind like some terrible premonition: 'the dense green screen sprang back to attention, obscuring my view of the harbour and closing the portal through which no man had ever returned.'

Captain Byrne popped his head out of the green thicket and called to him, 'Come ahead Mr Ruth, we've five miles to cover before dark.'

Daniel gasped as he heard those awful words spill from his lips, 'Needs must, Captain Byrne, needs must . . .' then felt cold dread clutch at his guts as he completed the old proverb, '. . . when the Devil drives.'

Epilogue

NEITHER DANIEL RUTH, NOR any of the crew of the stricken *Isabella,* reached civilisation. What became of them can only be a matter for speculation. It wasn't until some months later that a whaling crew, which had put in to Macquarie Harbour to wait out a storm, happened upon the decomposing remains of Michael Issacs and the wreck of the *Isabella*. It was assumed the ship had floundered in a storm and all hands lost overboard. The British authorities were duly informed, but given the area's remoteness and no evidence of foul play, the matter was allowed to rest.

As Daniel battled his way through the impenetrable scrub, trying desperately to stave off starvation and the terrible knowledge that they would soon have to sacrifice one of their party for nourishment, he couldn't have known that back in Philadelphia Dr Morton had suddenly taken ill. He fell into a coma and slipped away five days later on 25 May 1851, aged only fifty-two years.

The great and good gathered at Laurel Hill cemetery on Philadelphia's leafy outskirts, and the eulogies flowed. The *New York Tribune* proclaimed, 'Probably no scientific man in America enjoyed a higher reputation among scholars throughout the world.' Daniel's parents, William and Catherine Ruth, stood over the grave, little knowing that they were committing to the earth the only other person who knew of their son's whereabouts.

For years afterwards, Daniel's parents hoped for his return. His father, assuming that his brilliant but headstrong son had gone off in search of adventure, alerted all his shipping contacts to his son's disappearance and offered a £1000 reward for information leading to his whereabouts. For many years afterwards bedraggled castaways, dishevelled travellers and shipwrecked survivors would be greeted with the question, 'Are you perchance Daniel Ruth?' Though that question was asked many thousands of times in every corner of the known world, no one ever claimed the generous reward.

True romantics believe that a woman's heart has room enough for only one great love. Unable to countenance that Daniel would never return to her, Caroline Vandenberg hid herself away like some fairytale princess in the Gothic mansion she'd inherited from her parents and waited. She could've taken her pick of the eligible young men in Philadelphia who called on her regularly, but she sent them all away.

Though her fabled beauty slowly faded like a summer flower and then shrivelled away to nothing during the long autumn and winter of her life, her love for Daniel never grew cold. Reputedly, her dying words were, 'Why did Daniel never come back to me?'

No connection was ever made between Daniel's disappearance and Pearce's skull, which was found on Dr Morton's desk following his death. It was returned to its glass case where it gathered dust along with phrenology, craniology and polygenics, which are now only remembered as historical curiosities from that early period of scientific inquiry.

The 'American Golgotha', Morton's collection of one thousand human skulls, including that of Alexander Pearce, now resides in his *alma mater*, the University of Pennsylvania.

9 Cromwell Street,
Battery Point,
Hobart
28 October 1909

To whom it may concern,

I feel that some words of explanation are due to those who have read this remarkable story.

Some fifteen years ago, a surveyor by the name of Mr John Elliot called on me. He told me that he'd been working on the west coast of what since 1862 has been called Tasmania, which sounds much more benign of its previous name and does not have its convict stain. He had been commissioned by the Mount Lyell Mining Company to survey a route for a railway line to run down from Mount Lyell, where they'd started mining copper, to the coast where a port was to be built just inside Macquarie Harbour. The settlement that grew up clinging to the skirts of the unknown is now known as Strahan.

While working out in the forests, a group of his men discovered a skeleton of a man dressed in civilian clothes, not convict uniform. He had no means of identification, but they gave him a Christian burial and retrieved a knapsack containing an unsent letter to a Miss Caroline Vandenberg of Chestnut Hill, Philadelphia and two journals that made some mention of my late father and I.

As soon as I laid eyes on them I knew that one belonged to Alexander Pearce and the other to Daniel Ruth. I'd seen him writing in it and had admired its leatherwork the night I went to the Whalers' Return to warn him off. Though Mr

Elliot had obviously read both journals and was clearly curious to discover the identity of the man he'd found, I feigned innocence but promised faithfully to investigate the matter and write to him.

For many years I couldn't even bring myself to open them, perhaps for fear of what they might contain, but also because I felt some measure of guilt for sending Mr Ruth to that godforsaken place where he met his untimely end. It seems the proverb was true. By venturing through Hell's Gates he not only forfeited any hope of Heaven, but of life itself.

But now I've travelled around the sun nearly ninety times, I've stopped fearing death and given some thought to my legacy and tidying up any loose ends.

After reading both journals, I made enquires regarding the persons mentioned in the journals, particularly Miss Caroline Vandenberg who would have been greatly comforted by the letter in my possession, but, unfortunately, they had all passed on. I then realised it was incumbent on me, the last living person who knew all the circumstances of this extraordinary tale, to place all the material in my possession in a public archive so that the ancestors of those concerned might one day discover the fate of their loved ones and understand what drew them to that terrible place.

I deeply regret any part I played, unwitting though it was, in the events described; it is one of the few I shall carry to my grave.

I remain yours faithfully,
John Bisdee (Jnr)

THE END

Acknowledgements

This book was a tough assignment and the various drafts demanded a lot of time and commitment from people other than myself.

First, I'd like to thank my editor Nadine Davidoff for her sharp, insightful comments, which undoubtedly made the story clearer, tighter and more incisive.

My mother, Iris Bleszynski, provided some impeccable research and her usual, clear-sighted advice long after my objectivity and patience had deserted me and my agent, Margaret Gee, also provided invaluable advice about developing the story and kept the ship steady through a few tempests.

John Maltman, one of the very knowledgeable historical guides at the Old Hobart Penitentiary, very kindly showed me round this magnificent piece of colonial history and shared many of the old stories and legends attached to the place. This proved invaluable when writing the book.

My readers, Dorothy Frof, Sara Green, Paul Humphreys, Janet Leighton, and Ginny Maidment provided vital feedback on the first draft and many useful suggestions on how to improve later versions, which I did act on.

Thanks also to Jeanne Ryckmans and Katie Stackhouse at Random House for commissioning the book and guiding it through to publication.

Thanks to Hardie Grant Books for permission to reproduce the maps on pages xii–xv.

A mention in dispatches must also go to my long-suffering wife, Jill, and son Stefan whose sacrifices were by far the greatest.

Lastly, I'd like to thank CityRail for providing me with a 'studio' to write in every day. The 08.01 Waterfall to Bondi Junction 'cattle service' was a constant reminder of the suffering endured by our convict forebears and the close press of warm humanity provided many inspirational moments. Hopefully by my next book, rail transport in Sydney will have advanced from the nineteenth to the twenty-first century.

Also by bestselling author Nick Bleszynski . . .

SHOOT STRAIGHT, YOU BASTARDS!

The truth behind the killing of 'Breaker' Morant

UPDATED and EXPANDED EDITION

'An eye-opening version of the most controversial killing of two Australians in war time ever known'
DAILY TELEGRAPH

Nick Bleszynski

Foreword by Tim Fischer

SHOOT STRAIGHT, YOU BASTARDS!
The truth behind the killing of 'Breaker' Morant

Murder or justice? The question is still being fiercely debated more than a century after Lieutenant Harry 'Breaker' Morant and Lieutenant Peter Handcock were shot on a lonely veldt outside Pretoria at dawn on 27 February 1902 by a British military firing squad.

Shoot Straight, You Bastards! is a universal account of greed, ambition and the power of the political machine that crushes anyone who gets in the way.

In every war there is a character like Morant – a buckjumper, bush balladeer and rebellious spirit who ends up on the wrong side of the 'great cause'. This updated edition includes an appendix containing dramatic new evidence that Kitchener gave orders to 'take no prisoners'. Expert legal opinion supporting the belief that Morant and Handcock's convictions were 'unsafe' and a strong campaign to secure a proper judicial review combine here in a story Australians have waited more than a century to read.

'An eye-opening version of the most controversial killing of two Australians in war time ever known' – *Daily Telegraph*

'A ripper yarn' Bryce Courtenay

'You'll never take me alive'

The Life and Death of Bushranger BEN HALL

NICK BLESZYNSKI

'YOU'LL NEVER TAKE ME ALIVE'
The life and death of bushranger Ben Hall

'I'm not a criminal. I've been driven to this life . . . I was held for a month in gaol, an innocent man. While I was away me wife ran away with a policeman . . . Then I was arrested for the mail coach robbery and held another month before I was let out on bail. When I came home, I found my house burned down and cattle perished of thirst, left locked in yards . . . By Gawd, Mr Norton, it's your mob have driven me to it and, I tell you straight, you'll never take me alive!'

A powerful tale of betrayal and vengeance, *'You'll never take me alive'* tells the story of Ben Hall, a hero in the great outlaw tradition. Falsely imprisoned for bushranging by NSW police in 1863, Ben Hall declared, 'I might as well have the game as the blame'. He bailed up more banks, stations, squatters and towns than any other bushranger and masterminded the Eugowra escort robbery, netting the biggest haul in the colony's short history.

Known as 'the gentleman bushranger', Ben Hall was a chivalrous champion of the people. He told police, 'You'll never take me alive!' and they took him at his word. But 140 years later there is one last shocking revelation still to come . . .

Mixing archival research, folklore and the power of imagination, Nick Bleszynski brings Ben Hall out of the shadow of Ned Kelly and in vivid detail re-creates the life and struggles of the landowner who became an Australian bushranging legend.

'A ripper yarn' – Bryce Courtenay

More praise for Nick Bleszynski and his books . . .

SHOOT STRAIGHT, YOU BASTARDS!

'A ripping yarn that examines grave questions of morality and the value of human life' – *The Sydney Morning Herald*

'A comprehensive exploration of the legend of Breaker Morant . . . compelling reading' – *Sunday Times* (South Africa)

'YOU'LL NEVER TAKE ME ALIVE'

'. . . Bleszynski uses an inspired mix of archival research and the power of imagination to bring Ben Hall out of Ned Kelly's shadow.' – *Forbes Advocate*

'. . . Bleszynski's historical fiction offers a different and contemporary slant on the legend of Ben Hall . . . His book is the nearest thing to the stories I've been told by my parents and grand-parents.' – *Dubbo Daily Liberal*

'. . . a powerful tale of betrayal and vengeance, *'You'll Never Take Me Alive'* tells the story of Ben Hall, a hero in the great outlaw tradition . . . [Bleszynski] vividly re-creates the life and struggles of this landowner – the son of convicts – who became an Australian bushranging legend.' – *Griffth Area News*